T

THE T

AN

HENRY JAMES was born in New York in 1843 of ancestry both Irish and Scottish. He received a remarkably cosmopolitan education in New York, London, Paris and Geneva, and entered law school at Harvard in 1862. After 1869, he lived mostly in Europe, at first writing critical articles, reviews, and short stories for American periodicals. He lived in London for more than twenty years, and in 1898 moved to Rye, where his later novels were written. Under the influence of an ardent sympathy for the British cause in the First World War, Henry James was in 1915 naturalized a British subject. He died in 1916.

In his early novels, which include *Roderick Hudson* (1875) and *The Portrait of a Lady* (1881), he was chiefly concerned with the impact of the older civilisation of Europe upon American life. He analysed English character with extreme subtlety in such novels as *What Maisie Knew* (1897) and *The Awkward Age* (1899). In his last three great novels, *The Wings of the Dove* (1902), *The Ambassadors* (1903), and *The Golden Bowl* (1904), he returned to the 'international' theme of the confrontation of America and Europe.

T. J. LUSTIG is Lecturer in American Literature in the Department of American Studies at Keele University. He is the author of *Henry Jones and the Ghostly* (1994).

HENRY JAMES was born in New York in 1843 of ancestry both Irish and Scottish. He received a remarkably cosmopolitan education in New York, London, Paris and Geneva, and entered law school at Harvard in 1862. After 1869, he lived mostly in Europe, at first writing critical articles, reviews, and short stories for American periodicals. He lived in London for more than twenty years, and in 1898 moved to Rye, where his later novels were written. Under the influence of an ardent sympathy for the British cause in the First World War, Henry James was in 1915 naturalized a British subject. He died in 1916.

In his early novels, which include Roderick Hudson (1875) and The Portrait of a Lady (1881), he was chiefly concerned with the impact of the older civilisation of Europe upon American life. He analysed English character with extreme subtlety in such novels as What Maisie Knew (1897) and The Awkward Age (1899). In his last three great novels, The Wings of the Dove (1902), The Ambassadors (1903) and The Golden Bowl (1904), he returned to the 'international' theme of the confrontations of America and Europe.

T. J. Lustig is Lecturer in American Literature in the Department of American Studies at Keele University. He is the author of Henry James and the Ghostly (1994).

THE WORLD'S CLASSICS

HENRY JAMES

The Turn of the Screw
and Other Stories

Edited with an introduction and notes by
T. J. LUSTIG

Oxford · New York

OXFORD UNIVERSITY PRESS

Oxford University Press, Walton Street, Oxford OX2 6DP

Oxford New York
Athens Auckland Bangkok Bombay
Calcutta Cape Town Dar es Salaam Delhi
Florence Hong Kong Istanbul Karachi
Kuala Lumpur Madras Madrid Melbourne
Mexico City Nairobi Paris Singapore
Taipei Tokyo Toronto

and associated companies in
Berlin Ibadan

Oxford is a trade mark of Oxford University Press

'Sir Edmund Orme' first published 1891; published in the New York Edition 1909
'Owen Wingrave' first published 1892; published in the New York Edition 1909
'The Friends of the Friends' first published 1896; published in the New York Edition 1909
'The Turn of the Screw' first published 1898; published in the New York Edition 1908

Introduction, Note on the texts, Further reading, Notes and lists of Variant readings
© T. J. Lustig 1992
Chronology © Leon Edel 1963

First published as a World's Classics paperback 1992

British Library Cataloguing in Publication Data
Data available

Library of Congress Cataloging in Publication Data
James, Henry, 1843-1916.
The turn of the screw and other stories/Henry James; edited and
introduction notes by Tim Lustig.
p.   cm. — (The World's classics)
Includes bibliographical references (p.   ).
I. Lustig, Tim.   II. Title.   III. Series.
PS2116.T8   1992   813'.4—dc20   91-43679

ISBN 0-19-282927-0

9 10 8

Printed in Great Britain by
BPC Paperbacks Ltd
Aylesbury, Bucks

CONTENTS

CONTENTS

INTRODUCTION

' "The Turn of the Screw" is the most hopelessly evil story that we have ever read in any literature, ancient or modern.' So wrote the *Independent* (5 January 1899). Unsure whether to blame the ghosts of the tale or James himself for the story's 'refined subtlety of spiritual defilement', the reviewer's response foreshadows in its uncertainty as well as its ferocity the mystification and intense disagreement which have surrounded this intriguing tale ever since. In 'The Turn of the Screw' Henry James reached the pinnacle of his achievement in the field of supernatural fiction, treating his theme with a sophistication almost unprecedented in the genre. From 'The Romance of Certain Old Clothes', one of his earliest stories, to *The Sense of the Past*, the novel which he left unfinished at his death, James was to be repeatedly drawn to ghosts and the ghostly. His fascination was often a reluctant one, and in a letter of 27 April 1890 he remarked that 'the supernatural story . . . is not the *class* of fiction I myself most cherish', adding that he favoured instead 'a close connotation, or close observation, of the real—or whatever one may call it—the familiar, the inevitable'. It was fourteen years since the publication of James's last supernatural story, 'The Ghostly Rental'. Ten years later, however, he had completed nine tales which may broadly be characterized as 'ghostly'. Four of these—'Sir Edmund Orme', 'Owen Wingrave', 'The Friends of the Friends', and 'The Turn of the Screw'—make up the present volume.

At the beginning of the 1890s James was entering a period of crisis. He had to some extent lost interest in the 'international' fiction he had produced during the 1880s, and exhausted the social and political themes which had dominated *The Bostonians* (1885–6), *The Princess Casamassima* (1885–6), and *The Tragic Muse* (1889–90). The deaths of

friends, his ill-fated theatrical venture, and his disenchant-
ment with a culture which seemed to him increasingly
brazen and distorted were to prompt in him a growing sense
of otherness, of extinction, and of the general uncanniness
of life. 'I see ghosts everywhere,' he wrote to Francis Boott
on 11 October 1895. But the ghost stories of these troubled
years cannot be seen merely as a rearguard action against
what James called 'the great modern collapse of all the
forms and "superstitions" ' (*Notebooks*, 4 March 1895).
They were, rather, an impassioned exploration of the haunted
house of Victorian culture which brought James to the
threshold of his 'major phase' and laid much of the ground-
work for the more generally phantasmagoric and uncanny
experiences depicted in, for example, *The Ambassadors*
(1903). 'The Turn of the Screw' has an intensity and a
power to disturb which makes it at least the equal of works
like *Dr Jekyll and Mr Hyde* (1886), *The Picture of Dorian
Gray* (1891), *Dracula* (1897), and *Heart of Darkness* (1899).
All these novels examine the crumbling edges of the
Victorian edifice, the selves which lie behind its assumptions
of integrity, the violence and the discontent which both
created and terrified its civilization. The centres of unease
in these works of James's contemporaries, however, are
almost always at a distance, in the further reaches of
scientific, artistic, or geographical space. In 'The Turn of
the Screw', on the other hand, James limited himself to the
apparently mundane, showing what he called in his Preface
to 'Sir Edmund Orme' 'the strange and sinister embroidered
on the very type of the normal and easy'.

This concern for the formal and experiential relations
between the normal and the strange partially anticipated
Sigmund Freud's observation that the uncanny was 'that
class of the frightening which leads back to what is known
of old and long familiar' ('The "Uncanny" ', 1919). But
James was also capable of reversing Freud's paradox, since
he knew that the familiar possessed in its turn an ineffable

strangeness. Well before 'The Art of Fiction' (1884), he had been aware that his 'air of reality' was not simply a matter of transcribing everyday actuality in the way that he found so unsatisfactory in Trollope. Even the catalytic moments in his non-ghostly fiction were often uncanny ones. When, in the final chapter of *The Portrait of a Lady* (1881), Isabel briefly glimpses the spectral figure of Ralph Touchett in 'the cold, faint dawn', the scene is a powerful emblem of experience undergone. To see the ghost is a sign that through suffering Isabel has gained the 'miserable knowledge' which her cousin half-jokingly tells her is required before one can see the ghost of Gardencourt (ch. 5).

'Sir Edmund Orme' takes the tactical use of the super-natural in *The Portrait of a Lady* a step further, for here the ghostly is no longer, at least for the young man who narrates the story, a mere rite of passage. It is the passage itself, the very quintessence of experience. When the narrator follows Mrs Marden and her attractive daughter from the genteel and quietly anxious social world of Brighton to a country house party in Sussex, he is privileged with 'a mystic enlargement of vision'. Far from feeling the wordless horror of so many run-of-the-mill ghost stories, he exults in his experience 'as if it stood for all I had ever dreamt of', speculating that Orme is 'on my side, watching over my interest'. But what exactly is the narrator's 'interest'? Despite his sensitivity to the ghostly he is a somewhat dubious figure. He initially professes his love for Charlotte Marden in order, it seems, 'to keep her sense sealed'. Denying experience to others almost always has sinister implications in James, and it is the narrator as much as Orme who oppresses and coerces, who subjects Charlotte to 'a compulsion that was slightly painful'. His gallantry only partially conceals more predatory motives. Not tempted to tell Charlotte that he loves her, he entertains instead 'a strong impulse to say something intensely personal, some-thing violent and important'. To take up James's comment in his Preface, it is not so much that the strange and sinister are *embroidered on* the normal and easy as that the normal is itself sinister and Orme, ostensibly the sinister element in the tale, actually presents a front of complete normality. No Gothic monster, he is a discreet figure of 'perfect propriety' who if anything played the part of a victim in 'an old story, of love and pain and death'. This old story is in fact a very familiar, an archetypically Victorian tale of sexual unease. What haunts Mrs Marden's marred and repetitive speeches is the intimate and dishonourable secret of her own infidelity and transgression.

Old stories are again at work in 'Owen Wingrave'. The Wingraves are a military family who live on their legends of glorious battlefield deaths and less glorious deeds of violence within the home. Owen's father died when an Afghan sabre came 'crashing across his skull' and Colonel Wingrave killed his son with 'a blow on the head'. Owen wants to break with the centuries-old tradition of his family and thinks that war should be made a capital crime. The Wingraves begin a campaign to force him into conformity. 'Tactics' are adopted, an 'engine' is dragged into the field, and Owen goes off to see his aunt as if 'marching up to a battery'. So eager are the Wingraves to shed the blood of the family that they are scarcely capable of perpetuating it. The ritual by which they live consists in offering up their own members as sacrificial victims. These self-consuming practices find expression in the name of their house. 'Paramore' implies something both consistent with and contrary to 'mores', hinting at customs established both in spite and because of discontinuities. 'Paramore' suggests a similar ambivalence with regard to 'amore', hinting at the erotic conflict which also finds expression in Jane Wingrave's passion for the army, with its fusion of desire and suffering, aggression and remorse. Owen's aunt appears to associate 'Paramore' with her family's 'paramount valour', but the word also contains an extra-familial glimpse of 'paramour', making it perhaps appropriate that in rejecting the army it is as if Owen has 'fallen in love with a low girl' or is engaged in 'corrupting the youth of Athens'. So compendious are the paradoxes of the Wingrave family that these hinted improprieties, as well as the coolness between Owen and Kate Julian, are not the result of Owen's assertion of his independence but, rather, a symptomatic involvement with the broken engagements and violent passages of the Wingrave erotic mythology. It is impossible for Owen to break with his family's military past since in fighting it he inevitably perpetuates it. But his replication of the patterns of the past is also a transformation of those patterns. Displaying 'a military steadiness under fire', Owen wins a victory over the ghost of the family, becoming in death 'the young soldier on the gained field'.

Both 'Owen Wingrave' and 'Sir Edmund Orme' show the patterns of the past being simultaneously repeated and altered. In 'The Friends of the Friends', James shifts his subject from the field of history to that of hermeneutics, from the patterns of tradition to the patterns of interpretation. What, he seems to be asking, are the consequences of analysing life in terms of abstract oppositions and reflections? His narrator, a geometer of relationships, quickly draws attention to the similarities between her two friends. Both have seen a ghost and are in numerous ways alike. By some 'strange law', however, they are also 'alternate and incompatible': like mirror images they can approach but never meet. The narrator's manipulation of these patterns gradually becomes as life-threatening as the family traditions in 'Owen Wingrave', and it is no accident that a death almost immediately follows her arrangement and her postponement of a meeting between her two friends. Nevertheless her attempts to control events are doomed to failure. 'Laying the ghost' by sabotaging the projected meeting, she lends the patterns a vitality which escapes her. Shortly after the sudden death of her female friend the law of incompatibility which the narrator has tried to enforce is threatened when her fiancé claims to have seen the other woman on the night of her death. Determined that this meeting did not occur 'in the body', the narrator asserts that her fiancé has seen a ghost. This further attempt to impose patterns produces another perverse twist: by forcing her theories on her fiancé the narrator raises a ghost between them. Endeavouring to separate her two friends, she succeeds only in uniting them after death. In the final paragraph she greets the news of her ex-fiancé's demise as 'a direct contribution to my theory'. One might conclude that the tone of theoretical triumph struck in this closing comment verges on inhumanity if not insanity. To read the narrator's reading in such a way, however, is inevitably to risk repeating her own dubious attempts to map meaning.

'The Turn of the Screw' is a far more extensive study of the high price involved in constructing and enforcing rigid interpretations. A young woman obtains the post of governess to two children, abandoned at his country house by their uncle, and left by their previous preceptors, Peter Quint and Miss Jessel, in circumstances of some mystery. It is the first time that the new governess has known 'space and air and freedom'. Then, whilst taking a walk in the grounds one evening, she sees a figure on the tower. Who is he? Why is he there? Feeling that the scene has been 'stricken with death', she begins her investigations. Like the narrator of 'The Friends of the Friends', the governess seems intent above all on securing her univocal reading of events. With extraordinary tenacity and the utmost dexterity she struggles to confirm her hypothesis that the children are in the process of being corrupted by the ghosts of Quint and Miss Jessel.

For most of its earlier critics the central dilemma of the tale was whether or not to accept the interpretation of the governess. In 'The Ambiguity of Henry James' (1934) Edmund Wilson argued that she is 'a neurotic case of sex repression' whose reading is not to be trusted. For Wilson, the children are innocent and it is the governess who causes the death of Miles. The ghosts 'are not real ghosts at all but merely the governess's hallucinations'. James could hardly be cited as the first to have explored in fiction the possibility that ghosts are subjective phenomena. Such uncanny tales as George Eliot's 'The Lifted Veil' (1859), Guy de Maupassant's 'Le Horla' (1887) and Vernon Lee's 'A Wicked Voice' (1890) would lose much of their point if one failed to question the objectivity of their supernatural events. Unlike these tales, however, 'The Turn of the Screw' provides no clear indication either that Peter Quint and Miss Jessel are hallucinations or that they are apparitions. Yet it was perhaps inevitable that, in 'The Freudian Reading of *The Turn of the Screw*', Robert Heilman was provoked by Wilson's 'astonishingly *unambiguous* exegesis' into advancing a diametrically opposed one of his own. Heilman argued that Miles and Flora had indeed been corrupted by the ghosts, which were not hallucinations. For him the inability of the governess to defeat evil resulted from inexperience and not malevolence. Critical debate over the novel remained divided for several decades. A. J. A. Waldock, Glen A. Reed, and others sifted the text for evidence with which to refute the hallucination theory whilst Oscar Cargill and John Silver broadly agreed with Wilson.

This cursory survey inevitably caricatures the often subtle work of the critics mentioned above but it does not fundamentally misrepresent the prevailing assumption that to read 'The Turn of the Screw' is to establish *the* reading and if necessary to defeat other readings. This assumption is one that the governess shares; and even in the act of rejecting her interpretation, a critic like Wilson could be said to adopt a similarly single-minded defence of the coherence of his own position, demonizing the governess with something of the vehemence with which she herself demonizes Peter Quint and Miss Jessel. The circular relation between reading and counter-reading becomes even more remarkable when Heilman, who attacks psychopathological readings, himself accuses Wilson of 'hysterical blindness'. And when Heilman claims that 'The Turn of the Screw' is 'worth saving' the debate has, consciously or unconsciously, begun to take on the salvational overtones of the novel itself. One pictures Heilman desperately clutching the text in his arms and forcing it to confess to its ghosts as Wilson looms into view to deny that they exist.

At the beginning of 'The Turn of the Screw' Douglas, who introduces the story, deflects suggestions that the governess is motivated either by fear or desire, gently discouraging explanations in terms either of apparitions or hallucinations. 'The story *won't* tell,' he informs his audience, 'not in any literal vulgar way.' Yet, perhaps understandably, much of the criticism of 'The Turn of the Screw' has been devoted to making the story tell. James wrote in his Preface that he had set out 'to catch those not easily caught'. Edna Kenton anticipated Wilson by reading this comment as an admission that James was trying to trap his readers into a mistaken belief in the reality of the ghosts. When Kenton detects this 'story behind the "story" ' she implicitly claims to have avoided capture. Shoshana Felman, however, has argued more recently that critics like Kenton are trapped precisely by attempting to avoid being duped by the text. Positing a univocal reading and defining the evil which James only adumbrates, Kenton (like Wilson, Heilman, and others) ceases to draw meaning *out of* the text and instead proceeds, as James wrote in his Preface, to read *into* it 'more or less fantastic figures'. James meanwhile, both in the tale and in his evasive comments about it, neither provides nor claims to possess the supreme key to meaning. A ghost behind the ghosts, he establishes his mastery by disappearing from the scene, leaving in his wake eddies of unfixable significance.

In spite of the prevalent drive for the singular and the

discrete there is nevertheless a sense in which the sum of critical readings of this much-discussed novella remains faithful to what Felman describes as its 'incessant *sliding* of signification'. To reject the hallucination theory is not necessarily to share Heilman's belief that the governess is a tragically flawed protector: Joseph Firebaugh describes her as an 'inadequate priestess', Katherine Porter as a medium for evil, and John Lydenberg as a 'false saviour'. Nor are critics devoted to the hallucination theory united in their opinion of the governess: Cargill emphasizes her 'befuddled heroism' whilst Silver paints a picture of a calculating villainess. It does not follow that the hallucination theory requires Freudian underpinning, since Sidney Lind sees the tale in terms of a pre-Freudian psychology of the split consciousness, and nor is the Freudian approach inevitably linked to a belief in the innocence of the children: Mark Spilka suggests that a truly Freudian reading of the tale would recognize its investigation of infantile sexuality.

I have described this circuit of readings as if it was governed by a preliminary decision as to whether or not the ghosts are 'real', but there is a strong argument that the irreducibly hypothetical nature of literary statements renders such decisions meaningless. Firebaugh is quite right to argue that in an important sense 'the whole tale is illusion'. A similar difficulty attaches to disagreements over the reliability of the governess as a narrator. Her 'I' is certainly more opaque than the narrative voice of '*A Passionate Pilgrim*' and, arguably, less *reliably* unreliable than the 'I' of 'The Aspern Papers' (1888). But too often the question of reliability involves an odd assumption that fictional statements can in some way be verified. I am not suggesting that one must simply accept the text at face value and take the governess's word for everything, but once one raises the possibility of unreliability it is difficult to know where to stop: perhaps *nothing* the governess says is true. Or maybe Douglas is lying . . . and so on. Because the narrative could

be taken as an apologia consciously addressed to Douglas
(and not, as in 'Sir Edmund Orme' or 'The Friends of the
Friends', a private document without an intended recipient),
the reader cannot confidently look over the shoulder of the
governess. The detachment which made irony possible in
'The Friends of the Friends' gives way to a distance which is
all the more enigmatic because one expects first-person
narrative to be both immediate and intimate. It is to be
regretted that Marius Bewley and Wayne Booth took up
Allen Tate's potentially fruitful investigation of the dubiety
of first-person narrative only to dismiss Jamesian ambiguity
as perverse, unintentional, morally and structurally confused
and confusing. A similar hostility also emerges in the latter
part of Wilson's essay, and it is tempting to see such
attitudes as defensive reactions to the anxiety that a text like
'The Turn of the Screw' can create.

The anxiety I have mentioned springs not so much from
any definite action on the part of the ghosts, the governess,
or the children but from the fact that the values of the tale
are, as James wrote in his Preface, 'positively all blanks'.
The lack of definite information as to whether or not the
ghosts are real has led Shlomith Rimmon to write that it
possesses 'a central informational gap'. But the notion of an
absent core, a single, central enigma, does little to explain
the text's proliferating voids. The investigations of the
governess into what happened at Bly before her arrival
succeed only in bringing a series of absences to light: the
fact that waistcoats had gone missing, that Quint never wore
a hat, that Miles denied having been with Quint. The chain
of blanks culminates in the deaths of Quint and Miss Jessel
but is by no means restricted to events in the past. 'No
apparition', as Christine Brooke-Rose has pointed out, 'is
narrated *whole*.' The governess is unable to describe the
ghosts without breaking up the continuity of her narrative
and this as yet untitled tale is so curtailed at both ends that
Douglas must supply epilogue and prologue in the intro-

ductory chapter. Before the governess arrives at Bly, the children have passed through the hands of a series of relatives and servants, all of whom disappear or die. After the events described in the story, the governess's manuscript is also passed on to others at the deaths, first of the governess herself, and then of Douglas.

A series of spreading ripples, ghostly after-effects of an ever more distant origin, the narrative contains other writings which are also marked by loss, omission, and silence. The master writes to the governess only to sever all communication between them, enclosing a letter from Miles's headmaster which contains no explanation of why the boy has been sent back to Bly. The governess receives 'disturbing letters from home' but fails to communicate their contents. She does not post the children's letters to their uncle. When she finally decides to write to the master she describes herself only as sitting before 'a blank sheet of paper'. Her letter is destined never to be sent and Miles will later confess to having found 'nothing' in it. It is therefore appropriate that Flora's first lesson from the governess consists in copying out a sheet of 'nice "round O's" '. These O's resonate eerily with the sixty or so exclamations of 'oh', and approximately six hundred long dashes, which punctuate the narrative with the unsaid or unsayable.

'The Turn of the Screw' is, however, by no means impervious to interpretation: James's blanks perforate but do not destroy its play of meaning. Possessing an almost infinitely suggestive porousness, the tale is rich in fractured seams of reference to other texts. The governess seems to view her surroundings as a reservoir of literary archetypes, believing that her situation demands an 'extraordinary flight of heroism'. What sort of heroine does she want to be? In his Preface James compared 'The Turn of the Screw' to fairy-tales like 'Bluebeard' and 'Cinderella'. This suggests two roles for the governess: either, to put it schematically, she can defeat a threatening male figure, as in 'Bluebeard' or, as in 'Cinderella', marry an attractive one. But the tale opens these archetypal possibilities only to deviate from them: ultimately, in a perverse collision of both stories, it is the fairy prince who dies. When the governess refers to the 'gingerbread antiquity' of the towers at Bly one catches a brief glimpse of 'Hansel and Gretel'. Unfortunately, however, this story provides no role for the governess except that of the cruel stepmother who sends the children into the forest or the wicked witch who imprisons them. The archetypes either turn on the governess or elude her creative control. Shortly after the governess sees Quint for the first time she wonders whether there is 'a "secret" at Bly—a mystery of Udolpho or an insane, an unmentionable relative kept in unsuspected confinement'. The reference to Mrs Radcliffe's *The Mysteries of Udolpho* (1794) and the distinct allusion to Charlotte Brontë's *Jane Eyre* (1847) are, once again, not templates to map what the narrative is but quicksilver glints of what it fails to be. 'The Turn of the Screw' glances at, but does not pursue, the trails left by other texts. It depicts a socially alienated heroine but refuses to promote her to wealth and status through the discovery of lost relatives or missing wills. To read 'The Turn of the Screw' through *Udolpho* is to suspect that, despite a cynicism and shrewdness of which Emily St Aubert is incapable, the governess loses that balance of sensibility and sense which in Emily is threatened but ultimately preserved. In *Udolpho* it is the servants who recount ghostly legends to their mistresses. Although sensitive to 'ideal terrors', Emily warns her maid Annette that an undue interest in ghosts leads to 'the misery of superstition' (vol. ii, ch. 7), remaining silent about her own uncanny experiences (which are eventually explained naturalistically) in order to avoid seeming as credulous as a servant. 'The Turn of the Screw' turns these stable post-Enlightenment relations upside-down, for here the governess temporarily remains silent in order to make sure that she is not being 'practised upon by the servants', and then exposes the housekeeper to her own terrors. The irrational is not working from the bottom up but from the top down.

It would be easy to see the allusion to the insane, unmentionable relative of *Jane Eyre* as a mere flourish, an incidental enrichment of the *mise en scène*. James's portrait of the governess is certainly informed by Jane and Bly indubitably recalls Thornfield, but the numerous parallels between the two novels are neither inert nor unproblematic. Jane witnesses Rochester's arrival at Thornfield and renders assistance when his horse slips on a sheet of ice, but in 'The Turn of the Screw' this famous meeting is warped almost to the point of travesty. The governess is retrospectively informed of (and is not present at) the death (not injury) of the valet (not master) after a fall on the ice. *Jane Eyre* glissades into 'The Turn of the Screw' only to signal the later text's deviations. Rochester's arrival fills up 'the blanks of existence' for Jane (ch. 15), but for the governess the blanks remain because the master simply never turns up to be resisted, wounded, and redeemed. Marooned in a novel which refuses to satisfy her narrative desires, the governess seems to use Miles as a surrogate in the obscure ritual which she is enacting. In doing so she creates further ghostly echoes of *Jane Eyre* which defeat any attempt to become her literary predecessor. The image of Miles left indoors to finish a book 'on the red cushion of a deep window-seat' combines with the image of Flora concealed behind the window-blinds to recall the opening scene of *Jane Eyre* in which the young Jane sits in a window-seat behind a 'red moreen curtain', escaping from the oppressive environment of Gateshead into Bewick. Rather than progressing from Gateshead to Ferndean, the narrative thread of 'The Turn of the Screw' seems inexorably to wind back from Thornfield to Gateshead, so that one ends with Miles, forehead against the window, contemplating 'the dull things of November' just as Jane looked out, in the opening chapter of Charlotte Brontë's novel, at 'the drear November

day'. Shutting Flora up and later sending her away, the
governess displays a kinship not to Jane but to Mrs Reed,
who punishes Jane's demonic protests against injustice by
locking her into the red room and sending her away to
school at Lowood.

When the governess envisages herself as 'a screen'
between the children and the ghosts she seizes 'a magnificent
chance' not only to attract the master but also to enforce
distinctions. Unable, however, to create the sort of moral,
epistemological, or atmospheric chiaroscuro so dear to
Gothic literature, she seems quite literally to inhabit a
borderland between the light and the dark. Like a number
of scenes in the novel, her first encounter with Quint occurs
at twilight. This evening vision is paradoxically described as
her 'dawn of alarm'. Borderlines are more seriously
transgressed when 'the others, the outsiders' succeed in
getting in and Miles gets out. Characters repeatedly 'break
out' or 'break into' each other's speeches and the narrative
records numerous breakdowns, collapses, snaps, and bursts.
To be a screen seems to involve flattening one's identity to a
mirroring thinness and although the governess perhaps
seems only fretful when she talks of steadying, assuring, or
stiffening herself, the self-reflexive form becomes charged
with ontological anxiety when she speaks of finding,
hearing, feeling, or seeing herself. In her own eyes she
develops the opacity of another being, speculating that she
'seemed to see' something, that she 'seemed literally to be
running a race'. Towards the end of the tale she writes that
'I seemed to myself . . . . to have mastered it, to see it all'.
One wonders how a self so fractured can possibly achieve
mastery. Treating her intellectual and emotional states as
external presences, the governess notes that her fortitude
'revived' and that her doubts 'bristle'. On other occasions
she is 'possessed' by 'a portentous clearness', 'held' by a
'thought', and 'harassed' by her 'conclusions'. These would
usually be perfectly ordinary figures of speech but in 'The

Turn of the Screw' the dead metaphors spring to life.
Repeatedly unable to remember or express her experiences,
the governess resorts to strangely fused sensory formulations.
During Quint's first appearance she *hears* 'the intense hush
in which the sounds of evening dropped'. Later, on the
stairs at Bly, she *sees* him disappear into 'the silence itself'.
Any maintenance of discrete categories is extremely difficult
because hardly anything at Bly is unique: there are two
towers, two children, two scenes by the lake, two by the
dining-room window, and so on. Among numerous others,
words like 'turn' and 'repeat' insistently return and are
repeated. On occasions the narrative becomes trapped in a
tautologous circularity, so that the ghosts are said to come
'from where they come from' and Miles tells the governess
that 'when I'm bad I *am* bad'. This pervasive doubleness is
not the dualistic see-saw of the tale's opening lines but a
sequence of reflections which turn the actions of the
governess back upon herself. She sets Miles 'a sharp trap'
only to find that 'it was I who fell into the trap!' and later
provides against the 'danger of rebellion' only to encounter
'revolution'.

Yet it would be misleading to represent the governess as a
passive victim of the text's strange law. She bounds around
Bly, seizing and grasping characters and concepts, figurat-
ively smashing windows, delivering blows to the stomach,
pushing people to the wall, and holding them under fire.
Like the narrator of 'The Friends of the Friends', the
governess actively fills in the blanks, manipulating patterns
in accordance with her design. Her design may be consistent
but her arguments are less than straight. When Flora denies
seeing anything out of the window the governess 'absolutely
believed she lied'. Discovering the child again gazing into
the night, she now becomes convinced that Flora 'saw—as
she had not, I had satisfied myself, the previous time'. The
governess revises her interpretation yet again when she sees
Miles and not Miss Jessel on the lawn. These shifts in her

position are not accompanied by any retrospective exoneration of Flora. The governess assumes that blanks conceal meaning rather than indicating its absence, and the fact that his schoolmasters 'go into no particulars' about his dismissal can have 'only one meaning' for her: that the boy had been 'an injury to the others'. Following the departure of Flora and Mrs Grose, the governess observes that the servants 'looked blank'. For her this signifies their awareness of the 'crisis'. Yet when Mrs Grose is 'blank' in Chapter XVIII the governess sees only 'scared ignorance'. One can read blankness, in other words, either as ignorance or as portentous knowledge. Identical signs can support quite opposite readings, and one only needs to read 'with reflexion, with suspicion' (Chapter I) to conclude that all manifest signs of innocence are a pretence and must be reversed to reveal the guilty truth. Thus Miles's beauty and lack of a history initially suggest his innocence but later the children's 'more than earthly beauty' is said to be a 'fraud' and the fact that Miles has 'scarce even made a reference' to his previous life is precisely what arouses the governess's suspicions. If all manifestations of innocence are fraudulent, then there is simply no room for manifest innocence. But how does one explain manifest signs of guilt? To perform the usual turn on Flora's 'appalling language' or Miles's admission to having 'said things' would, vertiginously, be to see revealed guilt as a sign of latent innocence. In the final chapter, when the governess momentarily recognizes the possibility that Miles is innocent, she asks herself 'what then on earth was I?' It is difficult not to reply that she is guilty. To accuse her by simply inverting her interpretation is, however, to adopt the same dangerous logic. Arguing that the blanks are never suspect is as doubtful a strategy as maintaining that they always are. The polarized dialectic of the governess renders differences indiscriminable and opposites interchangeable. Her world of angels and demons can be converted into a mirror world of demons and angels, and her narrative is a gradually mounting crisis of distinctions. Shortly before Miss Jessel's final appearance the crisis culminates in pure oxymoron:

'He found the most divine little way to keep me quiet while she went off.'
' "Divine"?' Mrs Grose bewilderedly echoed.
'Infernal then!' I almost cheerfully rejoined.

Is the governess good or evil? If the divine and the infernal are interchangeable the question no longer makes much sense. Having seized her magnificent chance to become a screen, the governess ends up as a medium rather than a border. Gothic polarities become impacted paradoxes. Victim or violator? To an extent this choice underlies the depiction of governesses throughout Victorian literature. Was the nineteenth-century governess a mocked dogsbody like Miss Merry in *Daniel Deronda* (1876), or a Cinderella who defeated her Bluebeard before marrying him, as in *Jane Eyre*? A picaresque adventuress like Becky Sharp in *Vanity Fair* (1847), or a figure of pure malevolence, like Flora de Barral's governess in Conrad's *Chance* (1914)? The governess was of course potentially all these things, and the very openness of her role was itself a source of anxiety. In the governess of 'The Turn of the Screw', James addressed conflicts which went to the heart of nineteenth-century culture. Almost all of his previous ghost stories had in some way dealt with women who were not defined within the bourgeois family, with widows or the unmarried. These women tended to develop in opposite directions: either they could abuse or be abused, drain or be drained. Both in 'The Turn of the Screw' and in Victorian society at large, the figure of the governess focused, intensified, and ambiguated these polarized possibilities. An outsider within the family, the nineteenth-century governess belonged neither above nor below stairs, neither exclusively with the children nor with the adults, neither amongst women nor with men. The psychological conflicts which resulted from isolation and exploitation were to be treated by Freud in his analysis of Miss Lucy R. (*Studies on Hysteria*, 1895).

One of the correspondents in James's epistolary tale 'A Bundle of Letters' (1879) describes how Lady Battledown renames all her children's governesses 'Johnson' for her own convenience, paying them each £5 a year in compensation. But the name of another governess cited in the same story provides rather a different perspective. 'Miss Turnover' may well be the name of somebody who might, morally or sexually, be overturned, one of those governesses who, in the Victorian imagination at least, became 'fallen women'. Yet 'Turnover' could also be the name of somebody who overturns, who might even indeed bring Lady Battledown down in battle. The name certainly anticipates that of Miss Overmore, the upwardly-mobile governess of *What Maisie Knew*, but it also begins to hint at the more complex turns which James was later to weave in 'The Turn of the Screw'.

In the meantime, the uncertainty which affects one's estimation of the governess in 'The Turn of the Screw' was unfolded less ambiguously in two other stories by James. Mrs Ryves in 'Sir Dominick Ferrand' (1892) is the illegitimate daughter of a seduced governess, a rather tragic figure. In 'Master Eustace' (1871), on the other hand, the governess who narrates the tale is a quiet manipulator who wants to give her young charge 'a taste of bad luck'. Is the governess of 'The turn of the Screw' a later version of this pruriently puritanical figure? Possibly; she would certainly have been an unsympathetic reader of 'Sir Dominick Ferrand' and of the old stories 'of love and pain and death' mentioned in 'Sir Edmund Orme'. The governess shows little compassion for the 'infamous' predecessor she constructs from the shadowy details provided by Mrs Grose. She is in fact unique amongst James's ghost-seers in viewing the spectral as a manifestation of unmitigated evil. Even the narrator of 'The Friends of the Friends' accepts that ghosts generally return from motives of 'reparation, of admonition, or even of curiosity'. But, although James does seem to have been raising ghosts from his own previous work as well as from that of his literary predecessors, it is not sufficient to suggest that the two governesses in 'The Turn of the Screw' neatly reproduce the opposed possibilities which he envisaged for the figure elsewhere. For the governess and Miss Jessel are also twins. In the later chapters of the novel, the governess seems in her 'fierce rigour of confidence' to haunt Bly with something like the 'fury of intention' she attributes to Miss Jessel. On a number of occasions she both literally and metaphorically stands in the place of the apparitions. When Mrs Marden or Owen Wingrave encounter ghosts they become ghost-like. 'The Turn of the Screw' refines this insight: to see a ghost is potentially to become what one thinks ghosts are. Requiring a counterweight to found her own identity, the governess sees the ghosts as her mirror opposites and then, through the strange law of the text, becomes the very image of a ghost. The victim of meaning's ductility, she speaks in her narrative as a voice from the grave, from what Maurice Blanchot has called 'the imprecise space of narration—that unreal beyond where everything is apparition, slippery, evasive, present and absent'.

NOTE ON THE TEXTS

THE TALES which make up this volume were, as usual with James, published in magazines before being collected in book form. All four were among the 55 of James's 112 tales to be included in the New York Edition of The Novels and Tales of Henry James (issued in twenty-four volumes[1] between December 1907 and July 1909 by Charles Scribner's Sons), and it is the NYE versions which are reprinted here.

'Sir Edmund Orme' first appeared on 25 November 1891 in the Christmas number of *Black and White*. It was subsequently published with five other tales in *The Lesson of the Master* (London and New York: Macmillan, 1892). Revised for inclusion in NYE XVII, it followed 'The Altar of the Dead', 'The Beast in the Jungle', 'The Birthplace', 'The Private Life', 'Owen Wingrave', and 'The Friends of the Friends' and preceded 'The Real Right Thing', 'The Jolly Corner', and 'Julia Bride'.

'Owen Wingrave' was first published on 28 November 1892 in the Christmas number of the *Graphic*. It then reappeared with five other tales in *The Private Life* (London: Osgood, McIlvaine & Co., 1893) and as the third and final tale in *The Wheel of Time* (New York: Harper & Bros., 1893). It was revised for inclusion in NYE XVII. In December 1907 James converted the tale into a one-act play, *The Saloon*. This was rejected by the Incorporated Stage Society in 1909 and George Bernard Shaw, irritated by what he saw as the play's deference to the power of the past, asked James why he had written it. James replied on 20 January 1909 with a magisterial defence of the imagination, which for him 'absolutely enjoys and insists on and

---

[1] Two further volumes, the second comprising *The Sense of the Past*, were brought out in 1917.

incurably leads a life of its own'. In a second letter three days later, James argued that his hero had got 'the *best of everything*', thereby creating for the audience an 'intensity of impression and emotion'. *The Saloon* was eventually produced by Gertrude Kingston at the Little Theatre from January to February 1911.

'The Friends of the Friends' first appeared as 'The Way It Came' in the May 1896 issues of the *Chap Book* and *Chapman's Magazine of Fiction*. Under the original title it was then published with three other tales in *Embarrassments* (London: Heinemann, 1896). It was subsequently revised and retitled for inclusion in NYE XVII.

'The Turn of the Screw' was dictated to the stenographer William MacAlpine at 34 De Vere Gardens (James's flat in Kensington) during the autumn of 1897. MacAlpine had been engaged part-way through the composition of *What Maisie Knew* and, according to William Lyon Phelps, was said by James to have 'betrayed not the slightest shade of feeling' during the dictation of 'The Turn of the Screw': a story with which James meant 'to scare the whole world' ('Henry James', *Yale Review*, 5 (1916), 794). Work on the tale followed the completion of 'John Delavoy', preceded the composition of 'The Great Good Place' and 'In the Cage' and coincided with James's negotiations for a lease on Lamb House in Rye. The lease was signed by the end of September and the novella was certainly completed by 1 December 1897, when James wrote to his sister-in-law Alice, 'I *have*, at last, finished my little book.' 'The Turn of the Screw' was first published between January and April 1898 in *Collier's Weekly* where, although it displayed the same chapter divisions as later editions, it was also divided into twelve weekly instalments (the frame chapter, Chapters II–III, III–IV, IV–V, VI–VII, VIII–IX, X–XII, XIII–XV, XVI–XVIII, XIX–XX, XXI–XXII and XXIII–XXIV) and into five 'Parts' (the frame chapter to Chapter III, Chapters IV–VII, VIII–XIII, XIV–XVIII and XIX–XXIV). The tale was then published alongside 'Covering End' in *The Two Magics* (London: Heinemann, 1898). It was subsequently revised for inclusion in NYE XII, where it followed 'The Aspern Papers' and preceded 'The Liar' and 'The Two Faces'.

FURTHER READING

PRIMARY WORKS

MANY of James's works, particularly those written after about 1890, might broadly be characterized as 'ghostly'. In order to keep these suggestions for further reading within reasonable limits I have chosen to mention only those works which would customarily if crudely be classified as 'ghost stories' or which contain some form of ghostly encounter. The dates given are those of first publication. The original periodical texts are being republished in *The Tales of Henry James*, ed. Maqbool Aziz (Oxford, 1973–). The earliest book version of the tales can be found in *The Complete Tales of Henry James*, ed. Leon Edel, 12 vols (London, 1962–4). This edition is hereafter abbreviated to CT. Where revised New York Edition versions of the texts exist the relevant volumes are indicated.

i. Novels

The Portrait of a Lady (1880–1), NYE III–IV
The Sense of the Past (1917), NYE XXVI

ii. Tales

'The Romance of Certain Old Clothes' (1868), CT 1
'De Grey: A Romance' (1868), CT 1
'A Passionate Pilgrim' (1871), CT 2, NYE XIII
'The Ghostly Rental' (1876), CT 4
'Nona Vincent' (1892), CT 8
'The Private Life' (1892), CT 8, NYE XVII
'The Real Right Thing' (1899), CT 10, NYE XVII
'Maud-Evelyn' (1900), CT 11
'The Third Person' (1900), CT 11
'The Jolly Corner' (1908), CT 12, NYE XVII

iii. Plays

The Saloon, in *The Complete Plays of Henry James*, ed. Leon Edel (Philadelphia and New York, 1949).

iv. Other writings

'Is There a Life After Death?', in *In After Days: Thoughts on the Future Life*, by W. D. Howells, Henry James, and others (London, 1910), 199–233. Repr. in *The James Family*, ed. F. O. Matthiessen (New York, 1947), 602–14.

Henry James: Literary Criticism, ed. Leon Edel with Mark Wilson, Library of America, 2 vols (New York, 1984). See in particular James's comments on ghost story technique in his 1865 review of Mrs Braddon's *Aurora Floyd* (I. 742), on 'Howe's Masquerade' in his 1879 critical biography *Hawthorne* (I. 368–9), on Mérimée's handling of the supernatural in his 1874 review of *Dernières nouvelles* (II. 564), and on Balzac's interest in the supernatural in his 1875 essay (II. 47–8).

Letters, ed. Leon Edel, 4 vols (Cambridge, Mass., 1974–84). On 'Owen Wingrave' see in particular James's letters to George Bernard Shaw (20 Jan. 1909 and 23 Jan. 1909). On 'The Turn of the Screw' see his letters to Alice James (1 Dec. 1897), to A. C. Benson (11 Mar. 1898), to Dr Louis Waldstein (21 Oct. 1898), to H. G. Wells (9 Dec. 1898), to F. W. H. Myers (19 Dec. 1898), to W. D. Howells (29 June 1900, 9 Aug. 1900, and 11 Dec. 1902), and to J. B. Pinker (11 Sept. 1914).

SECONDARY WORKS

i. Bibliography

Edel, Leon, and Dan H. Laurence, with James Rambeau, *A Bibliography of Henry James*, The Soho Bibliographies, 8, third edn. (Oxford, 1982).

McColgan, Kristin Pruitt, *Henry James, 1917–1959: A Reference Guide* (Boston, 1979).

Scura, Dorothy McInnis, *Henry James, 1960–1974: A Reference Guide* (Boston, 1979).

ii. Biography

Edel, Leon, *The Life of Henry James*, revised edn., 2 vols (Harmondsworth, 1977).

iii. Criticism

'The Turn of the Screw' is probably the most extensively discussed of James's works and the critical history would in itself be the subject of no small book. I have tried to show a fair cross-section of the various approaches.

Armstrong, Paul B., 'History and Epistemology: The Example of *The Turn of the Screw*', *New Literary History*, 19 (1987–8), 693–712.

Banta, Martha, *Henry James and the Occult: The Great Extension* (Bloomington, Ind., 1972).

Bewley, Marius, *The Complex Fate* (London, 1952). See especially pp. 96–111, 134–48.

Blanchot, Maurice, 'The Turn of the Screw' (1959), in *The Sirens' Song: Selected Essays*, ed. Gabriel Josipovici, trans. Sacha Rabinovitch (Brighton, 1982).

Booth, Wayne C., *The Rhetoric of Fiction* (Chicago, 1961). See especially pp. 311–22, 339–46.

Brooke-Rose, Christine, *A Rhetoric of the Unreal* (Cambridge, 1981). See especially pp. 62–6, 117–227, 396–405.

Cargill, Oscar, '*The Turn of the Screw* and Alice James', *PMLA*, 78 (1963), 238–49; repr. in Kimbrough (q.v.).

Felman, Shoshana, 'Turning the Screw of Interpretation', *Yale French Studies*, 55 and 56 (1977), 94–207.

Firebaugh, Joseph J., 'Inadequacy in Eden: Knowledge and *The Turn of the Screw*', *Modern Fiction Studies*, 3 (1957), 57–63; repr. in Willen (q.v.).

Goddard, Harold C., 'A Pre-Freudian Reading of *The Turn*

of the Screw', *Nineteenth-Century Fiction*, 12 (1957), 1–36; repr. in Willen (q.v.).

Heilman, R. B., 'The Freudian Reading of *The Turn of the Screw'*, *Modern Language Notes*, 62 (1947), 433–45.

——, *'The Turn of the Screw* as Poem', *University of Kansas City Review*, 14 (1948), 277–89; repr. in Kimbrough and in Willen (qq.v.).

Kenton, Edna, 'Henry James to the Ruminant Reader: *The Turn of the Screw'*, *The Arts*, 6 (1924), 245–55; repr. in Willen (q.v.).

Kimbrough, Robert, ed., *Henry James: 'The Turn of the Screw'*, Norton Critical Edition (New York, 1966).

Lind, Sidney Edmund, 'The Supernatural Tales of Henry James: Conflict and Fantasy' (unpublished Ph.D. dissertation, New York University, 1948).

Lustig, T. J., *Henry James and the Ghostly* (Cambridge, 1994).

Lydenberg, John, 'The Governess Turns the Screws', *Nineteenth-Century Fiction*, 12 (1957), 37–58; repr. in Willen (q.v.).

O'Gorman, Donal, 'Henry James's Reading of *The Turn of the Screw'*, *Henry James Review*, 1 (1980), 125–38, 228–56.

Porter, Katherine Anne, Allen Tate, and Mark Van Doren, 'James: *The Turn of the Screw*' (transcript of a radio symposium broadcast on 3 May 1942), in Willen (q.v.).

Reed, Glenn A., 'Another Turn on James's *The Turn of the Screw'*, *American Literature*, 20 (1949), 413–23; repr. in Willen (q.v.).

Rimmon, Shlomith, *The Concept of Ambiguity: The Example of James* (Chicago, 1977).

Roellinger, Francis X., 'Psychical Research and *The Turn of the Screw'*, *American Literature*, 20 (1949), 401–12; repr. in Kimbrough (q.v.).

Rowe, John Carlos, *The Theoretical Dimensions of Henry James* (London, 1985). See especially pp. 120–44, 151–2.

Sheppard, E. A., *Henry James and 'The Turn of the Screw'* (Auckland, 1974).

Silver, John, 'A Note on the Freudian Reading of *The Turn of the Screw*', *American Literature*, 29 (1957), 207–11; repr. in Willen (q.v.).

Spilka, Mark, 'Turning the Freudian Screw: How Not to Do It', *Literature and Psychology*, 13 (1963), 105–11; repr. in Kimbrough (q.v.).

Tate, Allen, *see* Porter, Katherine.

Todorov, Tzvetan, *The Fantastic: A Structural Approach to a Literary Genre*, trans. Richard Howard (Ithaca, N.Y., 1975).

Waldock, A. J. A., 'Mr Edmund Wilson and *The Turn of the Screw*', *Modern Language Notes*, 62 (1947), 331–4; repr. in Willen (q.v.).

Willen, Gerald, ed., *A Casebook on Henry James's 'The Turn of the Screw'* (New York, 1960).

Wilson, Edmund, 'The Ambiguity of Henry James', *Hound and Horn*, 7 (1934), 385–406. This essay was republished with minor alterations in *The Triple Thinkers* (New York, 1938) and with major revisions and a postscript in *The Triple Thinkers*, enlarged edn. (New York, 1948). The 1948 text, with a further postscript dated 1959, is repr. in Willen (q.v.).

CHRONOLOGY OF HENRY JAMES

COMPILED BY LEON EDEL

1843   Born 15 April at No. 21 Washington Place, New York City.

1843–4   Taken abroad by parents to Paris and London: period of residence at Windsor.

1845–55 Childhood in Albany and New York.

1855–8   Attends schools in Geneva, London, Paris and Boulogne-sur-mer and is privately tutored.

1858   James family settles in Newport, Rhode Island.

1859   At scientific school in Geneva. Studies German in Bonn.

1860   At school in Newport. Receives back injury on eve of Civil War while serving as volunteer fireman. Studies art briefly. Friendship with John La Farge.

1862–3   Spends term in Harvard Law School.

1864   Family settles in Boston and then in Cambridge. Early anonymous story and unsigned reviews published.

1865   First signed story published in *Atlantic Monthly*.

1869–70 Travels in England, France and Italy. Death of his beloved cousin Minny Temple.

1870   Back in Cambridge, publishes first novel in *Atlantic, Watch and Ward*.

1872–4   Travels with sister Alice and aunt in Europe; writes impressionistic travel sketches for the *Nation*. Spends autumn in Paris and goes to Italy to write first large novel.

1874–5   On completion of *Roderick Hudson* tests New York City as residence; writes much literary journalism for *Nation*. First three books published: *Transatlantic Sketches*, *A Passionate Pilgrim* (tales), and *Roderick Hudson*.

1875–6   Goes to live in Paris. Meets Ivan Turgenev and through him Flaubert, Zola, Daudet, Maupassant and Edmond de Goncourt. Writes *The American*.

1876-7   Moves to London and settles in 3 Bolton Street, Picca-
          dilly. Revisits Paris, Florence, Rome.

1878   'Daisy Miller' published in London establishes fame on
          both sides of the Atlantic. Publishes first volume of essays,
          French Poets and Novelists.

1879-82   *The Europeans, Washington Square, Confidence, Portrait of
          a Lady*.

1882-3   Revisits Boston: First visit to Washington. Death of
          parents.

1884-6   Returns to London. Sister Alice comes to live near him.
          Fourteen-volume collection of novels and tales published.
          Writes *The Bostonians* and *The Princess Casamassima*,
          published in the following year.

1886   Moves to flat at 34 De Vere Gardens.

1887   Sojourn in Italy, mainly in Florence and Venice. 'The
          Aspern Papers', *The Reverberator*, 'A London Life'.
          Friendship with grand-niece of Fenimore Copper—
          Constance Fenimore Woolson.

1888   *Partial Portraits* and several collections of tales.

1889-90   *The Tragic Muse*.

1890-1   Dramatizes *The American*, which has a short run. Writes
          four comedies, rejected by producers.

1892   Alice James dies in London.

1894   Miss Woolson commits suicide in Venice. James journeys
          to Italy and visits her grave in Rome.

1895   He is booed at first night of his play *Guy Domville*. Deeply
          depressed, he abandons the theatre.

1896-7   *The Spoils of Poynton, What Maisie Knew*.

1898   Takes long lease of Lamb House, in Rye, Sussex. 'The
          Turn of the Screw' published.

1899-1900 *The Awkward Age, The Sacred Fount*. Friendship with
          Conrad and Wells.

1902-4   *The Ambassadors, The Wings of the Dove* and *The Golden
          Bowl*. Friendships with H. C. Andersen and Jocelyn
          Persse.

1905   Revisits U.S.A. after 20-year absence, lectures on Balzac
          and the speech of Americans.

1906–10   *The American Scene*. Edits selective and revised 'New York Edition' of his works in 24 volumes. Friendship with Hugh Walpole.

1910   Death of brother, William James.

1913   Sargent paints his portrait as 70th birthday gift from some 300 friends and admirers. Writes autobiographies, *A Small Boy and Others*, and *Notes of a Son and Brother*.

1914   *Notes on Novelists*. Visits wounded in hospitals.

1915   Becomes a British subject.

1916   Given Order of Merit. Dies 28 February in Chelsea, aged 72. Funeral in Chelsea Old Church. Ashes buried in Cambridge, Mass., family plot.

1976   Commemorative tablet unveiled in Poet's Corner of Westminster Abbey, 17 June.

PREFACES

The following extracts are taken from the Prefaces to Vols XVII and XII of the New York Edition.

I. 'SIR EDMUND ORME', 'OWEN WINGRAVE', AND 'THE FRIENDS OF THE FRIENDS'

I FEAR I can defend such doings but under the plea of my amusement in them—an amusement I of course hoped others might succeed in sharing. But so comes in exactly the principle under the wide strong wing of which several such matters are here harvested; things of a type that might move me, had I space, to a pleading eloquence. Such compositions as 'The Jolly Corner', printed here not for the first time, but printed elsewhere only as I write and after my quite ceasing to expect it; 'The Friends of the Friends', to which I here change the colourless title of 'The Way It Came' (1896), 'Owen Wingrave' (1893), 'Sir Edmund Orme' (1891), 'The Real Right Thing' (1900), would obviously never have existed but for that love of 'a story as a story' which had from far back beset and beguiled their author. To this passion, the vital flame at the heart of any sincere attempt to lay a scene and launch a drama, he flatters himself he has never been false; and he will indeed have done his duty but little by it if he has failed to let it, whether robustly or quite insidiously, fire his fancy and rule his scheme. He has consistently felt it (the appeal to wonder and terror and curiosity and pity and to the delight of fine recognitions, as well as to the joy, perhaps sharper still, of the mystified state) the very source of wise counsel and the very law of charming effect. He has revelled in the creation of alarm and suspense and surprise and relief, in all the arts that practise, with a scruple for nothing but any lapse of application, on the credulous soul of the candid or, immeasurably better, on the seasoned spirit of the cunning,

reader. He has built, rejoicingly, on that blest faculty of
wonder just named, in the latent eagerness of which the
novelist so finds, throughout, his best warrant that he can
but pin his faith and attach his car to it, rest in fine his
monstrous weight and his queer case on it, as on a strange
passion planted in the heart of man for his benefit, a
mysterious provision made for him in the scheme of nature.
He has seen this particular sensibility, the need and the love
of wondering and the quick response to any pretext for it, as
the beginning and the end of his affair—thanks to the
innumerable ways in which that chord may vibrate. His
prime care has been to master those most congruous with
his own faculty, to make it vibrate as finely as possible—or
in other words to the production of the interest appealing
most (by its kind) to himself. This last is of course the
particular clear light by which the genius of representation
ever best proceeds—with its beauty of adjustment to any
strain of attention whatever. Essentially, meanwhile, excited
wonder must have a subject, must face in a direction, must
be, increasingly, *about* something. Here comes in then the
artist's bias and his range—determined, these things, by his
own fond inclination. About what, good man, does he
himself most wonder?—for upon that, whatever it may be,
he will naturally most abound. Under that star will he
gather in what he shall most seek to represent; so that if you
follow thus his range of representation you will know how,
you will see where, again, good man, he for himself most
aptly vibrates.

All of which makes a desired point for the little group of
compositions here placed together; the point that, since the
question has ever been for me but of wondering and, with
all achievable adroitness, of causing to wonder, so the whole
fairy-tale side of life has used, for its tug at my sensibility, a
cord all its own. When we want to wonder there's no such
good ground for it as the wonderful—premising indeed
always, by an induction as prompt, that this element can

but be at best, to fit its different cases, a thing of appreciation. What is wonderful in one set of conditions may quite fail of its spell in another set; and, for that matter, the peril of the unmeasured strange, in fiction, being the silly, just as its strength, when it saves itself, is the charming, the wind of interest blows where it lists, the surrender of attention persists where it can. The ideal, obviously, on these lines, is the straight fairy-tale, the case that has purged in the crucible all its *bêtises* while keeping all its grace. It may seem odd, in a search for the amusing, to try to steer wide of the silly by hugging close the 'supernatural'; but one man's amusement is at the best (we have surely long had to recognise) another's desolation; and I am prepared with the confession that the 'ghost-story', as we for convenience call it, has ever been for me the most possible form of the fairy-tale. It enjoys, to my eyes, this honour by being so much the neatest—neat with that neatness without which *representation*, and therewith beauty, drops. One's working of the spell is of course—decently and effectively—but by the represented thing, and the grace of the more or less closely represented state is the measure of any success; a truth by the general smug neglect of which it's difficult not to be struck. To begin to wonder, over a case, I must begin to believe—to begin to give out (that is to attend) I must begin to take in, and to enjoy *that* profit I must begin to see and hear and feel. This wouldn't see, I allow, the general requirement—as appears from the fact that so many persons profess delight in the picture of marvels and prodigies which by any, even the easiest, critical measure *is* no picture; in the recital of wonderful horrific or beatific things that are neither represented nor, so far as one makes out, seen as representable: a weakness not invalidating, round about us, the most resounding appeals to curiosity. The main condition of interest—that of some appreciable rendering of sought effects—is absent from them; so that when, as often happens, one is asked

how one 'likes' such and such a 'story' one can but point
responsively to the lack of material for a judgement.

The apprehension at work, we thus see, would be of
certain projected conditions, and its first need therefore is
that these appearances be constituted in some other and
more colourable fashion than by the author's answering for
them on his more or less gentlemanly honour. This isn't
enough; *give* me your elements, *treat* me your subject, one
has to say—I must wait till then to tell you how I like them.
I might 'rave' about them all were they given and treated;
but there is no basis of opinion in such matters without a
basis of vision, and no ground for that, in turn, without
some communicated closeness of truth. There are portentous
situations, there are prodigies and marvels and miracles as
to which this communication, whether by necessity or by
chance, works comparatively straight—works, by our
measure, to some convincing consequence; there are others
as to which the report, the picture, the plea, answers no
tithe of the questions we would put. Those questions *may*
perhaps then, by the very nature of the case, be unanswer-
able—though often again, no doubt, the felt vice is but in
the quality of the provision made for them: on any showing,
my own instinct, even in the service of great adventures, is
all for the best *terms* of things; all for ground on which
touches and tricks may be multiplied, the greatest number
of questions answered, the greatest appearance of truth
conveyed. With the preference I have noted for the 'neat'
evocation—the image, of any sort, with fewest attendant
vaguenesses and cheapnesses, fewest loose ends dangling
and fewest features missing, the image kept in fine the most
susceptible of intensity—with this predilection, I say, the
safest arena for the play of moving accidents and mighty
mutations and strange encounters, or whatever odd matters,
is the field, as I may call it, rather of their second than of
their first exhibition. By which, to avoid obscurity, I mean
nothing more cryptic than I feel myself show them best by

showing almost exclusively the way they are felt, by recognising as their main interest some impression strongly made by them and intensely received. We but too probably break down, I have ever reasoned, when we attempt the prodigy, the appeal to mystification, in itself; with its 'objective' side too emphasised the report (it is ten to one) will practically run thin. We want it clear, goodness knows, but we also want it thick, and we get the thickness in the human consciousness that entertains and records, that amplifies and interprets it. That indeed, when the question is (to repeat) of the 'supernatural', constitutes the only thickness we do get; here prodigies, when they come straight, come with an effect imperilled; they keep all their character, on the other hand, by looming through some other history—the indispensable history of somebody's *normal* relation to something. It's in such connexions as these that they most interest, for what we are then mainly concerned with is their imputed and borrowed dignity. Intrinsic values they have none—as we feel for instance in such a matter as the would-be portentous climax of Edgar Poe's 'Arthur Gordon Pym', where the indispensable history is absent, where the phenomena evoked, the moving accidents, coming straight, as I say, are immediate and flat, and the attempt is all at the horrific in itself. The result is that, to my sense, the climax fails—fails because it stops short, and stops short for want of connexions. There *are* no connexions; not only, I mean, in the sense of further statement, but of our own further relation to the elements, which hang in the void: whereby we see the effect lost, the imaginative effort wasted.

I dare say, to conclude, that whenever, in quest, as I have noted, of the amusing, I have invoked the horrific, I have invoked it, in such air as that of 'The Turn of the Screw', that of 'The Jolly Corner', that of 'The Friends of the Friends', that of 'Sir Edmund Orme', that of 'The Real Right Thing', in earnest aversion to waste and from the sense that in art economy is always beauty. The apparitions of Peter Quint and Miss Jessel, in the first of the tales just named, the elusive presence nightly 'stalked' through the New York house by the poor gentleman in the second, are matters as to which in themselves, really, the critical challenge (essentially nothing ever but the spirit of fine attention) may take a hundred forms—and a hundred felt or possibly proved infirmities is too great a number. Our friends' respective minds about them, on the other hand, are a different matter—challengeable, and repeatedly, if you like, but never challengeable without some consequent further stiffening of the whole texture. Which proposition involves, I think, a moral. The moving accident, the rare conjunction, whatever it be, doesn't make the story—in the sense that the story is our excitement, our amusement, our thrill and our suspense; the human emotion and the human attestation, the clustering human conditions we expect presented, only make it. The extraordinary is most extraordinary in that it happens to you and me, and it's of value (of value for others) but so far as visibly brought home to us. At any rate, odd though it may sound to pretend that one feels on safer ground in tracing such an adventure as that of the hero of 'The Jolly Corner' than in pursuing a bright career among pirates or detectives, I allow that composition to pass as the measure or limit, on my own part, of any achievable comfort in the 'adventure-story'; and this not because I may 'render'—well, what my poor gentleman attempted and suffered in the New York house—better than I may render detectives or pirates or other splendid desperadoes, though even here too there would be something to say; but because the spirit engaged with the forces of violence interests me most when I can think of it as engaged most deeply, most finely and most 'subtly' (precious term!) For then it is that, as with the longest and firmest prongs of consciousness, I grasp and hold the throbbing subject; *there* it is above all that I find the steady light of the picture.

After which attempted demonstration I drop with scant grace perhaps to the admission here of a general vagueness on the article of my different little origins. I have spoken of these in three or four connexions, but ask myself to no purpose, I fear, what put such a matter as 'Owen Wingrave' or as 'The Friends of the Friends', such a fantasy as 'Sir Edmund Orme', into my head. The habitual teller of tales finds these things in old note-books—which however but shifts the burden a step; since how, and under what inspiration, did they first wake up in these rude cradles? One's notes, as all writers remember, sometimes explicitly mention, sometimes indirectly reveal, and sometimes wholly dissimulate, such clues and such obligations. The search for these last indeed, through faded or pencilled pages, is perhaps one of the sweetest of our more pensive pleasures. Then we chance on some idea we *have* afterwards treated; then, greeting it with tenderness, we wonder at the first form of a motive that was to lead us so far and to show, no doubt, to eyes not our own, for so other; then we heave the deep sigh of relief over all that is never, thank goodness, to be done again. Would we have embarked on *that* stream had we known?—and what mightn't we have made of this one *hadn't* we known! How, in a proportion of cases, could we have dreamed 'there might be something'?—and why, in another proportion, didn't we *try* what there might be, since there are sorts of trials (ah indeed more than one sort!) for which the day will soon have passed? Most of all, of a certainty, is brought back, before these promiscuities, the old burden of the much life and the little art, and of the portentous dose of the one it takes to make any show of the other. It isn't however that one 'minds' not recovering lost hints; the special pride of any tinted flower of fable, however small, is to be able to opine with the celebrated Topsy that it can only have 'growed'. Doesn't the fabulist himself indeed recall even as one of his best joys the particular pang (both quickening and, in a manner,

profaning possession) of parting with some conceit of which
he can give no account but that his sense—of beauty or
truth or whatever—has been for ever so long saturated with
it? Not, I hasten to add, that measurements of time mayn't
here be agreeably fallacious, and that the 'ever so long' of
saturation shan't often have consisted but of ten minutes of
perception. It comes back to me of 'Owen Wingrave', for
example, simply that one summer afternoon many years
ago, on a penny chair and under a great tree in Kensington
Gardens, I must at the end of a few such visionary moments
have been able to equip him even with details not involved
or not mentioned in the story. Would that adequate
intensity *all* have sprung from the fact that while I sat there
in the immense mild summer rustle and the ever so softened
London hum a young man should have taken his place on
another chair within my limit of contemplation, a tall quiet
slim studious young man, of admirable type, and have
settled to a book with immediate gravity? Did the young
man then, on the spot, just *become* Owen Wingrave,
establishing by the mere magic of type the situation,
creating at a stroke all the implications and filling out all the
picture? That he would have been capable of it is all I can
say—unless it be, otherwise put, that I should have been
capable of letting him; though there hovers the happy
alternative that Owen Wingrave, nebulous and fluid, may
only, at the touch, have found *himself* in this gentleman;
found, that is, a figure and a habit, a form, a face, a fate, the
interesting aspect presented and the dreadful doom recorded;
together with the required and multiplied connexions, not
least that presence of some self-conscious dangerous girl of
lockets and amulets offered by the full-blown idea to my
very first glance. These questions are as answerless as they
are, luckily, the reverse of pressing—since my poor point is
only that at the beginning of my session in the penny chair
the seedless fable hadn't a claim to make or an excuse to
give, and that, the very next thing, the pennyworth still

partly unconsumed, it was fairly bristling with pretexts. 'Dramatise it, dramatise it!' would seem to have rung with sudden intensity in my ears. But dramatise what? The young man in the chair? Him perhaps indeed—however disproportionately to his mere inoffensive stillness; though no imaginative response *can* be disproportionate, after all, I think, to any right, any really penetrating, appeal. Only, where and whence and why and how sneaked in, during so few seconds, so much penetration, so very much rightness? However, these mysteries are really irrecoverable; besides being doubtless of interest, in general, at the best, but to the infatuated author.

Moved to say that of 'Sir Edmund Orme' I remember absolutely nothing, I yet pull myself up ruefully to retrace the presumption that this morsel must first have appeared, with a large picture, in a weekly newspaper and, as then struck me, in the very smallest of all possible print—at sight of which I felt sure that, in spite of the picture (a thing, in its way, to be thankful for) no one would ever read it. I was never to hear in fact that anyone had done so—and I therefore surround it here with every advantage and give it without compunction a new chance. For as I meditate I do a little live it over, do a little remember in connexion with it the felt challenge of some experiment or two in one of the finer shades, the finest (*that* was the point) of the gruesome. The gruesome gross and obvious might be charmless enough; but why shouldn't one, with ingenuity, almost infinitely refine upon it?—as one was prone at any time to refine almost on anything? The study of certain of the situations that keep, as we say, the heart in the mouth might renew itself under this star; and in the recital in question, as in 'The Friends of the Friends', 'The Jolly Corner' and 'The Real Right Thing', the pursuit of such verily leads us into rarefied air. Two sources of effect must have seemed to me happy for 'Sir Edmund Orme'; one of these the bright thought of a state of *unconscious* obsession or, in romantic parlance, hauntedness, on the part of a given person; the consciousness of it on the part of some other, in anguish lest a wrong turn or forced betrayal shall determine a break in the blest ignorance, thus the subject of portrayal, with plenty of suspense for the occurrence or non-occurrence of the feared mischance. Not to be liable herself to a dark visitation, but to see such a danger play about her child as incessantly as forked lightning may play unheeded about the blind, this is the penalty suffered by the mother, in 'Sir Edmund Orme', for some hardness or baseness of her own youth. There I must doubtless have found my escape from the obvious; there I avoided a low directness and achieved one of those redoubled twists or sportive—by which I don't at all mean wanton—gambols dear to the fastidious, the creative fancy and that make for the higher interest. The higher interest—and this is the second of the two flowers of evidence that I pluck from the faded cluster—must further have dwelt, to my appraisement, in my placing my scene at Brighton, the old, the mid-Victorian, the Thackerayan Brighton; where the twinkling sea and the breezy air, the great friendly, fluttered, animated, many-coloured 'front', would emphasise the note I wanted; that of the strange and sinister embroidered on the very type of the normal and easy.

This was to be again, after years, the idea entertained for 'The Jolly Corner', about the composition of which there would be more to say than my space allows; almost more in fact than categorical clearness might see its way to. A very limited thing being on this occasion in question, I was moved to adopt as my motive an analysis of some one of the conceivably rarest and intensest grounds for an 'unnatural' anxiety, a *malaise* so incongruous and discordant, in the given prosaic prosperous conditions, as almost to be compromising. Spencer Brydon's adventure however is one of those finished fantasies that, achieving success or not, speak best even to the critical sense for themselves—which I leave it to do, while I apply the remark as well to 'The Friends of the Friends' (and all the more that this last piece allows probably for no other comment).

II. 'THE TURN OF THE SCREW'

That particular challenge at least 'The Turn of the Screw' doesn't incur; and this perfectly independent and irresponsible little fiction rejoices, beyond any rival on a like ground, in a conscious provision of prompt retort to the sharpest question that may be addressed to it. For it has the small strength—if I shouldn't say rather the unattackable ease—of a perfect homogeneity, of being, to the very last grain of its virtue, all of a kind; the very kind, as happens, least apt to be baited by earnest criticism, the only sort of criticism of which account need be taken. To have handled again this so full-blown flower of high fancy is to be led back by it to easy and happy recognitions. Let the first of these be that of the starting-point itself—the sense, all charming again, of the circle, one winter afternoon, round the hall-fire of a grave old country-house where (for all the world as if to resolve itself promptly and obligingly into convertible, into 'literary' stuff) the talk turned, on I forget what homely pretext, to apparitions and night-fears, to the marked and sad drop in the general supply, and still more in the general quality, of such commodities. The good, the really effective and heart-shaking ghost-stories (roughly so to term them) appeared all to have been told, and neither new crop nor new type in any quarter awaited us. The new type indeed, the mere modern 'psychical' case, washed clean of all queerness as by exposure to a flowing laboratory tap, and equipped with credentials vouching for this—the new type clearly promised little, for the more it was respectably certified the less it seemed of a nature to rouse the dear old sacred terror. Thus it was, I remember, that amid our lament for a beautiful lost form, our distinguished host expressed the wish that he might but have recovered for us

one of the scantest of fragments of this form at its best. He
had never forgotten the impression made on him as a young
man by the withheld glimpse, as it were, of a dreadful
matter that had been reported years before, and with as few
particulars, to a lady with whom he had youthfully talked.
The story would have been thrilling could she but have
found herself in better possession of it, dealing as it did with
a couple of small children in an out-of-the way place, to
whom the spirits of certain 'bad' servants, dead in the
employ of the house, were believed to have appeared with
the design of 'getting hold' of them. This was all, but there
had been more, which my friend's old converser had lost the
thread of: she could only assure him of the wonder of the
allegations as she had anciently heard them made. He
himself could give us but this shadow of a shadow—my own
appreciation of which, I need scarcely say, was exactly
wrapped up in that thinness. On the surface there wasn't
much, but another grain, none the less, would have spoiled
the precious pinch addressed to its end as neatly as some
modicum extracted from an old silver snuff-box and held
between finger and thumb. I was to remember the haunted
children and the prowling servile spirits as a 'value', of the
disquieting sort, in all conscience sufficient; so that when,
after an interval, I was asked for something seasonable by
the promoters of a periodical dealing in the time-honoured
Christmas-tide toy, I bethought myself at once of the
vividest little note for sinister romance that I had ever jotted
down.

Such was the private source of 'The Turn of the Screw';
and I wondered, I confess, why so fine a germ, gleaming
there in the wayside dust of life, had never been deftly
picked up. The thing had for me the immense merit of
allowing the imagination absolute freedom of hand, of
inviting it to act on a perfectly clear field, with no 'outside'
control involved, no pattern of the usual or the true or the
terrible 'pleasant' (save always of course the high pleasantry

of one's very form) to consort with. This makes in fact the charm of my second reference, that I find here a perfect example of an exercise of the imagination unassisted, unassociated—playing the game, making the score, in the phrase of our sporting day, off its own bat. To what degree the game was worth playing I needn't attempt to say: the exercise I have noted strikes me now, I confess, as the interesting thing, the imaginative faculty acting with the *whole* of the case on its hands. The exhibition involved is in other words a fairy-tale pure and simple—save indeed as to its springing not from an artless and measureless, but from a conscious and cultivated credulity. Yet the fairy-tale belongs mainly to either of two classes, the short and sharp and single, charged more or less with the compactness of anecdote (as to which let the familiars of our childhood, Cinderella and Blue-Beard and Hop o' my Thumb and Little Red Riding Hood and many of the gems of the Brothers Grimm directly testify), or else the long and loose, the copious, the various, the endless, where, dramatically speaking, roundness is quite sacrificed—sacrificed to fulness, sacrificed to exuberance, if one will: witness at hazard almost any one of the Arabian Nights. The charm of all these things for the distracted modern mind is in the clear field of experience, as I call it, over which we are thus led to roam; an annexed but independent world in which nothing is right save as we rightly imagine it. We have to do *that*, and we do it happily for the short spurt and in the smaller piece, achieving so perhaps beauty and lucidity; we flounder, we lose breath, on the other hand—that is we fail, not of continuity, but of an agreeable unity, of the 'roundness' in which beauty and lucidity largely reside— when we go in, as they say, for great lengths and breadths. And this, oddly enough, not because 'keeping it up' isn't abundantly within the compass of the imagination appealed to in certain conditions, but because the finer interest depends just on *how* it is kept up.

Nothing is so easy as improvisation, the running on and on of invention; it is sadly compromised, however, from the moment its stream breaks bounds and gets into flood. Then the waters may spread indeed, gathering houses and herds and crops and cities into their arms and wrenching off, for our amusement, the whole face of the land—only violating by the same stroke our sense of the course and the channel, which is our sense of the uses of a stream and the virtue of a story. Improvisation, as in the Arabian Nights, may keep on terms with encountered objects by sweeping them in and floating them on its breast; but the great effect it so loses—that of keeping on terms with itself. This is ever, I intimate, the hard thing for the fairy-tale; but by just so much as it struck me as hard did it in 'The Turn of the Screw' affect me as irresistibly prescribed. To improvise with extreme freedom and yet at the same time without the possibility of ravage, without the hint of a flood; to keep the stream, in a word, on something like ideal terms with itself: that was here my definite business. The thing was to aim at absolute singleness, clearness and roundness, and yet to depend on an imagination working freely, working (call it) with extravagance; by which law it wouldn't be thinkable except as free and wouldn't be amusing except as controlled. The merit of the tale, as it stands, is accordingly, I judge, that it has struggled successfully with its dangers. It is an excursion into chaos while remaining, like Blue-Beard and Cinderella, but an ancedote—though an anecdote amplified and highly emphasised and returning upon itself; as, for that matter, Cinderella and Blue-Beard return. I need scarcely add after this that it is a piece of ingenuity pure and simple, of cold artistic calculation, an *amusette* to catch those not easily caught (the 'fun' of the capture of the merely witless being ever but small), the jaded, the disillusioned, the fastidious. Otherwise expressed, the study is of a conceived 'tone', the tone of suspected and felt trouble, of an inordinate and incalculable sort—the tone of tragic, yet of exquisite, mystification. To knead the subject of my young friend's, the supposititious narrator's, mystification thick, and yet strain the expression of it so clear and fine that beauty would result: no side of the matter so revives for me as that endeavour. Indeed if the artistic value of such an experiment be measured by the intellectual echoes it may again, long after, set in motion, the case would make in favour of this little firm fantasy—which I seem to see draw behind it today a train of associations. I ought doubtless to blush for thus confessing them so numerous that I can but pick among them for reference. I recall for instance a reproach made me by a reader capable evidently, for the time, of some attention, but not quite capable of enough, who complained that I hadn't sufficiently 'characterised' my young woman engaged in her labyrinth; hadn't endowed her with signs and marks, features and humours, hadn't in a word invited her to deal with her own mystery as well as with that of Peter Quint, Miss Jessel and the hapless children. I remember well, whatever the absurdity of its now coming back to me, my reply to that criticism—under which one's artistic, one's ironic heart shook for the instant almost to breaking. 'You indulge in that stricture at your ease, and I don't mind confiding to you that—strange as it may appear!—one has to choose ever so delicately among one's difficulties, attaching one's self to the greatest, bearing hard on those and intelligently neglecting the others. If one attempts to tackle them all one is certain to deal completely with none; whereas the effectual dealing with a few casts a blest golden haze under cover of which, like wanton mocking goddesses in clouds, the others find prudent to retire. It was "déjà très-joli", in "The Turn of the Screw", please believe, the general proposition of our young woman's keeping crystalline her record of so many intense anomalies and obscurities—by which I don't of course mean her explanation of them, a different matter; and I saw no way, I feebly grant (fighting, at the best too, periodically, for every grudged inch of my space) to exhibit her in relations other than those; one of which, precisely, would have been her relation to her own nature. We have surely as much of her own nature as we can swallow in watching it reflect her anxieties and inductions. It constitutes no little of a character indeed, in such conditions, for a young person, as she says, "privately bred", that she is able to make her particular credible statement of such strange matters. She has "authority", which is a good deal to have given her, and I couldn't have arrived at so much had I clumsily tried for more.'

For which truth I claim part of the charm latent on occasion in the extracted reasons of beautiful things— putting for the beautiful always, in a work of art, the close, the curious, the deep. Let me place above all, however, under the protection of the presence the side by which this fiction appeals most to consideration: its choice of its way of meeting its gravest difficulty. There were difficulties not so grave: I had for instance simply to renounce all attempt to keep the kind and degree of impression I wished to produce on terms with the today so copious psychical record of cases of apparitions. Different signs and circumstances, in the reports, mark these cases; different things are done—though on the whole very little appears to be—by the persons appearing; the point is, however, that some things are never done at all: this negative quantity is large—certain reserves and proprieties and immobilities consistently impose themselves. Recorded and attested 'ghosts' are in other words as little expressive, as little dramatic, above all as little continuous and conscious and responsive, as is consistent with their taking the trouble—and an immense trouble they find it, we gather—to appear at all. Wonderful and interesting therefore at a given moment, they are inconceivable figures in an *action*—and 'The Turn of the Screw' was an action, desperately, or it was nothing. I had to decide in fine between having my apparitions correct and having my

story 'good'—that is producing my impression of the
dreadful, my designed horror. Good ghosts, speaking by
book, make poor subjects, and it was clear that from the
first my hovering prowling blighting presences, my pair of
abnormal agents, would have to depart altogether from the
rules. They would be agents in fact; there would be laid on
them the dire duty of causing the situation to reek with the
air of Evil. Their desire and their ability to do so, visibly
measuring meanwhile their effect, together with their
observed and described success—this was exactly my
central idea; so that, briefly, I cast my lot with pure
romance, the appearances conforming to the true type being
so little romantic.

This is to say, I recognise again, that Peter Quint and Miss
Jessel are not 'ghosts' at all, as we now know the ghost, but
goblins, elves, imps, demons as loosely constructed as those
of the old trials for witchcraft; if not, more pleasingly,
fairies of the legendary order, wooing their victims forth to
see them dance under the moon. Not indeed that I suggest
their reducibility to any form of the pleasing pure and
simple; they please at the best but through having helped
me to express my subject all directly and intensely. Here it
was—in the use made of them—that I felt a high degree of
art really required; and here it is that, on reading the tale
over, I find my precautions justified. The essence of the
matter was the villainy of motive in the evoked predatory
creatures; so that the result would be ignoble—by which I
mean would be trivial—were this element of evil but feebly
or inanely suggested. Thus arose on behalf of my idea the
lively interest of a possible suggestion and process of
adumbration; the question of how best to convey the sense of
the depths of the sinister without which my fable would so
woefully limp. Portentous evil—how was I to save that, as
an intention on the part of my demon-spirits, from the
drop, the comparative vulgarity, inevitably attending,
throughout the whole range of possible brief illustration,

the offered example, the imputed vice, the cited act, the limited deplorable presentable instance? To bring the bad dead back to life for a second round of badness is to warrant them as indeed prodigious, and to become hence as shy of specifications as of a waiting anti-climax. One had seen, in fiction, some grand form of wrong-doing, or better still of wrong-being, imputed, seen it promised and announced as by the hot breath of the Pit—and then, all lamentably, shrink to the compass of some particular brutality, some particular immorality, some particular infamy portrayed: with the result, alas, of the demonstration's falling sadly short. If *my* bad things, for 'The Turn of the Screw', I felt, should succumb to this danger, if they shouldn't seem sufficiently bad, there would be nothing for me but to hang my artistic head lower than I had ever known occasion to do.

The view of that discomfort and the fear of that dishonour, it accordingly must have been, that struck the proper light for my right, though by no means easy, short cut. What, in the last analysis, had I to give the sense of? Of their being, the haunting pair, capable, as the phrase is, of everything—that is of exerting, in respect to the children, the very worst action small victims so conditioned might be conceived as subject to. What would *be* then, on reflexion, this utmost conceivability?—a question to which the answer all admirably came. There is for such a case no eligible *absolute* of the wrong; it remains relative to fifty other elements, a matter of appreciation, speculation, imagination—these things moreover quite exactly in the light of the spectator's, the critic's the reader's experience. Only make the reader's general vision of evil intense enough, I said to myself—and that already is a charming job—and his own experience, his own imagination, his own sympathy (with the children) and horror (of their false friends) will supply him quite sufficiently with all the particulars. Make him *think* the evil, make him think it for himself, and you are released from weak specifications. This ingenuity I took pains—as indeed great pains were required—to apply; and with a success apparently beyond my liveliest hope. Droll enough at the same time, I must add, some of the evidence—even when most convincing—of this success. How can I feel my calculation to have failed, my wrought suggestion not to have worked, that is, on my being assailed, as has befallen me, with the charge of a monstrous emphasis, the charge of all indecently expatiating? There is not only from beginning to end of the matter not an inch of expatiation, but my values are positively all blanks save so far as an excited horror, a promoted pity, a created expertness—on which punctual effects of strong causes no writer can ever fail to plume himself—proceed to read into them more or less fantastic figures. Of high interest to the author meanwhile—and by the same stroke a theme for the moralist—the artless resentful reaction of the entertained person who has abounded in the sense of the situation. He visits his abundance, morally, on the artist—who has but clung to an ideal of faultlessness. Such indeed, for this latter, are some of the observations by which the prolonged strain of that clinging may be enlivened!

Sir Edmund Orme

SIR EDMUND ORME

THE STATEMENT appears to have been written, though the fragment is undated, long after the death of his wife, whom I take to have been one of the persons referred to. There is however nothing in the strange story to establish this point, now perhaps not of importance. When I took possession of his effects I found these pages, in a locked drawer, among papers relating to the unfortunate lady's too brief career—she died in childbirth a year after her marriage: letters, memoranda, accounts, faded photographs, cards of invitation. That's the only connexion I can point to, and you may easily, and will probably, think it too extravagant to have had a palpable basis. I can't, I allow, vouch for his having intended it as a report of real occurrence—I can only vouch for his general veracity. In any case it was written for himself, not for others. I offer it to others—having full option—precisely because of its oddity. Let them, in respect to the form of the thing, bear in mind that it was written quite for himself. I've altered nothing but the names.

If there's a story in the matter I recognise the exact moment at which it began. This was on a soft still Sunday noon in November, just after church, on the sunny Parade. Brighton was full of people; it was the height of the season and the day was even more respectable than lovely—which helped to account for the multitude of walkers. The blue sea itself was decorous; it seemed to doze with a gentle snore—if that *be* decorum—while nature preached a sermon. After writing letters all the morning I had come out to take a look at it before luncheon. I leaned over the rail dividing the King's

3

Road from the beach, and I think I had smoked a cigarette,
when I became conscious of an intended joke in the shape of
a light walking-stick laid across my shoulders. The idea, I
found, had been thrown off by Teddy Bostwick of the Rifles
and was intended as a contribution to talk. Our talk came
off as we strolled together—he always took your arm to
show you he forgave your obtuseness about his humour—
and looked at the people, and bowed to some of them, and
wondered who others were, and differed in opinion as to the
prettiness of girls. About Charlotte Marden we agreed,
however, as we saw her come toward us with her mother;
and there surely could have been no one who wouldn't have
concurred. The Brighton air used of old to make plain girls
pretty and pretty girls prettier still—I don't know whether
it works the spell now. The place was at any rate rare for
complexions, and Miss Marden's was one that made people
turn round. It made *us* stop, heaven knows—at least it was
one of the things, for we already knew the ladies.

   We turned with them, we joined them, we went where
they were going. They were only going to the end and
back—they had just come out of church. It was another
manifestation of Teddy's humour that he got immediate
possession of Charlotte, leaving me to walk with her
mother. However, I wasn't unhappy; the girl was before me
and I had her to talk about. We prolonged our walk; Mrs
Marden kept me and presently said she was tired and must
rest. We found a place on a sheltered bench—we gossiped as
the people passed. It had already struck me, in this pair,
that the resemblance between mother and daughter was
wonderful even among such resemblances, all the more that
it took so little account of a difference of nature. One often
hears mature mothers spoken of as warnings—sign-posts,
more or less discouraging, of the way daughters may go. But
there was nothing deterrent in the idea that Charlotte
should at fifty-five be as beautiful, even though it were
conditioned on her being as pale and preoccupied, as Mrs

Marden. At twenty-two she had a rosy blankness and was
admirably handsome. Her head had the charming shape of
her mother's and her features the same fine order. Then
there were looks and movements and tones—moments
when you could scarce say if it were aspect or sound—
which, between the two appearances, referred and reminded.

These ladies had a small fortune and a cheerful little
house at Brighton, full of portraits and tokens and
trophies—stuffed animals on the top of book-cases and
sallow varnished fish under glass—to which Mrs Marden
professed herself attached by pious memories. Her husband
had been 'ordered' there in ill health, to spend the last years
of his life, and she had already mentioned to me that it was a
place in which she felt herself still under the protection of
his goodness. His goodness appeared to have been great,
and she sometimes seemed to defend it from vague
innuendo. Some sense of protection, of an influence
invoked and cherished, was evidently necessary to her; she
had a dim wistfulness, a longing for security. She wanted
friends and had a good many. She was kind to me on our
first meeting, and I never suspected her of the vulgar
purpose of 'making up' to me—a suspicion of course unduly
frequent in conceited young men. It never struck me that
she wanted me for her daughter, nor yet, like some
unnatural mammas, for herself. It was as if they had had a
common deep shy need and had been ready to say: 'Oh be
friendly to us and be trustful! Don't be afraid—you won't
be expected to marry us.' 'Of course there's something
about mamma: that's really what makes her such a dear!'
Charlotte said to me, confidentially, at an early stage of our
acquaintance. She worshipped her mother's appearance. It
was the only thing she was vain of; she accepted the raised
eyebrows as a charming ultimate fact. 'She looks as if she
were waiting for the doctor, dear mamma,' she said on
another occasion. 'Perhaps *you're* the doctor; do you think

you are?' It appeared in the event that I had some healing power. At any rate when I learned, for she once dropped the remark, that Mrs Marden also held there was something 'awfully strange' about Charlotte, the relation of the two ladies couldn't but be interesting. It was happy enough, at bottom; each had the other so on her mind.

On the Parade the stream of strollers held its course, and Charlotte presently went by with Teddy Bostwick. She smiled and nodded and continued, but when she came back she stopped and spoke to us. Captain Bostwick positively declined to go in—he pronounced the occasion too jolly: might they therefore take another turn? Her mother dropped a 'Do as you like', and the girl gave me an impertinent smile over her shoulder as they quitted us. Teddy looked at me with his glass in one eye, but I didn't mind that: it was only of Miss Marden I was thinking as I laughed to my companion. 'She's a bit of a coquette, you know.'

'Don't say that—don't say that!' Mrs Marden murmured.

'The nicest girls always are—just a little,' I was magnanimous enough to plead.

'Then why are they always punished?'

The intensity of the question startled me—it had come out in a vivid flash. Therefore I had to think a moment before I put to her: 'What do you know of their punishment?'

'Well—I was a bad girl myself.'

'And were you punished?'

'I carry it through life,' she said as she looked away from me. 'Ah!' she suddenly panted in the next breath, rising to her feet and staring at her daughter, who had reappeared again with Captain Bostwick. She stood a few seconds, the queerest expression in her face; then she sank on the seat again and I saw she had blushed crimson. Charlotte, who had noticed it all, came straight up to her and, taking her hand with quick tenderness, seated herself at her other side. The girl had turned pale—she gave her mother a fixed scared look. Mrs Marden, who had had some shock that escaped our detection, recovered herself; that is she sat quiet and inexpressive, gazing at the indifferent crowd, the sunny air, the slumbering sea. My eye happened to fall nevertheless on the interlocked hands of the two ladies, and I quickly guessed the grasp of the elder to be violent. Bostwick stood before them, wondering what was the matter and asking me from his little vacant disk if *I* knew; which led Charlotte to say to him after a moment and with a certain irritation: 'Don't stand there that way, Captain Bostwick. Go away—*please* go away.'

I got up at this, hoping Mrs Marden wasn't ill; but she at once begged we wouldn't leave them, that we would particularly stay and that we would presently come home to luncheon. She drew me down beside her and for a moment I felt her hand press my arm in a way that might have been an involuntary betrayal of distress and might have been a private signal. What she should have wished to point out to me I couldn't divine: perhaps she had seen in the crowd somebody or something abnormal. She explained to us in a few minutes that she was all right, that she was only liable to palpitations: they came as quickly as they went. It was time to move—a truth on which we acted. The incident was felt to be closed. Bostwick and I lunched with our sociable friends, and when I walked away with him he professed, he had never seen creatures more completely to his taste.

Mrs Marden had made us promise to come back the next day to tea, and had exhorted us in general to come as often as we could. Yet the next day when, at five o'clock, I knocked at the door of the pretty house it was but to learn that the ladies had gone up to town. They had left a message for us with the butler: he was to say they had suddenly been called and much regretted it. They would be absent a few days. This was all I could extract from the dumb domestic. I went again three days later, but they were still away; and it was not till the end of a week that I got a note from Mrs Marden. 'We're back,' she wrote: 'do come and forgive us.' It was on this occasion, I remember—the occasion of my going just after getting the note—that she told me she had distinct intuitions. I don't know how many people there were in England at that time in that predicament, but there were very few who would have mentioned it; so that the announcement struck me as original, especially as her point was that some of these uncanny promptings were connected with myself. There were other people present—idle Brighton folk, old women with frightened eyes and irrelevant interjections—and I had too few minutes' talk with Charlotte; but the day after this I met them both at dinner and had the satisfaction of sitting next to Miss Marden. I recall this passage as the hour of its first fully coming over me that she was a beautiful liberal creature. I had seen her personality in glimpses and gleams, like a song sung in snatches, but now it was before me in a large rosy glow, as if it had been a full volume of sound. I heard the whole of the air, and it was sweet fresh music, which I was often to hum over.

After dinner I had a few words with Mrs Marden; it was at the time, late in the evening, when tea was handed about. A servant passed near us with a tray, I asked her if she would have a cup and, on her assenting, took one and offered it to her. She put out her hand for it and I gave it her, safely as I supposed; but as her fingers were about to secure it she started and faltered, so that both my frail vessel and its fine recipient dropped with a crash of porcelain and without, on the part of my companion, the usual woman's motion to save her dress. I stooped to pick up the fragments and when I raised myself Mrs Marden was looking across the room at her daughter, who returned it with lips of cheer but anxious eyes. 'Dear mamma, what on earth *is* the matter with you?' the silent question seemed to say. Mrs Marden coloured just as she had done after her strange movement on the Parade the other week, and I was therefore surprised when she said to me with unexpected assurance: 'You should really have a steadier hand!' I had begun to stammer a defence of my hand when I noticed her eyes fixed on me with an intense appeal. It was ambiguous at first and only added to my confusion; then suddenly I understood as plainly as if she had murmured 'Make believe it was you—make believe it was you.' The servant came back to take the morsels of the cup and wipe up the spilt tea, and while I was in the midst of making believe Mrs Marden abruptly brushed away from me and from her daughter's attention and went into another room. She gave no heed to the state of her dress.

I saw nothing more of either that evening, but the next morning, in the King's Road, I met the younger lady with a roll of music in her muff. She told me she had been a little way alone, to practise duets with a friend, and I asked her if she would go a little way further in company. She gave me leave to attend her to her door, and as we stood before it I enquired if I might go in. 'No, not today—I don't want you,' she said very straight, though not unamiably; while the words caused me to direct a wistful disconcerted gaze at one of the windows of the house. It fell on the white face of Mrs Marden, turned out at us from the drawing-room. She stood long enough to show it *was* she and not the apparition I had come near taking it for, and then she vanished before her daughter had observed her. The girl, during our walk, had said nothing about her. As I had been told they didn't want me I left them alone a little, after which certain hazards kept us still longer apart. I finally went up to London, and while there received a pressing invitation to come immediately down to Tranton, a pretty old place in Sussex belonging to a couple whose acquaintance I had lately made.

I went to Tranton from town, and on arriving found the Mardens, with a dozen other people, in the house. The first

thing Mrs Marden said was 'Will you forgive me?' and when
I asked what I had to forgive she answered 'My throwing
my tea over you.' I replied that it had gone over herself;
whereupon she said 'At any rate I was very rude—but some
time I think you'll understand, and then you'll make
allowances for me.' The first day I was there she dropped
two or three of these references—she had already indulged
in more than one—to the mystic initiation in store for me;
so that I began, as the phrase is, to chaff her about it, to say
I'd rather it were less wonderful and take it out at once. She
answered that when it should come to me I'd have indeed to
take it out—there would be little enough option. That it
would come was privately clear to her, a deep presentiment,
which was the only reason she had ever mentioned the
matter. Didn't I remember she had spoken to me of
intuitions? From the first of her seeing me she had been
sure there were things I shouldn't escape knowing. Meanwhile there was nothing to do but wait and keep cool, not to
be precipitate. She particularly wished not to become
extravagantly nervous. And I was above all not to be
nervous myself—one got used to everything. I returned that
though I couldn't make out what she was talking of I was
terribly frightened; the absence of a clue gave such a range
to one's imagination. I exaggerated on purpose; for if Mrs
Marden was mystifying I can scarcely say she was alarming.
I couldn't imagine what she meant, but I wondered more
than I shuddered. I might have said to myself that she was a
little wrong in the upper storey; but that never occurred to
me. She struck me as hopelessly right.

There were other girls in the house, but Charlotte the
most charming; which was so generally allowed that she
almost interfered with the slaughter of ground game. There
were two or three men, and I was of the number, who
actually preferred her to the society of the beaters. In short
she was recognised as a form of sport superior and exquisite.
She was kind to all of us—she made us go out late and come

in early. I don't know whether she flirted, but several other members of the party thought *they* did. Indeed as regards himself Teddy Bostwick, who had come over from Brighton, was visibly sure.

The third of these days was a Sunday, which determined a pretty walk to morning service over the fields. It was grey windless weather, and the bell of the little old church that nestled in the hollow of the Sussex down sounded near and domestic. We were a straggling procession in the mild damp air—which, as always at that season, gave one the feeling that after the trees were bare there was more of it, a larger sky—and I managed to fall a good way behind with Miss Marden. I remember entertaining, as we moved together over the turf, a strong impulse to say something intensely personal, something violent and important, important for *me*—such as that I had never seen her so lovely or that that particular moment was the sweetest of my life. But always, in youth, such words have been on the lips many times before they're spoken to any effect; and I had the sense, not that I didn't know her well enough—I cared little for that— but that she didn't sufficiently know *me*. In the church, a museum of old Tranton tombs and brasses, the big Tranton pew was full. Several of us were scattered, and I found a seat for Miss Marden, and another for myself beside it, at a distance from her mother and from most of our friends. There were two or three decent rustics on the bench, who moved in further to make room for us, and I took my place first, to cut off my companion from our neighbours. After she was seated there was still a space left, which remained empty till service was about half over.

This at least was the moment of my noting that another person had entered and had taken the seat. When I remarked him he had apparently been for some minutes in the pew—had settled himself and put down his hat beside him and, with his hands crossed on the knob of his cane, was gazing before him at the altar. He was a pale young man

in black and with the air of a gentleman. His presence
slightly startled me, for Miss Marden hadn't attracted my
attention to it by moving to make room for him. After a few
minutes, observing that he had no prayer-book, I reached
across my neighbour and placed mine before him, on the
ledge of the pew; a manœuvre the motive of which was not
unconnected with the possibility that, in my own destitution,
Miss Marden would give me one side of *her* velvet volume to
hold. The pretext however was destined to fail, for at the
moment I offered him the book the intruder—whose
intrusion I had so condoned—rose from his place without
thanking me, stepped noiselessly out of the pew, which had
no door, and, so discreetly as to attract no attention, passed
down the centre of the church. A few minutes had sufficed
for his devotions. His behaviour was unbecoming, his early
departure even more than his late arrival; but he managed
so quietly that we were not incommoded, and I found, on
turning a little to look after him, that nobody was disturbed
by his withdrawal. I only noticed, and with surprise, that
Mrs Marden had been so affected by it as to rise, all
involuntarily, in her place. She stared at him as he passed,
but he passed very quickly, and she as quickly dropped
down again, though not too soon to catch my eye across the
church. Five minutes later I asked her daughter, in a low
voice, if she would kindly pass me back my prayer-book—I
had waited to see if she would spontaneously perform the
act. The girl restored this aid to devotion, but had been so
far from troubling herself about it that she could say to me
as she did so: 'Why on earth did you put it there?' I was on
the point of answering her when she dropped on her knees,
and at this I held my tongue. I had only been going to say:
'To be decently civil.'

After the benediction, as we were leaving our places, I
was slightly surprised again to see that Mrs Marden, instead
of going out with her companions, had come up the aisle to
join us, having apparently something to say to her daughter.

She said it, but in an instant I saw it had been a pretext—her real business was with me. She pushed Charlotte forward and suddenly breathed to me: 'Did you see him?'

'The gentleman who sat down here? How could I help seeing him?'

'Hush!' she said with the intensest excitement; 'don't *speak* to her—don't tell her!' She slipped her hand into my arm, to keep me near her, to keep me, it seemed, away from her daughter. The precaution was unnecessary, for Teddy Bostwick had already taken possession of Miss Marden, and as they passed out of church in front of me I saw one of the other men close up on her other hand. It appeared to be felt that I had had my turn. Mrs Marden released me as soon as we got out, but not before I saw she had needed my support. 'Don't speak to anyone—don't tell anyone!' she went on.

'I don't understand. Tell anyone what?'

'Why that you saw him.'

'Surely they saw him for themselves.'

'Not one of them, not one of them.' She spoke with such passionate decision that I glanced at her—she was staring straight before her. But she felt the challenge of my eyes and stopped short, in the old brown timber porch of the church, with the others well in advance of us; where, looking at me now and in quite an extraordinary manner, 'You're the only person,' she said; 'the only person in the world.'

'But *you*, dear madam?'

'Oh me—of course. That's my curse!' And with this she moved rapidly off to join the rest of our group. I hovered at its outskirts on the way home—I had such food for rumination. Whom had I seen and why was the apparition— it rose before my mind's eye all clear again—invisible to the others? If an exception had been made for Mrs Marden why did it constitute a curse, and why was I to share so questionable a boon? This appeal, carried on in my own locked breast, kept me doubtless quiet enough at luncheon.

After the repast I went out on the old terrace to smoke a
cigarette, but had only taken a turn or two when I caught
Mrs Marden's moulded mask at the window of one of the
rooms open to the crooked flags. It reminded me of the
same flitting presence behind the pane at Brighton the day I
met Charlotte and walked home with her. But this time my
ambiguous friend didn't vanish; she tapped on the pane and
motioned me to come in. She was in a queer little
apartment, one of the many reception-rooms of which the
ground-floor at Tranton consisted; it was known as the
Indian room and had a style denominated Eastern—bamboo
lounges, lacquered screens, lanterns with long fringes and
strange idols in cabinets, objects not held to conduce to
sociability. The place was little used, and when I went
round to her we had it to ourselves. As soon as I appeared
she said to me: 'Please tell me this—are you in love with my
daughter?'

I really had a little to take my time. 'Before I answer your
question will you kindly tell me what gives you the idea? I
don't consider I've been very forward.'

Mrs Marden, contradicting me with her beautiful anxious
eyes, gave me no satisfaction on the point I mentioned; she
only went on strenuously: 'Did you say nothing to her on
the way to church?'

'What makes you think I said anything?'

'Why the fact that you saw him.'

'Saw whom, dear Mrs Marden?'

'Oh you know,' she answered gravely, even a little
reproachfully, as if I were trying to humiliate her by making
her name the unnameable.

'Do you mean the gentleman who formed the subject of
your strange statement in church—the one who came into
the pew?'

'You saw him, you saw him!' she panted with a strange
mixture of dismay and relief.

'Of course I saw him, and so did you.'

'It didn't follow. Did you feel it to be inevitable?'

I was puzzled again. 'Inevitable?'

'That you *should* see him?'

'Certainly, since I'm not blind.'

'You might have been. Everyone else is.' I was wonderfully at sea and I frankly confessed it to my questioner, but the case wasn't improved by her presently exclaiming: 'I knew you would, from the moment you should be really in love with her! I knew it would be the test—what do I mean?—the proof.'

'Are there such strange bewilderments attached to that high state?' I smiled to ask.

'You can judge for yourself. You see him, you see him!'— she quite exulted in it. 'You'll see him again.'

'I've no objection, but I shall take more interest in him if you'll kindly tell me who he is.'

She avoided my eyes—then consciously met them. 'I'll tell you if you'll tell me first what you said to her on the way to church.'

'Has she told you I said anything?'

'Do I need that?' she asked with expression.

'Oh yes, I remember—your intuitions! But I'm sorry to see they're at fault this time; because I really said nothing to your daughter that was the least out of the way.'

'Are you very very sure?'

'On my honour, Mrs Marden.'

'Then you consider you're not in love with her?'

'That's another affair!' I laughed.

'You are—you *are!* You wouldn't have seen him if you hadn't been.'

'Then who the deuce *is* he, madam?'—I pressed it with some irritation.

Yet she would still only question me back. 'Didn't you at least *want* to say something to her—didn't you come very near it?'

Well, this was more to the point; it justified the famous

intuitions. 'Ah "near" it as much as you like—call it the turn of a hair. I don't know what kept me quiet.'

'That was quite enough,' said Mrs Marden. 'It isn't what you say that makes the difference; it's what you feel. *That's* what he goes by.'

I was annoyed at last by her reiterated reference to an identity yet to be established, and I clasped my hands with an air of supplication which covered much real impatience, a sharper curiosity and even the first short throbs of a certain sacred dread. 'I entreat you to tell me whom you're talking about.'

She threw up her arms, looking away from me, as if to shake off both reserve and responsibility. 'Sir Edmund Orme.'

'And who may Sir Edmund Orme be?'

At the moment I spoke she gave a start. 'Hush—here they come.' Then as, following the direction of her eyes, I saw Charlotte, out on the terrace, by our own window, she added, with an intensity of warning: 'Don't notice him—*never!*'

The girl, who now had had her hands beside her eyes, peering into the room and smiling, signed to us, through the glass to admit her; on which I went and opened the long window. Her mother turned away and she came in with a laughing challenge: 'What plot in the world are you two hatching here?' Some plan—I forget what—was in prospect for the afternoon, as to which Mrs Marden's participation or consent was solicited, my own adhesion being taken for granted; and she had been half over the place in her quest. I was flurried, seeing the elder woman was—when she turned round to meet her daughter she disguised it to extravagance, throwing herself on the girl's neck and embracing her—so that, to pass it off, I overdid my gallantry.

'I've been asking your mother for your hand.'

'Oh indeed, and has she given it?' Miss Marden gaily returned.

'She was just going to when you appeared there.'

'Well, it's only for a moment—I'll leave you free.'

'Do you like him, Charlotte?' Mrs Marden asked with a candour I scarcely expected.

'It's difficult to say *before* him, isn't it?' the charming creature went on, entering into the humour of the thing, but looking at me as if she scarce liked me at all.

She would have had to say it before another person as well, for at that moment there stepped into the room from the terrace—the window had been left open—a gentleman who had come into sight, at least into mine, only within the instant. Mrs Marden had said 'Here *they* come', but he appeared to have followed her daughter at a certain distance. I recognised him at once as the personage who had sat beside us in church. This time I saw him better, saw his face and his carriage were strange. I speak of him as a personage, because one felt, indescribably, as if a reigning prince had come into the room. He held himself with something of the grand air and as if he were different from his company. Yet he looked fixedly and gravely at me, till I wondered what he expected. Did he consider that I should bend my knee or kiss his hand? He turned his eyes in the same way on Mrs Marden, but she knew what to do. After the first agitation produced by his approach she took no notice of him whatever; it made me remember her passionate adjuration to me. I had to achieve a great effort to imitate her, for though I knew nothing about him but that he was Sir Edmund Orme his presence acted as a strong appeal, almost as an oppression. He stood there without speaking—young pale handsome clean-shaven decorous, with extraordinary light blue eyes and something old-fashioned, like a portrait of years ago, in his head and in his manner of wearing his hair. He was in complete mourning—one immediately took him for very well dressed—and he carried his hat in his hand. He looked again strangely hard at me, harder than anyone in the world had ever looked before;

and I remember feeling rather cold and wishing he would say
something. No silence had ever seemed to me so soundless.
All this was of course an impression intensely rapid; but that
it had consumed some instants was proved to me suddenly by
the expression of countenance of Charlotte Marden, who
stared from one of us to the other—he never looked at her,
and she had no appearance of looking at him—and then
broke out with: 'What on earth is the matter with you?
You've such odd faces!' I felt the colour come back to mine,
and when she went on in the same tone, 'One would think
you had seen a ghost!' I was conscious I had turned very red.
Sir Edmund Orme never blushed, and I was sure no
embarrassment touched him. One had met people of that
sort, but never any one with so high an indifference.

'Don't be impertinent, and go and tell them all that I'll join
them,' said Mrs Marden with much dignity but with a tremor
of voice that I caught.

'And will you come—*you?*' the girl asked, turning away. I
made no answer, taking the question somehow as meant for
her companion. But he was more silent than I, and when she
reached the door—she was going out that way—she stopped,
her hand on the knob, and looked at me, repeating it. I
assented, springing forward to open the door for her, and as
she passed out she exclaimed to me mockingly: 'You haven't
got your wits about you—you shan't have my hand!'

I closed the door and turned round to find that Sir
Edmund Orme had during the moment my back was
presented to him retired by the window. Mrs Marden stood
there and we looked at each other long. It had only then—as
the girl flitted away—come home to me that her daughter
was unconscious of what had happened. It was *that*, oddly
enough, that gave me a sudden sharp shake—not my own
perception of our visitor, which felt quite natural. It made
the fact vivid to me that she had been equally unaware of
him in church, and the two facts together—now that they
were over—set my heart more sensibly beating. I wiped my

forehead, and Mrs Marden broke out with a low distressful wail: 'Now you know my life—now you know my life!'

'In God's name who is he—*what* is he?'

'He's a man I wronged.'

'How did you wrong him?'

'Oh awfully—years ago.'

'Years ago? Why, he's very young.'

'Young—young?' cried Mrs Marden. 'He was born before *I* was!'

'Then why does he look so?'

She came nearer to me, she laid her hand on my arm, and there was something in her face that made me shrink a little. 'Don't you understand—don't you *feel*?' she intensely put to me.

'I feel very queer!' I laughed; and I was conscious that my note betrayed it.

'He's dead!' said Mrs Marden from her white face.

'Dead?' I panted. 'Then that gentleman was—?' I couldn't even say a word.

'Call him what you like—there are twenty vulgar names. He's a perfect presence.'

'He's a splendid presence!' I cried. 'The place is haunted, *haunted!*' I exulted in the word as if it stood for all I had ever dreamt of.

'It isn't the place—more's the pity!' she instantly returned. 'That has nothing to do with it!'

'Then it's you, dear lady?' I said as if this were still better.

'No, nor me either—I wish it were!'

'Perhaps it's me,' I suggested with a sickly smile.

'It's nobody but my child—my innocent, innocent child!' And with this Mrs Marden broke down—she dropped into a chair and burst into tears. I stammered some question—I pressed on her some bewildered appeal, but she waved me off, unexpectedly and passionately. I persisted—couldn't I help her, couldn't I intervene? 'You *have* intervened,' she sobbed; 'you're *in* it, you're *in* it.'

'I'm very glad to be in anything so extraordinary,' I boldly declared.

'Glad or not, you can't get out of it.'

'I don't want to get out of it—it's too interesting.'

'I'm glad you like it!' She had turned from me, making haste to dry her eyes. 'And now go away.'

'But I want to know more about it.'

'You'll see all you want. Go away!'

'But I want to understand what I see.'

'How can you—when I don't understand myself?' she helplessly cried.

'We'll do so together—we'll make it out.'

At this she got up, doing what more she could to obliterate her tears. 'Yes, it will be better together—that's why I've liked you.'

'Oh we'll see it through!' I returned.

'Then you must control yourself better.'

'I will, I will—with practice.'

'You'll get used to it,' said my friend in a tone I never forgot. 'But go and join them—I'll come in a moment.'

I passed out to the terrace and felt I had a part to play. So far from dreading another encounter with the 'perfect presence', as she had called it, I was affected altogether in the sense of pleasure. I desired a renewal of my luck: I opened myself wide to the impression; I went round the house as quickly as if I expected to overtake Sir Edmund Orme. I didn't overtake him just then, but the day wasn't to close without my recognising that, as Mrs Marden had said, I should see all I wanted of him.

We took, or most of us took, the collective sociable walk which, in the English country-house, is—or was at that time—the consecrated pastime of Sunday afternoons. We were restricted to such a regulated ramble as the ladies were good for; the afternoons moreover were short, and by five o'clock we were restored to the fireside in the hall with a sense, on my part at least, that we might have done a little more for our tea. Mrs Marden had said she would join us, but she hadn't appeared; her daughter, who had seen her again before we went out, only explained that she was tired. She remained invisible all the afternoon, but this was a detail to which I gave as little heed as I had given to the circumstance of my not having Charlotte to myself, even for five minutes, during all our walk. I was too much taken up with another interest to care; I felt beneath my feet the threshold of the strange door, in my life, which had suddenly been thrown open and out of which came an air of a keenness I had never breathed and of a taste stronger than wine. I had heard all my days of apparitions, but it was a different thing to have seen one and to know that I should in all likelihood see it familiarly, as I might say, again. I was on the look-out for it as a pilot for the flash of a revolving light, and ready to generalise on the sinister subject, to answer for it to all and sundry that ghosts were much less alarming and much more amusing than was commonly supposed. There's no doubt that I was much uplifted. I couldn't get over the distinction conferred on me, the exception—in the way of mystic enlargement of vision—made in my favour. At the same time I think I did justice to Mrs Marden's absence—a commentary, when I came to think, on what she had said to me: 'Now you know my life.' She had probably been exposed to our hoverer for years, and, not having my firm fibre, had broken down under it. Her nerve was gone, though she had also been able to attest that, in a degree, one got used to it. She had got used to breaking down.

Afternoon tea, when the dusk fell early, was a friendly hour at Tranton; the firelight played into the wide white last-century hall; sympathies almost confessed themselves, lingering together, before dressing, on deep sofas, in muddy boots, for last words after walks; and even solitary absorption in the third volume of a novel that was wanted by someone else seemed a form of geniality. I watched my moment and went over to Charlotte when I saw her about to withdraw. The ladies had left the place one by one, and after I had addressed myself to her particularly the three men who had been near gradually dispersed. We had a little vague talk—she might have been a good deal preoccupied, and heaven knows *I* was—after which she said she must go: she should be late for dinner. I proved to her by book that she had plenty of time, and she objected that she must at any rate go up to see her mother, who, she feared, was unwell.

'On the contrary, she's better than she has been for a long time—I'll guarantee that,' I said. 'She has found out she can have confidence in me, and that has done her good.' Miss Marden had dropped into her chair again, I was standing before her, and she looked up at me without a smile, with a dim distress in her beautiful eyes: not exactly as if I were hurting her, but as if she were no longer disposed to treat as a joke what had passed—whatever it was, it would give at the same time no ground for the extreme of solemnity—between her mother and myself. But I could answer her enquiry in all kindness and candour, for I was really conscious that the poor lady had put off a part of her burden on me and was proportionately relieved and eased. 'I'm sure she has slept all the afternoon as she hasn't slept for years,' I went on. 'You've only to ask her.'

Charlotte got up again. 'You make yourself out very useful.'

'You've a good quarter of an hour,' I said. 'Haven't I a right to talk to you a little this way, alone, when your mother has given me your hand?'

'And is it *your* mother who has given me yours? I'm much obliged to her, but I don't want it. I think our hands are not our mothers'—they happen to be our own!' laughed the girl.

'Sit down, sit down and let me tell you!' I pleaded.

I still stood there urgently, to see if she wouldn't oblige me. She cast about, looking vaguely this way and that, as if under a compulsion that was slightly painful. The empty hall was quiet—we heard the loud ticking of the great clock. Then she slowly sank down and I drew a chair close to her. This made me face round to the fire again, and with the movement I saw disconcertedly that we weren't alone. The next instant, more strangely than I can say, my discomposure, instead of increasing, dropped, for the person before the fire was Sir Edmund Orme. He stood there as I had seen him in the Indian room, looking at me with the expressionless attention that borrowed gravity from his sombre distinction. I knew so much more about him now that I had to check a movement of recognition, an acknowledgement of his presence. When once I was aware of it, and that it lasted, the sense that we had company, Charlotte and I, quitted me: it was impressed on me on the contrary that we were but the more markedly thrown together. No influence from our companion reached her, and I made a tremendous and very nearly successful effort to hide from her that my own sensibility was other and my nerves as tense as harp-strings. I say 'very nearly', because she watched me an instant—while my words were arrested—in a way that made me fear she was going to say again, as she had said in the Indian room: 'What on earth is the matter with you?'

What the matter with me was I quickly told her, for the full knowledge of it rolled over me with the touching sight of her unconsciousness. It was touching that she became in the presence of this extraordinary portent. What was portended, danger or sorrow, bliss or bane, was a minor question; all I saw, as she sat there, was that, innocent and charming, she was close to a horror, as she might have thought it, that happened to be veiled from her but that might at any moment be disclosed. I didn't mind it now, as I found—at least more than I could bear; but nothing was more possible than she should, and if it wasn't curious and interesting it might easily be appalling. If I didn't mind it for myself, I afterwards made out, this was largely because I

was so taken up with the idea of protecting her. My heart,
all at once, beat high with this view; I determined to do
everything I could to keep her sense sealed. What I could do
might have been all obscure to me if I hadn't, as the minutes
lapsed, become more aware than of anything else that I
loved her. The way to save her was to love her, and the way
to love her was to tell her, now and here, that I did so. Sir
Edmund Orme didn't prevent me, especially as after a
moment he turned his back to us and stood looking
discreetly at the fire. At the end of another moment he
leaned his head on his arm, against the chimney-piece, with
an air of gradual dejection, like a spirit still more weary than
discreet. Charlotte Marden rose with a start at what I said to
her—she jumped up to escape it; but she took no offence:
the feeling I expressed was too real. She only moved about
the room with a deprecating murmur, and I was so busy
following up any little advantage I might have obtained that
I didn't notice in what manner Sir Edmund Orme disappeared. I only found his place presently vacant. This
made no difference—he had been so small a hindrance; I
only remember being suddenly struck with something
inexorable in the sweet sad headshake Charlotte gave me.

'I don't ask for an answer now,' I said; 'I only want you to
be sure—to know how much depends on it.'

'Oh I don't want to give it to you now or ever!' she
replied. 'I hate the subject, please—I wish one could be let
alone.' And then, since I might have found something harsh
in this irrepressible artless cry of beauty beset, she added,
quickly vaguely kindly, as she left the room: 'Thank you,
thank you—thank you so very much!'

At dinner I was generous enough to be glad for her that,
on the same side of the table with me, she hadn't me in
range. Her mother was nearly opposite me, and just after we
had sat down Mrs Marden gave me a long deep look that
expressed, and to the utmost, our strange communion. It
meant of course 'She has told me', but it meant other things

beside. At any rate I know what my mute response to her conveyed: 'I've seen him again—I've seen him again!' This didn't prevent Mrs Marden from treating her neighbours with her usual scrupulous blandness. After dinner, when, in the drawing-room, the men joined the ladies and I went straight up to her to tell her how I wished we might have some quiet words, she said at once, in a low tone, looking down at her fan while she opened and shut it: 'He's here—he's here.'

'Here?' I looked round the room, but was disappointed.

'Look where *she* is,' said Mrs Marden just with the faintest asperity. Charlotte was in fact not in the main saloon, but in a smaller into which it opened and which was known as the morning-room. I took a few steps and saw her, through a doorway, upright in the middle of the room, talking with three gentlemen whose backs were practically turned to me. For a moment my quest seemed vain; then I knew one of the gentlemen—the middle one—could but be Sir Edmund Orme. This time it *was* surprising that the others didn't see him. Charlotte might have seemed absolutely to have her eyes on him and to be addressing him straight. She saw me after an instant, however, and immediately averted herself. I returned to her mother with a sharpened fear the girl might think I was watching *her*, which would be unjust. Mrs Marden had found a small sofa—a little apart—and I sat down beside her. There were some questions I had so wanted to go into that I wished we were once more in the Indian room. I presently gathered however that our privacy quite sufficed. We communicated so closely and completely now, and with such silent reciprocities, that it would in every circumstance be adequate.

'Oh yes, he's there,' I said; 'and at about a quarter-past seven he was in the hall.'

'I knew it at the time—and I was so glad!' she answered straight.

'So glad?'

'That it was your affair this time and not mine. It's a rest for me.'

'Did you sleep all the afternoon?' I then asked.

'As I haven't done for months. But how did you know that?'

'As *you* knew, I take it, that Sir Edmund was in the hall. We shall evidently each of us know things now—where the other's concerned.'

'Where *he's* concerned,' Mrs Marden amended. 'It's a blessing, the way you take it,' she added with a long mild sigh.

'I take it', I at once returned, 'as a man who's in love with your daughter.'

'Of course—of course.' Intense as I now felt my desire for the girl to be I couldn't help laughing a little at the tone of these words; and it led my companion immediately to say: 'Otherwise you wouldn't have seen him.'

Well, I esteemed my privilege, but I saw an objection to this. 'Does everyone see him who's in love with her? If so there would be dozens.'

'They're not in love with her as you are.'

I took this in and couldn't but accept it. 'I can of course only speak for myself—and I found a moment before dinner to do so.'

'She told me as soon as she saw me,' Mrs Marden replied.

'And have I any hope—any chance?'

'That you may have is what I long for, what I pray for.'

The sore sincerity of this touched me. 'Ah how can I thank you enough?' I murmured.

'I believe it will all pass—if she only loves you,' the poor woman pursued.

'It will all pass?' I was a little at a loss.

'I mean we shall then be rid of him—shall never see him again.'

'Oh if she loves me I don't care how often I see him!' I roundly returned.

'Ah you take it better than *I* could,' said my companion. 'You've the happiness not to know—not to understand.'

'I don't indeed. What on earth does he want?'

'He wants to make me suffer.' She turned her wan face upon me with it, and I saw now for the first time, and saw well, how perfectly, if this had been our visitant's design, he had done his work. 'For what I did to him,' she explained.

'And what did you do to him?'

She gave me an unforgettable look. 'I killed him.' As I had seen him fifty yards off only five minutes before, the words gave me a start. 'Yes, I make you jump; be careful. He's there still, but he killed himself. I broke his heart—he thought me awfully bad. We were to have been married, but I broke it off—just at the last. I saw someone I liked better; I had no reason but that. It wasn't for interest or money or position or any of that baseness. All the good things were his. It was simply that I fell in love with Major Marden. When I saw *him* I felt I couldn't marry any one else. I wasn't in love with Edmund Orme; my mother and my elder, my married, sister had brought it about. But he did love me and I knew—that is almost knew!—how much! But I told him I didn't care—that I couldn't, that I wouldn't ever. I threw him over, and he took something, some abominable drug or draught that proved fatal. It was dreadful, it was horrible, he was found that way—he died in agony. I married Major Marden, but not for five years. I was happy, perfectly happy—time obliterates. But when my husband died I began to see him.'

I had listened intently, wondering. 'To see your husband?'

'Never, never—*that* way, thank God! To see *him*—and with Chartie, always with Chartie. The first time it nearly killed me—about seven years ago, when she first came out. Never when I'm by myself—only with her. Sometimes not for months, then every day for a week. I've tried everything to break the spell—doctors and *régimes* and climates; I've prayed to God on my knees. That day at Brighton, on the Parade with you, when you thought I was ill, that was the first for an age. And then in the evening, when I knocked my tea over you, and the day you were at the door with her and I saw you from the window—each time he was there.'

'I see, I see.' I was more thrilled than I could say. 'It's an apparition like another.'

'Like another? Have you ever seen another?' she cried.

'No, I mean the sort of thing one has heard of. It's tremendously interesting to encounter a case.'

'Do you call me a "case"?' my friend cried with exquisite resentment.

'I was thinking of myself.'

'Oh you're the right one!' she went on. 'I was right when I trusted you.'

'I'm devoutly grateful you did; but what made you do it?' I asked.

'I had thought the whole thing out. I had had time to in those dreadful years while he was punishing me in my daughter.'

'Hardly that,' I objected, 'if Miss Marden never knew.'

'That has been my terror, that she *will*, from one occasion to another. I've an unspeakable dread of the effect on her.'

'She shan't, she shan't!' I engaged in such a tone that several people looked round. Mrs Marden made me rise, and our talk dropped for that evening. The next day I told her I must leave Tranton—it was neither comfortable nor considerate to remain as a rejected suitor. She was disconcerted, but accepted my reasons, only appealing to me with mournful eyes: 'You'll leave me alone then with my burden?' It was of course understood between us that for many weeks to come there would be no discretion in 'worrying poor Charlotte': such were the terms in which, with odd feminine and maternal inconsistency, she alluded to an attitude on my part that she favoured. I was prepared to be heroically considerate, but I held that even this delicacy permitted me to say a word to Miss Marden before I went. I begged her after breakfast to take a turn with me on the terrace, and as she hesitated, looking at me distantly, I let her know it was only to ask her a question and to say goodbye—I was going away for *her*.

She came out with me and we passed slowly round the house three or four times. Nothing is finer than this great airy platform, from which every glance is a sweep of the country with the sea on the furthest edge. It might have been that as we passed the windows we were conspicuous to our friends in the house, who would make out sarcastically why I was so significantly bolting. But I didn't care; I only wondered if they mightn't really this time receive the impression of Sir Edmund Orme, who joined us on one of our turns and strolled slowly on the other side of Charlotte. Of what odd essence he was made I know not; I've no theory about him—leaving that to others—any more than about such or such another of my fellow mortals (and *his* law of being) as I have elbowed in life. He was as positive, as individual and ultimate a fact as any of these. Above all he was, by every seeming, of as fine and as sensitive, of as thoroughly honourable, a mixture; so that I should no more have thought of taking a liberty, of practising an experiment, with him, of touching him, for instance, or of addressing him, since he set the example of silence, than I should have thought of committing any other social grossness. He had always, as I saw more fully later, the perfect propriety of his position—looked always arrayed and anointed, and carried himself ever, in each particular, exactly as the occasion demanded. He struck me as strange, incontestably, but somehow always struck me as right. I very soon came to attach an idea of beauty to his unrecognised presence, the beauty of an old story, of love and pain and death. What I ended by feeling was that he was on my side, watching over my interest, looking to it that no trick should be played me and that my heart at least shouldn't be broken. Oh he had taken them seriously, his own wound and his own loss—he had certainly proved this in his day. If poor Mrs Marden, responsible for these things, had, as she told me, thought the case out, I also treated it to the finest analysis I could bring to bear. It was a case of retributive justice, of the visiting on the children of the sins of the mothers, since not of the fathers. This wretched mother was to pay, in suffering, for the suffering she had inflicted, and as the disposition to trifle with an honest man's just expectations might crop up again, to my detriment, in the child, the latter young person was to be studied and watched, so that *she* might be made to suffer should she do an equal wrong. She might emulate her parent by some play of characteristic perversity not less than she resembled her in charm; and if that impulse should be determined in her, if she should be caught, that is to say, in some breach of faith or some heartless act, her eyes would on the spot, by an insidious logic, be opened suddenly and unpitiedly to the 'perfect presence', which she would then have to work as she could into her conception of a young lady's universe. I had no great fear for her, because I hadn't felt her lead me on from vanity, and I knew that if I was disconcerted it was because I had myself gone too fast. We should have a good deal of ground to get over at least before I should be in a position to be sacrificed by her. She couldn't take back what she had given before she had given rather more. Whether I asked for more was indeed another matter, and the question I put to her on the terrace that morning was whether I might continue during the winter to come to Mrs Marden's house. I promised not to come too often and not to speak to her for three months of the issue I had raised the day before. She replied that I might do as I liked, and on this we parted.

I carried out the vow I had made her; I held my tongue for my three months. Unexpectedly to myself there were moments of this time when she did strike me as capable of missing my homage even though she might be indifferent to my happiness. I wanted so to make her like me that I became subtle and ingenious, wonderfully alert, patiently diplomatic. Sometimes I thought I had earned my reward, brought her to the point of saying: 'Well, well, you're the best of them all—you may speak to me now.' Then there was a greater blankness than ever in her beauty and on certain days a mocking light in her eyes, a light of which the meaning seemed to be: 'If you don't take care I *will* accept you, to have done with you the more effectually.' Mrs Marden was a great help to me simply by believing in me, and I valued her faith all the more that it continued even through a sudden intermission of the miracle that had been wrought for me. After our visit to Tranton Sir Edmund Orme gave us a holiday, and I confess it was at first a disappointment to me. I felt myself by so much less designated, less involved and connected—all with Charlotte I mean to say. 'Oh don't cry till you're out of the wood,' was her mother's comment; 'he has let me off sometimes for six months. He'll break out again when you least expect it—he understands his game.' For her these weeks were happy, and she was wise enough not to talk about me to the girl. She was so good as to assure me I was taking the right line, that I looked as if I felt secure and that in the long run women give way to this. She had known them do it even when the man was a fool for that appearance, for that confidence—a fool indeed on any terms. For herself she felt it a good time, almost her best, a Saint Martin's summer of the soul. She was better than she had been for years, and had me to thank for it. The sense of visitation was light on her—she wasn't in anguish every time she looked round. Charlotte contradicted me repeatedly, but contradicted herself still more. That winter by the old Sussex sea was a wonder of mildness, and we often sat out in the sun. I walked up and down with my young woman, and Mrs Marden, sometimes on a bench, sometimes in a Bath-chair, waited for us and smiled at us as we passed. I always looked out for a sign in her face—'He's with you, he's with you' (she would see him before I should) but nothing came; the season had brought us as well a sort of spiritual softness. Toward the end of April the air was so like June that, meeting my two friends one night at some Brighton sociability—an evening party with amateur music—I drew the younger unresistingly out upon a balcony to which a window in one of the rooms stood open. The night was close and thick, the stars dim, and below us under the cliff we heard the deep rumble of the tide. We listened to it a little and there came to us, mixed with it from within the house, the sound of a violin accompanied by a piano—a performance that had been our pretext for escaping.

'Do you like me a little better?' I broke out after a minute. 'Could you listen to me again?'

I had no sooner spoken than she laid her hand quickly, with a certain force, on my arm. 'Hush!—isn't there someone there?' She was looking into the gloom of the far end of the balcony. This balcony ran the whole width of the house, a width very great in the best of the old houses at Brighton. We were to some extent lighted by the open window behind us, but the other windows, curtained within, left the darkness undiminished, so that I made out but dimly the figure of a gentleman standing there and looking at us. He was in evening dress, like a guest—I saw the vague sheen of his white shirt and the pale oval of his face—and he might perfectly have been a guest who had stepped out in advance of us to take the air. Charlotte took him for one at first—then evidently, even in a few seconds, saw that the intensity of his gaze was unconventional. What else she saw I couldn't determine; I was too occupied with my own impression to do more than feel the quick contact of her uneasiness. My own impression was in fact the strongest of sensations, a sensation of horror; for what could the thing mean but that the girl at last *saw?* I heard her give a sudden, gasping 'Ah!' and move quickly into the house. It was only afterwards I knew that I myself had had a totally new emotion—my horror passing into anger and my anger into a stride along the balcony with a gesture of reprobation. The case was simplified to the vision of an adorable girl menaced and terrified. I advanced to vindicate her security, but I found nothing there to meet me. It was either all a mistake or Sir Edmund Orme had vanished.

I followed her at once, but there were symptoms of confusion in the drawing-room when I passed in. A lady had fainted, the music had stopped; there was a shuffling of chairs and a pressing forward. The lady was not Charlotte, as I feared, but Mrs Marden, who had suddenly been taken ill. I remember the relief with which I learned this, for to see Charlotte stricken would have been anguish, and her mother's condition gave a channel to her agitation. It was of course all a matter for the people of the house and for the ladies, and I could have no share in attending to my friends or in conducting them to their carriage. Mrs Marden revived and insisted on going home, after which I uneasily withdrew.

I called the next morning for better news and I learnt she was more at ease, but on my asking if Charlotte would see me the message sent down was an excuse. There was nothing for me to do all day but roam with a beating heart. Toward evening however I received a line in pencil, brought by hand—'Please come; mother wishes you.' Five minutes later I was at the door again and ushered into the drawing-room. Mrs Marden lay on the sofa, and as soon as I looked at her I saw the shadow of death in her face. But the first thing she said was that she was better, ever so much better; her poor old fluttered heart had misbehaved again, but now was decently quiet. She gave me her hand and I bent over her, my eyes on her eyes, and in this way was able to read what she didn't speak—'I'm really very ill, but appear to take what I say exactly as I say it.' Charlotte stood there beside her, looking not frightened now, but intensely grave, and meeting no look of my own. 'She has told me—she has told me!' her mother went on.

'She has told you?' I stared from one of them to the other, wondering if my friend meant that the girl had named to her the unexplained appearance on the balcony.

'That you spoke to her again—that you're admirably faithful.'

I felt a thrill of joy at this; it showed me that memory uppermost, and also that her daughter had wished to say the thing that would most soothe her, not the thing that would alarm her. Yet I was myself now sure, as sure as if Mrs Marden had told me, that she knew and had known at the moment what her daughter had seen. 'I spoke—I spoke, but she gave me no answer,' I said.

'She will now, won't you, Chartie? I want it so, I want it!' our companion murmured with ineffable wistfulness.

'You're very good to me'—Charlotte addressed me, seriously and sweetly, but with her eyes fixed on the carpet. There was something different in her, different from all the past. She had recognised something, she felt a coercion. I could see her uncontrollably tremble.

'Ah if you would let me show you *how* good I can be!' I cried as I held out my hands to her. As I uttered the words I was touched with the knowledge that something had happened. A form had constituted itself on the other side of the couch, and the form leaned over Mrs Marden. My whole being went forth into a mute prayer that Charlotte shouldn't see it and that I should be able to betray nothing. The impulse to glance toward her mother was even stronger than the involuntary movement of taking in Sir Edmund Orme; but I could resist even that, and Mrs Marden was perfectly still. Charlotte got up to give me her hand, and then—with the definite act—she dreadfully saw. She gave, with a shriek, one stare of dismay, and another sound, the wail of one of the lost, fell at the same instant on my ear. But

I had already sprung toward the creature I loved, to cover her, to veil her face, and she had as passionately thrown herself into my arms. I held her there a moment—pressing her close, given up to her, feeling each of her throbs with my own and not knowing which was which; then all of a sudden, coldly, I was sure we were alone. She released herself. The figure beside the sofa had vanished, but Mrs Marden lay in her place with closed eyes, with something in her stillness that gave us both a fresh terror. Charlotte expressed it in the cry of 'Mother, mother!' with which she flung herself down. I fell on my knees beside her—Mrs Marden had passed away.

Was the sound I heard when Chartie shrieked—the other and still more tragic sound I mean—the despairing cry of the poor lady's death-shock or the articulate sob (it was like a waft from a great storm) of the exorcised and pacified spirit? Possibly the latter, for that was mercifully the last of Sir Edmund Orme.

I had already sprung toward the creature I loved; to cover her, to veil her face; and she had as passionately thrown herself into my arms. I held her there a moment—pressing her close, given up to her, feeling each of her throbs with my own and not knowing which was which, then all of a sudden, coldly, I was sure we were alone. She released herself. The figure beside the sofa had vanished; but Mrs Marden lay in her place with closed eyes, with something in her stillness that gave us both a fresh terror. Charlotte expressed it in the cry of 'Mother, mother!' with which she flung herself down. I fell on my knees beside her—Mrs Marden had passed away.

Was the sound I heard when Charlotte shrieked—the other and still more tragic sound I mean—the despairing cry of the poor lady's death-shock or the articulate sob (it was like a wail from a great storm) of the exposed and pacified spirit? Possibly the latter, for that was mercifully the last of Sir Edmund Orme.

Owen Wingrave

OWEN WINGRAVE

I

'UPON MY honour you must be off your head!' cried Spencer Coyle as the young man, with a white face, stood there panting a little and repeating 'Really I've quite decided,' and 'I assure you I've thought it all out.' They were both pale, but Owen Wingrave smiled in a manner exasperating to his supervisor, who however still discriminated sufficiently to feel his grimace—it was like an irrelevant leer—the result of extreme and conceivable nervousness.

'It was certainly a mistake to have gone so far; but that's exactly why it strikes me I mustn't go further,' poor Owen said, waiting mechanically, almost humbly—he wished not to swagger, and indeed had nothing to swagger about—and carrying through the window to the stupid opposite houses the dry glitter of his eyes.

'I'm unspeakably disgusted. You've made me dreadfully ill'—and Mr Coyle looked in truth thoroughly upset.

'I'm very sorry. It was the fear of the effect on you that kept me from speaking sooner.'

'You should have spoken three months ago. Don't you know your mind from one day to the other?' the elder of the pair demanded.

The young man for a moment held himself: then he quavered his plea. 'You're very angry with me and I expected it. I'm awfully obliged to you for all you've done for me. I'll do anything else for you in return, but I can't do that. Everyone else will let me have it of course. I'm prepared for that—I'm prepared for everything. It's what has taken the time: to be sure I was prepared. I think it's your displeasure I feel most and regret most. But little by little you'll get over it,' Owen wound up.

'*You'll* get over it rather faster, I suppose!' the other satirically exclaimed. He was quite as agitated as his young friend, and they were evidently in no condition to prolong an encounter in which each drew blood. Mr Coyle was a professional 'coach'; he prepared aspirants for the army, taking only three or four at a time, to whom he applied the irresistible stimulus the possession of which was both his secret and his fortune. He hadn't a great establishment; he would have said himself that it was not a wholesale business. Neither his system, his health nor his temper could have concorded with numbers; so he weighed and measured his pupils and turned away more applicants than he passed. He was an artist in his line, caring only for picked subjects and capable of sacrifices almost passionate for the individual. He liked ardent young men—there were types of facility and kinds of capacity to which he was indifferent—and he had taken a particular fancy to Owen Wingrave. This young man's particular shade of ability, to say nothing of his whole personality, almost cast a spell and at any rate worked a charm. Mr Coyle's candidates usually did wonders, and he might have sent up a multitude. He was a person exactly of the stature of the great Napoleon, with a certain flicker of genius in his light blue eye: it had been said of him that he looked like a concert-giving pianist. The tone of his favourite pupil now expressed, without intention indeed, a superior wisdom that irritated him. He hadn't at all suffered before from Wingrave's high opinion of himself, which had seemed justified by remarkable parts; but today, of a sudden, it struck him as intolerable. He cut short the discussion, declining absolutely to regard their relations as terminated, and remarked to his pupil that he had better go off somewhere—down to Eastbourne, say: the sea would bring him round—and take a few days to find his feet and come to his senses. He could afford the time, he was so well

up: when Spencer Coyle remembered how well up he was
he could have boxed his ears. The tall athletic young man
wasn't physically a subject for simplified reasoning; but a
troubled gentleness in his handsome face, the index of
compunction mixed with resolution, virtually signified that
if it could have done any good he would have turned both
cheeks. He evidently didn't pretend that his wisdom was
superior; he only presented it as his own. It was his own
career after all that was in question. He couldn't refuse to go
through the form of trying Eastbourne or at least of holding
his tongue, though there was that in his manner which
implied that if he should do so it would be really to give
Mr Coyle a chance to recuperate. He didn't feel a bit
overworked, but there was nothing more natural than that,
with their tremendous pressure, Mr Coyle should be.
Mr Coyle's own intellect would derive an advantage from
his pupil's holiday. Mr Coyle saw what he meant, but
controlled himself; he only demanded, as his right, a truce
of three days. Owen granted it, though as fostering sad
illusions this went visibly against his conscience; but before
they separated the famous crammer remarked: 'All the same
I feel I ought to see someone. I think you mentioned to me
that your aunt had come to town?'

'Oh yes—she's in Baker Street. Do go and see her,' the
boy said for comfort.

His tutor sharply eyed him. 'Have you broached this folly
to her?'

'Not yet—to no one. I thought it right to speak to you
first.'

'Oh what you "think right"!' cried Spencer Coyle,
outraged by his young friend's standards. He added that he
would probably call on Miss Wingrave; after which the
recreant youth got out of the house.

The latter didn't, none the less, start at once for
Eastbourne; he only directed his steps to Kensington
Gardens, from which Mr Coyle's desirable residence—he

was terribly expensive and had a big house—was not far removed. The famous coach 'put up' his pupils, and Owen had mentioned to the butler that he would be back to dinner. The spring day was warm to his young blood, and he had a book in his pocket which, when he had passed into the Gardens and, after a short stroll, dropped into a chair, he took out wth the slow soft sigh that finally ushers in a pleasure postponed. He stretched his long legs and began to read it; it was a volume of Goethe's poems. He had been for days in a state of the highest tension, and now that the cord had snapped the relief was proportionate; only it was characteristic of him that this deliverance should take the form of an intellectual pleasure. If he had thrown up the probability of a magnificent career it wasn't to dawdle along Bond Street nor parade his indifference in the window of a club. At any rate he had in a few moments forgotten everything—the tremendous pressure, Mr Coyle's disappointment and even his formidable aunt in Baker Street. If these watchers had overtaken him there would surely have been some excuse for their exasperation. There was no doubt he was perverse, for his very choice of a pastime only showed how he had got up his German.

'What the devil's the matter with him, do *you* know?' Spencer Coyle asked that afternoon of young Lechmere, who had never before observed the head of the establishment to set a fellow such an example of bad language. Young Lechmere was not only Wingrave's fellow pupil, he was supposed to be his intimate, indeed quite his best friend, and had unconsciously performed for Mr Coyle the office of making the promise of his great gifts more vivid by contrast. He was short and sturdy and as a general thing uninspired, and Mr Coyle, who found no amusement in believing in him, had never thought him less exciting than as he stared now out of a face from which you could no more guess whether he had caught an idea than you could judge of your dinner by looking at a dish-cover. Young Lechmere concealed such achievements as if they had been youthful indiscretions. At any rate he could evidently conceive no reason why it should be thought there was anything more than usual the matter with the companion of his studies; so Mr Coyle had to continue: 'He declines to go up. He chucks the whole shop!'

The first thing that struck young Lechmere in the case was the freshness, as of a forgotten vernacular, it had imparted to the governor's vocabulary. 'He doesn't want to go to Sandhurst?'

'He doesn't want to go anywhere. He gives up the army altogether. He objects', said Mr Coyle in a tone that made young Lechmere almost hold his breath, 'to the military profession.'

'Why it has been the profession of all his family!'

'Their profession? It has been their religion! Do you know Miss Wingrave?'

'Oh yes. Isn't she awful?' young Lechmere candidly ejaculated.

His instructor demurred. 'She's formidable, if you mean that, and it's right she should be; because somehow in her very person, good maiden lady as she is, she represents the might, she represents the traditions and the exploits, of the British army. She represents the expansive property of the English name. I think his family can be trusted to come down on him, but every influence should be set in motion. I want to know what yours is. Can *you* do anything in the matter?'

'I can try a couple of rounds with him,' said young Lechmere reflectively. 'But he knows a fearful lot. He has the most extraordinary ideas.'

'Then he has told you some of them—he has taken you into his confidence?'

'I've heard him jaw by the yard,' smiled the honest youth. 'He has told me he despises it.'

'What *is* it he despises? I can't make out.'

The most consecutive of Mr Coyle's nurslings considered a moment, as if he were conscious of a responsibility. 'Why I think just soldiering, don't you know? He says we take the wrong view of it.'

'He oughtn't to talk to *you* that way. It's corrupting the youth of Athens. It's sowing sedition.'

'Oh I'm all right!' said young Lechmere. 'And he never told me he meant to chuck it. I always thought he meant to see it through, simply because he had to. He'll argue to any side you like. He can talk your head off—I will say *that* for him. But it's a tremendous pity—I'm sure he'd have a big career.'

'Tell him so then; plead with him; struggle with him—for God's sake.'

'I'll do what I can—I'll tell him it's a regular shame.'

'Yes, strike *that* note—insist on the disgrace of it.'

The young man gave Mr Coyle a queer look. 'I'm sure he wouldn't do anything dishonourable.'

'Well—it won't look right. He must be made to feel *that*—work it up. Give him a comrade's point of view—that of a brother-in-arms.'

'That's what I thought we were going to be!' young Lechmere mused romantically, much uplifted by the nature of the mission imposed on him. 'He's an awfully good sort.'

'No one will think so if he backs out!' said Spencer Coyle.

'Well, they mustn't say it to *me*!' his pupil rejoined with a flush.

Mr Coyle debated, noting his tone and aware that in the perversity of things, though this young man was a born soldier, no excitement would ever attach to *his* alternatives save perhaps on the part of the nice girl to whom at an early day he was sure to be placidly united. 'Do you like him very much—do you believe in him?'

Young Lechmere's life in these days was spent in

answering terrible questions, but he had never been put through so straight a lot as these. 'Believe in him? Rather!' 'Then *save* him!'

The poor boy was puzzled, as if it were forced upon him by this intensity that there was more in such an appeal than could appear on the surface; and he doubtless felt that he was but apprehending a complex situation when after another moment, with his hands in his pockets, he replied hopefully but not pompously: 'I dare say I can bring him round!'

II

BEFORE seeing young Lechmere Mr Coyle had determined to telegraph an enquiry to Miss Wingrave. He had prepaid the answer, which, being promptly put into his hand, brought the interview we have just related to a close. He immediately drove off to Baker Street, where the lady had said she awaited him, and five minutes after he got there, as he sat with Owen Wingrave's remarkable aunt, he repeated several times over, in his angry sadness and with the infallibility of his experience: 'He's so intelligent—he's so intelligent!' He had declared it had been a luxury to put such a fellow through.

'Of course he's intelligent; what else could he be? We've never, that I know of, had but *one* idiot in the family!' said Jane Wingrave. This was an allusion that Mr Coyle could understand, and it brought home to him another of the reasons for the disappointment, the humiliation as it were, of the good people at Paramore, at the same time that it gave an example of the conscientious coarseness he had on former occasions observed in his hostess. Poor Philip Wingrave, her late brother's eldest son, was literally imbecile and banished from view; deformed, unsocial, irretrievable, he had been relegated to a private asylum and

had become among the friends of the family only a little
hushed lugubrious legend. All the hopes of the house,
picturesque Paramore, now unintermittently old Sir Philip's
rather melancholy home—his infirmities would keep him
there to the last—were therefore gathered on the second
boy's head, which nature, as if in compunction for her
previous botch, had, in addition to making it strikingly
handsome, filled with a marked and general readiness.
These two had been the only children of the old man's only
son, who, like so many of his ancestors, had given up a
gallant young life to the service of his country. Owen
Wingrave the elder had received his death-cut, in close
quarters, from an Afghan sabre; the blow had come
crashing across his skull. His wife, at that time in India, was
about to give birth to her third child; and when the event
took place, in darkness and anguish, the baby came lifeless
into the world and the mother sank under the multiplication
of her woes. The second of the little boys in England, who
was at Paramore with his grandfather, became the peculiar
charge of his aunt, the only unmarried one, and during the
interesting Sunday that, by urgent invitation, Spencer
Coyle, busy as he was, had, after consenting to put Owen
through, spent under that roof, the celebrated crammer
received a vivid impression of the influence exerted at least
in intention by Miss Wingrave. Indeed the picture of this
short visit remained with the observant little man a curious
one—the vision of an impoverished Jacobean house, shabby
and remarkably 'creepy', but full of character still and full
of felicity as a setting for the distinguished figure of the
peaceful old soldier. Sir Philip Wingrave, a relic rather than
a celebrity, was a small brown erect octogenarian, with
smouldering eyes and a studied courtesy. He liked to do the
diminished honours of his house, but even when with a
shaky hand he lighted a bedroom candle for a deprecating
guest it was impossible not to feel him, beneath the surface,
a merciless old man of blood. The eye of the imagination

could glance back into his crowded Eastern past—back at episodes in which his scrupulous forms would only have made him more terrible. He had his legend—and oh there were stories about him!

Mr Coyle remembered also two other figures—a faded inoffensive Mrs Julian, domesticated there by a system of frequent visits as the widow of an officer and a particular friend of Miss Wingrave, and a remarkably clever little girl of eighteen, who was this lady's daughter and who struck the speculative visitor as already formed for other relations. She was very impertinent to Owen, and in the course of a long walk that he had taken with the young man and the effect of which, in much talk, had been to clinch his high opinion of him, he had learned—for Owen chattered confidentially—that Mrs Julian was the sister of a very gallant gentleman, Captain Hume-Walker of the Artillery, who had fallen in the Indian Mutiny and between whom and Miss Wingrave (it had been that lady's one known concession) a passage of some delicacy, taking a tragic turn, was believed to have been enacted. They had been engaged to be married, but she had given way to the jealousy of her nature—had broken with him and sent him off to his fate, which had been horrible. A passionate sense of having wronged him, a hard eternal remorse had thereupon taken possession of her, and when his poor sister, linked also to a soldier, had by a still heavier blow been left almost without resources, she had devoted herself grimly to a long expiation. She had sought comfort in taking Mrs Julian to live much of the time at Paramore, where she became an unremunerated though not uncriticised housekeeper, and Spencer Coyle rather fancied it a part of this comfort that she could at leisure trample on her. The impression of Jane Wingrave was not the faintest he had gathered on that intensifying Sunday—an occasion singularly tinged for him with the sense of bereavement and mourning and memory, of names never mentioned, of the far-away plaint of widows

and the echoes of battles and bad news. It was all military
indeed, and Mr Coyle was made to shudder a little at the
profession of which he helped to open the door to otherwise
harmless young men. Miss Wingrave might moreover have
made such a bad conscience worse—so cold and clear a good
one looked at him out of her hard fine eyes and trumpeted
in her sonorous voice.

   She was a high distinguished person, angular but not
awkward, with a large forehead and abundant black hair
arranged like that of a woman conceiving perhaps excusably
of her head as 'noble', and today irregularly streaked with
white. If however she represented for our troubled friend
the genius of a military race it was not that she had the step
of a grenadier or the vocabulary of a camp-follower; it was
only that such sympathies were vividly implied in the
general fact to which her very presence and each of her
actions and glances and tones were a constant and direct
allusion—the paramount valour of her family. If she was
military it was because she sprang from a military house and
because she wouldn't for the world have been anything but
what the Wingraves had been. She was almost vulgar about
her ancestors, and if one had been tempted to quarrel with
her one would have found a fair pretext in her defective
sense of proportion. This temptation however said nothing
to Spencer Coyle, for whom, as a strong character revealing
itself in colour and sound, she was almost a 'treat' and who
was glad to regard her as a force exerted on his own side. He
wished her nephew had more of her narrowness instead of
being almost cursed with the tendency to look at things in
their relations. He wondered why when she came up to
town she always resorted to Baker Street for lodgings. He
had never known nor heard of Baker Street as a residence—
he associated it only with bazaars and photographers. He
divined in her a rigid indifference to everything that was
not the passion of her life. Nothing really mattered to her
but that, and she would have occupied apartments in

Whitechapel if they had been an item in her tactics. She had
received her visitor in a large cold faded room, furnished
with slippery seats and decorated with alabaster vases and
wax-flowers. The only little personal comfort for which she
appeared to have looked out was a fat catalogue of the Army
and Navy Stores, which reposed on a vast desolate table-
cover of false blue. Her clear forehead—it was like a
porcelain slate, a receptacle for addresses and sums—had
flushed when her nephew's crammer told her the extraordinary news; but he saw she was fortunately more angry
than frightened. She had essentially, she would always
have, too little imagination for fear, and the healthy habit
moreover of facing everything had taught her that the
occasion usually found her a quantity to reckon with. He
saw that her only present fear could have been that of the
failure to prevent her nephew's showing publicly for an ass,
or for worse, and that to such an apprehension as this she
was in fact inaccessible. Practically too she was not troubled
by surprise; she recognised none of the futile, none of the
subtle sentiments. If Owen had for an hour made a fool of
himself she was angry; disconcerted as she would have been
on learning that he had confessed to debts or fallen in love
with a low girl. But there remained in any annoyance the
saving fact that no one could make a fool of *her*.

'I don't know when I've taken such an interest in a young
man—I think I've never done it since I began to handle
them,' Mr Coyle said. 'I like him, I believe in him. It's been
a delight to see how he was going.'

'Oh I know how they go!' Miss Wingrave threw back her
head with an air as acquainted as if a headlong array of the
generations had flashed before her with a rattle of their
scabbards and spurs. Spencer Coyle recognised the intima-
tion that she had nothing to learn from anybody about the
natural carriage of a Wingrave, and he even felt convicted
by her next words of being, in her eyes, with the troubled
story of his check, his weak complaint of his pupil, rather a

poor creature. 'If you like him,' she exclaimed, 'for mercy's
sake keep him quiet!'

Mr Coyle began to explain to her that this was less easy
than she appeared to imagine; but it came home to him that
she really grasped little of what he said. The more he
insisted that the boy had a kind of intellectual independence,
the more this struck her as a conclusive proof that her
nephew was a Wingrave and a soldier. It was not till he
mentioned to her that Owen had spoken of the profession of
arms as of something that would be 'beneath' him, it was
not till her attention was arrested by this intenser light on
the complexity of the problem, that she broke out after a
moment's stupefied reflexion: 'Send him to see me at once!'

'That's exactly what I wanted to ask your leave to do. But
I've wanted also to prepare you for the worst, to make you
understand that he strikes me as really obstinate, and to
suggest to you that the most powerful arguments at your
command—especially if you should be able to put your
hand on some intensely practical one—will be none too
effective.'

'I think I've got a powerful argument'—and Miss
Wingrave looked hard at her visitor. He didn't know in the
least what this engine might be, but he begged her to drag it
without delay into the field. He promised their young man
should come to Baker Street that evening, mentioning
however that he had already urged him to spend a couple of
the very next days at Eastbourne. This led Jane Wingrave to
enquire with surprise what virtue there might be in *that*
expensive remedy, and to reply with decision when he had
said 'The virtue of a little rest, a little change, a little relief
to overwrought nerves', 'Ah don't coddle him—he's costing
us a great deal of money! I'll talk to him and I'll take him
down to Paramore; he'll be dealt with there, and I'll send
him back to you straightened out.'

Spencer Coyle hailed this pledge superficially with
satisfaction, but before he quitted the strenuous lady he

knew he had really taken on a new anxiety—a restlessness
that made him say to himself, groaning inwardly: 'Oh she *is*
a grenadier at bottom, and she'll have no tact. I don't know
what her powerful argument is; I'm only afraid she'll be
stupid and make him worse. The old man's better—*he's*
capable of tact, though he's not quite an extinct volcano.
Owen will probably put him in a rage. In short it's a
difficulty that the boy's the best of them.'

He felt afresh that evening at dinner that the boy was the
best of them. Young Wingrave—who, he was pleased to
observe, had not yet proceeded to the seaside—appeared at
the repast as usual, looking inevitably a little self-conscious,
but not too original for Bayswater. He talked very naturally
to Mrs Coyle, who had thought him from the first the most
beautiful young man they had ever received; so that the
person most ill at ease was poor Lechmere, who took great
trouble, as if from the deepest delicacy, not to meet the eye
of his misguided mate. Spencer Coyle however paid the
price of his own profundity in feeling more and more
worried; he could so easily see that there were all sorts of
things in his young friend that the people of Paramore
wouldn't understand. He began even already to react
against the notion of his being harassed—to reflect that after
all he had a right to his ideas—to remember that he was of a
substance too fine to be handled with blunt fingers. It was
in this way that the ardent little crammer, with his
whimsical perceptions and complicated sympathies, was
generally condemned not to settle down comfortably either
to his displeasures or to his enthusiasms. His love of the real
truth never gave him a chance to enjoy them. He mentioned
to Wingrave after dinner the propriety of an immediate visit
to Baker Street, and the young man, looking 'queer', as he
thought—that is smiling again with the perverse high spirit
in a wrong cause that he had shown in their recent
interview—went off to face the ordeal. Spencer Coyle was
sure he was scared—he was afraid of his aunt; but somehow

this didn't strike him as a sign of pusillanimity. *He* should have been scared, he was well aware, in the poor boy's place, and the sight of his pupil marching up to the battery in spite of his terrors was a positive suggestion of the temperament of the soldier. Many a plucky youth would have funked this special exposure.

'He *has* got ideas!' young Lechmere broke out to his instructor after his comrade had quitted the house. He was bewildered and rather rueful—he had an emotion to work off. He had before dinner gone straight at his friend, as Mr Coyle had requested, and had elicited from him that his scruples were founded on an overwhelming conviction of the stupidity—the 'crass barbarism' he called it—of war. His great complaint was that people hadn't invented anything cleverer, and he was determined to show, the only way he could, that *he* wasn't so dull a brute.

'And he thinks all the great generals ought to have been shot, and that Napoleon Bonaparte in particular, the greatest, was a scoundrel, a criminal, a monster for whom language has no adequate name!' Mr Coyle rejoined, completing young Lechmere's picture. 'He favoured you, I see, with exactly the same pearls of wisdom that he produced for me. But I want to know what *you* said.'

'I said they were awful rot!' Young Lechmere spoke with emphasis and was slightly surprised to hear Mr Coyle laugh, out of tune, at this just declaration, and then after a moment continue:

'It's all very curious—I dare say there's something in it. But it's a pity!'

'He told me when it was that the question began to strike him in that light. Four or five years ago, when he did a lot of reading about all the great swells and their campaigns— Hannibal and Julius Cæsar, Marlborough and Frederick and Bonaparte. He *has* done a lot of reading, and he says it opened his eyes. He says that a wave of disgust rolled over him. He talked about the "immeasurable misery" of wars, and asked me why nations don't tear to pieces the governments, the rulers that go in for them. He hates poor old Bonaparte worst of all.'

'Well, poor old Bonaparte *was* a scoundrel. He was a frightful ruffian,' Mr Coyle unexpectedly declared. 'But I suppose you didn't admit that.'

'Oh I dare say he was objectionable, and I'm very glad we laid him on his back. But the point I made to Wingrave was that his own behaviour would excite no end of remark.' And young Lechmere hung back but an instant before adding: 'I told him he must be prepared for the worst.'

'Of course he asked you what you meant by the "worst",' said Spencer Coyle.

'Yes, he asked me that, and do you know what I said? I said people would call his conscientious scruples and his wave of disgust a mere pretext. Then he asked "A pretext for what?"'

'Ah he rather had you there!' Mr Coyle returned with a small laugh that was mystifying to his pupil.

'Not a bit—for I told him.'

'What did you tell him?'

Once more, for a few seconds, with his conscious eyes in his instructor's, the young man delayed. 'Why what we spoke of a few hours ago. The appearance he'd present of not having—' The honest youth faltered afresh, but brought it out: 'The military temperament, don't you know? But do you know how he cheeked us on that?' young Lechmere went on.

'Damn the military temperament!' the crammer promptly replied.

Young Lechmere stared. Mr Coyle's tone left him uncertain if he were attributing the phrase to Wingrave or uttering his own opinion, but he exclaimed: 'Those were exactly his words!'

'He doesn't care,' said Mr Coyle.

'Perhaps not. But it isn't fair for him to abuse *us* fellows. I told him it's the finest temperament in the world, and that there's nothing so splendid as pluck and heroism.'

'Ah there you had *him!*'

'I told him it was unworthy of him to abuse a gallant, a magnificent profession. I told him there's no type so fine as that of the soldier doing his duty.'

'That's essentially *your* type, my dear boy.' Young Lechmere blushed; he couldn't make out—and the danger was naturally unexpected to him—whether at that moment he didn't exist mainly for the recreation of his friend. But he was partly reassured by the genial way this friend continued, laying a hand on his shoulder: 'Keep *at* him that way! We may do something. I'm in any case extremely obliged to you.'

Another doubt however remained unassuaged—a doubt which led him to overflow yet again before they dropped the painful subject: 'He *doesn't* care! But it's awfully odd he shouldn't!'

'So it is, but remember what you said this afternoon—I mean about your not advising people to make insinuations to *you*.'

'I believe I should knock the beggar down!' said young Lechmere. Mr Coyle had got up; the conversation had taken place while they sat together after Mrs Coyle's withdrawal from the dinner-table, and the head of the establishment administered to his candid charge, on principles that were a part of his thoroughness, a glass of excellent claret. The disciple in question, also on his feet, lingered an instant, not for another 'go', as he would have called it, at the decanter, but to wipe his microscopic moustache with prolonged and unusual care. His companion saw he had something to bring out which required a final effort, and waited for him an instant with a hand on the knob of the door. Then as young Lechmere drew nearer Spencer Coyle grew conscious of an unwonted intensity in the round and ingenuous face. The boy was nervous, but tried to behave like a man of the world. 'Of course it's between ourselves,' he stammered, 'and I wouldn't breathe such a word to any one who wasn't interested in poor Wingrave as you are. But do you think he funks it?'

Mr Coyle looked at him so hard an instant that he was visibly frightened at what he had said. 'Funks it! Funks what?'

'Why what we're talking about—the service.' Young Lechmere gave a little gulp and added with a want of active wit almost pathetic to Spencer Coyle: 'The dangers, you know!'

'Do you mean he's thinking of his skin?'

Young Lechmere's eyes expanded appealingly, and what his instructor saw in his pink face—even thinking he saw a tear—was the dread of a disappointment shocking in the degree in which the loyalty of admiration had been great.

'Is he—is he beastly *afraid?*' repeated the honest lad with a quaver of suspense.

'Dear no!' said Spencer Coyle, turning his back.

On which young Lechmere felt a little snubbed and even a little ashamed. But still more he felt relieved.

III

LESS than a week after this the elder man received a note from Miss Wingrave, who had immediately quitted London with her nephew. She proposed he should come down to Paramore for the following Sunday—Owen was really so tiresome. On the spot, in that house of examples and memories and in combination with her poor dear father, who was 'dreadfully annoyed', it might be worth their while to make a last stand. Mr Coyle read between the lines of this letter that the party at Paramore had got over a good deal of ground since Miss Wingrave, in Baker Street, had treated his despair as superficial. She wasn't an insinuating woman, but she went so far as to put the question on the ground of his conferring a particular favour on an afflicted family; and she expressed the pleasure it would give them should he be accompanied by Mrs Coyle, for whom she enclosed a separate invitation. She mentioned that she was also writing, subject to Mr Coyle's approval, to young Lechmere. She thought such a nice manly boy might do her wretched nephew some good. The celebrated crammer decided to embrace this occasion; and now it was the case not so much that he was angry as that he was anxious. As he directed his answer to Miss Wingrave's letter he caught himself smiling at the thought that at bottom he was going to defend his ex-pupil rather than to give him away. He said to his wife, who was a fair fresh slow woman—a person of much more presence than himself—that she had better take Miss Wingrave at her word: it was such an extraordinary, such a fascinating specimen of an old English home. This last allusion was softly sarcastic—he had accused the good lady more than once of being in love with Owen Wingrave. She admitted that she was, she even gloried in her passion; which shows that the subject, between them, was treated in a liberal spirit. She carried out the joke by accepting the invitation with eagerness. Young Lechmere was delighted to do the same; his instructor had good-naturedly taken the view that the little break would freshen him up for his last spurt.

It was the fact that the occupants of Paramore did indeed take their trouble hard that struck our friend after he had been an hour or two in that fine old house. This very short second visit, beginning on the Saturday evening, was to constitute the strangest episode of his life. As soon as he found himself in private with his wife—they had retired to dress for dinner—they called each other's attention with effusion and almost with alarm to the sinister gloom diffused through the place. The house was admirable from its old grey front, which came forward in wings so as to form three sides of a square, but Mrs Coyle made no scruple to declare that if she had known in advance the sort of impression she was going to receive she would never have put her foot in it. She characterised it as 'uncanny' and as looking wicked and weird, and she accused her husband of not having warned her properly. He had named to her in advance some of the appearances she was to expect, but while she almost feverishly dressed she had innumerable questions to ask. He hadn't told her about the girl, the extraordinary girl, Miss Julian—that is, he hadn't told her that this young lady, who in plain terms was a mere dependent, would be in effect, and as a consequence of the way she carried herself, the most important person in the house. Mrs Coyle was already prepared to announce that she hated Miss Julian's affectations. Her husband above all hadn't told her that they should find their young charge looking five years older.

'I couldn't imagine that,' Spencer said, 'nor that the character of the crisis here would be quite so perceptible. But I suggested to Miss Wingrave the other day that they should press her nephew in real earnest, and she has taken me at my word. They've cut off his supplies—they're trying to starve him out. That's not what I meant—but indeed I don't quite *know* today what I meant. Owen feels the pressure, but he won't yield.' The strange thing was that, now he was there, the brooding little coach knew still better, even while half-closing his eyes to it, that his own spirit had been caught up by a wave of reaction. If he was there it was because he was on poor Owen's side. His whole impression, his whole apprehension, had on the spot become much deeper. There was something in the young fanatic's very resistance that began to charm him. When his wife, in the intimacy of the conference I have mentioned, threw off the mask and commended even with extravagance the stand his pupil had taken (he was too good to be a horrid soldier and it was noble of him to suffer for his convictions—

wasn't he as upright as a young hero, even though as pale as a Christian martyr?) the good lady only expressed the sympathy which, under cover of regarding his late inmate as a rare exception, he had already recognised in his own soul.

For, half an hour ago, after they had had superficial tea in the brown old hall of the house, that searcher into the reasons of things had proposed to him, before going to dress, a short turn outside, and had even, on the terrace, as they walked together to one of the far ends, passed his hand entreatingly into his companion's arm, permitting himself thus a familiarity unusual between pupil and master and calculated to show he had guessed whom he could most depend on to be kind to him. Spencer Coyle had on his own side guessed something, so that he wasn't surprised at the boy's having a particular confidence to make. He had felt on arriving that each member of the party would want to get hold of him first, and he knew that at that moment Jane Wingrave was peering through the ancient blur of one of the windows—the house had been modernised so little that the thick dim panes were three centuries old—to see whether her nephew looked as if he were poisoning the visitor's mind. Mr Coyle lost no time therefore in reminding the youth—though careful to turn it to a laugh as he did so—that he hadn't come down to Paramore to be corrupted. He had come down to make, face to face, a last appeal, which he hoped wouldn't be utterly vain. Owen smiled sadly as they went, asking him if he thought he had the general air of a fellow who was going to knock under.

'I think you look odd—I think you look ill,' Spencer Coyle said very honestly. They had paused at the end of the terrace.

'I've had to exercise a great power of resistance, and it rather takes it out of one.'

'Ah my dear boy, I wish your great power—for you evidently possess it—were exerted in a better cause!'

Owen Wingrave smiled down at his small but erect

instructor. 'I don't believe that!' Then he added, to explain
why: 'Isn't what you want (if you're so good as to think well
of my character) to see me exert *most* power, in whatever
direction? Well, this is the way I exert most.' He allowed he
had had some terrible hours with his grandfather, who had
denounced him in a way to make his hair stand up on his
head. He had expected them not to like it, not a bit, but had
had no idea they would make such a row. His aunt was
different, but she was equally insulting. Oh they had made
him feel they were ashamed of him; they accused him of
putting a public dishonour on their name. He was the only
one who had ever backed out—he was the first for three
hundred years. Every one had known he was to go up, and
now every one would know him for a young hypocrite who
suddenly pretended to have scruples. They talked of his
scruples as you wouldn't talk of a cannibal's god. His
grandfather had called him outrageous names. 'He called
me—he called me—' Here Owen faltered and his voice
failed him. He looked as haggard as was possible to a young
man in such splendid health.

'I probably know!' said Spencer Coyle with a nervous
laugh.

His companion's clouded eyes, as if following the last
strange consequences of things, rested for an instant on a
distant object. Then they met his own and for another
moment sounded them deeply. 'It isn't true. No, it isn't.
It's not *that!*'

'I don't suppose it is! But what *do* you propose instead of
it?'

'Instead of what?'

'Instead of the stupid solution of war. If you take that
away you should suggest at least a substitute.'

'That's for the people in charge, for governments and
cabinets,' said Owen. '*They'll* arrive soon enough at a
substitute, in the particular case, if they're made to
understand that they'll be hanged—and also drawn and

quartered—if they don't find one. Make it a capital crime; *that* will quicken the wits of ministers!' His eyes brightened as he spoke, and he looked assured and exalted. Mr Coyle gave a sigh of sad surrender—it was really a stiff obsession. He saw the moment after this when Owen was on the point of asking if he too thought him a coward; but he was relieved to be able to judge that he either didn't suspect him of it or shrank uncomfortably from putting the question to the test. Spencer Coyle wished to show confidence, but somehow a direct assurance that he didn't doubt of his courage was too gross a compliment—it would be like saying he didn't doubt of his honesty. The difficulty was presently averted by Owen's continuing: 'My grandfather can't break the entail, but I shall have nothing but this place, which, as you know, is small and, with the way rents are going, has quite ceased to yield an income. He has some money—not much, but such as it is he cuts me off. My aunt does the same—she has let me know her intentions. She was to have left me her six hundred a year. It was all settled, but now what's definite is that I don't get a penny of it if I give up the army. I must add in fairness that I have from my mother three hundred a year of my own. And I tell you the simple truth when I say I don't care a rap for the loss of the money.' The young man drew the long slow breath of a creature in pain; then he added: '*That's* not what worries me!'

'What are you going to do instead then?' his friend asked without other comment.

'I don't know—perhaps nothing. Nothing great at all events. Only something peaceful!'

Owen gave a weary smile, as if, worried as he was, he could yet appreciate the humorous effect of such a declaration from a Wingrave; but what it suggested to his guest, who looked up at him with a sense that he was after all not a Wingrave for nothing and had a military steadiness under fire, was the exasperation that such a profession, made in such a way and striking them as the last word of the inglorious, might well have produced on the part of his grandfather and his aunt. 'Perhaps nothing'—when he might carry on the great tradition! Yes, he wasn't weak, and he was interesting; but there was clearly a point of view from which he was provoking. 'What *is* it then that worries you?' Mr Coyle demanded.

'Oh the house—the very air and feeling of it. There are strange voices in it that seem to mutter at me—to say dreadful things as I pass. I mean the general consciousness and responsibility of what I'm doing. Of course it hasn't been easy for me—anything rather! I assure you I don't enjoy it.' With a light in them that was like a longing for justice Owen again bent his eyes on those of the little coach; then he pursued: 'I've started up all the old ghosts. The very portraits glower at me on the walls. There's one of my great-great-grandfather (the one the extraordinary story you know is about—the old fellow who hangs on the second landing of the big staircase) that fairly stirs on the canvas, just heaves a little, when I come near it. I have to go up and down stairs—it's rather awkward! It's what my aunt calls the family circle, and they sit, ever so grimly, in judgement. The circle's all constituted here, it's a kind of awful encompassing presence, it stretches away into the past, and when I came back with her the other day Miss Wingrave told me I wouldn't have the impudence to stand in the midst of it and say such things. I *had* to say them to my grandfather; but now that I've said them it seems to me the question's ended. I want to go away—I don't care if I never come back again.'

'Oh you *are* a soldier; you must fight it out!' Mr Coyle laughed.

The young man seemed discouraged at his levity, but as they turned around, strolling back in the direction from which they had come, he himself smiled faintly after an instant and replied: 'Ah we're tainted all!'

They walked in silence part of the way to the old portico; then the elder of the pair, stopping short after having assured himself he was at a sufficient distance from the house not to be heard, suddenly put the question: 'What does Miss Julian say?'

'Miss Julian?' Owen had perceptibly coloured.

'I'm sure *she* hasn't concealed her opinion.'

'Oh it's the opinion of the family-circle, for she's a member of it of course. And then she has her own as well.'

'Her own opinion?'

'Her own family-circle.'

'Do you mean her mother—that patient lady?'

'I mean more particularly her father, who fell in battle. And her grandfather, and *his* father, and her uncles and great-uncles—they all fell in battle.'

Mr Coyle, his face now rather oddly set, took it in. 'Hasn't the sacrifice of so many lives been sufficient? Why should she sacrifice *you*?'

'Oh she *hates* me!' Owen declared as they resumed their walk.

'Ah the hatred of pretty girls for fine young men!' cried Spencer Coyle.

He didn't believe in it, but his wife did, it appeared perfectly, when he mentioned this conversation while, in the fashion that has been described, the visitors dressed for dinner. Mrs Coyle had already discovered that nothing could have been nastier than Miss Julian's manner to the disgraced youth during the half-hour the party had spent in the hall; and it was this lady's judgement that one must have had no eyes in one's head not to see that she was already trying outrageously to flirt with young Lechmere. It was a pity they had brought that silly boy: he was down in the hall with the creature at that moment. Spencer Coyle's version was different—he believed finer elements involved. The girl's footing in the house was inexplicable on any ground save that of her being predestined to Miss Wingrave's nephew. As the niece of Miss Wingrave's own unhappy intended she had been devoted early by this lady to the office of healing by a union with the hope of the race the tragic breach that had separated their elders; and if in reply to this it was to be said that a girl of spirit couldn't enjoy in such a matter having her duty cut out for her, Owen's enlightened friend was ready with the argument that a young person in Miss Julian's position would never be such a fool as really to quarrel with a capital chance. She was familiar at Paramore and she felt safe; therefore she might treat herself to the amusement of pretending she had her option. It was all innocent tricks and airs. She had a curious charm, and it was vain to pretend that the heir of that house wouldn't seem good enough to a girl, clever as she might be, of eighteen. Mrs Coyle reminded her husband that their late charge was precisely now *not* of that house: this question was among the articles that exercised their wits after the two men had taken the turn on the terrace. Spencer then mentioned to his wife that Owen was afraid of the portrait of his great-great-grandfather. He would show it to her, since she hadn't noticed it, on their way downstairs.

'Why of his great-great-grandfather more than of any of the others?'

'Oh because he's the most formidable. He's the one who's sometimes seen.'

'Seen where?' Mrs Coyle had turned round with a jerk.

'In the room he was found dead in—the White Room they've always called it.'

'Do you mean to say the house has a proved *ghost?*' Mrs Coyle almost shrieked. 'You brought me here without telling me?'

'Didn't I mention it after my other visit?'

'Not a word. You only talked about Miss Wingrave.'

'Oh I was full of the story—you've simply forgotten.'

'Then you should have reminded me!'

'If I had thought of it I'd have held my peace—for you wouldn't have come.'

'I wish indeed I hadn't!' cried Mrs Coyle. 'But what', she immediately asked, '*is* the story?'

'Oh a deed of violence that took place here ages ago. I think it was in George the Second's time that Colonel Wingrave, one of their ancestors, struck in a fit of passion one of his children, a lad just growing up, a blow on the head of which the unhappy child died. The matter was hushed up for the hour and some other explanation put about. The poor boy was laid out in one of those rooms on the other side of the house, and amid strange smothered rumours the funeral was hurried on. The next morning, when the household assembled, Colonel Wingrave was missing; he was looked for vainly, and at last it occurred to someone that he might perhaps be in the room from which his child had been carried to burial. The seeker knocked without an answer—then opened the door. The poor man lay dead on the floor, in his clothes, as if he had reeled and fallen back, without a wound, without a mark, without anything in his appearance to indicate that he had either struggled or suffered. He was a strong sound man—there was nothing to account for such a stroke. He's supposed to have gone to the room during the night, just before going to bed, in some fit of compunction or some fascination of dread. It was only after this that the truth about the boy came out. But no one ever sleeps in the room.'

Mrs Coyle had fairly turned pale. 'I hope not indeed! Thank heaven they haven't put *us* there!'

'We're at a comfortable distance—I know the scene of the event.'

'Do you mean you've been *in*—?'

'For a few moments. They're rather proud of the place and my young friend showed it me when I was here before.'

Mrs Coyle stared. 'And what is it like?'

'Simply an empty dull old-fashioned bedroom, rather big

and furnished with the things of the "period". It's panelled
from floor to ceiling, and the panels evidently, years and
years ago, were painted white. But the paint has darkened
with time and there are three or four quaint little ancient
"samplers", framed and glazed, hung on the walls.'

Mrs Coyle looked round with a shudder. 'I'm glad there
are no samplers here! I never heard anything so jumpy!
Come down to dinner.'

On the staircase as they went her husband showed her the
portrait of Colonel Wingrave—a representation, with some
force and style, for the place and period, of a gentleman
with a hard handsome face, in a red coat and a peruke.
Mrs Coyle pronounced his descendant old Sir Philip
wonderfully like him; and her husband could fancy, though
he kept it to himself, that if one should have the courage to
walk the old corridors of Paramore at night one might meet
a figure that resembled him roaming, with the restlessness
of a ghost, hand in hand with the figure of a tall boy. As he
proceeded to the drawing-room with his wife he found
himself suddenly wishing he had made more of a point of
his pupil's going to Eastbourne. The evening however
seemed to have taken upon itself to dissipate any such
whimsical forebodings, for the grimness of the family-
circle, as he had preconceived its composition, was mitigated
by an infusion of the 'neighbourhood'. The company at
dinner was recruited by two cheerful couples, one of them
the vicar and his wife, and by a silent young man who had
come down to fish. This was a relief to Mr Coyle, who had
begun to wonder what was after all expected of him and why
he had been such a fool as to come, and who now felt that
for the first hours at least the situation wouldn't have
directly to be dealt with. Indeed he found, as he had found
before, sufficient occupation for his ingenuity in reading the
various symptoms of which the social scene that spread
about him was an expression. He should probably have a
trying day on the morrow: he foresaw the difficulty of the

long decorous Sunday and how dry Jane Wingrave's ideas, elicited in strenuous conference, would taste. She and her father would make him feel they depended upon him for the impossible, and if they should try to associate him with too tactless a policy he might end by telling them what he thought of it—an accident not required to make his visit a depressed mistake. The old man's actual design was evidently to let their friends see in it a positive mark of their being all right. The presence of the great London coach was tantamount to a profession of faith in the results of the impending examination. It had clearly been obtained from Owen, rather to the principal visitor's surprise, that he would do nothing to interfere with the apparent concord. He let the allusions to his hard work pass and, holding his tongue about his affairs, talked to the ladies as amicably as if he hadn't been 'cut off'. When Mr Coyle looked at him once or twice across the table, catching his eye, which showed an indefinable passion, he found a puzzling pathos in his laughing face: one couldn't resist a pang for a young lamb so visibly marked for sacrifice. 'Hang him, what a pity he's such a fighter!' he privately sighed—and with a want of logic that was only superficial.

This idea however would have absorbed him more if so much of his attention hadn't been for Kate Julian, who now that he had her well before him struck him as a remarkable and even as a possibly interesting young woman. The interest resided not in any extraordinary prettiness, for if she was handsome, with her long Eastern eyes, her magnificent hair and her general unabashed originality, he had seen complexions rosier and features that pleased him more: it dwelt in a strange impression that she gave of being exactly the sort of person whom, in her position, common considerations, those of prudence and perhaps even a little those of decorum, would have enjoined on her not to be. She was what was vulgarly termed a dependent—penniless patronised tolerated; but something in all her air conveyed that if her situation was inferior her spirit, to make up for it, was above precautions or submissions. It wasn't in the least that she was aggressive—she was too indifferent for that; it was only as if, having nothing either to gain or to lose, she could afford to do as she liked. It occurred to Spencer Coyle that she might really have had more at stake than her imagination appeared to take account of; whatever this quantity might be, at any rate, he had never seen a young woman at less pains to keep the safe side. He wondered inevitably what terms prevailed between Jane Wingrave and such an inmate as this; but those questions of course were unfathomable deeps. Perhaps keen Kate lorded it even over her protectress. The other time he was at Paramore he had received an impression that, with Sir Philip beside her, the girl could fight with her back to the wall. She amused Sir Philip, she charmed him, and he liked people who weren't afraid; between him and his daughter moreover there was no doubt which was the higher in command. Miss Wingrave took many things for granted, and most of all the rigour of discipline and the fate of the vanquished and the captive.

But between their clever boy and so original a companion of his childhood what odd relation would have grown up? It couldn't be indifference, and yet on the part of happy handsome youthful creatures it was still less likely to be aversion. They weren't Paul and Virginia, but they must have had their common summer and their idyll: no nice girl could have disliked such a nice fellow for anything but not liking *her*, and no nice fellow could have resisted such propinquity. Mr Coyle remembered indeed that Mrs Julian had spoken to him as if the propinquity had been by no means constant, owing to her daughter's absences at school, to say nothing of Owen's; her visits to a few friends who were so kind as to 'take' her from time to time; her sojourns in London—so difficult to manage, but still managed by God's help—for 'advantages', for drawing and singing,

especially drawing, or rather painting in oils, for which she
had gained high credit. But the good lady had also
mentioned that the young people were quite brother and
sister, which *was* a little, after all, like Paul and Virginia.
Mrs Coyle had been right, and it was apparent that Virginia
was doing her best to make the time pass agreeably for
young Lechmere. There was no such whirl of conversation
as to render it an effort for our critic to reflect on these
things: the tone of the occasion, thanks principally to the
other guests, was not disposed to stray—it tended to the
repetition of anecdote and the discussion of rents, topics
that huddled together like uneasy animals. He could judge
how intensely his hosts wished the evening to pass off as if
nothing had happened; and this gave him the measure of
their private resentment. Before dinner was over he found
himself fidgety about his second pupil. Young Lechmere,
since he began to cram, had done all that might have been
expected of him; but this couldn't blind his instructor to a
present perception of his being in moments of relaxation as
innocent as a babe. Mr Coyle had considered that the
amusements of Paramore would probably give him a fillip,
and the poor youth's manner testified to the soundness of
the forecast. The fillip had been unmistakeably administered;
it had come in the form of a revelation. The light on young
Lechmere's brow announced with a candour that was
almost an appeal for compassion, or at least a deprecation of
ridicule, that he had never seen anything like Miss Julian.

IV

In the drawing-room after dinner the girl found a chance to
approach Owen's late preceptor. She stood before him a
moment, smiling while she opened and shut her fan, and
then said abruptly, raising her strange eyes: 'I know what
you've come for, but it isn't any use.'

'I've come to look after *you* a little. Isn't *that* any use?'

'It's very kind. But I'm not the question of the hour. You won't do anything with Owen.'

Spencer Coyle hesitated a moment. 'What will *you* do with his young friend?'

She stared, looked around her. 'Mr Lechmere? Oh poor little lad! We've been talking about Owen. He admires him so.'

'So do I. I should tell you that.'

'So do we all. That's why we're in such despair.'

'Personally then you'd *like* him to be a soldier?' the visitor asked.

'I've quite set my heart on it. I adore the army and I'm awfully fond of my old playmate,' said Miss Julian.

Spencer recalled the young man's own different version of her attitude; but he judged it loyal not to challenge her. 'It's not conceivable that your old playmate shouldn't be fond of you. He must therefore wish to please you; and I don't see why—between you, such clever young people as you are!—you don't set the matter right.'

'Wish to please me!' Miss Julian echoed. 'I'm sorry to say he shows no such desire. He thinks me an impudent wretch. I've told him what I think of *him*, and he simply hates me.'

'But you think so highly! You just told me you admire him.'

'His talents, his possibilities, yes; even his personal appearance, if I may allude to such a matter. But I don't admire his present behaviour.'

'Have you had the question out with him?' Spencer asked.

'Oh yes, I've ventured to be frank—the occasion seemed to excuse it. He couldn't like what I said.'

'What did you say?'

The girl, thinking a moment, opened and shut her fan again. 'Why—as we're such good old friends—that such conduct doesn't begin to be that of a gentleman!'

After she had spoken her eyes met Mr Coyle's who looked

into their ambiguous depths. 'What then would you have said without that tie?'

'How odd for *you* to ask that—in such a way!' she returned with a laugh. 'I don't understand your position: I thought your line was to make soldiers!'

'You should take my little joke. But, as regards Owen Wingrave, there's no "making" needed,' he declared. 'To my sense'—and the little crammer paused as with a consciousness of responsibility for his paradox—'to my sense he *is*, in a high sense of the term, a fighting man.'

'Ah let him prove it!' she cried with impatience and turning short off.

Spencer Coyle let her go; something in her tone annoyed and even not a little shocked him. There had evidently been a violent passage between these young persons, and the reflexion that such a matter was after all none of his business but troubled him the more. It was indeed a military house, and she was at any rate a damsel who placed her ideal of manhood—damsels doubtless always had their ideals of manhood—in the type of the belted warrior. It was a taste like another; but even a quarter of an hour later, finding himself near young Lechmere, in whom this type was embodied, Spencer Coyle was still so ruffled that he addressed the innocent lad with a certain magisterial dryness. 'You're under no pressure to sit up late, you know. That's not what I brought you down for.' The dinner-guests were taking leave and the bedroom candles twinkled in a monitory row. Young Lechmere however was too agreeably agitated to be accessible to a snub: he had a happy preoccupation which almost engendered a grin.

'I'm only too eager for bedtime. Do you know there's an awfully jolly room?'

Coyle debated a moment as to whether he should take the allusion—then spoke from his general tension. 'Surely they haven't put you there?'

'No indeed: no one has passed a night in it for ages. But

that's exactly what I want to do—it would be tremendous fun.'

'And have you been trying to get Miss Julian's leave?'

'Oh *she* can't give it she says. But she believes in it, and she maintains that no man has ever dared.'

'No man *shall* ever!' said Spencer with decision. 'A fellow in your critical position in particular must have a quiet night.'

Young Lechmere gave a disappointed but reasonable sigh. 'Oh all right. But mayn't I sit up for a little go at Wingrave? I haven't had any yet.'

Mr Coyle looked at his watch. 'You may smoke *one* cigarette.'

He felt a hand on his shoulder and turned round to see his wife tilting candle-grease upon his coat. The ladies were going to bed and it was Sir Philip's inveterate hour; but Mrs Coyle confided to her husband that after the dreadful things he had told her she positively declined to be left alone, for no matter how short an interval, in any part of the house. He promised to follow her within three minutes, and after the orthodox handshakes the ladies rustled away. The forms were kept up at Paramore as bravely as if the old house had no present intensity of heartache. The only one of which Coyle noticed the drop was some salutation to himself from Kate Julian. She gave him neither a word nor a glance, but he saw her look hard at Owen. Her mother, timid and pitying, was apparently the only person from whom this young man caught an inclination of the head. Miss Wingrave marshalled the three ladies—her little procession of twinkling tapers—up the wide oaken stairs and past the watching portrait of her ill-fated ancestor. Sir Philip's servant appeared and offered his arm to the old man, who turned a perpendicular back on poor Owen when the boy made a vague movement to anticipate this office. Mr Coyle learned later that before Owen had forfeited favour it had always, when he was at home, been his privilege at bedtime

to conduct his grandfather ceremoniously to rest.
Sir Philip's habits were contemptuously different now. His
apartments were on the lower floor and he shuffled stiffly
off to them with his valet's help, after fixing for a moment
significantly on the most responsible of his visitors the thick
red ray, like the glow of stirred embers, that always made
his eyes conflict oddly with his mild manners. They seemed
to say to poor Spencer 'We'll let the young scoundrel have it
tomorrow!' One might have gathered from them that the
young scoundrel, who had now strolled to the other end of
the hall, had at least forged a cheque. His friend watched
him an instant, saw him drop nervously into a chair and
then with a restless movement get up. The same movement
brought him back to where Mr Coyle stood addressing a last
injunction to young Lechmere.

'I'm going to bed and I should like you particularly to
conform to what I said to you a short time ago. Smoke a
single cigarette with our host here and then go to your
room. You'll have me down on you if I hear of your having,
during the night, tried any preposterous games.' Young
Lechmere, looking down with his hands in his pockets, said
nothing—he only poked at the corner of a rug with his toe;
so that his fellow visitor, dissatisfied with so tacit a pledge,
presently went on to Owen: 'I must request you, Wingrave,
not to keep so sensitive a subject sitting up—and indeed to
put him to bed and turn his key in the door.' As Owen
stared an instant, apparently not understanding the motive
of so much solicitude, he added: 'Lechmere has a morbid
curiosity about one of your legends—of your historic rooms.
Nip it in the bud.'

'Oh the legend's rather good, but I'm afraid the room's an
awful sell!' Owen laughed.

'You know you don't *believe* that, my boy!' young
Lechmere returned.

'I don't think he does'—Mr Coyle noticed Owen's
mottled flush.

'He wouldn't try a night there himself!' their companion pursued.

'I know who told you that,' said Owen, lighting a cigarette in an embarrassed way at the candle, without offering one to either of his friends.

'Well, what if she did?' asked the younger of these gentlemen, rather red. 'Do you want them *all* yourself?' he continued facetiously, fumbling in the cigarette-box.

Owen Wingrave only smoked quietly; then he brought out: 'Yes—what if she did? But she doesn't know,' he added.

'She doesn't know what?'

'She doesn't know anything!—I'll tuck him in!' Owen went on gaily to Mr Coyle, who saw that his presence, now a certain note had been struck, made the young men uncomfortable. He was curious, but there were discretions and delicacies, with his pupils, that he had always pretended to practise; scruples which however didn't prevent, as he took his way upstairs, his recommending them not to be donkeys.

At the top of the staircase, to his surprise, he met Miss Julian, who was apparently going down again. She hadn't begun to undress, nor was she perceptibly disconcerted at seeing him. She nevertheless, in a manner slightly at variance with the rigour with which she had overlooked him ten minutes before, dropped the words: 'I'm going down to look for something. I've lost a jewel.'

'A jewel?'

'A rather good turquoise, out of my locket. As it's the only *real* ornament I've the honour to possess—!' And she began to descend.

'Shall I go with you and help you?' asked Spencer Coyle.

She paused a few steps below him, looking back with her Oriental eyes. 'Don't I hear our friends' voices in the hall?'

'Those remarkable young men are there.'

'*They'll* help me.' And Kate Julian passed down.

Spencer Coyle was tempted to follow her, but remembering his standard of tact he rejoined his wife in their apartment. He delayed nevertheless to go to bed and, though he looked into his dressing-room, couldn't bring himself even to take off his coat. He pretended for half an hour to read a novel; after which, quietly, or perhaps I should say agitatedly, he stepped from the dressing-room into the corridor. He followed his passage to the door of the room he knew to have been assigned to young Lechmere and was comforted to see it closed. Half an hour earlier he had noticed it stand open; therefore he could take for granted the bewildered boy had come to bed. It was of this he had wished to assure himself, and having done so he was on the point of retreating. But at the same instant he heard a sound in the room—the occupant was doing, at the window, something that showed him he might knock without the reproach of waking his pupil up. Young Lechmere came in fact to the door in his shirt and trousers. He admitted his visitor in some surprise, and when the door was closed again the latter said: 'I don't want to make your life a burden, but I had it on my conscience to see for myself that you're not exposed to undue excitement.'

'Oh there's plenty of that!' said the ingenuous youth. 'Miss Julian came down again.'

'To look for a turquoise?'

'So she said.'

'Did she find it?'

'I don't know. I came up. I left her with poor Owen.'

'Quite the right thing,' said Spencer Coyle.

'I don't know,' young Lechmere repeated uneasily. 'I left them quarrelling.'

'What about?'

'I don't understand. They're a quaint pair!'

Spencer turned it over. He had, fundamentally, principles and high decencies, but what he had in particular just now was a curiosity, or rather, to recognise it for what it was, a sympathy, which brushed them away. 'Does it strike you that *she's* down on him?' he permitted himself to enquire.

'Rather!—when she tells him he lies!'

'What do you mean?'

'Why before *me*. It made me leave them; it was getting too hot. I stupidly brought up the question of that bad room again, and said how sorry I was I had had to promise you not to try my luck with it.'

'You can't pry about in that gross way in other people's houses—you can't take such liberties, you know!' Mr Coyle interjected.

'I'm all right—see how good I am. I don't want to go *near* the place!' said young Lechmere confidingly. 'Miss Julian said to me "Oh I dare say *you'd* risk it, but"—and she turned and laughed at poor Owen—"that's more than we can expect of a gentleman who has taken *his* extraordinary line." I could see that something had already passed between them on the subject—some teasing or challenging of hers. It may have been only chaff, but his chucking the profession had evidently brought up the question of the white feather—I mean of his pluck.'

'And what did Owen say?'

'Nothing at first; but presently he brought out very quietly: "I spent all last night in the confounded place." We both stared and cried out at this and I asked him what he had seen there. He said he had seen nothing, and Miss Julian replied that he ought to tell his story better than that—he ought to make something good of it. "It's not a story—it's a simple fact," said he; on which she jeered at him and wanted to know why, if he had done it, he hadn't told her in the morning, since he knew what she thought of him, "I know, my dear, but I don't care," the poor devil said. This made her angry, and she asked him quite seriously whether he'd care if he should know she believed him to be trying to deceive us.'

'Ah what a brute!' cried Spencer Coyle.

'She's a most extraordinary girl—I don't know what she's up to,' young Lechmere quite panted.

'Extraordinary indeed—to be romping and bandying words at that hour of the night with fast young men!'

But young Lechmere made his distinction. 'I mean because I think she likes him.'

Mr Coyle was so struck with this unwonted symptom of subtlety that he flashed out: 'And do you think he likes *her?*'

It produced on his pupil's part a drop and a plaintive sigh. 'I don't know—I give it up!—But I'm sure he *did* see something or hear something,' the youth added.

'In that ridiculous place? What makes you sure?'

'Well, because he looks as if he had. I've an idea you can tell—in such a case. He behaves as if he had.'

'Why then shouldn't he name it?'

Young Lechmere wondered and found. 'Perhaps it's too bad to mention.'

Spencer Coyle gave a laugh. 'Aren't you glad then *you're* not in it?'

'Uncommonly!'

'Go to bed, you goose,' Spencer said with renewed nervous derision. 'But before you go tell me how he met her charge that he was trying to deceive you.'

' "Take me there yourself then and lock me in!" '

'And *did* she take him?'

'I don't know—I came up.'

He exchanged a long look with his pupil. 'I don't think they're in the hall now. Where's Owen's own room?'

'I haven't the least idea.'

Mr Coyle was at a loss; he was in equal ignorance and he couldn't go about trying doors. He bade young Lechmere sink to slumber; after which he came out into the passage. He asked himself if he should be able to find his way to the room Owen had formerly shown him, remembering that in common with many of the others it had its ancient name painted on it. But the corridors of Paramore were intricate;

moreover some of the servants would still be up, and he
didn't wish to appear unduly to prowl. He went back to his
own quarters, where Mrs Coyle soon noted the continuance
of his inability to rest. As she confessed for her own part, in
the dreadful place, to an increased sense of 'creepiness',
they spent the early part of the night in conversation, so that
a portion of their vigil was inevitably beguiled by her
husband's account of his colloquy with little Lechmere and
by their exchange of opinions upon it. Toward two o'clock
Mrs Coyle became so nervous about their persecuted young
friend, and so possessed by the fear that that wicked girl had
availed herself of his invitation to put him to an abominable
test, that she begged her husband to go and look into the
matter at whatever cost to his own tranquility. But Spencer,
perversely, had ended, as the perfect stillness of the night
settled upon them, by charming himself into a pale
acceptance of Owen's readiness to face God knew what
unholy strain—an exposure the more trying to excited
sensibilities as the poor boy had now learned by the ordeal
of the previous night how resolute an effort he should have
to make. 'I hope he *is* there,' he said to his wife: 'it puts
them all so hideously in the wrong!' At any rate he couldn't
take on himself to explore a house he knew so little. He was
inconsequent—he didn't prepare for bed. He sat in the
dressing-room with his light and his novel—he waited to
find himself nod. At last however Mrs Coyle turned over
and ceased to talk, and at last too he fell asleep in his chair.
How long he slept he only knew afterwards by computation;
what he knew to begin with was that he had started up in
confusion and under the shock of an appalling sound. His
consciousness cleared itself fast, helped doubtless by a
confirmatory cry of horror from his wife's room. But he
gave no heed to his wife; he had already bounded into the
passage. There the sound was repeated—it was the 'Help!
help!' of a woman in agonised terror. It came from a distant
quarter of the house, but the quarter was sufficiently

indicated. He rushed straight before him, the sound of opening doors and alarmed voices in his ears and the faintness of the early dawn in his eyes. At a turn of one of the passages he came upon the white figure of a girl in a swoon on a bench, and in the vividness of the revelation he read as he went that Kate Julian, stricken in her pride too late with a chill of compunction for what she had mockingly done, had, after coming to release the victim of her derision, reeled away, overwhelmed, from the catastrophe that was her work—the catastrophe that the next moment he found himself aghast at on the threshold of an open door. Owen Wingrave, dressed as he had last seen him, lay dead on the spot on which his ancestor had been found. He was all the young soldier on the gained field.

The Friends of
the Friends

THE FRIENDS OF THE FRIENDS

I

I FIND, as you prophesied, much that's interesting, but little that helps the delicate question—the possibility of publication. Her diaries are less systematic than I hoped; she only had a blessed habit of noting and narrating. She summarised, she saved; she appears seldom indeed to have let a good story pass without catching it on the wing. I allude of course not so much to things she heard as to things she saw and felt. She writes sometimes of herself, sometimes of others, sometimes of the combination. It's under this last rubric that she's usually most vivid. But it's not, you'll understand, when she's most vivid that she's always most publishable. To tell the truth she's fearfully indiscreet, or has at least all the material for making *me* so. Take as an instance the fragment I send you after dividing it for your convenience into several small chapters. It's the contents of a thin blank-book which I've had copied out and which has the merit of being nearly enough a rounded thing, an intelligible whole. These pages evidently date from years ago. I've read with the liveliest wonder the statement they so circumstantially make and done my best to swallow the prodigy they leave to be inferred. These things would be striking, wouldn't they? to any reader; but can you imagine for a moment my placing such a document before the world, even though, as if she herself had desired the world should have the benefit of it, she has given her friends neither name nor initials? Have you any sort of clue to their identity? I leave her the floor.

I

I KNOW perfectly of course that I brought it upon myself; but that doesn't make it any better. I was the first to speak of her to him—he had never even heard her mentioned. Even if I had happened not to speak someone else would have made up for it: I tried afterwards to find comfort in that reflexion. But the comfort of reflexions is thin: the only comfort that counts in life is not to have been a fool. That's a beatitude I shall doubtless never enjoy. 'Why you ought to meet her and talk it over' is what I immediately said. 'Birds of a feather flock together.' I told him who she was and that they were birds of a feather because if he had had in youth a strange adventure she had had about the same time just such another. It was well known to her friends—an incident she was constantly called on to describe. She was charming clever pretty unhappy; but it was none the less the thing to which she had originally owed her reputation.

Being at the age of eighteen somewhere abroad with an aunt she had had a vision of one of her parents at the moment of death. The parent was in England hundreds of miles away and so far as she knew neither dying nor dead. It was by day, in the museum of some great foreign town. She had passed alone, in advance of her companions, into a small room containing some famous work of art and occupied at that moment by two other persons. One of these was an old custodian; the second, before observing him, she took for a stranger, a tourist. She was merely conscious that he was bareheaded and seated on a bench. The instant her eyes rested on him however she beheld to her amazement her father, who, as if he had long waited for her, looked at her in singular distress and an impatience that was akin to reproach. She rushed to him with a bewildered cry, 'Papa, what *is* it?' but this was followed by an exhibition of still livelier feeling when on her movement he simply vanished, leaving the custodian and her relations, who were by that time at her heels, to gather round her in dismay. These persons, the official, the aunt, the cousins, were therefore in a manner witnesses of the fact—the fact at least of the impression made on her; and there was the further testimony of a doctor who was attending one of the party and to whom it was immediately afterwards communicated. He gave her a remedy for hysterics, but said to the aunt privately: 'Wait and see if something doesn't happen at home.' Something *had* happened—the poor father, suddenly and violently seized, had died that morning. The aunt, the mother's sister, received before the day was out a telegram announcing the event and requesting her to prepare her niece for it. Her niece was already prepared, and the girl's sense of this visitation remained of course indelible. We had all, as her friends, had it conveyed to us and had conveyed it creepily to each other. Twelve years had elapsed, and as a woman who had made an unhappy marriage and lived apart from her husband she had become interesting from other sources; but since the name she now bore was a name frequently borne, and since moreover her judicial separation, as things were going, could hardly count as a distinction, it was usual to qualify her as 'the one, you know, who saw her father's ghost'.

As for him, dear man, he had seen his mother's—so there you are! I had never heard of that till this occasion on which our closer, our pleasanter acquaintance led him, through some turn of the subject of our talk, to mention it and to inspire me in so doing with the impulse to let him know that he had a rival in the field—a person with whom he could compare notes. Later on his story became for him, perhaps because of my unduly repeating it, likewise a convenient worldly label; but it hadn't a year before been the ground on which he was introduced to me. He had other merits, just as she, poor thing, had others. I can honestly say that I was quite aware of them from the first—I discovered them sooner than he discovered mine. I remember how it struck me even at the time that his sense of mine was quickened by my having been able to match, though not indeed straight from my own experience, his curious anecdote. It dated, this anecdote, as hers did, from some dozen years before—a year in which, at Oxford, he had for some reason of his own been staying on into the 'Long'. He had been in the August afternoon on the river. Coming back into his room while it was still distinct daylight he found his mother standing there as if her eyes had been fixed on the door. He had had a letter from her that morning out of Wales, where she was staying with her father. At the sight of him she smiled with extraordinary radiance and extended her arms to him, and then as he sprang forward and joyfully opened his own she vanished from the place. He wrote to her that night, telling her what had happened; the letter had been carefully preserved. The next morning he heard of her death. He was through this chance of our talk extremely struck with the little prodigy I was able to produce for him. He had never encountered another case. Certainly they ought to meet, my friend and he; certainly they would have something in common. I would arrange this, wouldn't I?—if *she* didn't mind; for himself he didn't mind in the least. I had promised to speak to her of the matter as soon as possible, and within the week I was able to do so. She 'minded' as little as he; she was perfectly willing to see him. And yet no meeting was to occur—as meetings are commonly understood.

II

THAT'S just half my tale—the extraordinary way it was hindered. This was the fault of a series of accidents; but the accidents, persisting for years, became, to me and to others, a subject of mirth with either party. They were droll enough at first, then they grew rather a bore. The odd thing was that both parties were amenable: it wasn't a case of their being indifferent, much less of their being indisposed. It was one of the caprices of chance, aided I suppose by some rather settled opposition of their interests and habits. His were centred in his office, his eternal inspectorship, which left him small leisure, constantly calling him away and making him break engagements. He liked society, but he found it everywhere and took it at a run. I never knew at a given moment where he was, and there were times when for months together I never saw him. She was on her side practically suburban: she lived at Richmond and never went 'out'. She was a woman of distinction, but not of fashion, and felt, as people said, her situation. Decidedly proud and rather whimsical, she lived her life as she had planned it. There were things one could do with her, but one couldn't make her come to one's parties. One went indeed a little more than seemed quite convenient to hers, which consisted of her cousin, a cup of tea and the view. The tea was good; but the view was familiar, though perhaps not, like the cousin—a disagreeable old maid who had been of the group at the museum and with whom she now lived—offensively so. This connexion with an inferior relative, which had partly an economic motive—she proclaimed her companion a marvellous manager—was one of the little perversities we had to forgive her. Another was her estimate of the proprieties created by her rupture with her husband. That was extreme—many persons called it even morbid. She made no advances; she cultivated scruples; she suspected, or I should perhaps rather say she remembered, slights: she was one of the few women I've known whom that particular predicament had rendered modest rather than bold. Dear thing, she had some delicacy! Especially marked were the limits she had set to possible attentions from men: it was always her thought that her husband only waited to pounce on her. She discouraged if she didn't forbid the visits of male persons not senile: she said she could never be too careful.

When I first mentioned to her that I had a friend whom fate had distinguished in the same weird way as herself I put her quite at liberty to say 'Oh bring him out to see me!' I should probably have been able to bring him, and a situation perfectly innocent or at any rate comparatively simple would have been created. But she uttered no such word; she only said: 'I must meet him certainly; yes, I shall look out for him!' That caused the first delay, and meanwhile various things happened. One of them was that as time went on she made, charming as she was, more and more friends, and that it regularly befell that these friends were sufficiently also friends of his to bring him up in conversation. It was odd that without belonging, as it were, to the same world or, according to the horrid term, the same set, my baffled pair should have happened in so many cases to fall in with the same people and make them join in the droll chorus. She had friends who didn't know each other but who inevitably and punctually recommended *him*. She had also the sort of originality, the intrinsic interest, that led her to be kept by each of us as a private resource, cultivated jealously, more or less in secret, as a person whom one didn't meet in society, whom it was not for everyone— whom it was not for the vulgar—to approach, and with whom therefore acquaintance was particularly difficult and particularly precious. We saw her separately, with appointments and conditions, and found it made on the whole for harmony not to tell each other. Somebody had always had a note from her still later than somebody else. There was some silly woman who for a long time, among the unprivileged, owed to three simple visits to Richmond a reputation for being intimate with 'lots of awfully clever out-of-the-way people'.

Everyone has had friends it has seemed a happy thought to bring together, and everyone remembers that his happiest thoughts have not been his greatest successes; but I doubt if there was ever a case in which the failure was in such direct proportion to the quantity of influence set in motion. It's really perhaps here the quantity of influence that was most remarkable. My lady and my gentleman each pronounced it to me and others quite a subject for a roaring farce. The reason first given had with time dropped out of sight and fifty better ones flourished on top of it. They were so awfully alike: they had the same ideas and tricks and tastes, the same prejudices and superstitions and heresies; they said the same things and sometimes did them; they liked and disliked the same persons and places, the same books, authors and styles; there were touches of resemblance even in their looks and features. It established much of a propriety that they were in common parlance equally 'nice' and almost equally handsome. But the great sameness, for wonder and chatter, was their rare perversity in regard to being photographed. They were the only persons ever heard of who had never been 'taken' and who had a passionate objection to it. They just *wouldn't* be—no, not for anything anyone could say. I had loudly complained of this; him in particular I had so vainly desired to be able to show on my drawing-room chimney-piece in a Bond Street frame. It was at any rate the very liveliest of all the reasons why they ought to know each other—all the lively reasons reduced to naught by the strange law that had made them bang so many doors in each other's face, made them the buckets in the well, the two ends of the see-saw, the two parties in the State, so that when one was up the other was down, when one was out the other was in; neither by any possibility entering a house till the other had left it or leaving it all unawares till the other was at hand. They only arrived when they had been given up, which was precisely also when they departed. They were in a word alternate and incompatible; they missed each other with an inveteracy that could be explained only by its being preconcerted. It was however so far from preconcerted that it had ended—literally after several years—by disappointing and annoying them. I don't think their curiosity was lively till it had been proved utterly vain. A great deal was of course done to help them, but it merely laid wires for them to trip. To give examples I should have to have taken notes; but I happen to remember that neither had ever been able to dine on the right occasion. The right occasion for each was the occasion that would be wrong for the other. On the wrong one they were most punctual, and there were never any but wrong ones. The very elements conspired and the constitution of man re-enforced them. A cold, a headache, a bereavement, a storm, a fog, an earthquake, a cataclysm, infallibly intervened. The whole business was beyond a joke.

Yet as a joke it had still to be taken, though one couldn't help feeling that the joke had made the situation serious, had produced on the part of each a consciousness, an awkwardness, a positive dread of the last accident of all, the only one with any freshness left, the accident that *would* bring them together. The final effect of its predecessors had been to kindle this instinct. They were quite ashamed— perhaps even a little of each other. So much preparation, so much frustration: what indeed could be good enough for it all to lead up to? A mere meeting would be mere flatness. Did I see them at the end of years, they often asked, just stupidly confronted? If they were bored by the joke they might be worse bored by something else. They made exactly the same reflexions, and each in some manner was sure to hear of the other's. I really think it was this peculiar diffidence that finally controlled the situation. I mean that if they had failed for the first year or two because they couldn't help it, they kept up the habit because they had— what shall I call it?—grown nervous. It really took some lurking volition to account for anything both so regular and so ridiculous.

III

WHEN to crown our long acquaintance I accepted his renewed offer of marriage it was humorously said, I know, that I had made the gift of his photograph a condition. This was so far true that I had refused to give him mine without it. At any rate I had him at last, in his high distinction, on the chimney-piece, where the day she called to congratulate me she came nearer than she had ever done to seeing him. He had in being taken set her an example that I invited her to follow; he had sacrificed his perversity—wouldn't she sacrifice hers? She too must give me something on my engagement—wouldn't she give me the companion-piece? She laughed and shook her head; she had headshakes whose impulse seemed to come from as far away as the breeze that stirs a flower. The companion-piece to the portrait of my future husband was the portrait of his future wife. She had taken her stand—she could depart from it as little as she could explain it. It was a prejudice, an *entêtement*, a vow— she would live and die unphotographed. Now too she was alone in that state: this was what she liked; it made her so much more original. She rejoiced in the fall of her late associate and looked a long time at his picture, about which she made no memorable remark, though she even turned it over to see the back. About our engagement she was charming—full of cordiality and sympathy. 'You've known him even longer than I've *not*,' she said, 'and that seems a very long time.' She understood how we had jogged together over hill and dale and how inevitable it was that we should now rest together. I'm definite about all this because what followed is so strange that it's a kind of relief to me to mark the point up to which our relations were as natural as ever. It was I myself who in a sudden madness altered and destroyed them. I see now that she gave me no pretext and that I only found one in the way she looked at the fine face in the Bond Street frame. How then would I have had her look at it? What I had wanted from the first was to make her care for him. Well, that was what I still wanted—up to the moment of her having promised me she would on this occasion really aid me to break the silly spell that had kept them asunder. I had arranged with him to do his part if she would as triumphantly do hers. I was on a different footing now—I was on a footing to answer for him. I would positively engage that at five on the following Saturday he should be on that spot. He was out of town on pressing business, but, pledged to keep his promise to the letter, would return on purpose and in abundant time. 'Are you perfectly sure?' I remember she asked, looking grave and considering: I thought she had turned a little pale. She was tired, she was indisposed: it was a pity he was to see her after all at so poor a moment. If he only *could* have seen her five years before! However, I replied that this time I was sure and that success therefore depended simply on herself. At five o'clock on the Saturday she would find him in a particular chair I pointed out, the one in which he usually sat and in which—though this I didn't mention—he had been sitting when, the week before, he put the question of our future to me in the way that had brought me round. She looked at it in silence, just as she had looked at the photograph, while I repeated for the twentieth time that it was too preposterous one shouldn't somehow succeed in introducing to one's dearest friend one's second self. '*Am* I your dearest friend?' she asked with a smile that for a moment brought back her beauty. I replied by pressing her to my bosom; after which she said: 'Well, I'll come. I'm extraordinarily afraid, but you may count on me.'

When she had left me I began to wonder what she was afraid of, for she had spoken as if she fully meant it. The next day, late in the afternoon, I had three lines from her: she had found on getting home the announcement of her husband's death. She hadn't seen him for seven years, but she wished me to know it in this way before I should hear of it in another. It made however in her life, strange and sad to say, so little difference that she would scrupulously keep her appointment. I rejoiced for her—I supposed it would make at least the difference of her having more money; but even in this diversion, far from forgetting she had said she was afraid, I seemed to catch sight of a reason for her being so. Her fear, as the evening went on, became contagious, and the contagion took in my breast the form of a sudden panic. It wasn't jealousy—it just was the dread of jealousy. I called myself a fool for not having been quiet till we were man and wife. After that I should somehow feel secure. It was only a question of waiting another month—a trifle surely for people who had waited so long. It had been plain enough she was nervous, and now she was free her nervousness wouldn't be less. What was it therefore but a sharp foreboding? She had been hitherto the victim of interference, but it was quite possible she would henceforth be the source of it. The victim in that case would be my simple self. What had the interference been but the finger of Providence pointing out a danger? The danger was of course for poor *me*. It had been kept at bay by a series of accidents unexampled in their frequency; but the reign of accident was now visibly at an end. I had an intimate conviction that both parties would keep the tryst. It was more and more impressed on me that they were approaching, converging. They were like the seekers for the hidden object in the game of blindfold; they had one and the other begun to 'burn'. We had talked about breaking the spell; well, it would be effectually broken—unless indeed it should merely take another form and overdo their encounters as it had overdone their escapes. This was something I couldn't sit still for thinking of; it kept me awake—at midnight I was full of unrest. At last I felt there was only one way of laying the ghost. If the reign of accident was over I must just take up the succession. I sat down and wrote a hurried note which would meet him on his return and which as the servants had gone to bed I sallied forth bareheaded into the empty gusty street to drop into the nearest pillar-box. It was to tell him that I shouldn't be able to be at home in the afternoon as I had hoped and that he must postpone his visit till dinner-time. This was an implication that he would find me alone.

IV

WHEN accordingly at five she presented herself I naturally felt false and base. My act had been a momentary madness, but I had at least, as they say, to live up to it. She remained an hour; he of course never came; and I could only persist in my perfidy. I had thought it best to let her come; singular as this now seems to me I held it diminished my guilt. Yet as she sat there so visibly white and weary, stricken with a sense of everything her husband's death had opened up, I felt a really piercing pang of pity and remorse. If I didn't tell her on the spot what I had done it was because I was too ashamed. I feigned astonishment—I feigned it to the end; I protested that if ever I had had confidence I had had it that day. I blush as I tell my story—I take it as my penance. There was nothing indignant I didn't say about him; I invented suppositions, attenuations; I admitted in stupefaction, as the hands of the clock travelled, that their luck hadn't turned. She smiled at this vision of their 'luck', but she looked anxious—she looked unusual: the only thing that kept me up was the fact that, oddly enough, she wore mourning—no great depths of crape, but simple and scrupulous black. She had in her bonnet three small black feathers. She carried a little muff of astrachan. This put me, by the aid of some acute reflexion, a little in the right. She had written to me that the sudden event made no difference for her, but apparently it made as much difference as that.

If she was inclined to the usual forms why didn't she observe that of not going the first day or two out to tea? There was someone she wanted so much to see that she couldn't wait till her husband was buried. Such a betrayal of eagerness made me hard and cruel enough to practise my odious deceit, though at the same time, as the hour waxed and waned, I suspected in her something deeper still than disappointment and somewhat less successfully concealed. I mean a strange underlying relief, the soft low emission of the breath that comes when a danger is past. What happened as she spent her barren hour with me was that at last she gave him up. She let him go for ever. She made the most graceful joke of it that I've ever seen made of anything; but it was for all that a great date in her life. She spoke with her mild gaiety of all the other vain times, the long game of hide-and-seek, the unprecedented queerness of such a relation. For it *was*, or had been, a relation, wasn't it, hadn't it? That was just the absurd part of it. When she got up to go I said to her that it was more a relation than ever, but that I hadn't the face after what had occurred to propose to her for the present another opportunity. It was plain that the only valid opportunity would be my accomplished marriage. Of course she would be at my wedding? It was even to be hoped that *he* would.

'If *I* am, he won't be!'—I remember the high quaver and the little break of her laugh. I admitted there might be something in that. The thing was therefore to get us safely married first. 'That won't help us. Nothing will help us!' she said as she kissed me farewell. 'I shall never, never see him!' It was with those words she left me.

I could bear her disappointment as I've called it; but when a couple of hours later I received him at dinner I discovered I couldn't bear his. The way my manœuvre might have affected him hadn't been particularly present to me; but the result of it was the first word of reproach that had ever yet dropped from him. I say 'reproach' because that expression is scarcely too strong for the terms in which he conveyed to me his surprise that under the extraordinary circumstances I shouldn't have found some means not to deprive him of such an occasion. I might really have managed either not to be obliged to go out or to let their meeting take place all the same. They would probably have got on, in my drawing-room, well enough without me. At this I quite broke down—I confessed my iniquity and the miserable reason of it. I hadn't put her off and I hadn't gone out; she had been there and, after waiting for him an hour, had departed in the belief that he had been absent by his own fault.

'She must think me a precious brute!' he exclaimed. 'Did she say of me'—and I remember the just perceptible catch of breath in his pause—'What she had a right to say?'

'I assure you she said nothing that showed the least feeling. She looked at your photograph, she even turned round the back of it, on which your address happens to be inscribed. Yet it provoked her to no demonstration. She doesn't care so much as all that.'

'Then why are you afraid of her?'

'It wasn't of her I was afraid. It was of you.'

'Did you think I'd be so sure to fall in love with her? You never alluded to such a possibility before,' he went on as I remained silent. 'Admirable person as you pronounced her, that wasn't the light in which you showed her to me.'

'Do you mean that if it *had* been you'd have managed by this time to catch a glimpse of her? I didn't fear things then,' I added. 'I hadn't the same reason.'

He kissed me at this, and when I remembered that she had done so an hour or two before I felt for an instant as if he were taking from my lips the very pressure of hers. In spite of kisses the incident had shed a certain chill, and I suffered horribly from the sense that he had seen me guilty of a fraud. He had seen it only through my frank avowal, but I was as unhappy as if I had a stain to efface. I couldn't get over the manner of his looking at me when I spoke of her apparent indifference to his not having come. For the first time since I had known him he seemed to have expressed a doubt of my word. Before we parted I told him that I'd undeceive her—start the first thing in the morning for Richmond and there let her know he had been blameless. At this he kissed me again. I'd expiate my sin, I said; I'd humble myself in the dust; I'd confess and ask to be forgiven. At this he kissed me once more.

V

IN the train the next day this struck me as a good deal for him to have consented to; but my purpose was firm enough to carry me on. I mounted the long hill to where the view begins, and then I knocked at her door. I was a trifle mystified by the fact that her blinds were still drawn, reflecting that if in the stress of my compunction I had come early I had certainly yet allowed people time to get up.

'At home, mum? She has left home for ever.'

I was extraordinarily startled by this announcement of the elderly parlour-maid. 'She has gone away?'

'She's dead, mum, please.' Then as I gasped at the horrible word: 'She died last night.'

The loud cry that escaped me sounded even in my own ears like some harsh violation of the hour. I felt for the moment as if I had killed her; I turned faint and saw through a vagueness the woman hold out her arms to me. Of what next happened I've no recollection, nor of anything but my friend's poor stupid cousin, in a darkened room, after an interval that I suppose very brief, sobbing at me in a smothered accusatory way. I can't say how long it took me to understand, to believe and then to press back with an immense effort that pang of responsibility which, superstitiously, insanely, had been at first almost all I was

conscious of. The doctor, after the fact, had been super-
latively wise and clear: he was satisfied of a long-latent
weakness of the heart, determined probably years before by
the agitations and terrors to which her marriage had
introduced her. She had had in those days cruel scenes with
her husband, she had been in fear of her life. All emotion,
everything in the nature of anxiety and suspense had been
after that to be strongly deprecated, as in her marked
cultivation of a quiet life she was evidently well aware; but
who could say that anyone, especially a 'real lady', might be
successfully protected from *every* little rub? She had had one
a day or two before in the news of her husband's death—
since there were shocks of all kinds, not only those of grief
and surprise. For that matter she had never dreamed of so
near a release: it had looked uncommonly as if he would live
as long as herself. Then in the evening, in town, she had
manifestly had some misadventure: something must have
happened there that it would be imperative to clear up. She
had come back very late—it was past eleven o'clock, and on
being met in the hall by her cousin, who was extremely
anxious, had allowed she was tired and must rest a moment
before mounting the stairs. They had passed together into
the dining-room, her companion proposing a glass of wine
and bustling to the sideboard to pour it out. This took but a
moment, and when my informant turned round our poor
friend had not had time to seat herself. Suddenly, with a
small moan that was barely audible, she dropped upon the
sofa. She was dead. What unknown 'little rub' had dealt her
the blow? What concussion, in the name of wonder, *had*
awaited her in town? I mentioned immediately the one
thinkable ground of disturbance—her having failed to meet
at my house, to which by invitation for the purpose she had
come at five o'clock, the gentleman I was to be married to,
who had been accidentally kept away and with whom she
had no acquaintance whatever. This obviously counted for
little; but something else might easily have occurred:

nothing in the London streets was more possible than an accident, especially an accident in those desperate cabs. What had she done, where had she gone on leaving my house? I had taken for granted she had gone straight home. We both presently remembered that in her excursions to town she sometimes, for convenience, for refreshment, spent an hour or two at the 'Gentlewomen', the quiet little ladies' club, and I promised that it should be my first care to make at that establishment an earnest appeal. Then we entered the dim and dreadful chamber where she lay locked up in death and where, asking after a little to be left alone with her, I remained for half an hour. Death had made her, had kept her beautiful; but I felt above all, as I kneeled at her bed, that it had made her, had kept her silent. It had turned the key on something I was concerned to know.

On my return from Richmond and after another duty had been performed I drove to his chambers. It was the first time, but I had often wanted to see them. On the staircase, which, as the house contained twenty sets of rooms, was unrestrictedly public, I met his servant, who went back with me and ushered me in. At the sound of my entrance he appeared in the doorway of a further room, and the instant we were alone I produced my news: 'She's dead!'

'Dead?' He was tremendously struck, and I noticed he had no need to ask whom, in this abruptness, I meant.

'She died last evening—just after leaving me.'

He stared with the strangest expression, his eyes searching mine as for a trap. 'Last evening—after leaving you?' He repeated my words in stupefaction. Then he brought out, so that it was in stupefaction I heard, 'Impossible! I saw her.'

'You "saw" her?'

'On that spot—where you stand.'

This called back to me after an instant, as if to help me to take it in, the great wonder of the warning of his youth. 'In the hour of death—I understand: as you so beautifully saw your mother.'

'Ah *not* as I saw my mother—not that way, not that way!' He was deeply moved by my news—far more moved, it was plain, than he would have been the day before: it gave me a vivid sense that, as I had then said to myself, there was indeed a relation between them and that he had actually been face to face with her. Such an idea, by its reassertion of his extraordinary privilege, would have suddenly presented him as painfully abnormal hadn't he vehemently insisted on the difference. 'I saw her living. I saw her to speak to her. I saw her as I see you now.'

It's remarkable that for a moment, though only for a moment, I found relief in the more personal, as it were, but also the more natural, of the two odd facts. The next, as I embraced this image of her having come to him on leaving me and of just what it accounted for in the disposal of her time, I demanded with a shade of harshness of which I was aware: 'What on earth did she come for?'

He had now had a minute to think—to recover himself and judge of effects, so that if it was still with excited eyes he spoke he showed a conscious redness and made an inconsequent attempt to smile away the gravity of his words. 'She came just to see me. She came—after what had passed at your house—so that we *should*, nevertheless at last meet. The impulse seemed to me exquisite, and that was the way I took it.'

I looked round the room where she had been—where *she* had been and I never had till now. 'And was the way you took it the way she expressed it?'

'She only expressed it by being here and by letting me look at her. That was enough!' he cried with an extraordinary laugh.

I wondered more and more. 'You mean she didn't speak to you?'

'She said nothing. She only looked at me as I looked at her.'

'And you didn't speak either?'

He gave me again his painful smile. 'I thought of *you*. The situation was every way delicate. I used the finest tact. But she saw she had pleased me.' He even repeated his dissonant laugh.

'She evidently "pleased" you!' Then I thought a moment. 'How long did she stay?'

'How can I say? It seemed twenty minutes, but it was probably a good deal less.'

'Twenty minutes of silence!' I began to have my definite view and now in fact quite to clutch at it. 'Do you know you're telling me a thing positively monstrous?'

He had been standing with his back to the fire; at this, with a pleading look, he came to me. 'I beseech you, dearest, to take it kindly.'

I could take it kindly, and I signified as much; but I couldn't somehow, as he rather awkwardly opened his arms, let him draw me to him. So there fell between us for an appreciable time the discomfort of a great silence.

VI

HE broke it by presently saying: 'There's absolutely no doubt of her death?'

'Unfortunately none. I've just risen from my knees by the bed where they've laid her out.'

He fixed his eyes hard on the floor; then he raised them to mine. 'How does she look?'

'She looks—at peace.'

He turned away again while I watched him; but after a moment he began: 'At what hour then—?'

'It must have been near midnight. She dropped as she reached her house—from an affection of the heart which she knew herself and her physician knew her to have, but of which, patiently, bravely, she had never spoken to me.'

He listened intently and for a minute was unable to speak. At last he broke out with an accent of which the almost boyish confidence, the really sublime simplicity, rings in my ears as I write: 'Wasn't she *wonderful*!' Even at the time I was able to do it justice enough to answer that I had always told him so; but the next minute, as if after speaking he had caught a glimpse of what he might have made me feel, he went on quickly: 'You can easily understand that if she didn't get home till midnight—'

I instantly took him up. 'There was plenty of time for you to have seen her? How so,' I asked, 'when you didn't leave my house till late? I don't remember the very moment—I was preoccupied. But you know that though you said you had lots to do you sat for some time after dinner. She, on her side, was all the evening at the 'Gentlewomen', I've just come from there—I've ascertained. She had tea there; she remained a long long time.'

'What was she doing all the long long time?'

I saw him eager to challenge at every step my account of the matter; and the more he showed this the more I was moved to emphasise that version, to prefer with apparent perversity an explanation which only deepened the marvel and the mystery, but which, of the two prodigies it had to choose from, my reviving jealousy found easiest to accept. He stood there pleading with a candour that now seems to me beautiful for the privilege of having in spite of supreme defeat known the living woman; while I, with a passion I wonder at today, though it still smoulders in a manner in its ashes, could only reply that, through a strange gift shared by her with his mother and on her own side likewise hereditary, the miracle of his youth had been renewed for him, the miracle of hers for her. She had been to him—yes, and by an impulse as charming as he liked; but oh she hadn't been in the body! It was a simple question of evidence. I had had, I maintained, a definite statement of what she had done—most of the time—at the little club.

The place was almost empty, but the servants had noticed her. She had sat motionless in a deep chair by the drawing-room fire; she had leaned back her head, she had closed her eyes, she had seemed softly to sleep.

'I see. But till what o'clock?'

'There', I was obliged to answer, 'the servants fail me a little. The portress in particular is unfortunately a fool, even though she too is supposed to be a Gentlewoman. She was evidently at that period of the evening, without a substitute and against regulations, absent for some little time from the cage in which it's her business to watch the comings and goings. She's muddled, she palpably prevaricates; so I can't positively, from her observation, give you an hour. But it was remarked toward half-past ten that our poor friend was no longer in the club.'

It suited him down to the ground. 'She came straight here, and from here she went straight to the train.'

'She couldn't have run it so close,' I declared. 'That was a thing she particularly never did.'

'There was no need of running it close, my dear—she had plenty of time. Your memory's at fault about my having left you late: I left you, as it happens, unusually early. I'm sorry my stay with you seemed long, for I was back here by ten.'

'To put yourself into your slippers', I retorted, 'and fall asleep in your chair. You slept till morning—you saw her in a dream!' He looked at me in silence and with sombre eyes—eyes that showed me he had some irritation to repress. Presently I went on: 'You had a visit, at an extraordinary hour, from a lady—*soit:* nothing in the world's more probable. But there are ladies and ladies. How in the name of goodness, if she was unannounced and dumb and you had into the bargain never seen the least portrait of her—how could you identify the person we're talking of?'

'Haven't I to absolute satiety heard her described? I'll describe her for you in every particular.'

'Don't!' I cried with a promptness that made him laugh

once more. I coloured at this, but I continued: 'Did your servant introduce her?'

'He wasn't here—he's always away when he's wanted. One of the features of this big house is that from the street-door the different floors are accessible practically without challenge. My servant makes love to a young person employed in the rooms above these, and he had a long bout of it last evening. When he's out on that job he leaves my outer door, on the staircase, so much ajar as to enable him to slip back without a sound. The door then only requires a push. She pushed it—that simply took a little courage.'

'A little? It took tons! And it took all sorts of impossible calculations.'

'Well, she had them—she made them. Mind you, I don't deny for a moment', he added, 'that it was very very wonderful!'

Something in his tone kept me a time from trusting myself to speak. At last I said: 'How did she come to know where you live?'

'By remembering the address on the little label the shop-people happily left sticking to the frame I had had made for my photograph.'

'And how was she dressed?'

'In mourning, my own dear. No great depths of crape, but simple and scrupulous black. She had in her bonnet three small black feathers. She carried a little muff of astrachan. She has near the left eye', he continued, 'a tiny vertical scar—'

I stopped him short. 'The mark of a caress from her husband.' Then I added: 'How close you must have been to her!' He made no answer to this, and I thought he blushed, observing which I broke straight off. 'Well, goodbye.'

'You won't stay a little?' He came to me again tenderly, and this time I suffered him. 'Her visit had its beauty,' he murmured as he held me, 'but yours has a greater one.'

I let him kiss me, but I remembered, as I had

remembered the day before, that the last kiss she had given, as I supposed, in this world had been for the lips he touched. 'I'm life, you see,' I answered. 'What you saw last night was death.'

'It was life—it was life!'

He spoke with a soft stubbornness—I disengaged myself. We stood looking at each other hard. 'You describe the scene—so far as you describe it at all—in terms that are incomprehensible. She was in the room before you knew it?'

'I looked up from my letter-writing—at that table under the lamp I had been wholly absorbed in it—and she stood before me.'

'Then what did you do?'

'I sprang up with an ejaculation, and she, with a smile, laid her finger, ever so warningly, yet with a sort of delicate dignity, to her lips. I knew it meant silence, but the strange thing was that it seemed immediately to explain and to justify her. We at any rate stood for a time that, as I've told you, I can't calculate, face to face. It was just as you and I stand now.'

'Simply staring?'

He shook an impatient head. 'Ah! *we're* not staring!'

'Yes, but we're talking.'

'Well, *we* were—after a fashion.' He lost himself in the memory of it. 'It was as friendly at this.' I had on my tongue's end to ask if that was saying much for it, but I made the point instead that what they had evidently done was to gaze in mutual admiration. Then I asked if his recognition of her had been immediate. 'Not quite,' he replied, 'for of course I didn't expect her; but it came to me long before she went who she was—who only she could be.'

I thought a little. 'And how did she at last go?'

'Just as she arrived. The door was open behind her and she passed out.'

'Was she rapid—slow?'

'Rather quick. But looking behind her,' he smiled to add. 'I let her go, for I perfectly knew I was to take it as she wished.'

I was conscious of exhaling a long vague sigh. 'Well, you must take it now as *I* wish—you must let *me* go.'

At this he drew near me again, detaining and persuading me, declaring with all due gallantry that I was a very different matter. I'd have given anything to have been able to ask him if he had touched her, but the words refused to form themselves: I knew to the last tenth of a tone how horrid and vulgar they'd sound. I said something else—I forget exactly what; it was feebly tortuous and intended, meanly enough, to make him tell me without my putting the question. But he didn't tell me; he only repeated, as from a glimpse of the propriety of soothing and consoling me, the sense of his declaration of some minutes before—the assurance that she was indeed exquisite, as I had always insisted, but that I was his 'real' friend and his very own for ever. This led me to reassert, in the spirit of my previous rejoinder, that I had at least the merit of being alive; which in turn drew from him again the flash of contradiction I dreaded. 'Oh *she* was live! She was, she was!'

'She was dead, she was dead!' I asseverated with an energy, a determination it should *be* so, which comes back to me now almost as grotesque. But the sound of the word as it rang out filled me suddenly with horror, and all the natural emotion the meaning of it might have evoked in other conditions gathered and broke in a flood. It rolled over me that here was a great affection quenched and how much I had loved and trusted her. I had a vision at the same time of the lonely beauty of her end. 'She's gone—she's lost to us for ever!' I burst into sobs.

'That's exactly what I feel,' he exclaimed, speaking with extreme kindness and pressing me to him for comfort. 'She's gone; she's lost to us for ever: so what does it matter now?' He bent over me, and when his face had touched mine I scarcely knew if it were wet with my tears or with his own.

VII

IT was my theory, my conviction, it became, as I may say, my attitude, that they had still never 'met'; and it was just on this ground I felt it generous to ask him to stand with me at her grave. He did so very modestly and tenderly, and I assumed, though he himself clearly cared nothing for the danger, that the solemnity of the occasion, largely made up of persons who had known them both and had a sense of the long joke, would sufficiently deprive his presence of all light association. On the question of what had happened the evening of her death little more passed between us; I had been taken by a horror of the element of evidence. On either hypothesis it was gross and prying. He on his side lacked producible corroboration—everything, that is, but a statement of his house-porter, on his own admission a most casual and intermittent personage—that between the hours of ten o'clock and midnight no less than three ladies in deep black had flitted in and out of the place. This proved far too much; we had neither of us any use for three. He knew I considered I had accounted for every fragment of her time, and we dropped the matter as settled; we abstained from further discussion. What *I* knew however was that he abstained to please me rather than because he yielded to my reasons. He didn't yield—he was only indulgent; he clung to his interpretation because he liked it better. He liked it better, I held, because it had more to say to his vanity. That, in a similar position, wouldn't have been its effect on me, though I had doubtless quite as much; but these are things of individual humour and as to which no person can judge for another. I should have supposed it more gratifying to be the subject of one of those inexplicable occurrences

that are chronicled in thrilling books and disputed about at
learned meetings; I could conceive, on the part of a being
just engulfed in the infinite and still vibrating with human
emotion, of nothing more fine and pure, more high and
august, than such an impulse of reparation, of admonition,
or even of curiosity. *That* was beautiful, if one would, and I
should in his place have thought more of myself for being so
distinguished and so selected. It was public that he had
already, that he had long figured in that light, and what was
such a fact in itself but almost a proof? Each of the strange
visitations contributed to establish the other. He had a
different feeling; but he had also, I hasten to add, an
unmistakeable desire not to make a stand or, as they say, a
fuss about it. I might believe what I liked—the more so that
the whole thing was in a manner a mystery of my
producing. It was an event of my history, a puzzle of my
consciousness, not of his; therefore he would take about it
any tone that struck me as convenient. We had both at all
events other business on hand; we were pressed with
preparations for our marriage.

Mine were assuredly urgent, but I found as the days went
on that to believe what I 'liked' was to believe what I was
more and more intimately convinced of. I found also that I
didn't like it so much as that came to, or that the pleasure at
all events was far from being the cause of my conviction. My
obsession, as I may really call it and as I began to perceive,
refused to be elbowed away, as I had hoped, by my sense of
paramount duties. If I had a great deal to do I had still more
to think of, and the moment came when my occupations
were gravely menaced by my thoughts. I see it all now, I feel
it, I live it over. It's terribly void of joy, it's full indeed to
overflowing of bitterness; and yet I must do myself justice—
I couldn't have been other than I was. The same strange
impressions, had I to meet them again, would produce the
same deep anguish, the same sharp doubts, the same still
sharper certainties. Oh it's all easier to remember than to

write, but even could I retrace the business hour by hour, could I find terms for the inexpressible, the ugliness and the pain would quickly stay my hand. Let me then note very simply and briefly that a week before our wedding-day, three weeks after her death, I knew in all my fibres that I had something very serious to look in the face and that if I was to make this effort I must make it on the spot and before another hour should elapse. My unextinguished jealousy—that was the Medusa-mask. It hadn't died with her death, it had lividly survived, and it was fed by suspicions unspeakable. They *would* be unspeakable today, that is, if I hadn't felt the sharp need of uttering them at the time. This need took possession of me—to save me, as it seemed, from my fate. When once it had done so I saw—in the urgency of the case, the diminishing hours and shrinking interval—only one issue, that of absolute promptness and frankness. I could at least not do him the wrong of delaying another day; I could at least treat my difficulty as too fine for a subterfuge. Therefore very quietly, but none the less abruptly and hideously, I put it before him on a certain evening that we must reconsider our situation and recognise that it had completely altered.

He stared bravely. 'How in the world altered?'

'Another person has come between us.'

He took but an instant to think. 'I won't pretend not to know whom you mean.' He smiled in pity for my aberration, but he meant to be kind. 'A woman dead and buried!'

'She's buried, but she's not dead. She's dead for the world—she's dead for me. But she's not dead for you.'

'You hark back to the different construction we put on her appearance that evening?'

'No,' I answered, 'I hark back to nothing. I've no need of it. I've more than enough with what's before me.'

'And pray, darling, what may that be?'

'You're completely changed.'

'By that absurdity?' he laughed.

'Not so much by that one as by other absurdities that have followed it.'

'And what may *they* have been?'

We had faced each other fairly, with eyes that didn't flinch; but his had a dim strange light, and my certitude triumphed in his perceptible paleness. 'Do you really pretend', I asked, 'not to know what they are?'

'My dear child,' he replied, 'you describe them too sketchily!'

I considered a moment. 'One may well be embarrassed to finish the picture! But from that point of view—and from the beginning—what was ever more embarrassing than your idiosyncrasy?'

He invoked his vagueness—a thing he always did beautifully. 'My idiosyncrasy?'

'Your notorious, your peculiar power.'

He gave a great shrug of impatience, a groan of overdone disdain. 'Oh my peculiar power!'

'Your accessibility to forms of life,' I coldly went on, 'your command of impressions, appearances, contacts, closed—for our gain or our loss—to the rest of us. That was originally a part of the deep interest with which you inspired me—one of the reasons I was amused, I was indeed positively proud, to know you. It was a magnificent distinction; it's a magnificent distinction still. But of course I had no prevision then of the way it would operate now; and even had that been the case I should have had none of the extraordinary way in which its action would affect me.'

'To what in the name of goodness', he pleadingly enquired, 'are you fantastically alluding?' Then as I remained silent, gathering a tone for my charge, 'How in the world *does* it operate?' he went on; 'and how in the world are you affected?'

'She missed you for five years,' I said, 'but she never misses you now. You're making it up!'

'Making it up?' He had begun to turn from white to red.

'You see her—you see her: you see her every night!' He gave a loud sound of derision, but I felt it ring false. 'She comes to you as she came that evening,' I declared; 'having tried it she found she liked it!' I was able, with God's help, to speak without blind passion or vulgar violence; but those were the exact words—and far from 'sketchy' they then appeared to me—that I uttered. He had turned away in his laughter, clapping his hands at my folly, but in an instant he faced me again with a change of expression that struck me. 'Do you dare to deny', I then asked, 'that you habitually see her?'

He had taken the line of indulgence, of meeting me halfway and kindly humouring me. At all events he to my astonishment suddenly said: 'Well, my dear, what if I do?'

'It's your natural right: it belongs to your constitution and to your wonderful if not perhaps quite enviable fortune. But you'll easily understand that it separates us. I unconditionally release you.'

'Release me?'

'You must choose between me and her.'

He looked at me hard. 'I see.' Then he walked away a little, as if grasping what I had said and thinking how he had best treat it. At last he turned on me afresh. 'How on earth do you know such an awfully private thing?'

'You mean because you've tried so hard to hide it? It *is* awfully private, and you may believe I shall never betray you. You've done your best, you've acted your part, you've behaved, poor dear! loyally and admirably. Therefore I've watched you in silence, playing my part too; I've noted every drop in your voice, every absence in your eyes, every effort in your indifferent hand: I've waited till I was utterly sure and miserably unhappy. How *can* you hide it when you're abjectly in love with her, when you're sick almost to death with the joy of what she gives you?' I checked his quick protest with a quicker gesture. 'You love her as you've *never* loved, and, passion for passion, she gives it straight back! She rules you, she holds you, she has you all! A woman, in such a case as mine, divines and feels and sees; she's not a dull dunce who has to be "credibly informed". You come to me mechanically, compunctiously, with the dregs of your tenderness and the remnant of your life. I can renounce you, but I can't share you: the best of you is hers, I know what it is and freely give you up to her for ever!'

He made a gallant fight, but it couldn't be patched up; he repeated his denial, he retracted his admission, he ridiculed my charge, of which I freely granted him moreover the indefensible extravagance. I didn't pretend for a moment that we were talking of common things; I didn't pretend for a moment that he and she were common people. Pray, if they *had* been, how should I ever have cared for them? They had enjoyed a rare extension of being and they had caught me up in their flight; only I couldn't breathe in such air and I promptly asked to be set down. Everything in the facts was monstrous, and most of all my lucid perception of them; the only thing allied to nature and truth was my having to act on that perception. I felt after I had spoken in this sense that my assurance was complete; nothing had been wanting to it but the sight of my effect on him. He disguised indeed the effect in a cloud of chaff, a diversion that gained him time and covered his retreat. He challenged my sincerity, my sanity, almost my humanity, and that of course widened our breach and confirmed our rupture. He did everything in short but convince me either that I was wrong or that he was unhappy: we separated and I left him to his inconceivable communion.

He never married, any more than I've done. When six years later, in solitude and silence, I heard of his death I hailed it as a direct contribution to my theory. It was sudden, it was never properly accounted for, it was surrounded by circumstances in which—for oh I took them to pieces!—I distinctly read an intention, the mark of his own hidden hand. It was the result of a long necessity, of an unquenchable desire. To say exactly what I mean, it was a response to an irresistible call.

The Turn of
the Screw

THE TURN OF THE SCREW

THE STORY had held us, round the fire, sufficiently breathless, but except the obvious remark that it was gruesome, as on Christmas Eve in an old house a strange tale should essentially be, I remember no comment uttered till somebody happened to note it as the only case he had met in which such a visitation had fallen on a child. The case, I may mention, was that of an apparition in just such an old house as had gathered us for the occasion—an appearance, of a dreadful kind, to a little boy sleeping in the room with his mother and waking her up in the terror of it; waking her not to dissipate his dread and soothe him to sleep again, but to encounter also herself, before she had succeeded in doing so, the same sight that had shocked him. It was this observation that drew from Douglas—not immediately, but later in the evening—a reply that had the interesting consequence to which I call attention. Someone else told a story not particularly effective, which I saw he was not following. This I took for a sign that he had himself something to produce and that we should only have to wait. We waited in fact till two nights later; but that same evening, before we scattered, he brought out what was in his mind.

'I quite agree—in regard to Griffin's ghost, or whatever it was—that its appearing first to the little boy, at so tender an age, adds a particular touch. But it's not the first occurrence of its charming kind that I know to have been concerned with a child. If the child gives the effect another turn of the screw, what do you say to *two* children—?'

'We say of course,' somebody exclaimed, 'that two children give two turns! Also that we want to hear about them.'

I can see Douglas there before the fire, to which he had got up to present his back, looking down at this converser with his hands in his pockets. 'Nobody but me, till now, has ever heard. It's quite too horrible.' This was naturally declared by several voices to give the thing the utmost price, and our friend, with quiet art, prepared his triumph by turning his eyes over the rest of us and going on: 'It's beyond everything. Nothing at all that I know touches it.'

'For sheer terror?' I remember asking.

He seemed to say it wasn't so simple as that; to be really at a loss how to qualify it. He passed his hand over his eyes, made a little wincing grimace. 'For dreadful—dreadfulness!'

'Oh how delicious!' cried one of the women.

He took no notice of her; he looked at me, but as if, instead of me, he saw what he spoke of. 'For general uncanny ugliness and horror and pain.'

'Well then,' I said, 'just sit right down and begin.'

He turned round to the fire, gave a kick to a log, watched it an instant. Then as he faced us again: 'I can't begin. I shall have to send to town.' There was a unanimous groan at this, and much reproach; after which, in his preoccupied way, he explained. 'The story's written. It's in a locked drawer—it has not been out for years. I could write to my man and enclose the key; he could send down the packet as he finds it.' It was to me in particular that he appeared to propound this—appeared almost to appeal for aid not to hesitate. He had broken a thickness of ice, the formation of many a winter; had had his reasons for a long silence. The others resented postponement, but it was just his scruples that charmed me. I adjured him to write by the first post and to agree with us for an early hearing; then I asked him if the experience in question had been his own. To this his answer was prompt. 'Oh thank God, no!'

'And is the record yours? You took the thing down?'

'Nothing but the impression. I took that *here*'—he tapped his heart. 'I've never lost it.'

'Then your manuscript—?'

'Is in old faded ink and in the most beautiful hand.' He hung fire again. 'A woman's. She has been dead these twenty years. She sent me the pages in question before she died.' They were all listening now, and of course there was somebody to be arch, or at any rate to draw the inference. But if he put the inference by without a smile it was also without irritation. 'She was a most charming person, but she was ten years older than I. She was my sister's governess,' he quietly said. 'She was the most agreeable woman I've ever known in her position; she'd have been worthy of any whatever. It was long ago, and this episode was long before. I was at Trinity, and I found her at home on my coming down the second summer. I was much there that year—it was a beautiful one; and we had, in her off-hours, some strolls and talks in the garden—talks in which she struck me as awfully clever and nice. Oh yes; don't grin: I liked her extremely and am glad to this day to think she liked me too. If she hadn't she wouldn't have told me. She had never told anyone. It wasn't simply that she said so, but that I knew she hadn't. I was sure; I could see. You'll easily judge why when you hear.'

'Because the thing had been such a scare?'

He continued to fix me. 'You'll easily judge,' he repeated: '*you* will.'

I fixed him too. 'I see. She was in love.'

He laughed for the first time. 'You *are* acute. Yes, she was in love. That is she *had* been. That came out—she couldn't tell her story without its coming out. I saw it, and she saw I saw it; but neither of us spoke of it. I remember the time and the place—the corner of the lawn, the shade of the great beeches and the long hot summer afternoon. It wasn't a scene for a shudder; but oh—!' He quitted the fire and dropped back into his chair.

'You'll receive the packet Thursday morning?' I said.

'Probably not till the second post.'

'Well then; after dinner—'

'You'll all meet me here?' He looked us round again. 'Isn't anybody going?' It was almost the tone of hope.

'Everybody will stay!'

'*I* will—and *I* will!' cried the ladies whose departure had been fixed. Mrs Griffin, however, expressed the need for a little more light. 'Who was it she was in love with?'

'The story will tell,' I took upon myself to reply.

'Oh I can't wait for the story!'

'The story *won't* tell,' said Douglas; 'not in any literal vulgar way.'

'More's the pity then. That's the only way I ever understand.'

'Won't *you* tell, Douglas?' somebody else enquired.

He sprang to his feet again. 'Yes—tomorrow. Now I must go to bed. Goodnight.' And, quickly catching up a candlestick, he left us slightly bewildered. From our end of the great brown hall we heard his step on the stair; whereupon Mrs Griffin spoke. 'Well, if I don't know who she was in love with I know who *he* was.'

'She was ten years older,' said her husband.

'*Raison de plus*—at that age! But it's rather nice, his long reticence.'

'Forty years!' Griffin put in.

'With this outbreak at last.'

'The outbreak', I returned, 'will make a tremendous occasion of Thursday night'; and everyone so agreed with me that in the light of it we lost all attention for everything else. The last story, however incomplete and like the mere opening of a serial, had been told; we handshook and 'candlestuck', as somebody said, and went to bed.

I knew the next day that a letter containing the key had, by the first post, gone off to his London apartments; but in spite of—or perhaps just on account of the eventual diffusion of this knowledge we quite let him alone till after dinner, till such an hour of the evening in fact as might best accord with the kind of emotion on which our hopes were fixed. Then he became as communicative as we could desire, and indeed gave us his best reason for being so. We had it from him again before the fire in the hall, as we had had our mild wonders of the previous night. It appeared that the narrative he had promised to read us really required for a proper intelligence a few words of prologue. Let me say here distinctly, to have done with it, that this narrative, from an exact transcript of my own made much later, is what I shall presently give. Poor Douglas, before his death—when it was in sight—committed to me the manuscript that reached him on the third of these days and that, on the same spot, with immense effect, he began to read to our hushed little circle on the night of the fourth. The departing ladies who had said they would stay didn't, of course, thank heaven, stay: they departed, in consequence of arrangements made, in a rage of curiosity, as they professed, produced by the touches with which he had already worked us up. But that only made his little final auditory more compact and select, kept it, round the hearth, subject to a common thrill.

The first of these touches conveyed that the written statement took up the tale at a point after it had, in a manner, begun. The fact to be in possession of was therefore that his old friend, the youngest of several daughters of a poor country parson, had at the age of twenty, on taking service for the first time in the schoolroom, come up to London, in trepidation, to answer in person an advertisement that had already placed her in brief correspondence with the advertiser. This person proved, on her presenting herself for judgement at a house in Harley Street that impressed her as vast and imposing—this prospective partron proved a gentleman, a bachelor in the prime of life, such a figure as had never risen, save in a dream or an old novel, before a fluttered anxious girl out of a Hampshire vicarage. One could easily fix his type; it never, happily, dies out. He was handsome and bold and pleasant, off-hand and gay and kind. He struck her, inevitably, as gallant and splendid, but what took her most of all and gave her the courage she afterwards showed was that he put the whole thing to her as a favour, an obligation he should gratefully incur. She figured him as rich, but as fearfully extravagant— saw him all in a glow of high fashion, of good looks, of expensive habits, of charming ways with women. He had for his town residence a big house filled with the spoils of travel and the trophies of the chase; but it was to his country home, an old family place in Essex, that he wished her immediately to proceed.

He had been left, by the death of his parents in India, guardian to a small nephew and a small niece, children of a younger, military brother whom he had lost two years before. These children were, by the strangest of chances for a man in his position—a lone man without the right sort of experience or a grain of patience—very heavy on his hands. It had all been a great worry and, on his own part doubtless, a series of blunders, but he immensely pitied the poor chicks and had done all he could; had in particular sent them down to his other house, the proper place for them being of course the country, and kept them there from the first with the best people he could find to look after them, parting even with his own servants to wait on them and going down himself, whenever he might, to see how they were doing. The awkward thing was that they had practically no other relations and that his own affairs took up all his time. He had put them in possession of Bly, which was healthy and secure, and had placed at the head of their little establishment—but belowstairs only—an excellent woman, Mrs Grose, whom he was sure his visitor would like and who had formerly been maid to his mother. She was now housekeeper and was also acting for the time as superintendent to the little girl, of whom, without children of her own, she was by good luck extremely fond. There were plenty of people to help, but of course the young lady who should go down as governess would be in supreme authority. She would also have, in holidays, to look after the small boy, who had been for a term at school—young as he was to be sent, but what else could be done?—and who, as the holidays were about to begin, would be back from one day to the other. There had been for the two children at first a young lady whom they had had the misfortune to lose. She had done for them quite beautifully—she was a most respectable person—till her death, the great awkwardness of which had, precisely, left no alternative but the school for little Miles. Mrs Grose, since then, in the way of manners and things, had done as she could for Flora; and there were, further, a cook, a housemaid, a dairywoman, an old pony, an old groom and an old gardener, all likewise thoroughly respectable.

So far had Douglas presented his picture when someone put a question. 'And what did the former governess die of? Of so much respectability?'

Our friend's answer was prompt. 'That will come out. I don't anticipate.'

'Pardon me—I thought that was just what you *are* doing.'

'In her successor's place', I suggested, 'I should have wished to learn if the office brought with it—'

'Necessary danger to life?' Douglas completed my thought. 'She did wish to learn, and she did learn. You shall hear tomorrow what she learnt. Meanwhile of course the prospect struck her as slightly grim. She was young, untried, nervous: it was a vision of serious duties and little company, of really great loneliness. She hesitated—took a couple of days to consult and consider. But the salary offered much exceeded her modest measure, and on a second interview she faced the music, she engaged.' And Douglas, with this, made a pause that, for the benefit of the company, moved me to throw in—

'The moral of which was of course the seduction exercised by the splendid young man. She succumbed to it.'

He got up and, as he had done the night before, went to the fire, gave a stir to a log with his foot, then stood a moment with his back to us. 'She saw him only twice.'

'Yes, but that's just the beauty of her passion.'

A little to my surprise, on this, Douglas turned round to me. 'It *was* the beauty of it. There were others', he went on, 'who hadn't succumbed. He told her frankly all his difficulty—that for several applicants the conditions had been prohibitive. They were somehow simply afraid. It sounded dull—it sounded strange; and all the more so because of his main condition.'

'Which was——?'

'That she should never trouble him—but never, never: neither appeal nor complain nor write about anything; only meet all questions herself, receive all moneys from his solicitor, take the whole thing over and let him alone. She promised to do this, and she mentioned to me that when, for a moment, disburdened, delighted, he held her hand, thanking her for the sacrifice, she already felt rewarded.'

'But was that all her reward?' one of the ladies asked.

'She never saw him again.'

'Oh!' said the lady; which, as our friend immediately again left us, was the only other word of importance contributed to the subject till, the next night, by the corner of the hearth, in the best chair, he opened the faded red cover of a thin old-fashioned gilt-edged album. The whole thing took indeed more nights than one, but on the first occasion the same lady put another question. 'What's your title?'

'I haven't one.'

'Oh *I* have!' I said. But Douglas, without heeding me, had begun to read with a fine clearness that was like a rendering to the ear of the beauty of his author's hand.

to the younger of my pupils. The little girl who accompanied Mrs Grose affected me on the spot as a creature too charming not to make it a great fortune to have to do with

I

I REMEMBER the whole beginning as a succession of flights and drops, a little see-saw of the right throbs and the wrong. After rising, in town, to meet his appeal I had at all events a couple of very bad days—found all my doubts bristle again, felt indeed sure I had made a mistake. In this state of mind I spent the long hours of bumping swinging coach that carried me to the stopping-place at which I was to be met by a vehicle from the house. This convenience, I was told, had been ordered, and I found, toward the close of the June afternoon, a commodious fly in waiting for me. Driving at that hour, on a lovely day, through a country the summer sweetness of which served as a friendly welcome, my fortitude revived and, as we turned into the avenue, took a flight that was probably but a proof of the point to which it had sunk. I suppose I had expected, or had dreaded, something so dreary that what greeted me was a good surprise. I remember as a thoroughly pleasant impression the broad clear front, its open windows and fresh curtains and the pair of maids looking out; I remember the lawn and the bright flowers and the crunch of my wheels on the gravel and the clustered tree-tops over which the rooks circled and cawed in the golden sky. The scene had a greatness that made it a different affair from my own scant home, and there immediately appeared at the door, with a little girl in her hand, a civil person who dropped me as decent a curtsey as if I had been the mistress or a distinguished visitor. I had received in Harley Street a narrower notion of the place, and that, as I recalled it, made me think the proprietor still more of a gentleman, suggested that what I was to enjoy might be a matter beyond his promise.

I had no drop again till the next day, for I was carried triumphantly through the following hours by my introduction to the younger of my pupils. The little girl who accompanied Mrs Grose affected me on the spot as a creature too charming not to make it a great fortune to have to do with her. She was the most beautiful child I had ever seen and I afterwards wondered why my employer hadn't made more of a point to me of this. I slept little that night—I was too much excited; and this astonished me too, I recollect, remained with me, adding to my sense of the liberality with which I was treated. The large impressive room, one of the best in the house, the great state bed, as I almost felt it, the figured full draperies, the long glasses in which, for the first time, I could see myself from head to foot, all struck me— like the wonderful appeal of my small charge—as so many things thrown in. It was thrown in as well, from the first moment, that I should get on with Mrs Grose in a relation over which, on my way, in the coach, I fear I had rather brooded. The one appearance indeed that in this early outlook might have made me shrink again was that of her being so inordinately glad to see me. I felt within half an hour that she was so glad—stout simple plain clean wholesome woman—as to be positively on her guard against showing it too much. I wondered even then a little why she should wish *not* to show it, and that, with reflexion, with suspicion, might of course have made me uneasy.

But it was a comfort that there could be no uneasiness in a connexion with anything so beatific as the radiant image of my little girl, the vision of whose angelic beauty had probably more than anything else to do with the restlessness that, before morning, made me several times rise and wander about my room to take in the whole picture and prospect; to watch from my open window the faint summer dawn, to look at such stretches of the rest of the house as I could catch, and to listen, while in the fading dusk the first birds began to twitter, for the possible recurrence of a sound or two, less natural and not without but within, that I had fancied I heard. There had been a moment when I believed

I recognised, faint and far, the cry of a child; there had been another when I found myself just consciously starting as at the passage, before my door, of a light footstep. But these fancies were not marked enough not to be thrown off, and it is only in the light, or the gloom, I should rather say, of other and subsequent matters that they now come back to me. To watch, teach, 'form' little Flora would too evidently be the making of a happy and useful life. It had been agreed between us downstairs that after this first occasion I should have her as a matter of course at night, her small white bed being already arranged, to that end, in my room. What I had undertaken was the whole care of her, and she had remained just this last time with Mrs Grose only as an effect of our consideration for my inevitable strangeness and her natural timidity. In spite of this timidity—which the child herself, in the oddest way in the world, had been perfectly frank and brave about, allowing it, without a sign of uncomfortable consciousness, with the deep sweet serenity indeed of one of Raphael's holy infants, to be discussed, to be imputed to her and to determine us—I felt quite sure she would presently like me. It was part of what I already liked Mrs Grose herself for, the pleasure I could see her feel in my admiration and wonder as I sat at supper with four tall candles and with my pupil, in a high chair and a bib, brightly facing me between them over bread and milk. There were naturally things that in Flora's presence could pass between us only as prodigious and gratified looks, obscure and round-about allusions.

'And the little boy—does he look like her? Is he too so very remarkable?'

One wouldn't, it was already conveyed between us, too grossly flatter a child. 'Oh Miss, *most* remarkable. If you think well of this one!'—and she stood there with a plate in her hand, beaming at our companion, who looked from one of us to the other with placid heavenly eyes that contained nothing to check us.

'Yes; if I do—?'

'You *will* be carried away by the little gentleman!'

'Well, that, I think, is what I came for—to be carried away. I'm afraid, however,' I remember feeling the impulse to add, 'I'm rather easily carried away. I was carried away in London!'

I can still see Mrs Grose's broad face as she took this in. 'In Harley Street?'

'In Harley Street.'

'Well, Miss, you're not the first—and you won't be the last.'

'Oh I've no pretensions', I could laugh, 'to being the only one. My other pupil, at any rate, as I understand, comes back tomorrow?'

'Not tomorrow—Friday, Miss. He arrives, as you did, by the coach, under care of the guard, and is to be met by the same carriage.'

I forthwith wanted to know if the proper as well as the pleasant and friendly thing wouldn't therefore be that on the arrival of the public conveyance I should await him with his little sister; a proposition to which Mrs Grose assented so heartily that I somehow took her manner as a kind of comforting pledge—never falsified, thank heaven!—that we should on every question be quite at one. Oh she was glad I was there!

What I felt the next day was, I suppose, nothing that could be fairly called a reaction from the cheer of my arrival; it was probably at the most only a slight oppression produced by a fuller measure of the scale, as I walked round them, gazed up at them, took them in, of my new circumstances. They had, as it were, an extent and mass for which I had not been prepared and in the presence of which I found myself, freshly, a little scared not less than a little proud. Regular lessons, in this agitation, certainly suffered some wrong; I reflected that my first duty was, by the gentlest arts I could contrive, to win the child into the sense of knowing me. I spent the day with her out of doors; I arranged with her, to her great satisfaction, that it should be she, she only, who might show me the place. She showed it step by step and room by room and secret by secret, with droll delightful childish talk about it and with the result, in half an hour, of our becoming tremendous friends. Young as she was I was struck, throughout our little tour, with her confidence and courage, with the way, in empty chambers and dull corridors, on crooked staircases that made me pause and even on the summit of an old machicolated square tower that made me dizzy, her morning music, her disposition to tell me so many more things than she asked, rang out and led me on. I have not seen Bly since the day I left it, and I dare say that to my present older and more informed eyes it would show a very reduced importance. But as my little conductress, with her hair of gold and her frock of blue, danced before me round corners and pattered down passages, I had the view of a castle of romance inhabited by a rosy sprite, such a place as would somehow, for diversion of the young idea, take all colour out of story-books and fairy-tales. Wasn't it just a story-book over which I had fallen a-doze and a-dream? No; it was a big ugly antique but convenient house, embodying a few features of a building still older, half-displaced and half-utilised, in which I had the fancy of our being almost as lost as a handful of passengers in a great drifting ship. Well, I was strangely at the helm!

II

THIS came home to me when, two days later, I drove over with Flora to meet, as Mrs Grose said, the little gentleman; and all the more for an incident that, presenting itself the the second evening, had deeply disconcerted me. The first day had been, on the whole, as I have expressed, reassuring;

but I was to see it wind up to a change of note. The postbag that evening—it came late—contained a letter for me which, however, in the hand of my employer, I found to be composed but of a few words enclosing another, addressed to himself, with a seal still unbroken. 'This, I recognise, is from the head-master, and the head-master's an awful bore. Read him, please; deal with him; but mind you don't report. Not a word. I'm off!' I broke the seal with a great effort—so great a one that I was a long time coming to it; took the unopened missive at last up to my room and only attacked it just before going to bed. I had better have let it wait till morning, for it gave me a second sleepless night. With no counsel to take, the next day, I was full of distress; and it finally got so the better of me that I determined to open myself at least to Mrs Grose.

'What does it mean? The child's dismissed his school.'

She gave me a look that I remarked at the moment; then, visibly, with a quick blankness, seemed to try to take it back. 'But aren't they all—?'

'Sent home—yes. But only for the holidays. Miles may never go back at all.'

Consciously, under my attention, she reddened. 'They won't take him?'

'They absolutely decline.'

At this she raised her eyes, which she had turned from me; I saw them fill with good tears. 'What has he done?'

I cast about; then I judged best simply to hand her my document—which, however, had the effect of making her, without taking it, simply put her hands behind her. She shook her head sadly. 'Such things are not for me, Miss.'

My counsellor couldn't read! I winced at my mistake, which I attenuated as I could, and opened the letter again to repeat it to her; then, faltering in the act and folding it up once more, I put it back in my pocket. 'Is he really *bad*?'

The tears were still in her eyes. 'Do the gentlemen say so?'

'They go into no particulars. They simply express their

regret that it should be impossible to keep him. They can have but one meaning.' Mrs Grose listened with dumb emotion; she forbore to ask me what this meaning might be; so that, presently, to put the thing with some coherence and with the mere aid of her presence to my own mind, I went on: 'That he's an injury to the others.'

At this, with one of the quick turns of simple folk, she suddenly flamed up. 'Master Miles!—*him* an injury?'

There was such a flood of good faith in it that, though I had not yet seen the child, my very fears made me jump to the absurdity of the idea. I found myself, to meet my friend the better, offering it, on the spot, sarcastically. 'To his poor little innocent mates!'

'It's too dreadful', cried Mrs Grose, 'to say such cruel things! Why he's scarce ten years old.'

'Yes, yes; it would be incredible.'

She was evidently grateful for such a profession. 'See him, Miss, first. *Then* believe it!' I felt forthwith a new impatience to see him; it was the beginning of a curiosity that, all the next hours, was to deepen almost to pain. Mrs Grose was aware, I could judge, of what she had produced in me, and she followed it up with assurance. 'You might as well believe it of the little lady. Bless her,' she added the next moment—'*look* at her!'

I turned and saw that Flora, whom, ten minutes before, I had established in the schoolroom with a sheet of white paper, a pencil and a copy of nice 'round O's', now presented herself to view at the open door. She expressed in her little way an extraordinary detachment from disagreeable duties, looking at me, however, with a great childish light that seemed to offer it as a mere result of the affection she had conceived for my person, which had rendered necessary that she should follow me. I needed nothing more than this to feel the full force of Mrs Grose's comparison, and, catching my pupil in my arms, covered her with kisses in which there was a sob of atonement.

None the less, the rest of the day, I watched for further occasion to approach my colleague, especially as, toward evening, I began to fancy she rather sought to avoid me. I overtook her, I remember, on the staircase; we went down together and at the bottom I detained her, holding her there with a hand on her arm. 'I take what you said to me at noon as a declaration that *you've* never known him to be bad.'

She threw back her head; she had clearly by this time, and very honestly, adopted an attitude. 'Oh never known him—I don't pretend *that!*'

I was upset again. 'Then you *have* known him—?'

'Yes indeed, Miss, thank God!'

On reflexion I accepted this. 'You mean that a boy who never is—?'

'Is no boy for *me*!'

I held her tighter. 'You like them with the spirit to be naughty?' Then, keeping pace with her answer, 'So do I!' I eagerly brought out. 'But not to the degree to contaminate—'

'To contaminate?'—my big word left her at a loss.

I explained it. 'To corrupt.'

She stared, taking my meaning in; but it produced in her an odd laugh. 'Are you afraid he'll corrupt *you*?' She put the question with such a fine bold humour that with a laugh, a little silly doubtless, to match her own, I gave way for the time to the apprehension of ridicule.

But the next day, as the hour for my drive approached, I cropped up in another place. 'What was the lady who was here before?'

'The last governess? She was also young and pretty—almost as young and almost as pretty, Miss, even as you.'

'Ah then I hope her youth and her beauty helped her!' I recollect throwing off. 'He seems to like us young and pretty!'

'Oh he *did*', Mrs Grose assented: 'it was the way he liked everyone!' She had no sooner spoken indeed than she caught herself up. 'I mean that's *his* way—the master's.'

I was struck. 'But of whom did you speak first?'

She looked blank, but she coloured. 'Why of *him*.'

'Of the master?'

'Of who else?'

There was so obviously no one else that the next moment I had lost my impression of her having accidentally said more than she meant; and I merely asked what I wanted to know. 'Did *she* see anything in the boy—?'

'That wasn't right? She never told me.'

I had a scruple, but I overcame it. 'Was she careful—particular?'

Mrs Grose appeared to try to be conscientious. 'About some things—yes.'

'But not about all?'

Again she considered. 'Well, Miss—she's gone. I won't tell tales.'

'I quite understand your feeling,' I hastened to reply; but I thought it after an instant not opposed to this concession to pursue: 'Did she die here?'

'No—she went off.'

I don't know what there was in this brevity of Mrs Grose's that struck me as ambiguous. 'Went off to die?' Mrs Grose looked straight out of the window, but I felt that, hypothetically, I had a right to know what young persons engaged for Bly were expected to do. 'She was taken ill, you mean, and went home?'

'She was not taken ill, so far as appeared, in this house. She left it, at the end of the year, to go home, as she said, for a short holiday, to which the time she had put in had certainly given her a right. We had then a young woman—a nursemaid who had stayed on and who was a good girl and clever; and *she* took the children altogether for the interval. But our young lady never came back, and at the very moment I was expecting her I heard from the master that she was dead.'

I turned this over, 'But of what?'

'He never told me! But please, Miss,' said Mrs Grose, 'I must get to my work.'

III

HER thus turning her back on me was fortunately not, for my just preoccupations, a snub that could check the growth of our mutual esteem. We met, after I had brought home little Miles, more intimately than ever on the ground of my stupefaction, my general emotion: so monstrous was I then ready to pronounce it that such a child as had now been revealed to me should be under an interdict. I was a little late on the scene of his arrival, and I felt, as he stood wistfully looking out for me before the door of the inn at which the coach had put him down, that I had seen him on the instant, without and within, in the great glow of freshness, the same positive fragrance of purity, in which I had from the first moment seen his little sister. He was incredibly beautiful, and Mrs Grose had put her finger on it: everything but a sort of passion of tenderness for him was swept away by his presence. What I then and there took him to my heart for was something divine that I have never found to the same degree in any child—his indescribable little air of knowing nothing in the world but love. It would have been impossible to carry a bad name with a greater sweetness of innocence, and by the time I had got back to Bly with him I remained merely bewildered—so far, that is, as I was not outraged—by the sense of the horrible letter locked up in one of the drawers of my room. As soon as I could compass a private word with Mrs Grose I declared to her that it was grotesque.

She promptly understood me. 'You mean the cruel charge?'

'It doesn't live an instant. My dear woman, *look* at him!'

She smiled at my pretension to have discovered his charm. 'I assure you, Miss, I do nothing else! What will you say then?' she immediately added.

'In answer to the letter?' I had made up my mind. 'Nothing at all.'

'And to his uncle?'

I was incisive. 'Nothing at all.'

'And to the boy himself?'

I was wonderful. 'Nothing at all.'

She gave with her apron a great wipe to her mouth. 'Then I'll stand by you. We'll see it out.'

'We'll see it out!' I ardently echoed, giving her my hand to make it a vow.

She held me there a moment, then whisked up her apron again with her detached hand. 'Would you mind, Miss, if I used the freedom—'

'To kiss me? No!' I took the good creature in my arms and after we had embraced like sisters felt still more fortified and indignant.

This at all events was for the time: a time so full that as I recall the way it went it reminds me of all the art I now need to make it a little distinct. What I look back at with amazement is the situation I accepted. I had undertaken, with my companion, to see it out, and I was under a charm apparently that could smooth away the extent and the far and difficult connexions of such an effort. I was lifted aloft on a great wave of infatuation and pity. I found it simple, in my ignorance, my confusion and perhaps my conceit, to assume that I could deal with a boy whose education for the world was all on the point of beginning. I am unable even to remember at this day what proposal I framed for the end of his holidays and the resumption of his studies. Lessons with me indeed, that charming summer, we all had a theory that he was to have; but I now feel that for weeks the lessons must have been rather my own. I learnt something—at first certainly—that had not been one of the teachings of my small smothered life; learnt to be amused, and even amusing, and not to think for the morrow. It was the first time, in a manner, that I had known space and air and freedom, all the music of summer and all the mystery of nature. And then there was consideration—and consideration was sweet. Oh it was a trap—not designed but deep—to my imagination, to my delicacy, perhaps to my vanity; to whatever in me was most excitable. The best way to picture it all is to say that I was off my guard. They gave me so little trouble—they were of a gentleness so extraordinary. I used to speculate—but even this with a dim disconnectedness— as to how the rough future (for all futures are rough!) would handle them and might bruise them. They had the bloom of health and happiness; and yet, as if I had been in charge of a pair of little grandees, of princes of the blood, for whom everything, to be right, would have to be fenced about and ordered and arranged; the only form that in my fancy the after-years could take for them was that of a romantic, a really royal extension of the garden and the park. It may be of course above all that what suddenly broke into this gives the previous time a charm of stillness—that hush in which something gathers or crouches. The change was actually like the spring of a beast.

In the first weeks the days were long; they often, at their finest, gave me what I used to call my own hour, the hour when, for my pupils, tea-time and bed-time having come and gone, I had before my final retirement a small interval alone. Much as I liked my companions this hour was the thing in the day I liked most; and I liked it best of all when, as the light faded—or rather, I should say, the day lingered and the last calls of the last birds sounded, in a flushed sky, from the old trees—I could take a turn into the grounds and enjoy, almost with a sense of property that amused and flattered me, the beauty and dignity of the place. It was a pleasure at these moments to feel myself tranquil and justified; doubtless perhaps also to reflect that by my discretion, my quiet good sense and general high propriety, I was giving pleasure—if he ever thought of it!—to the person to whose pressure I had yielded. What I was doing was what he had earnestly hoped and directly asked of me, and that I *could*, after all, do it proved even a greater joy than I had expected. I dare say I fancied myself in short a remarkable young woman and took comfort in the faith that this would more publicly appear. Well, I needed to be remarkable to offer a front to the remarkable things that presently gave their first sign.

It was plump, one afternoon, in the middle of my very hour: the children were tucked away and I had come out for my stroll. One of the thoughts that, as I don't in the least shrink now from noting, used to be with me in these wanderings was that it would be as charming as a charming story suddenly to meet someone. Someone would appear there at the turn of a path and would stand before me and smile and approve. I didn't ask more than that—I only asked that he should *know*; and the only way to be sure he knew would be to see it, and the kind light of it, in his handsome face. That was exactly present to me—by which I mean the face was—when, on the first of these occasions, at the end of a long June day, I stopped short on emerging from one of the plantations and coming into view of the house. What arrested me on the spot—and with a shock much greater than any vision had allowed for—was the sense that my imagination had, in a flash, turned real. He did stand there!—but high up, beyond the lawn and at the very top of the tower to which, on the first morning, little Flora had conducted me. This tower was one of a pair— square incongruous crenellated structures—that were distinguished, for some reason, though I could see little difference, as the new and the old. They flanked opposite ends of the house and were probably architectural absurd- ities, redeemed in a measure indeed by not being wholly disengaged nor of a height too pretentious, dating, in their gingerbread antiquity, from a romantic revival that was already a respectable past. I admired them, had fancies about them, for we could all profit in a degree, especially when they loomed through the dusk, by the grandeur of their actual battlements; yet it was not at such an elevation that the figure I had so often invoked seemed most in place.

It produced in me, this figure, in the clear twilight, I remember, two distinct gasps of emotion, which were, sharply, the shock of my first and that of my second surprise. My second was a violent perception of the mistake of my first: the man who met my eyes was not the person I had precipitately supposed. There came to me thus a bewilderment of vision of which, after these years, there is no living view that I can hope to give. An unknown man in a lonely place is a permitted object of fear to a young woman privately bred; and the figure that faced me was—a few more seconds assured me—as little anyone else I knew as it was the image that had been in my mind. I had not seen it in Harley Street—I had not seen it anywhere. The place moreover, in the strangest way of the world, had on the instant and by the very fact of its appearance become a solitude. To me at least, making my statement here with a deliberation with which I have never made it, the whole feeling of the moment returns. It was as if, while I took in, what I did take in, all the rest of the scene had been stricken with death. I can hear again, as I write, the intense hush in which the sounds of evening dropped. The rooks stopped cawing in the golden sky and the friendly hour lost for the unspeakable minute all its voice. But there was no other change in nature, unless indeed it were a change that I saw with a stranger sharpness. The gold was still in the sky, the clearness in the air, and the man who looked at me over the battlements was as definite as a picture in a frame. That's how I thought, with extraordinary quickness, of each person he might have been and that he wasn't. We were confronted across our distance quite long enough for me to ask myself with intensity who then he was and to feel, as an effect of my inability to say, a wonder that in a few seconds more became intense.

The great question, or one of these, is afterwards, I know, with regard to certain matters, the question of how long they have lasted. Well, this matter of mine, think what you will of it, lasted while I caught at a dozen possibilities, none of which made a difference for the better, that I could see, in there having been in the house—and for how long, above all?—a person of whom I was in ignorance. It lasted while I just bridled a little with the sense of how my office seemed to require that there should be no such ignorance and no such person. It lasted while this visitant, at all events—and there was a touch of the strange freedom, as I remember, in the sign of familiarity of his wearing no hat—seemed to fix me, from his position, with just the question, just the scrutiny through the fading light, that his own presence provoked. We were too far apart to call to each other, but there was a moment at which, at shorter range, some challenge between us, breaking the hush, would have been the right result of our straight mutual stare. He was in one of the angles, the one away from the house, very erect, as it struck me, and with both hands on the ledge. So I saw him as I see the letters I form on this page; then, exactly, after a minute, as if to add to the spectacle, he slowly changed his place—passed, looking at me hard all the while, to the opposite corner of the platform. Yes, it was intense to me that during this transit he never took his eyes from me, and I can see at this moment the way his hand, as he went, moved from one of the crenellations to the next. He stopped at the other corner, but less long, and even as he turned away still markedly fixed me. He turned away; that was all I knew.

IV

IT was not that I didn't wait, on this occasion, for more, since I was as deeply rooted as shaken. Was there a 'secret' at Bly—a mystery of Udolpho or an insane, an unmentionable relative kept in unsuspected confinement? I can't say how long I turned it over, or how long, in a confusion of curiosity and dread, I remained where I had had my collision; I only recall that when I re-entered the house darkness had quite closed in. Agitation, in the interval, certainly had held me and driven me, for I must, in circling about the place, have walked three miles; but I was to be later on so much more overwhelmed that this mere dawn of alarm was a comparatively human chill. The most singular part of it in fact—singular as the rest had been—was the part I became, in the hall, aware of in meeting Mrs Grose. This picture comes back to me in the general train—the impression, as I received it on my return, of the wide white panelled space, bright in the lamplight and with its portraits and red carpet, and of the good surprised look of my friend, which immediately told me she had missed me. It came to me straightway, under her contact, that, with plain heartiness, mere relieved anxiety at my appearance, she knew nothing whatever that could bear upon the incident I had there ready for her. I had not suspected in advance that her comfortable face would pull me up, and I somehow measured the importance of what I had seen by my thus finding myself hesitate to mention it. Scarce anything in the whole history seems to me so odd as this fact that my real beginning of fear was one, as I may say, with the instinct of sparing my companion. On the spot, accordingly, in the pleasant hall and with her eyes on me, I, for a reason that I couldn't then have phrased, achieved an inward revolution—offered a vague pretext for my lateness and, with the plea of the beauty of the night and of the heavy dew and wet feet, went as soon as possible to my room.

Here it was another affair; here, for many days after, it was a queer affair enough. There were hours, from day to day—or at least there were moments, snatched even from clear duties—when I had to shut myself up to think. It wasn't so much yet that I was more nervous than I could bear to be as that I was remarkably afraid of becoming so; for the truth I had now to turn over was simply and clearly the truth that I could arrive at no account whatever of the visitor with whom I had been so inexplicably and yet, as it seemed to me, so intimately concerned. It took me little time to see that I might easily sound, without forms of enquiry and without exciting remark, any domestic complication. The shock I had suffered must have sharpened all my senses; I felt sure, at the end of three days and as the result of mere closer attention, that I had not been practised upon by the servants nor made the object of any 'game'. Of whatever it was that I knew nothing was known around me. There was but one sane inference: someone had taken a liberty rather monstrous. That was what, repeatedly, I dipped into my room and locked the door to say to myself. We had been, collectively, subject to an intrusion; some unscrupulous traveller, curious in old houses, had made his way in unobserved, enjoyed the prospect from the best point of view and then stolen out as he came. If he had given me such a bold hard stare, that was but a part of his indiscretion. The good thing, after all, was that we should surely see no more of him.

This was not so good a thing, I admit, as not to leave me to judge that what, essentially, made nothing else much signify was simply my charming work. My charming work was just my life with Miles and Flora and through nothing could I so like it as through feeling that to throw myself into it was to throw myself out of trouble. The attraction of my small charges was a constant joy, leading me to wonder afresh at the vanity of my original fears, the distaste I had begun by entertaining for the probable grey prose of my office. There was to be no grey prose, it appeared, and no long grind; so how could work not be charming that presented itself as daily beauty? It was all the romance of the nursery and the poetry of the school-room. I don't mean by this of course that we studied only fiction and verse; I mean that I can express no otherwise the sort of interest my companions inspired. How can I describe that except by saying that instead of growing deadly used to them—and it's a marvel for a governess: I call the sisterhood to witness!—I made constant fresh discoveries. There was one direction, assuredly, in which these discoveries stopped: deep obscurity continued to cover the region of the boy's conduct at school. It had been promptly given me, I have noted, to face that mystery without a pang. Perhaps even it would be nearer the truth to say that—without a word—he himself had cleared it up. He had made the whole charge absurd. My conclusion bloomed there with the real rose-flush of his innocence: he was only too fine and fair for the little horrid unclean school-world, and he had paid a price for it. I reflected acutely that the sense of such individual differences, such superiorities of quality, always, on the part of the majority—which could include even stupid sordid head-masters—turns infallibly to the vindictive.

Both the children had a gentleness—it was their own fault, and it never made Miles a muff—that kept them (how shall I express it?) almost impersonal and certainly quite unpunishable. They were like those cherubs of the anecdote who had—morally at any rate—nothing to whack! I remember feeling with Miles in especial as if he had had, as it were, nothing to call even an infinitesimal history. We expect of a small child scant enough 'antecedents', but there was in this beautiful little boy something extraordinarily sensitive, yet extraordinarily happy, that, more than in any creature of his age I have seen, struck me as beginning anew each day. He had never for a second suffered. I took this as a direct disproof of his having really been chastised. If he had been wicked he would have 'caught' it, and I should have caught it by the rebound—I should have found the trace, should have felt the wound and the dishonour. I could reconstitute nothing at all, and he was therefore an angel. He never spoke of his school, never mentioned a comrade or a master; and I, for my part, was quite too much disgusted to allude to them. Of course I was under the spell, and the wonderful part is that, even at the time, I perfectly knew I was. But I gave myself up to it; it was an antidote to any pain, and I had more pains than one. I was in receipt in these days of disturbing letters from home, where things were not going well. But with this joy of my children what things in the world mattered? That was the question I used to put to my scrappy retirements. I was dazzled by their loveliness.

There was a Sunday—to get on—when it rained with such force and for so many hours that there could be no procession to church; in consequence of which, as the day declined, I had arranged with Mrs Grose that, should the evening show improvement, we would attend together the late service. The rain happily stopped, and I prepared for our walk, which, through the park and by the good road to the village, would be a matter of twenty minutes. Coming downstairs to meet my colleague in the hall, I remembered a pair of gloves that had required three stitches and that had received them—with a publicity perhaps not edifying—while I sat with the children at their tea, served on Sundays, by exception, in that cold clean temple of mahogany and brass, the 'grown-up' dining-room. The gloves had been dropped there, and I turned in to recover them. The day was grey enough, but the afternoon light still lingered, and it enabled me, on crossing the threshold, not only to recognise, on a chair near the wide window, then closed, the articles I wanted, but to become aware of a person on the other side of the window and looking straight in. One step into the room had sufficed; my vision was instantaneous; it was all there. The person looking straight in was the person who had already appeared to me. He appeared thus again with I won't say greater distinctness, for that was impossible, but with a nearness that represented a forward stride in our intercourse and made me, as I met him, catch my breath and turn cold. He was the same—he was the same, and seen, this time, as he had been seen before, from the waist up, the window, though the dining-room was on the ground floor, not going down to the terrace on which he stood. His face was close to the glass, yet the effect of this better view was, strangely, just to show me how intense the former had been. He remained but a few seconds—long enough to convince me he also saw and recognised; but it was as if I had always been looking at him for years and had known him always. Something, however, happened this time that had not happened before; his stare into my face, through the glass and across the room, was as deep and hard as then, but it quitted me for a moment during which I could still watch it, see it fix successively several other things. On the spot there came to me the added shock of the certitude that it was not for me he had come. He had come for someone else.

The flash of this knowledge—for it was knowledge in the midst of dread—produced in me the most extraordinary effect, starting, as I stood there, a sudden vibration of duty and courage. I say courage because I was beyond all doubt already far gone. I bounded straight out of the door again, reached that of the house, got in an instant upon the drive and, passing along the terrace as fast as I could rush, turned a corner and came full in sight. But it was in sight of nothing now—my visitor had vanished. I stopped, almost dropped, with the real relief of this; but I took in the whole scene—I gave him time to reappear. I call it time, but how long was it? I can't speak to the purpose today of the duration of these things. That kind of measure must have left me: they couldn't have lasted as they actually appeared to me to last.

The terrace and the whole place, the lawn and the garden beyond it, all I could see of the park, were empty with a great emptiness. There were shrubberies and big trees, but I remember the clear assurance I felt that none of them concealed him. He was there or was not there: not there if I didn't see him. I got hold of this; then instinctively, instead of returning as I had come, went to the window. It was confusedly present to me that I ought to place myself where he had stood. I did so; I applied my face to the pane and looked, as he had looked, into the room. As if, at this moment, to show me exactly what his range had been, Mrs Grose, as I had done for himself just before, came in from the hall. With this I had the full image of the repetition of what had already occurred. She saw me as I had seen my own visitant; she pulled up short as I had done; I gave her something of the shock that I had received. She turned white, and this made me ask myself if I had blanched as much. She started, in short, and retreated just on *my* lines, and I knew she had then passed out and come round to me and that I should presently meet her. I remained where I was, and while I waited I thought of more things than one. But there's only one I take space to mention. I wondered why *she* should be scared.

V

OH she let me know as soon as, round the corner of the house, she loomed again into view. 'What in the name of goodness is the matter—?' She was now flushed and out of breath.

I said nothing till she came quite near. 'With me?' I must have made a wonderful face. 'Do I show it?'

'You're as white as a sheet. You look awful.'

I considered; I could meet on this, without scruple, any degree of innocence. My need to respect the bloom of Mrs

Grose's had dropped, without a rustle, from my shoulders, and if I wavered for the instant it was not with what I kept back. I put out my hand to her and she took it; I held her hard a little, liking to feel her close to me. There was a kind of support in the shy heave of her surprise. 'You came for me for church, of course, but I can't go.'

'Has anything happened?'

'Yes. You must know now. Did I look very queer?'

'Through this window? Dreadful!'

'Well,' I said, 'I've been frightened.' Mrs Grose's eyes expressed plainly that *she* had no wish to be, yet also that she knew too well her place not to be ready to share with me any marked inconvenience. Oh it was quite settled that she *must* share! 'Just what you saw from the dining-room a minute ago was the effect of that. What *I* saw—just before—was much worse.'

Her hand tightened. 'What was it?'

'An extraordinary man. Looking in.'

'What extraordinary man?'

'I haven't the least idea.'

Mrs Grose gazed round us in vain. 'Then where is he gone?'

'I know still less.'

'Have you seen him before?'

'Yes—once. On the old tower.'

She could only look at me harder. 'Do you mean he's a stranger?'

'Oh very much!'

'Yet you didn't tell me?'

'No—for reasons. But now that you've guessed—'

Mrs Grose's round eyes encountered this charge. 'Ah I haven't guessed!' she said very simply. 'How can I if *you* don't imagine?'

'I don't in the very least.'

'You've seen him nowhere but on the tower?'

'And on this spot just now.'

Mrs Grose looked round again. 'What was he doing on the tower?'

'Only standing there and looking down at me.'

She thought a minute. 'Was he a gentleman?'

I found I had no need to think. 'No.' She gazed in deeper wonder. 'No.'

'Then nobody about the place? Nobody from the village?'

'Nobody—nobody. I didn't tell you, but I made sure.'

She breathed a vague relief: this was, oddly, so much to the good. It only went indeed a little way. 'But if he isn't a gentleman—'

'What *is* he? He's a horror.'

'A horror?'

'He's—God help me if I know *what* he is!'

Mrs Grose looked round once more; she fixed her eyes on the duskier distance and then, pulling herself together, turned to me with full inconsequence. 'It's time we should be at church.'

'Oh I'm not fit for church!'

'Won't it do you good?'

'It won't do *them*—!' I nodded at the house.

'The children?'

'I can't leave them now.'

'You're afraid—?'

I spoke boldly. 'I'm afraid of *him*.'

Mrs Grose's large face showed me, at this, for the first time, the far-away faint glimmer of a consciousness more acute: I somehow made out in it the delayed dawn of an idea I myself had not given her and that was as yet quite obscure to me. It comes back to me that I thought instantly of this as something I could get from her; and I felt it to be connected with the desire she presently showed to know more. 'When was it—on the tower?'

'About the middle of the month. At this same hour.'

'Almost at dark,' said Mrs Grose.

'Oh no, not nearly. I saw him as I see you.'

'Then how did he get in?'

'And how did he get out?' I laughed. 'I had no opportunity to ask him! This evening, you see,' I pursued, 'he has not been able to get in.'

'He only peeps?'

'I hope it will be confined to that!' She had now let go my hand; she turned away a little. I waited an instant; then I brought out: 'Go to church. Goodbye. I must watch.'

Slowly she faced me again. 'Do you fear for them?'

We met in another long look. 'Don't *you*?' Instead of answering she came nearer to the window and, for a minute, applied her face to the glass. 'You see how he could see,' I meanwhile went on.

She didn't move. 'How long was he here?'

'Till I came out. I came to meet him.'

Mrs Grose at last turned round, and there was still more in her face. '*I* couldn't have come out.'

'Neither could I!' I laughed again. 'But I did come. I've my duty.'

'So have I mine,' she replied; after which she added: 'What's he like?'

'I've been dying to tell you. But he's like nobody.'

'Nobody?' she echoed.

'He has no hat.' Then seeing in her face that she already, in this, with a deeper dismay, found a touch of picture, I quickly added stroke to stroke. 'He has red hair, very red, close-curling, and a pale face, long in shape, with straight good features and little rather queer whiskers that are as red as his hair. His eyebrows are somehow darker; they look particularly arched and as if they might move a good deal. His eyes are sharp, strange—awfully; but I only know clearly that they're rather small and very fixed. His mouth's wide, and his lips are thin, and except for his little whiskers he's quite clean-shaven. He gives me a sort of sense of looking like an actor.'

'An actor!' It was impossible to resemble one less, at least, than Mrs Grose at that moment.

'I've never seen one, but so I suppose them. He's tall, active, erect,' I continued, 'but never—no, never!—a gentleman.'

My companion's face had blanched as I went on; her round eyes started and her mild mouth gaped. 'A gentleman?' she gasped, confounded, stupefied: 'A gentleman *he*?'

'You know him then?'

She visibly tried to hold herself. 'But he *is* handsome?'

I saw the way to help her. 'Remarkably!'

'And dressed—?'

'In somebody's clothes. They're smart, but they're not his own.'

She broke into a breathless affirmative groan. 'They're the master's!'

I caught it up. 'You *do* know him?'

She faltered but a second. 'Quint!' she cried.

'Quint?'

'Peter Quint—his own man, his valet, when he was here!'

'When the master was?'

Gaping still, but meeting me, she pieced it all together. 'He never wore his hat, but he did wear—well, there were waistcoats missed! They were both here—last year. Then the master went, and Quint was alone.'

I followed, but halting a little. 'Alone?'

'Alone with *us*.' Then as from a deeper depth, 'In charge,' she added.

'And what became of him?'

She hung fire so long that I was still more mystified. 'He went too,' she brought out at last.

'Went where?'

Her expression, at this, became extraordinary. 'God knows where! He died.'

'Died?' I almost shrieked.

She seemed fairly to square herself, plant herself more firmly to express the wonder of it. 'Yes. Mr Quint's dead.'

VI

IT took of course more than that particular passage to place us together in presence of what we had now to live with as we could, my dreadful liability to impressions of the order so vividly exemplified, and my companion's knowledge henceforth—a knowledge half consternation and half compassion—of that liability. There had been this evening, after the revelation that left me for an hour so prostrate—there had been for either of us no attendance on any service but a little service of tears and vows, of prayers and promises, a climax to the series of mutual challenges and pledges that had straightway ensued on our retreating together to the schoolroom and shutting ourselves up there to have everything out. The result of our having everything out was simply to reduce our situation to the last rigour of its elements. She herself had seen nothing, not the shadow of a shadow, and nobody in the house but the governess was in the governess's plight; yet she accepted without directly impugning my sanity the truth as I gave it to her, and ended by showing me on this ground an awestricken tenderness, a deference to my more than questionable privilege, of which the very breath has remained with me as that of the sweetest of human charities.

What was settled between us accordingly that night was that we thought we might bear things together; and I was not even sure that in spite of her exemption it was she who had the best of the burden. I knew this hour, I think, as well as I knew later, what I was capable of meeting to shelter my pupils; but it took me some time to be wholly sure of what my honest comrade was prepared for to keep terms with so stiff an agreement. I was queer company enough—quite as queer as the company I received; but as I trace over what we went through I see how much common ground we must have found in the one idea that, by good fortune, *could* steady us. It was the idea, the second movement, that led me straight out, as I may say, of the inner chamber of my dread. I could take the air in the court, at least, and there Mrs Grose could join me. Perfectly can I recall now the particular way strength came to me before we separated for the night. We had gone over and over every feature of what I had seen.

'He was looking for someone else, you say—someone who was not you?'

'He was looking for little Miles.' A portentous clearness now possessed me. '*That's* whom he was looking for.'

'But how do you know?'

'I know, I know, I know!' My exaltation grew. 'And *you* know, my dear!'

She didn't deny this, but I required, I felt, not even so much telling as that. She took it up again in a moment. 'What if *he* should see him?'

'Little Miles? That's what he wants!'

She looked immensely scared again. 'The child?'

'Heaven forbid! The man. He wants to appear to *them*.' That he might was an awful conception, and yet somehow I could keep it at bay; which moreover, as we lingered there, was what I succeeded in practically proving. I had an absolute certainty that I should see again what I had already seen, but something within me said that by offering myself bravely as the sole subject of such experience, by accepting, by inviting, by surmounting it all, I should serve as an expiatory victim and guard the tranquillity of the rest of the household. The children in especial I should thus fence about and absolutely save. I recall one of the last things I said that night to Mrs Grose.

'It does strike me that my pupils have never mentioned—!'

She looked at me hard as I musingly pulled up. 'His having been here and the time they were with him?'

'The time they were with him, and his name, his presence, his history, in any way. They've never alluded to it'

'Oh the little lady doesn't remember. She never heard or knew.'

'The circumstances of his death?' I thought with some intensity. 'Perhaps not. But Miles would remember—Miles would know.'

'Ah don't try him!' broke from Mrs Grose.

I returned her the look she had given me. 'Don't be afraid.' I continued to think. 'It *is* rather odd.'

'Never by the least reference. And you tell me they were "great friends".'

'Oh it wasn't *him!*' Mrs Grose with emphasis declared. 'It was Quint's own fancy. To play with him, I mean—to spoil him.' She paused a moment; then she added: 'Quint was much too free.'

This gave me, straight from my vision of his face—*such* a face!—a sudden sickness of disgust. 'Too free with *my* boy?'

'Too free with everyone!'

I forbore for the moment to analyse this description further than by the reflexion that a part of it applied to several of the members of the household, of the half-dozen maids and men who were still of our small colony. But there was everything, for our apprehension, in the lucky fact that no discomfortable legend, no perturbation of scullions, had ever, within anyone's memory, attached to the kind old place. It had neither bad name nor ill fame, and Mrs Grose, most apparently, only desired to cling to me and to quake in silence. I even put her, the very last thing of all, to the test. It was when, at midnight, she had her hand on the schoolroom door to take leave. 'I *have* it from you then—for it's of great importance—that he was definitely and admittedly bad?'

'Oh not admittedly. *I* knew it—but the master didn't.'

'And you never told him?'

'Well, he didn't like tale-bearing—he hated complaints. He was terribly short with anything of that kind, and if people were all right to *him*—'

'He wouldn't be bothered with more?' This squared well enough with my impression of him: he was not a trouble-loving gentleman, nor so very particular perhaps about some of the company he himself kept. All the same, I pressed my informant. 'I promise you *I* would have told!'

She felt my discrimination. 'I dare say I was wrong. But really I was afraid.'

'Afraid of what?'

'Of things that man could do. Quint was so clever—he was so deep.'

I took this in still more than I probably showed. 'You weren't afraid of anything else? Not of his effect—?'

'His effect?' she repeated with a face of anguish and waiting while I faltered.

'On innocent little precious lives. They were in your charge.'

'No, they weren't in mine!' she roundly and distressfully returned. 'The master believed in him and placed him here because he was supposed not to be quite in health and the country air so good for him. So he had everything to say. Yes'—she let me have it—'even about *them*.'

'Them—that creature?' I had to smother a kind of howl. 'And you could bear it?'

'No. I couldn't—and I can't now!' And the poor woman burst into tears.

A rigid control, from the next day, was, as I have said, to follow them; yet how often and how passionately, for a week, we came back together to the subject! Much as we had discussed it that Sunday night. I was, in the immediate later hours in especial—for it may be imagined whether I slept—still haunted with the shadow of something she had not told me. I myself had kept back nothing, but there was a word Mrs Grose had kept back. I was sure moreover by morning that this was not from a failure of frankness, but because on every side there were fears. It seems to me indeed, in raking it all over, that by the time the morrow's sun was high I had restlessly read into the facts before us almost all the meaning they were to receive from subsequent and more cruel occurrences. What they gave me above all was just the sinister figure of the living man—the dead one would keep a while!—and of the months he had continuously passed at Bly, which, added up, made a formidable stretch. The limit of this evil time had arrived only when, on the dawn of a winter's morning, Peter Quint was found, by a labourer going to early work, stone dead on the the road from the village: a catastrophe explained—superficially at least—by a visible wound to his head; such a wound as might have been produced (and as, on the final evidence, *had* been) by a fatal slip, in the dark and after leaving the public-house, on the steepish icy slope, a wrong path altogether, at the bottom of which he lay. The icy slope, the turn mistaken at night and in liquor, accounted for much— practically, in the end and after the inquest and boundless chatter, for everything; but there had been matters in his life, strange passages and perils, secret disorders, vices more than suspected, that would have accounted for a good deal more.

I scarce know how to put my story into words that shall be a credible picture of my state of mind; but I was in these days literally able to find a joy in the extraordinary flight of heroism the occasion demanded of me. I now saw that I had been asked for a service admirable and difficult; and there would be a greatness in letting it be seen—oh in the right quarter!—that I could succeed where many another girl might have failed. It was an immense help to me—I confess I rather applaud myself as I look back!—that I saw my response so strongly and so simply. I was there to protect and defend the little creatures in the world the most bereaved and the most loveable, the appeal of whose helplessness had suddenly become only too explicit, a deep constant ache of one's own engaged affection. We were cut off, really, together; we were united in our danger. They had nothing but me, and I—well, I had *them*. It was in short a magnificent chance. This chance presented itself to me in an image richly material. I was a screen—I was to stand before them. The more I saw the less they would. I began to watch them in a stifled suspense, a disguised tension, that might well, had it continued too long, have turned to something like madness. What saved me, as I now see, was that it turned to another matter altogether. It didn't last as suspense—it was superseded by horrible proofs. Proofs, I say, yes—from the moment I really took hold.

This moment dated from an afternoon hour that I happened to spend in the grounds with the younger of my pupils alone. We had left Miles indoors, on the red cushion of a deep window-seat; he had wished to finish a book, and I had been glad to encourage a purpose so laudable in a young man whose only defect was a certain ingenuity of restlessness. His sister, on the contrary, had been alert to come out, and I strolled with her half an hour, seeking the shade, for the sun was still high and the day exceptionally warm. I was aware afresh with her, as we went, of how, like her brother, she contrived—it was the charming thing in both children—to let me alone without appearing to drop me and to accompany me without appearing to oppress. They were never importunate and yet never listless. My attention to them all really went to seeing them amuse themselves immensely without me: this was a spectacle they seemed actively to prepare and that employed me as an active admirer. I walked in a world of their invention—they had no occasion whatever to draw upon mine; so that my time was taken only with being for them some remarkable person or thing that the game of the moment required and that was merely, thanks to my superior, my exalted stamp, a happy and highly distinguished sinecure. I forget what I was on the present occasion; I only remember that I was something very important and very quiet and that Flora was playing very hard. We were on the edge of the lake, and, as we had lately begun geography, the lake was the Sea of Azof.

Suddenly, amid these elements, I became aware that on the other side of the Sea of Azof we had an interested spectator. The way this knowledge gathered in me was the strangest thing in the world—the strangest, that is, except the very much stranger in which it quickly merged itself. I had sat down with a piece of work—for I was something or other that could sit—on the old stone bench which overlooked the pond; and in this position I began to take in with certitude and yet without direct vision the presence, a good way off, of a third person. The old trees, the thick shrubbery, made a great and pleasant shade, but it was all suffused with the brightness of the hot still hour. There was no ambiguity in anything; none whatever at least in the conviction I from one moment to another found myself forming as to what I should see straight before me and across the lake as a consequence of raising my eyes. They were attached at this juncture to the stitching in which I was engaged, and I can feel once more the spasm of my effort not to move them till I should so have steadied myself as to be able to make up my mind what to do. There was an alien object in view—a figure whose right of presence I instantly and passionately questioned. I recollect counting over perfectly the possibilities, reminding myself that nothing was more natural for instance than the appearance of one of the men about the place, or even of a messenger, a postman or a tradesman's boy, from the village. That reminder had as little effect on my practical certitude as I was conscious—still even without looking—of its having upon the character and attitude of our visitor. Nothing was more natural than that these things should be the other things they absolutely were not.

Of the positive identity of the apparition I would assure myself as soon as the small clock of my courage should have ticked out the right second; meanwhile, with an effort that was already sharp enough, I transferred my eyes straight to little Flora, who, at the moment, was about ten yards away. My heart had stood still for an instant with the wonder and terror of the question whether she too would see; and I held my breath while I waited for what a cry from her, what some sudden innocent sign either of interest or of alarm, would tell me. I waited, but nothing came; then in the first place—and there is something more dire in this, I feel, than in anything I have to relate—I was determined by a sense that within a minute all spontaneous sounds from her had dropped; and in the second by the circumstance that also within the minute she had, in her play, turned her back to the water. This was her attitude when I at last looked at her—looked with the confirmed conviction that we were still, together, under direct personal notice. She had picked up a small flat piece of wood which happened to have in it a little hole that had evidently suggested to her the idea of sticking in another fragment that might figure as a mast and make the thing a boat. This second morsel, as I watched her, she was very markedly and intently attempting to tighten in its place. My apprehension of what she was doing sustained me so that after some seconds I felt I was ready for more. Then I again shifted my eyes—I faced what I had to face.

VII

I GOT hold of Mrs Grose as soon after this as I could; and I can give no intelligible account of how I fought out the interval. Yet I still hear myself cry as I fairly threw myself into her arms: 'They *know*—it's too monstrous: they know, they know!'

'And what on earth—?' I felt her incredulity as she held me.

'Why all that *we* know—and heaven knows what more besides!' Then as she released me I made it out to her, made it out perhaps only now with full coherency even to myself. 'Two hours ago, in the garden'—I could scarce articulate—'Flora *saw!*'

Mrs Grose took it as she might have taken a blow in the stomach. 'She has told you?' she panted.

'Not a word—that's the horror. She kept it to herself! The child of eight, *that* child!' Unutterable still for me was the stupefaction of it.

Mrs Grose of course could only gape the wider. 'Then how do you know?'

'I was there—I saw with my eyes: saw she was perfectly aware.'

'Do you mean aware of *him?*'

'No—of *her.*' I was conscious as I spoke that I looked prodigious things, for I got the slow reflexion of them in my companion's face. 'Another person—this time; but a figure of quite as unmistakeable horror and evil: a woman in black, pale and dreadful—with such an air also, and such a face!—on the other side of the lake. I was there with the child—quiet for the hour; and in the midst of it she came.'

'Came how—from where?'

'From where they come from! She just appeared and stood there—but not so near.'

'And without coming nearer?'

'Oh for the effect and the feeling she might have been as close as you!'

My friend, with an odd impulse, fell back a step. 'Was she someone you've never seen?'

'Never. But someone the child has. Someone *you* have.'

Then to show how I had thought it all out: 'My predecessor—the one who died.'

'Miss Jessel?'

'Miss Jessel. You don't believe me?' I pressed.

She turned right and left in her distress. 'How can you be sure?'

This drew from me, in the state of my nerves, a flash of impatience. 'Then ask Flora—*she's* sure!' But I had no sooner spoken than I caught myself up. 'No, for God's sake *don't!* She'll say she isn't—she'll lie!'

Mrs Grose was not too bewildered instinctively to protest. 'Ah how *can* you?'

'Because I'm clear. Flora doesn't want me to know.'

'It's only then to spare you.'

'No, no—there are depths, depths! The more I go over it the more I see in it, and the more I see in it the more I fear. I don't know what I *don't* see, what I *don't* fear!'

Mrs Grose tried to keep up with me. 'You mean you're afraid of seeing her again?'

'Oh no; that's nothing—now!' Then I explained. 'It's of *not* seeing her.'

But my companion only looked wan. 'I don't understand.'

'Why, it's that the child may keep it up—and that the child assuredly *will*—without my knowing it.'

At the image of this possibility Mrs Grose for a moment collapsed, yet presently to pull herself together again as from the positive force of the sense of what, should we yield an inch, there would really be to give way to. 'Dear, dear—we must keep our heads! And after all, if she doesn't mind it—!' She even tried a grim joke. 'Perhaps she likes it!'

'Like *such* things—a scrap of an infant!'

'Isn't it just a proof of her blest innocence?' my friend bravely enquired.

She brought me, for the instant, almost round. 'Oh we must clutch at *that*—we must cling to it! If it isn't a proof of what you say, it's a proof of—God knows what! For the woman's a horror of horrors.'

Mrs Grose, at this, fixed her eyes a minute on the ground; then at last raising them, 'Tell me how you know,' she said.

'Then you admit it's what she was?' I cried.

'Tell me how you know,' my friend simply repeated.

'Know? By seeing her! By the way she looked.'

'At you, do you mean—so wickedly?'

'Dear me, no—I could have borne that. She gave me never a glance. She only fixed the child.'

Mrs Grose tried to see it. 'Fixed her?'

'Ah with such awful eyes!'

She stared at mine as if they might really have resembled them. 'Do you mean of dislike?'

'God help us, no. Of something much worse.'

'Worse than dislike?'—this left her indeed at a loss.

'With a determination—indescribable. With a kind of fury of intention.'

I made her turn pale. 'Intention?'

'To get hold of her.' Mrs Grose—her eyes just lingering on mine—gave a shudder and walked to the window; and while she stood there looking out I completed my statement. '*That's* what Flora knows.'

After a little she turned round. 'The person was in black, you say?'

'In mourning—rather poor, almost shabby. But—yes—with extraordinary beauty.' I now recognised to what I had at last, stroke by stroke, brought the victim of my confidence, for she quite visibly weighed this. 'Oh handsome—very, very,' I insisted; 'wonderfully handsome. But infamous.'

She slowly came back to me. 'Miss Jessel—*was* infamous.' She once more took my hand in both her own, holding it as tight as if to fortify me against the increase of alarm I might draw from this disclosure. 'They were both infamous,' she finally said.

So for a little we faced it once more together; and I found absolutely a degree of help in seeing it now so straight. 'I appreciate', I said, 'the great decency of your not having hitherto spoken; but the time has certainly come to give me the whole thing.' She appeared to assent to this, but still only in silence; seeing which I went on: 'I must have it now. Of what did she die? Come, there was something between them.'

'There was everything.'

'In spite of the difference—?'

'Oh of their rank, their condition'—she brought it woefully out. '*She* was a lady.'

I turned it over; I again saw. 'Yes—she was a lady.'

'And he so dreadfully below,' said Mrs Grose.

I felt that I doubtless needn't press too hard, in such company, on the place of a servant in the scale; but there was nothing to prevent an acceptance of my companion's own measure of my predecessor's abasement. There was a way to deal with that, and I dealt; the more readily for my full vision—on the evidence—of our employer's late clever good-looking 'own' man; impudent, assured, spoiled, depraved. 'The fellow was a hound.'

Mrs Grose considered as if it were perhaps a little a case for a sense of shades. 'I've never seen one like him. He did what he wished.'

'With *her*?'

'With them all.'

It was as if now in my friend's own eyes Miss Jessel had again appeared. I seemed at any rate for an instant to trace their evocation of her as distinctly as I had seen her by the pond; and I brought out with decision: 'It must have been also what *she* wished!'

Mrs Grose's face signified that it had been indeed, but she said at the same time: 'Poor woman—she paid for it!'

'Then you do know what she died of?' I asked.

'No—I know nothing. I wanted not to know; I was glad

enough I didn't; and I thanked heaven she was well out of this!'

'Yet you had then your idea—'

'Of her real reason for leaving? Oh yes—as to that. She couldn't have stayed. Fancy it here—for a governess! And afterwards I imagined—and I still imagine. And what I imagine is dreadful.'

'Not so dreadful as what *I* do,' I replied; on which I must have shown her—as I was indeed but too conscious—a front of miserable defeat. It brought out again all her compassion for me, and at the renewed touch of her kindness my power to resist broke down. I burst, as I had the other time made her burst, into tears; she took me to her motherly breast, where my lamentation overflowed. 'I don't do it!' I sobbed in despair; 'I don't save or shield them! It's far worse than I dreamed. They're lost!'

VIII

WHAT I had said to Mrs Grose was true enough: there were in the matter I had put before her depths and possibilities that I lacked resolution to sound; so that when we met once more in the wonder of it we were of a common mind about the duty of resistance to extravagant fancies. We were to keep our heads if we should keep nothing else—difficult indeed as that might be in the face of all that, in our prodigious experience, seemed least to be questioned. Late that night, while the house slept, we had another talk in my room; when she went all the way with me as to its being beyond doubt that I had seen exactly what I had seen. I found that to keep her thoroughly in the grip of this I had only to ask her how, if I had 'made it up', I came to be able to give, of each of the persons appearing to me, a picture disclosing, to the last detail, their special marks—a portrait on the exhibition of which she had instantly recognised and named them. She wished, of course—small blame to her!—to sink the whole subject; and I was quick to assure her that my own interest in it had now violently taken the form of a search for the way to escape from it. I closed with her cordially on the article of the likelihood that with recurrence—for recurrence we took for granted—I should get used to my danger; distinctly professing that my personal exposure had suddenly become the least of my discomforts. It was my new suspicion that was intolerable; and yet even to this complication the later hours of the day had brought a little ease.

On leaving her, after my first outbreak, I had of course returned to my pupils, associating the right remedy for my dismay with that sense of their charm which I had already recognised as a resource I could positively cultivate and which had never failed me yet. I had simply, in other words, plunged afresh into Flora's special society and there become aware—it was almost a luxury!—that she could put her little conscious hand straight upon the spot that ached. She had looked at me in sweet speculation and then had accused me to my face of having 'cried'. I had supposed the ugly signs of it brushed away; but I could literally—for the time at all events—rejoice, under this fathomless charity, that they had not entirely disappeared. To gaze into the depths of blue of the child's eyes and pronounce their loveliness a trick of premature cunning was to be guilty of a cynicism in preference to which I naturally preferred to abjure my judgement and, so far as might be, my agitation. I couldn't abjure for merely wanting to, but I could repeat to Mrs Grose—as I did there, over and over, in the small hours— that with our small friends' voices in the air, their pressure on one's heart and their fragrant faces against one's cheek, everything fell to the ground but their incapacity and their beauty. It was a pity that, somehow, to settle this once for all, I had equally to re-enumerate the signs of subtlety that, in the afternoon, by the lake, had made a miracle of my show of self-possession. It was a pity to be obliged to re-investigate the certitude of the moment itself and repeat how it had come to me as a revelation that the inconceivable communion I then surprised must have been for both parties a matter of habit. It was a pity I should have had to quaver out again the reasons for my not having, in my delusion, so much as questioned that the little girl saw our visitant even as I actually saw Mrs Grose herself, and that she wanted, by just so much as she did thus see, to make me suppose she didn't, and at the same time, without showing anything, arrive at a guess as to whether I myself did! It was a pity I needed to recapitulate the portentous little activities by which she sought to divert my attention—the perceptible increase of movement, the greater intensity of play, the singing, the gabbling of nonsense and the invitation to romp.

Yet if I had not indulged, to prove there was nothing in it, in this review, I should have missed the two or three dim elements of comfort that still remained to me. I shouldn't for instance have been able to asseverate to my friend that I was certain—which was so much to the good—that *I* at least had not betrayed myself. I shouldn't have been prompted, by stress of need, by desperation of mind—I scarce know what to call it—to invoke such further aid to intelligence as might spring from pushing my colleague fairly to the wall. She had told me, bit by bit, under pressure, a great deal; but a small shifty spot on the wrong side of it all still sometimes brushed my brow like the wing of a bat; and I remember how on this occasion—for the sleeping house and the concentration alike of our danger and our watch seemed to help—I felt the importance of giving the last jerk to the curtain. 'I don't believe anything so horrible,' I recollect saying; 'no, let us put it definitely, my dear, that I don't. But if I did, you know, there's a thing I should require now, just without sparing you the least bit more—oh not a scrap, come!—to get out of you. What was it you had in mind

when, in our distress, before Miles came back, over the
letter from his school, you said, under my insistence, that
you didn't pretend for him he hadn't literally *ever* been
"bad"? He has *not*, truly, "ever", in these weeks that I
myself have lived with him and so closely watched him; he
has been an imperturbable little prodigy of delightful
loveable goodness. Therefore you might perfectly have
made the claim for him if you had not, as it happened, seen
an exception to take. What was your exception, and to what
passage in your personal observation of him did you refer?'

It was a straight question enough, but levity was not our
note, and in any case I had before the grey dawn
admonished us to separate got my answer. What my friend
had had in mind proved immensely to the purpose. It was
neither more nor less than the particular fact that for a
period of several months Quint and the boy had been
perpetually together. It was indeed the very appropriate
item of evidence of her having ventured to criticise the
propriety, to hint at the incongruity, of so close an alliance,
and even to go so far on the subject as a frank overture to
Miss Jessel would take her. Miss Jessel had, with a very
high manner about it, requested her to mind her business,
and the good woman had on this directly approached little
Miles. What she had said to him, since I pressed, was that
she liked to see young gentlemen not forget their station.

I pressed again, of course, the closer for that, 'You
reminded him that Quint was only a base menial?'

'As you might say! And it was his answer, for one thing,
that was bad.'

'And for another thing?' I waited. 'He repeated your
words to Quint?'

'No, not that. It's just what he *wouldn't!*' she could still
impress on me. 'I was sure, at any rate,' she added, 'that he
didn't. But he denied certain occasions.'

'What occasions?'

'When they had been about together quite as if Quint

were his tutor—and a very grand one—and Miss Jessel only for the little lady. When he had gone off with the fellow, I mean, and spent hours with him.'

'He then prevaricated about it—he said he hadn't?' Her assent was clear enough to cause me to add in a moment: 'I see. He lied.'

'Oh!' Mrs Grose mumbled. This was a suggestion that it didn't matter; which indeed she backed up by a further remark. 'You see, after all, Miss Jessel didn't mind. She didn't forbid him.'

I considered. 'Did he put that to you as a justification?'

At this she dropped again. 'No, he never spoke of it.'

'Never mentioned her in connexion with Quint?'

She saw, visibly flushing, where I was coming out. 'Well, he didn't show anything. He denied,' she repeated; 'he denied.'

Lord, how I pressed her now! 'So that you could see he knew what was between the two wretches?'

'I don't know—I don't know!' the poor woman wailed.

'You do know, you dear thing,' I replied; 'only you haven't my dreadful boldness of mind, and you keep back, out of timidity and modesty and delicacy, even the impression that in the past, when you had, without my aid, to flounder about in silence, most of all made you miserable. But I shall get it out of you yet! There was something in the boy that suggested to you,' I continued, 'his covering and concealing their relation.'

'Oh he couldn't prevent—'

'Your learning the truth? I dare say! But, heavens,' I fell, with vehemence, a-thinking, 'what it shows that they must, to that extent, have succeeded in making of him!'

'Ah nothing that's not nice *now*!' Mrs Grose lugubriously pleaded.

'I don't wonder you looked queer,' I persisted, 'when I mentioned to you the letter from his school!'

'I doubt if I looked as queer as you!' she retorted with homely force. 'And if he was so bad then as that comes to, how is he such an angel now?'

'Yes indeed—and if he was a fiend at school! How, how, how? Well,' I said in my torment, 'you must put it to me again, though I shall not be able to tell you for some days. Only put it to me again!' I cried in a way that made my friend stare. 'There are directions in which I mustn't for the present let myself go.' Meanwhile I returned to her first example—the one to which she had just previously referred—of the boy's happy capacity for an occasional slip. 'If Quint—on your remonstrance at the time you speak of—was a base menial, one of the things Miles said to you, I find myself guessing, was that you were another.' Again her admission was so adequate that I continued: 'And you forgave him that?'

'Wouldn't *you*?'

'Oh yes!' And we exchanged there, in the stillness, a sound of the oddest amusement. Then I went on: 'At all events, while he was with the man—'

'Miss Flora was with the woman. It suited them all!'

It suited me too, I felt, only too well; by which I mean that it suited exactly the particular deadly view I was in the very act of forbidding myself to entertain. But I so far succeeded in checking the expression of this view that I will throw, just here, no further light on it than may be offered by the mention of my final observation to Mrs Grose. 'His having lied and been impudent are, I confess, less engaging specimens than I had hoped to have from you of the outbreak in him of the little natural man. Still', I mused, 'they must do, for they make me feel more than ever that I must watch.'

It made me blush, the next minute, to see in my friend's face how much more unreservedly she had forgiven him than her anecdote struck me as pointing out to my own tenderness any way to do. This was marked when, at the

schoolroom door, she quitted me. 'Surely you don't accuse
him—'

'Of carrying on an intercourse that he conceals from me?
Ah remember that, until further evidence, I now accuse
nobody.' Then before shutting her out to go by another
passage to her own place, 'I must just wait,' I wound up.

IX

I WAITED and waited, and the days took as they elapsed
something from my consternation. A very few of them, in
fact, passing, in constant sight of my pupils, without a fresh
incident, sufficed to give to grievous fancies and even to
odious memories a kind of brush of the sponge. I have
spoken of the surrender to their extraordinary childish grace
as a thing I could actively promote in myself, and it may be
imagined if I neglected now to apply at this source for
whatever balm it would yield. Stranger than I can express,
certainly, was the effort to struggle against my new lights. It
would doubtless have been a greater tension still, however,
had it not been so frequently successful. I used to wonder
how my little charges could help guessing that I thought
strange things about them; and the circumstance that these
things only made them more interesting was not by itself a
direct aid to keeping them in the dark. I trembled lest they
should see that they *were* so immensely more interesting.
Putting things at the worst, at all events, as in meditation I
so often did, any clouding of their innocence could only
be—blameless and foredoomed as they were—a reason the
more for taking risks. There were moments when I knew
myself to catch them up by an irresistible impulse and press
them to my heart. As soon as I had done so I used to
wonder—'What will they think of that? Doesn't it betray
too much?' It would have been easy to get into a sad wild
tangle about how much I might betray; but the real account,

I feel, of the hours of peace I could still enjoy was that the immediate charm of my companions was a beguilement still effective even under the shadow of the possibility that it was studied. For if it occurred to me that I might occasionally excite suspicion by the little outbreaks of my sharper passion for them, so too I remember asking if I mightn't see a queerness in the traceable increase of their own demonstrations.

They were at this period extravagantly and preternaturally fond of me; which, after all, I could reflect, was no more than a graceful response in children perpetually bowed down over and hugged. The homage of which they were so lavish succeeded in truth for my nerves quite as well as if I never appeared to myself, as I may say, literally to catch them at a purpose in it. They had never, I think, wanted to do so many things for their poor protectress; I mean—though they got their lessons better and better, which was naturally what would please her most—in the way of diverting, entertaining, surprising her; reading her passages, telling her stories, acting her charades, pouncing out at her, in disguises, as animals and historical characters, and above all astonishing her by the 'pieces' they had secretly got by heart and could interminably recite. I should never get to the bottom—were I to let myself go even now—of the prodigious private commentary, all under still more private correction, with which I in these days overscored their full hours. They had shown me from the first a facility for everything, a general faculty which, taking a fresh start, achieved remarkable flights. They got their little tasks as if they loved them; they indulged, from the mere exuberance of the gift, in the most unimposed little miracles of memory. They not only popped out at me as tigers and as Romans, but as Shakespeareans, astronomers and navigators. This was so singularly the case that it had presumably much to do with the fact as to which, at the present day, I am at a loss for a different explanation: I allude to my unnatural composure on the subject of another school for Miles. What I remember is that I was content for the time not to open the question, and that contentment must have sprung from the sense of his perpetually striking show of cleverness. He was too clever for a bad governess, for a parson's daughter, to spoil; and the strangest if not the brightest thread in the pensive embroidery I just spoke of was the impression I might have got, if I had dared to work it out, that he was under some influence operating in his small intellectual life as a tremendous incitement.

If it was easy to reflect, however, that such a boy could postpone school, it was at least as marked that for such a boy to have been 'kicked out' by a school-master was a mystification without end. Let me add that in their company now—and I was careful almost never to be out of it—I could follow no scent very far. We lived in a cloud of music and affection and success and private theatricals. The musical sense in each of the children was of the quickest, but the elder in especial had a marvellous knack of catching and repeating. The schoolroom piano broke into all gruesome fancies; and when that failed there were confabulations in corners, with a sequel of one of them going out in the highest spirits in order to 'come in' as something new. I had had brothers myself, and it was no revelation to me that little girls could be slavish idolaters of little boys. What surpassed everything was that there was a little boy in the world who could have for the inferior age, sex and intelligence so fine a consideration. They were extraordinarily at one, and to say that they never either quarrelled or complained is to make the note of praise coarse for their quality of sweetness. Sometimes perhaps indeed (when I dropped into coarseness) I came across traces of little understandings between them by which one of them should keep me occupied while the other slipped away. There is a naïf side, I suppose, in all diplomacy; but if my pupils practised upon me it was surely with the minimum of grossness. It was all in the other quarter that, after a lull, the grossness broke out.

I find that I really hang back; but I must take my horrid plunge. In going on with the record of what was hideous at Bly I not only challenge the most liberal faith—for which I little care; but (and this is another matter) I renew what I myself suffered, I again push my dreadful way through it to the end. There came suddenly an hour after which, as I look back, the business seems to me to have been all pure suffering; but I have at least reached the heart of it, and the straightest road out is doubtless to advance. One evening—with nothing to lead up or prepare it—I felt the cold touch of the impression that had breathed on me the night of my arrival and which, much lighter then as I have mentioned, I should probably have made little of in memory had my subsequent sojourn been less agitated. I had not gone to bed; I sat reading by a couple of candles. There was a roomful of old books at Bly—last-century fiction some of it, which, to the extent of a distinctly deprecated renown, but never to so much as that of a stray specimen, had reached the sequestered home and appealed to the unavowed curiosity of my youth. I remember that the book I had in my hand was Fielding's 'Amelia'; also that I was wholly awake. I recall further both a general conviction that it was horribly late and a particular objection to looking at my watch. I figure finally that the white curtain draping, in the fashion of those days, the head of Flora's little bed, shrouded, as I had assured myself long before, the perfection of childish rest. I recollect in short that though I was deeply interested in my author I found myself, at the turn of a page and with his spell all scattered, looking straight up from him and hard at the door of my room. There was a moment during which I listened, reminded of the faint sense I had had, the first night, of there being something undefinably astir in the house, and noted the soft breath of the open casement just move the half-drawn blind.

Then, with all the marks of a deliberation that must have seemed magnificent had there been any one to admire it, I laid down my book, rose to my feet and, taking a candle, went straight out of the room and, from the passage, on which my light made little impression, noiselessly closed and locked the door.

I can say now neither what determined nor what guided me, but I went straight along the lobby, holding my candle high, till I came within sight of the tall window that presided over the great turn of the staircase. At this point I precipitately found myself aware of three things. They were practically simultaneous, yet they had flashes of succession. My candle, under a bold flourish, went out, and I perceived, by the uncovered window, that the yielding dusk of earliest morning rendered it unnecessary. Without it, the next instant, I knew that there was a figure on the stair. I speak of sequences, but I required no lapse of seconds to stiffen myself for a third encounter with Quint. The apparition had reached the landing halfway up and was therefore on the spot nearest the window, where, at sight of me, it stopped short and fixed me exactly as it had fixed me from the tower and from the garden. He knew me as well as I knew him; and so, in the cold faint twilight, with a glimmer in the high glass and another on the polish of the oak stair below, we faced each other in our common intensity. He was absolutely, on this occasion, a living detestable dangerous presence. But that was not the wonder of wonders; I reserve this distinction for quite another circumstance: the circumstance that dread had unmistakeably quitted me and that there was nothing in me unable to meet and measure him.

I had plenty of anguish after that extraordinary moment, but I had, thank God, no terror. And he knew I hadn't—I found myself at the end of an instant magnificently aware of this. I felt, in a fierce rigour of confidence, that if I stood my ground a minute I should cease—for the time at least—to have him to reckon with; and during the minute, accordingly, the thing was as human and hideous as a real interview: hideous just because it *was* human, as human as to have met alone, in the small hours, in a sleeping house, some enemy, some adventurer, some criminal. It was the dead silence of our long gaze at such close quarters that gave the whole horror, huge as it was, its only note of the unnatural. If I had met a murderer in such a place and at such an hour we still at least would have spoken. Something would have passed, in life, between us; if nothing had passed one of us would have moved. The moment was so prolonged that it would have taken but little more to make me doubt if even *I* were in life. I can't express what followed it save by saying that the silence itself—which was indeed in a manner an attestation of my strength—became the element into which I saw the figure disappear; in which I definitely saw it turn, as I might have seen the low wretch to which it had once belonged turn on receipt of an order, and pass, with my eyes on the villainous back that no hunch could have more disfigured, straight down the staircase and into the darkness in which the next bend was lost.

X

I REMAINED a while at the top of the stair, but with the effect presently of understanding that when my visitor had gone, he had gone; then I returned to my room. The foremost thing I saw there by the light of the candle I had left burning was that Flora's little bed was empty; and on this I caught my breath with all the terror that, five minutes before, I had been able to resist. I dashed at the place in which I had left her lying and over which—for the small silk counterpane and the sheets were disarranged—the white curtains had been deceivingly pulled forward; then my step, to my unutterable relief, produced an answering sound: I noticed an agitation of the window-blind, and the child, ducking down, emerged rosily from the other side of it. She stood there in so much of her candour and so little of her night-gown, with her pink bare feet and the golden glow of her curls. She looked intensely grave, and I had never had such a sense of losing an advantage acquired (the thrill of which had just been so prodigious) as on my consciousness that she addressed me with a reproach—'You naughty: where *have* you been?' Instead of challenging her own irregularity I found myself arraigned and explaining. She herself explained, for that matter, with the loveliest eagerest simplicity. She had known suddenly, as she lay there, that I was out of the room, and had jumped up to see what had become of me. I had dropped, with the joy of her reappearance, back into my chair—feeling then, and then only, a little faint; and she had pattered straight over to me, thrown herself upon my knee, given herself to be held with the flame of the candle full in the wonderful little face that was still flushed with sleep. I remember closing my eyes an instant, yieldingly, consciously, as before the excess of something beautiful that shone out of the blue of her own. 'You were looking for me out of the window?' I said. 'You thought I might be walking in the grounds?'

'Well, you know, I thought someone was'—she never blanched as she smiled out that at me.

Oh how I looked at her now! 'And did you see anyone?'

'Ah *no!*' she returned almost (with the full privilege of childish inconsequence) resentfully, though with a long sweetness in her little drawl of the negative.

At that moment, in the state of my nerves, I absolutely believed she lied; and if I once more closed my eyes it was before the dazzle of the three or four possible ways in which I might take this up. One of these for a moment tempted me with such singular force that, to resist it, I must have gripped my little girl with a spasm that, wonderfully, she submitted to without a cry or a sign of fright. Why not break out at her on the spot and have it all over?—give it to her straight in her lovely little lighted face? 'You see, you see, you *know* that you do and that you already quite suspect I believe it; therefore why not frankly confess it to me, so that we may at least live with it together and learn perhaps, in the strangeness of our fate, where we are and what it means?' This solicitation dropped, alas, as it came: if I could immediately have succumbed to it I might have spared myself—well, you'll see what. Instead of succumbing I sprang again to my feet, looked at her bed and took a helpless middle way. 'Why did you pull the curtain over the place to make me think you were still there?'

Flora luminously considered; after which, with her little divine smile: 'Because I don't like to frighten you!'

'But if I had, by your idea, gone out—?'

She absolutely declined to be puzzled; she turned her eyes to the flame of the candle as if the question were as irrelevant, or at any rate as impersonal, as Mrs Marcet or nine-times-nine. 'Oh but you know', she quite adequately answered, 'that you might come back, you dear, and that you *have!*' And after a little, when she had got into bed, I had, a long time, by almost sitting on her for the retention of her hand, to show how I recognised the pertinence of my return.

You may imagine the general complexion, from that moment, of my nights. I repeatedly sat up till I didn't know when; I selected moments when my room-mate unmistakeably slept, and, stealing out, took noiseless turns in the passage. I even pushed as far as to where I had last met Quint. But I never met him there again, and I may as well say at once that I on no other occasion saw him in the house. I just missed, on the staircase, nevertheless, a different adventure. Looking down it from the top I once recognised the presence of a woman seated on one of the lower steps with her back presented to me, her body half-bowed and her head, in an attitude of woe, in her hands. I had been there but an instant, however, when she vanished without looking round at me. I knew, for all that, exactly what dreadful face she had to show; and I wondered whether, if instead of being above I had been below, I should have had the same nerve for going up that I had lately shown Quint. Well, there continued to be plenty of call for nerve. On the eleventh night after my latest encounter with that gentleman—they were all numbered now—I had an alarm that perilously skirted it and that indeed, from the particular quality of its unexpectedness, proved quite my sharpest shock. It was precisely the first night during this series that, weary with vigils, I had conceived I might again without laxity lay myself down at my old hour. I slept immediately and, as I afterwards knew, till about one o'clock; but when I woke it was to sit straight up, as completely roused as if a hand had shaken me. I had left a light burning, but it was now out, and I felt an instant certainty that Flora had extinguished it. This brought me to my feet and straight, in the darkness, to her bed, which I found she had left. A glance at the window enlightened me further, and the striking of a match completed the picture.

The child had again got up—this time blowing out the taper, and had again, for some purpose of observation or response, squeezed in behind the blind and was peering out into the night. That she now saw—as she had not, I had satisfied myself, the previous time—was proved to me by the fact that she was disturbed neither by my re-illumination nor by the haste I made to get into slippers and into a wrap. Hidden, protected, absorbed, she evidently rested on the sill—the casement opened forward—and gave herself up. There was a great still moon to help her, and this fact had counted in my quick decision. She was face to face with the apparition we had met at the lake, and could now communicate with it as she had not then been able to do. What I, on my side, had to care for was, without disturbing her, to reach, from the corridor, some other window turned to the same quarter. I got to the door without her hearing me; I got out of it, closed it and listened, from the other side, for some sound from her. While I stood in the passage I had my eyes on her brother's door, which was but ten steps off and which, indescribably, produced in me a renewal of the strange impulse that I lately spoke of as my temptation. What if I should go straight in and march to *his* window?—what if, by risking to his boyish bewilderment a revelation of my motive, I should throw across the rest of the mystery the long halter of my boldness?

This thought held me sufficiently to make me cross to his threshold and pause again. I preternaturally listened; I figured to myself what might portentously be; I wondered if his bed were also empty and he also secretly at watch. It was a deep soundless minute, at the end of which my impulse failed. He was quiet; he might be innocent; the risk was hideous; I turned away. There was a figure in the grounds— a figure prowling for a sight, the visitor with whom Flora was engaged; but it wasn't the visitor most concerned with my boy. I hesitated afresh, but on other grounds and only a few seconds; then I had made my choice. There were empty rooms enough at Bly, and it was only a question of choosing the right one. The right one suddenly presented itself to me as the lower one—though high above the gardens—in the solid corner of the house that I have spoken of as the old tower. This was a large square chamber, arranged with some state as a bedroom, the extravagant size of which made it so inconvenient that it had not for years, though kept by Mrs Grose in exemplary order, been occupied. I had often admired it and I knew my way about in it; I had only, after just faltering at the first chill gloom of its disuse, to pass across it and unbolt in all quietness one of the shutters. Achieving this transit I uncovered the glass without a sound and, applying my face to the pane, was able, the darkness without being much less than within, to see that I commanded the right direction. Then I saw something more. The moon made the night extraordinarily penetrable and showed me on the lawn a person, diminished by distance, who stood there motionless and as if fascinated, looking up to where I had appeared—looking, that is, not so much straight at me as at something that was apparently above me. There was clearly another person above me— there was a person on the tower; but the presence on the lawn was not in the least what I had conceived and had confidently hurried to meet. The presence on the lawn—I felt sick as I made it out—was poor little Miles himself.

XI

IT was not till late next day that I spoke to Mrs Grose; the rigour with which I kept my pupils in sight making it often difficult to meet her privately: the more as we each felt the importance of not provoking—on the part of the servants quite as much as on that of the children—any suspicion of a secret flurry or of a discussion of mysteries. I drew a great security in this particular from her mere smooth aspect. There was nothing in her fresh face to pass on to others the least of my horrible confidences. She believed me, I was sure, absolutely: if she hadn't I don't know what would have become of me, for I couldn't have borne the strain alone. But she was a magnificent monument to the blessing of a want of imagination, and if she could see in our little charges nothing but their beauty and amiability, their happiness and cleverness, she had no direct communication with the sources of my trouble. If they had been at all visibly blighted or battered she would doubtless have grown, on tracing it back, haggard enough to match them; as matters stood, however, I could feel her, when she surveyed them with her large white arms folded and the habit of serenity in all her look, thank the Lord's mercy that if they were ruined the pieces would still serve. Flights of fancy gave place, in her mind, to a steady fireside glow, and I had already begun to perceive how, with the development of the conviction that—as time went on without a public accident—our young things could, after all, look out for themselves, she addressed her greatest solicitude to the sad case presented by their deputy-guardian. That, for myself, was a sound simplification: I could engage that, to the world, my face should tell no tales, but it would have been, in the conditions, an immense added worry to find myself anxious about hers.

At the hour I now speak of she had joined me, under pressure, on the terrace, where, with the lapse of the season, the afternoon sun was now agreeable; and we sat there together while before us and at a distance, yet within call if we wished, the children strolled to and fro in one of their most manageable moods. They moved slowly, in unison, below us, over the lawn, the boy, as they went, reading aloud from a story-book and passing his arm round his sister to keep her quite in touch. Mrs Grose watched them with positive placidity; then I caught the suppressed intellectual creak with which she conscientiously turned to take from me a view of the back of the tapestry. I had made her a receptacle of lurid things, but there was an odd recognition of my superiority—my accomplishments and my function— in her patience under my pain. She offered her mind to my disclosures as, had I wished to mix a witch's broth and proposed it with assurance, she would have held out a large clean saucepan. This had become thoroughly her attitude by the time that, in my recital of the events of the night, I reached the point of what Miles had said to me when, after seeing him, at such a monstrous hour, almost on the very spot where he happened now to be, I had gone down to bring him in; choosing then, at the window, with a concentrated need of not alarming the house, rather that method than any noisier process. I had left her meanwhile in little doubt of my small hope of representing with success even to her actual sympathy my sense of the real splendour of the little inspiration with which, after I had got him into the house, the boy met my final articulate challenge. As soon as I appeared in the moonlight on the terrace he had come to me as straight as possible; on which I had taken his hand without a word and led him, through the dark spaces, up the staircase where Quint had so hungrily hovered for him, along the lobby where I had listened and trembled, and so to his forsaken room.

Not a sound, on the way, had passed between us, and I had wondered—oh *how* I had wondered!—if he were groping about in his dreadful little mind for something plausible and not too grotesque. It would tax his invention certainly, and I felt, this time, over his real embarrassment, a curious thrill of triumph. It was a sharp trap for any game hitherto successful. He could play no longer at perfect propriety, nor could he pretend to it; so how the deuce would he get out of the scrape? There beat in me indeed, with the passionate throb of this question, an equal dumb appeal as to how the deuce *I* should. I was confronted at last, as never yet, with all the risk attached even now to sounding my own horrid note. I remember in fact that as we pushed into his little chamber, where the bed had not been slept in at all and the window, uncovered to the moonlight, made the place so clear that there was no need of striking a match—I remember how I suddenly dropped, sank upon the edge of the bed from the force of the idea that he must know how he really, as they say, 'had' me. He could do what he liked, with all his cleverness to help him, so long as I should continue to defer to the old tradition of the criminality of those caretakers of the young who minister to superstitions and fears. He 'had' me indeed, and in a cleft stick; for who would ever absolve me, who would consent that I should go unhung, if, by the faintest tremor of an overture, I were the first to introduce into our perfect intercourse an element so dire? No, no: it was useless to attempt to convey to Mrs Grose, just as it is scarcely less so to attempt to suggest here, how, during our short stiff brush there in the dark, he fairly shook me with admiration. I was of course thoroughly kind and merciful; never, never yet had I placed on his small shoulders hands of such tenderness as those with which, while I rested against the bed, I held him there well under fire. I had no alternative but, in form at least, to put it to him.

'You must tell me now—and all the truth. What did you go out for? What were you doing there?'

I can still see his wonderful smile, the whites of his beautiful eyes and the uncovering of his clear teeth, shine to me in the dusk. 'If I tell you why, will you understand?' My heart, at this, leaped into my mouth. *Would* he tell me why? I found no sound on my lips to press it, and I was aware of answering only with a vague repeated grimacing nod. He was gentleness itself, and while I wagged my head at him he stood there more than ever a little fairy prince. It was his brightness indeed that gave me a respite. Would it be so great if he were really going to tell me? 'Well,' he said at last, 'just exactly in order that you should do this.'

'Do what?'

'Think me—for a change—*bad!*' I shall never forget the sweetness and gaiety with which he brought out the word, nor how, on top of it, he bent forward and kissed me. It was practically the end of everything. I met his kiss and I had to make, while I folded him for a minute in my arms, the most stupendous effort not to cry. He had given exactly the account of himself that permitted least my going behind it, and it was only with the effect of confirming my acceptance of it that, as I presently glanced about the room, I could say—

'Then you didn't undress at all?'

He fairly glittered in the gloom. 'Not at all, I sat up and read.'

'And when did you go down?'

'At midnight. When I'm bad I *am* bad!'

'I see, I see—it's charming. But how could you be sure I should know it?'

'Oh I arranged that with Flora.' His answers rang out with a readiness! 'She was to get up and look out.'

'Which is what she did do.' It was I who fell into the trap!

'So she disturbed you, and, to see what she was looking at, you also looked—you saw.'

'While you', I concurred, 'caught your death in the night air!'

He literally bloomed so from this exploit that he could afford radiantly to assent. 'How otherwise should I have been bad enough?' he asked. Then, after another embrace, the incident and our interview closed on my recognition of all the reserves of goodness that, for his joke, he had been able to draw upon.

XII

THE particular impression I had received proved in the morning light, I repeat, not quite successfully presentable to Mrs Grose, though I re-enforced it with the mention of still another remark that he had made before we separated. 'It all lies in half a dozen words,' I said to her, 'words that really settle the matter. "Think, you know, what I *might* do!" He threw that off to show me how good he is. He knows down to the ground what he "might do". That's what he gave them a taste of at school.'

'Lord, you do change!' cried my friend.

'I don't change—I simply make it out. The four, depend upon it, perpetually meet. If on either of these last nights you had been with either child you'd clearly have understood. The more I've watched and waited the more I've felt that if there were nothing else to make it sure it would be made so by the systematic silence of each. *Never*, by a slip of the tongue, have they so much as alluded to either of their old friends, any more than Miles has alluded to his expulsion. Oh yes, we may sit here and look at them, and they may show off to us there to their fill; but even while they pretend to be lost in their fairy-tale they're steeped in their vision of the dead restored to them. He's not reading to her,' I declared; 'they're talking of *them*—they're talking horrors! I go on, I know, as if I were crazy; and it's a wonder I'm not. What I've seen would have made *you* so; but it has only made me more lucid, made me get hold of still other things.'

My lucidity must have seemed awful, but the charming creatures who were victims of it, passing and repassing in their interlocked sweetness, gave my colleague something to hold on by; and I felt how tight she held as, without stirring in the breath of my passion, she covered them still with her eyes. 'Of what other things have you got hold?'

'Why of the very things that have delighted, fascinated and yet, at bottom, as I now so strangely see, mystified and troubled me. Their more than earthly beauty, their absolutely unnatural goodness. It's a game,' I went on; 'it's a policy and a fraud!'

'On the part of little darlings—?'

'As yet mere lovely babies? Yes, mad as that seems!' The very act of bringing it out really helped me to trace it—follow it all up and piece it all together. 'They haven't been good—they've only been absent. It has been easy to live with them because they're simply leading a life of their own. They're not mine—they're not ours. They're his and they're hers!'

'Quint's and that woman's?'

'Quint's and that woman's. They want to get to them.'

Oh how, at this, poor Mrs Grose appeared to study them! 'But for what?'

'For the love of all the evil that, in those dreadful days, the pair put into them. And to ply them with that evil still, to keep up the work of demons, is what brings the others back.'

'Laws!' said my friend under her breath. The exclamation

was homely, but it revealed a real acceptance of my further proof of what, in the bad time—for there had been a worse even than this!—must have occurred. There could have been no such justification for me as the plain assent of her experience to whatever depth of depravity I found credible in our brace of scoundrels. It was in obvious submission of memory that she brought out after a moment: 'They *were* rascals! But what can they now do?' she pursued.

'Do?' I echoed so loud that Miles and Flora, as they passed at their distance, paused an instant in their walk and looked at us. 'Don't they do enough?' I demanded in a lower tone, while the children, having smiled and nodded and kissed hands to us, resumed their exhibition. We were held by it a minute; then I answered: 'They can destroy them!' At this my companion did turn, but the appeal she launched was a silent one, the effect of which was to make me more explicit. 'They don't know as yet quite how—but they're trying hard. They're seen only across, as it were, and beyond—in strange places and on high places, the top of towers, the roof of houses, the outside of windows, the further edge of pools; but there's a deep design, on either side, to shorten the distance and overcome the obstacle: so the success of the tempters is only a question of time. They've only to keep to their suggestions of danger.'

'For the children to come?'

'And perish in the attempt!' Mrs Grose slowly got up, and I scrupulously added: 'Unless, of course, we can prevent!'

Standing there before me while I kept my seat she visibly turned things over. 'Their uncle must do the preventing. He must take them away.'

'And who's to make him?'

She had been scanning the distance, but she now dropped on me a foolish face. 'You, Miss.'

'By writing to him that his house is poisoned and his little nephew and niece mad?'

'But if they *are*, Miss?'

'And if I am myself, you mean? That's charming news to be sent him by a person enjoying his confidence and whose prime undertaking was to give him no worry.'

Mrs Grose considered, following the children again. 'Yes, he do hate worry. That was the great reason—'

'Why those fiends took him in so long? No doubt, though his indifference must have been awful. As I'm not a fiend, at any rate, I shouldn't take him in.'

My companion, after an instant and for all answer, sat down again and grasped my arm. 'Make him at any rate come to you.'

I stared. 'To *me*?' I had a sudden fear of what she might do. ' "Him"?'

'He ought to *be* here—he ought to help.'

I quickly rose and I think I must have shown her a queerer face than ever yet. 'You see me asking him for a visit?' No, with her eyes on my face she evidently couldn't. Instead of it even—as a woman reads another—she could see what I myself saw: his derision, his amusement, his contempt for the breakdown of my resignation at being left alone and for the fine machinery I had set in motion to attract his attention to my slighted charms. She didn't know—no one knew—how proud I had been to serve him and to stick to our terms; yet she none the less took the measure, I think, of the warning I now gave her. 'If you should so lose your head as to appeal to him for me—'

She was really frightened. 'Yes, Miss?'

'I would leave, on the spot, both him and you.'

XIII

IT was all very well to join them, but speaking to them proved quite as much as ever an effort beyond my strength—offered, in close quarters, difficulties as insurmountable as before. This situation continued a month, and with new aggravations and particular notes, the note above all, sharper and sharper, of the small ironic consciousness on the part of my pupils. It was not, I am as sure today as I was sure then, my mere infernal imagination: it was absolutely traceable that they were aware of my predicament and that this strange relation made, in a manner, for a long time, the air in which we moved. I don't mean that they had their tongues in their cheeks or did anything vulgar, for that was not one of their dangers: I do mean, on the other hand, that the element of the unnamed and untouched became, between us, greater than any other, and that so much avoidance couldn't have been made successful without a great deal of tacit arrangement. It was as if, at moments, we were perpetually coming into sight of subjects before which we must stop short, turning suddenly out of alleys that we perceived to be blind, closing with a little bang that made us look at each other—for, like all bangs, it was something louder than we had intended—the doors we had indiscreetly opened. All roads lead to Rome, and there were times when it might have struck us that almost every branch of study or subject of conversation skirted forbidden ground. Forbidden ground was the question of the return of the dead in general and of whatever, in especial, might survive, for memory, of the friends little children had lost. There were days when I could have sworn that one of them had, with a small invisible nudge, said to the other: 'She thinks she'll do it this time—but she *won't!*' To 'do it' would have been to indulge for instance—and for once in a way—in some direct reference to the lady who had prepared them for my discipline. They had a delightful endless appetite for passages in my own history to which I had again and again treated them; they were in possession of everything that had ever happened to me, had had, with every circumstance, the story of my smallest adventures and of those of my brothers and sisters and of the cat and the dog at home, as well as many particulars of the whimsical bent of my father, of the furniture and arrangement of our house and of the conversation of the old women of our village. There were things enough, taking one with another, to chatter about, if one went very fast and knew by instinct when to go round. They pulled with an art of their own the strings of my invention and my memory; and nothing else perhaps, when I thought of such occasions afterwards, gave me so the suspicion of being watched from under cover. It was in any case over *my* life, *my* past and *my* friends alone that we could take anything like our ease; a state of affairs that led them sometimes without the least pertinence to break out into sociable reminders. I was invited—with no visible connexion—to repeat afresh Goody Gosling's celebrated *mot* or to confirm the details already supplied as to the cleverness of the vicarage pony.

It was partly at such junctures as these and partly at quite different ones that, with the turn my matters had now taken, my predicament, as I have called it, grew most sensible. The fact that the days passed for me without another encounter ought, it would have appeared, to have done something toward soothing my nerves. Since the light brush, that second night on the upper landing, of the presence of a woman at the foot of the stair, I had seen nothing, whether in or out of the house, that one had better not have seen. There was many a corner round which I expected to come upon Quint, and many a situation that, in a merely sinister way, would have favoured the appearance of Miss Jessel. The summer had turned, the summer had gone; the autumn had dropped upon Bly and had blown out half our lights. The place, with its grey sky and withered garlands, its bared spaces and scattered dead leaves, was like a theatre after the performance—all strewn with crumpled playbills. There were exactly states of the air, conditions of sound and of stillness, unspeakable impressions of the *kind* of ministering moment, that brought back to me, long enough to catch it, the feeling of the medium in which, that June evening out of doors, I had had my first sight of Quint, and in which too, at those other instants, I had, after seeing him through the window, looked for him in vain in the circle of shrubbery. I recognised the signs, the portents—I recognised the moment, the spot. But they remained unaccompanied and empty, and I continued unmolested; if unmolested one could call a young woman whose sensibility had, in the most extraordinary fashion, not declined but deepened. I had said in my talk with Mrs Grose on that horrid scene of Flora's by the lake—and had perplexed her by so saying—that it would from that moment distress me much more to lose my power than to keep it. I had then expressed what was vividly in my mind: the truth that, whether the children really saw or not— since, that is, it was not yet definitely proved—I greatly preferred, as a safeguard, the fulness of my own exposure. I was ready to know the very worst that was to be known. What I had then had an ugly glimpse of was that my eyes might be sealed just while theirs were most opened. Well, my eyes *were* sealed, it appeared, at present—a consumma- tion for which it seemed blasphemous not to thank God. There was, alas, a difficulty about that: I would have thanked him with all my soul had I not had in a proportionate measure this conviction of the secret of my pupils.

How can I retrace today the strange steps of my obsession? There were times of our being together when I would have been ready to swear that, literally, in my presence, but with my direct sense of it closed, they had visitors who were known and were welcome. Then it was that, had I not been deterred by the very chance that such an injury might prove greater than the injury to be averted, my exaltation would have broken out. 'They're here, they're here, you little wretches,' I would have cried, 'and you can't deny it now!' The little wretches denied it with all the added volume of their sociability and their tenderness, just in the crystal depths of which—like the flash of a fish in a stream—the mockery of their advantage peeped up. The shock had in truth sunk into me still deeper than I knew on the night when, looking out either for Quint or for Miss Jessel under the stars, I had seen there the boy over whose rest I watched and who had immediately brought in with him—had straightway there turned on me—the lovely upward look with which, from the battlements above us, the hideous apparition of Quint had played. If it was a question of a scare my discovery on this occasion had scared me more than any other, and it was essentially in the scared state that I drew my actual conclusions. They harassed me so that sometimes, at odd moments, I shut myself up audibly to rehearse—it was at once a fantastic relief and a renewed despair—the manner in which I might come to the point. I approached it from one side and the other while, in my room, I flung myself about, but I always broke down in the monstrous utterance of names. As they died away on my lips I said to myself that I should indeed help them to represent something infamous if by pronouncing them I should violate as rare a little case of instinctive delicacy as any schoolroom probably had ever known. When I said to myself: '*They* have the manners to be silent, and you, trusted as you are, the baseness to speak!' I felt myself crimson and covered my face with my hands. After these secret scenes I chattered more than ever, going on volubly enough till one of our prodigious palpable hushes occurred— I can call them nothing else—the strange dizzy lift or swim (I try for terms!) into a stillness, a pause of all life, that had nothing to do with the more or less noise we at the moment might be engaged in making and that I could hear through any intensified mirth or quickened recitation or louder strum of the piano. Then it was that the others, the outsiders, were there. Though they were not angels they 'passed', as the French say, causing me, while they stayed, to tremble with the fear of their addressing to their younger victims some yet more infernal message or more vivid image than they had thought good enough for myself.

What it was least possible to get rid of was the cruel idea that, whatever I had seen, Miles and Flora saw *more*—things terrible and unguessable and that sprang from dreadful passages of intercourse in the past. Such things naturally left on the surface, for the time, a chill that we vociferously denied we felt; and we had all three with repetition, got into such splendid training that we went, each time, to mark the close of the incident, almost automatically through the very same movements. It was striking of the children at all events to kiss me inveterately with a wild irrelevance and never to fail—one or the other—of the precious question that had helped us through many a peril. 'When do you think he *will* come? Don't you think we *ought* to write?'—there was nothing like that enquiry, we found by experience, for carrying off an awkwardness. 'He' of course was their uncle in Harley Street; and we lived in much profusion of theory that he might at any moment arrive to mingle in our circle. It was impossible to have given less encouragement than he had administered to such a doctrine, but if we had not had the doctrine to fall back upon we should have deprived each other of some of our finest exhibitions. He never wrote to them—that may have been selfish, but it was a part of the flattery of his trust of myself; for the way in which a man pays his highest tribute to a woman is apt to be but the more festal celebration of one of the sacred laws of his comfort. So I held that I carried out the spirit of the pledge given not to appeal to him when I let our young friends understand that their own letters were but charming literary exercises. They were too beautiful to be posted; I kept them myself; I have them all to this hour. This was a rule indeed which only added to the satiric effect of my being plied with the supposition that he might at any moment be among us. It was exactly as if our young friends knew how almost more awkward than anything else that might be for me. There appears to me moreover as I look back no note in all this more extraordinary than the mere fact that, in spite of my tension and of their triumph, I never lost patience with them. Adorable they must in truth have been, I now feel, since I didn't in these days hate them! Would exasperation, however, if relief had longer been postponed, finally have betrayed me? It little matters, for relief arrived. I call it relief though it was only the relief that a snap brings to a strain or the burst of a thunderstorm to a day of suffocation. It was at least change, and it came with a rush.

XIV

WALKING to church a certain Sunday morning, I had little Miles at my side and his sister, in advance of us and at Mrs Grose's, well in sight. It was a crisp clear day, the first of its order for some time; the night had brought a touch of frost and the autumn air, bright and sharp, made the church-bells almost gay. It was an odd accident of thought that I should have happened at such a moment to be particularly and very gratefully struck with the obedience of my little charges. Why did they never resent my inexorable, my perpetual society? Something or other had brought nearer home to me that I had all but pinned the boy to my shawl, and that in the way our companions were marshalled before me I might have appeared to provide against some danger of rebellion. I was like a gaoler with an eye to possible surprises and escapes. But all this belonged—I mean their magnificent little surrender—just to the special array of the facts that were most abysmal. Turned out for Sunday by his uncle's tailor, who had had a free hand and a notion of pretty waistcoats and of his grand little air, Miles's whole title to independence, the rights of his sex and situation, were so stamped upon him that if he had suddenly struck for freedom I should have had nothing to say. I was by the strangest of chances wondering how I should meet him when the revolution unmistakeably occurred. I call it a revolution because I now see how, with the word he spoke, the curtain rose on the last act of my dreadful drama and the catastrophe was precipitated. 'Look here, my dear, you know,' he charmingly said, 'when in the world, please, am I going back to school?'

Transcribed here the speech sounds harmless enough, particularly as uttered in the sweet, high, casual pipe with which, at all interlocutors, but above all at his eternal governess, he threw off intonations as if he were tossing roses. There was something in them that always made one 'catch', and I caught at any rate now so effectually that I stopped as short as if one of the trees of the park had fallen across the road. There was something new, on the spot, between us, and he was perfectly aware I recognised it, though to enable me to do so he had no need to look a whit less candid and charming than usual. I could feel in him how he already, from my at first finding nothing to reply, perceived the advantage he had gained. I was so slow to find anything that he had plenty of time, after a minute, to continue with his suggestive but inconclusive smile: 'You know, my dear, that for a fellow to be with a lady *always*—!' His 'my dear' was constantly on his lips for me, and nothing could have expressed more the exact shade of the sentiment which I desired to inspire my pupils than its fond familiarity. It was so respectfully easy.

But oh how I felt that at present I must pick my own phrases! I remember that, to gain time, I tried to laugh, and I seemed to see in the beautiful face with which he watched me how ugly and queer I looked. 'And always with the same lady?' I returned.

He neither blenched nor winked. The whole thing was virtually out between us. 'Ah of course she's a jolly "perfect" lady; but after all I'm a fellow, don't you see? who's—well, getting on.'

I lingered there with him an instant ever so kindly. 'Yes, you're getting on.' Oh but I felt helpless!

I have kept to this day the heartbreaking little idea of how he seemed to know that and to play with it. 'And you can't say I've not been awfully good, can you?'

I laid my hand on his shoulder, for though I felt how much better it would have been to walk on I was not yet quite able. 'No, I can't say that, Miles.'

'Except just that one night, you know—!'

'That one night?' I couldn't look as straight as he.

'Why when I went down—went out of the house.'

'Oh yes. But I forget what you did it for.'

'You forget?'—he spoke with the sweet extravagance of childish reproach. 'Why it was just to show you I could!'

'Oh yes—you could.'

'And I can again.'

I felt I might perhaps after all succeed in keeping my wits about me. 'Certainly. But you won't.'

'No, not *that* again. It was nothing.'

'It was nothing,' I said. 'But we must go on.'

He resumed our walk with me, passing his hand into my arm. 'Then when *am* I going back?'

I wore, in turning it over, my most responsible air. 'Were you very happy at school?'

He just considered. 'Oh I'm happy enough anywhere!'

'Well then,' I quavered, 'if you're just as happy here—!'

'Ah but that isn't everything! Of course *you* know a lot—'

'But you hint that you know almost as much?' I risked as he paused.

'Not half I want to!' Miles honestly professed. 'But it isn't so much that.'

'What is it then?'

'Well—I want to see more life.'

'I see; I see.' We had arrived within sight of the church and of various persons, including several of the household of Bly, on their way to it and clustered about the door to see

us go in. I quickened our step; I wanted to get there before
the question between us opened up much further; I
reflected hungrily that he would have for more than an hour
to be silent; and I thought with envy of the comparative
dusk of the pew and of the almost spiritual help of the
hassock on which I might bend my knees. I seemed literally
to be running a race with some confusion to which he was
about to reduce me, but I felt he had got in first when,
before we had even entered the churchyard, he threw
out—

'I want my own sort!'

It literally made me bound forward. 'There aren't many
of your own sort, Miles!' I laughed. 'Unless perhaps dear
little Flora!'

'You really compare me to a baby girl?'

This found me singularly weak. 'Don't you then *love* our
sweet Flora?'

'If I didn't—and you too; if I didn't—!' he repeated as if
retreating for a jump, yet leaving his thought so unfinished
that, after we had come into the gate, another stop, which
he imposed on me by the pressure of his arm, had become
inevitable. Mrs Grose and Flora had passed into the church,
the other worshippers had followed and we were, for the
minute, alone among the old thick graves. We had paused,
on the path from the gate, by a low oblong table-like tomb.

'Yes, if you didn't—?'

He looked, while I waited, about at the graves. 'Well,
you know what!' But he didn't move, and he presently
produced something that made me drop straight down on
the stone slab as if suddenly to rest. 'Does my uncle think
what *you* think?'

I markedly rested. 'How do you know what I think?'

'Ah well, of course I don't; for it strikes me you never tell
me. But I mean does *he* know?'

'Know what, Miles?'

'Why the way I'm going on.'

I recognised quickly enough that I could make, to this enquiry, no answer that wouldn't involve something of a sacrifice of my employer. Yet it struck me that we were all, at Bly, sufficiently sacrificed to make that venial. 'I don't think your uncle much cares.'

Miles, on this, stood looking at me. 'Then don't you think he can be made to?'

'In what way?'

'Why by his coming down.'

'But who'll get him to come down?'

'*I* will!' the boy said with extraordinary brightness and emphasis. He gave me another look charged with that expression and then marched off alone into church.

XV

THE business was practically settled from the moment I never followed him. It was a pitiful surrender to agitation, but my being aware of this had somehow no power to restore me. I only sat there on my tomb and read into what our young friend had said to me the fulness of its meaning; by the time I had grasped the whole of which I had also embraced, for absence, the pretext that I was ashamed to offer my pupils and the rest of the congregation such an example of delay. What I said to myself above all was that Miles had got something out of me and that the gage of it for him would be just this awkward collapse. He had got out of me that there was something I was much afraid of, and that he should probably be able to make use of my fear to gain, for his own purpose, more freedom. My fear was of having to deal with the intolerable question of the grounds of his dismissal from school, since that was really but the question of the horrors gathered behind. That his uncle should arrive to treat with me of these things was a solution that, strictly speaking, I ought now to have desired to bring on; but I could so little face the ugliness and the pain of it that I simply procrastinated and lived from hand to mouth. The boy, to my deep discomposure, was immensely in the right, was in a position to say to me: 'Either you clear up with my guardian the mystery of this interruption of my studies, or you cease to expect me to lead with you a life that's so unnatural for a boy.' What was so unnatural for the particular boy I was concerned with was this sudden revelation of a consciousness and a plan.

That was what really overcame me, what prevented my going in. I walked round the church, hesitating, hovering; I reflected that I had already, with him, hurt myself beyond repair. Therefore I could patch up nothing and it was too extreme an effort to squeeze beside him into the pew: he would be so much more sure than ever to pass his arm into mine and make me sit there for an hour in close mute contact with his commentary on our talk. For the first minute since his arrival I wanted to get away from him. As I paused beneath the high east window and listened to the sounds of worship I was taken with an impulse that might master me, I felt, and completely, should I give it the least encouragement. I might easily put an end to my ordeal by getting away altogether. Here was my chance; there was no one to stop me; I could give the whole thing up—turn my back and bolt. It was only a question of hurrying again, for a few preparations, to the house which the attendance at church of so many of the servants would practically have left unoccupied. No one, in short, could blame me if I should just drive desperately off. What was it to get away if I should get away only till dinner? That would be in a couple of hours, at the end of which—I had the acute prevision— my little pupils would play at innocent wonder about my non-appearance in their train.

'What *did* you do, you naughty bad thing? Why in the world, to worry us so—and take our thoughts off too, don't know?—did you desert us at the very door?' I couldn't meet such questions nor, as they asked them, their false little lovely eyes; yet it was all so exactly what I should have to meet that, as the prospect grew sharp to me, I at last let myself go.

I got, so far as the immediate moment was concerned, away; I came straight out of the churchyard and, thinking hard, retraced my steps through the park. It seemed to me that by the time I reached the house I had made up my mind to cynical flight. The Sunday stillness both of the approaches and of the interior, in which I met no one, fairly stirred me with a sense of opportunity. Were I to get off quickly this way I should get off without a scene, without a word. My quickness would have to be remarkable, however, and the question of a conveyance was the great one to settle. Tormented, in the hall, with difficulties and obstacles, I remember sinking down at the foot of the staircase—suddenly collapsing there on the lowest step and then, with a revulsion, recalling that it was exactly where, more than a month before, in the darkness of night and just so bowed with evil things, I had seen the spectre of the most horrible of women. At this I was able to straighten myself; I went the rest of the way up; I made, in my turmoil, for the schoolroom, where there were objects belonging to me that I should have to take. But I opened the door to find again, in a flash, my eyes unsealed. In the presence of what I saw I reeled straight back upon resistance.

Seated at my own table in the clear noonday light I saw a person whom, without my previous experience, I should have taken at the first blush for some housemaid who might have stayed at home to look after the place and who, availing herself of rare relief from observation and of the schoolroom table and my pens, ink and paper, had applied herself to the considerable effort of a letter to her sweetheart. There was an effort in the way that, while her arms rested on the table, her hands, with evident weariness, supported her head; but at the moment I took this in I had already become aware that, in spite of my entrance, her attitude strangely persisted. Then it was—with the very act of its announcing itself—that her identity flared up in a change of posture. She rose, not as if she had heard me, but with an indescribable grand melancholy of indifference and detachment, and, within a dozen feet of me, stood there as my vile predecessor. Dishonoured and tragic, she was all before me; but even as I fixed and, for memory, secured it, the awful image passed away. Dark as midnight in her black dress, her haggard beauty and her unutterable woe, she had looked at me long enough to appear to say that her right to sit at my table was as good as mine to sit at hers. While these instants lasted indeed I had the extraordinary chill of a feeling that it was I who was the intruder. It was as a wild protest against it that, actually addressing her—'You terrible miserable woman!'—I heard myself break into a sound that, by the open door, rang through the long passage and the empty house. She looked at me as if she heard me, but I had recovered myself and cleared the air. There was nothing in the room the next minute but the sunshine and the sense that I must stay.

XVI

I HAD so perfectly expected the return of the others to be marked by a demonstration that I was freshly upset at having to find them merely dumb and discreet about my desertion. Instead of gaily denouncing and caressing me they made no allusion to my having failed them, and I was left, for the time, on perceiving that she too said nothing, to study Mrs Grose's odd face. I did this to such purpose that I made sure they had in some way bribed her to silence; a silence that, however, I would engage to break down on the first private opportunity. This opportunity came before tea:

I secured five minutes with her in the housekeeper's room, where, in the twilight, amid a smell of lately-baked bread, but with the place all swept and garnished, I found her sitting in pained placidity before the fire. So I see her still, so I see her best: facing the flame from her straight chair in the dusky shining room, a large clean picture of the 'put away'—of drawers closed and locked and rest without a remedy.

'Oh yes, they asked me to say nothing; and to please them—so long as they were there—of course I promised. But what had happened to you?'

'I only went with you for the walk,' I said. 'I had then to come back to meet a friend.'

She showed her surprise. 'A friend—*you?*'

'Oh yes, I've a couple!' I laughed. 'But did the children give you a reason?'

'For not alluding to your leaving us? Yes; they said you'd like it better. *Do* you like it better?'

My face had made her rueful. 'No, I like it worse!' But after an instant I added: 'Did they say why I should like it better?'

'No; Master Miles only said "We must do nothing but what she likes!"'

'I wish indeed he would! And what did Flora say?'

'Miss Flora was too sweet. She said "Oh of course, of course!"—and I said the same.'

I thought a moment. 'You were too sweet too—I can hear you all. But none the less, between Miles and me, it's now all out.'

'All out?' My companion stared. 'But what, Miss?'

'Everything. It doesn't matter. I've made up my mind. I came home, my dear,' I went on, 'for a talk with Miss Jessel.'

I had by this time formed the habit of having Mrs Grose literally well in hand in advance of my sounding that note; so that even now, as she bravely blinked under the signal of my word, I could keep her comparatively firm. 'A talk! Do you mean she spoke?'

'It came to that. I found her, on my return, in the schoolroom.'

'And what did she say?' I can hear the good woman still, and the candour of her stupefaction.

'That she suffers the torments—!'

It was this, of a truth, that made her, as she filled out my picture, gape. 'Do you mean', she faltered '—of the lost?'

'Of the lost. Of the damned. And that's why, to share them—' I faltered myself with the horror of it.

But my companion, with less imagination, kept me up. 'To share them—?'

'She wants Flora.' Mrs Grose might, as I gave it to her, fairly have fallen away from me had I not been prepared. I still held her there, to show I was. 'As I've told you, however, it doesn't matter.'

'Because you've made up your mind? But to what?'

'To everything.'

'And what do you call "everything"?'

'Why to sending for their uncle.'

'Oh Miss, in pity do,' my friend broke out.

'Ah but I will, I *will*! I see it's the only way. What's "out", as I told you, with Miles is that if he thinks I'm afraid to—and has ideas of what he gains by that—he shall see he's mistaken. Yes, yes; his uncle shall have it here from me on the spot (and before the boy himself if necessary) that if I'm to be reproached with having done nothing again about more school—'

'Yes, Miss—' my companion pressed me.

'Well, there's that awful reason.'

There were now clearly so many of these for my poor colleague that she was excusable for being vague. 'But—a—which?'

'Why the letter from his old place.'

'You'll show it to the master?'

'I ought to have done so on the instant.'

'Oh no!' said Mrs Grose with decision.

'I'll put it before him', I went on inexorably, 'that I can't undertake to work the question on behalf of a child who has been expelled—'

'For we've never in the least known what!' Mrs Grose declared.

'For wickedness. For what else—when he's so clever and beautiful and perfect? Is he stupid? Is he untidy? Is he infirm? Is he ill-natured? He's exquisite—so it can be only *that*; and that would open up the whole thing. After all,' I said, 'it's their uncle's fault. If he left here such people—!'

'He didn't really in the least know them. The fault's mine.' She had turned quite pale.

'Well, you shan't suffer,' I answered.

'The children shan't!' she emphatically returned.

I was silent a while; we looked at each other. 'Then what am I to tell him?'

'You needn't tell him anything. *I'll* tell him.'

I measured this. 'Do you mean you'll write—?' Remembering she couldn't, I caught myself up. 'How do you communicate?'

'I tell the bailiff. *He* writes.'

'And should you like him to write our story?'

My question had a sarcastic force that I had not fully intended, and it made her after a moment inconsequently break down. The tears were again in her eyes. 'Ah Miss, *you* write!'

'Well—tonight,' I at last returned; and on this we separated.

XVII

I WENT so far, in the evening, as to make a beginning. The weather had changed back, a great wind was abroad, and beneath the lamp, in my room, with Flora at peace beside me, I sat for a long time before a blank sheet of paper and listened to the lash of the rain and the batter of the gusts. Finally I went out, taking a candle; I crossed the passage and listened a minute at Miles's door. What, under my endless obsession, I had been impelled to listen for was some betrayal of his not being at rest, and I presently caught one, but not in the form I had expected. His voice tinkled out. 'I say, you there—come in.' It was gaiety in the gloom!

I went in with my light and found him in bed, very wide awake but very much at his ease. 'Well, what are *you* up to?' he asked with a grace of sociability in which it occurred to me that Mrs Grose, had she been present, might have looked in vain for proof that anything was 'out'.

I stood over him with my candle. 'How did you know I was there?'

'Why of course I heard you. Did you fancy you made no noise? You're like a troop of cavalry!' he beautifully laughed.

'Then you weren't asleep?'

'Not much! I lie awake and think.'

I had put my candle, designedly, a short way off, and then, as he held out his friendly old hand to me, had sat down on the edge of his bed. 'What is it', I asked, 'that you think of?'

'What in the world, my dear, but *you?*'

'Ah the pride I take in your appreciation doesn't insist on that! I had so far rather you slept.'

'Well, I think also, you know, of this queer business of ours.'

I marked the coolness of his firm little hand. 'Of what queer business, Miles?'

'Why the way you bring me up. And all the rest!'

I fairly held my breath a minute, and even from my glimmering taper there was light enough to show how he smiled up at me from his pillow. 'What do you mean by all the rest?'

'Oh you know, you know!'

I could say nothing for a minute, though I felt as I held his hand and our eyes continued to meet that my silence had all the air of admitting his charge and that nothing in the whole world of reality was perhaps at that moment so fabulous as our actual relation. 'Certainly you shall go back to school,' I said, 'if it be that that troubles you. But not to the old place—we must find another, a better. How could I know it did trouble you, this question, when you never told me so, never spoke of it at all?' His clear listening face, framed in its smooth whiteness, made him for the minute as appealing as some wistful patient in a children's hospital; and I would have given, as the resemblance came to me, all I possessed on earth really to be the nurse or the sister of charity who might have helped to cure him. Well, even as it was I perhaps might help! 'Do you know you've never said a word to me about your school—I mean the old one; never mentioned it in any way?'

He seemed to wonder; he smiled with the same loveliness. But he clearly gained time; he waited, he called for guidance. 'Haven't I?' It wasn't for *me* to help him—it was for the thing I had met!

Something in his tone and the expression of his face, as I got this from him, set my heart aching with such a pang as it had never yet known; so unutterably touching was it to see his little brain puzzled and his little resources taxed to play, under the spell laid on him, a part of innocence and consistency. 'No, never—from the hour you came back. You've never mentioned to me one of your masters, one of your comrades, nor the least little thing that ever happened to you at school. Never, little Miles—no never—have you given me an inkling of anything that *may* have happened there. Therefore you can fancy how much I'm in the dark. Until you came out, that way, this morning, you had since the first hour I saw you scarce even made a reference to anything in your previous life. You seemed so perfectly to accept the present.' It was extraordinary how my absolute conviction of his secret precocity—or whatever I might call the poison of an influence that I dared but half-phrase— made him, in spite of the faint breath of his inward trouble, appear as accessible as an older person, forced me to treat him as an intelligent equal. 'I thought you wanted to go on as you are.'

It struck me that at this he just faintly coloured. He gave, at any rate, like a convalescent slightly fatigued, a languid shake of his head. 'I don't—I don't. I want to get away.'

'You're tired of Bly?'

'Oh no, I like Bly.'

'Well then—?'

'Oh *you* know what a boy wants!'

I felt I didn't know so well as Miles, and I took temporary refuge. 'You want to go to your uncle?'

Again, at this, with his sweet ironic face, he made a movement on the pillow. 'Ah you can't get off with that!'

I was silent a little, and it was I now, I think, who changed colour. 'My dear, I don't want to get off!'

'You can't even if you do. You can't, you can't!'—he lay beautifully staring. 'My uncle must come down and you must completely settle things.'

'If we do', I returned with some spirit, 'you may be sure it will be to take you quite away.'

'Well, don't you understand that that's exactly what I'm working for? You'll have to *tell* him—about the way you've let it all drop: you'll have to tell him a tremendous lot!'

The exultation with which he uttered this helped me somehow for the instant to meet him rather more. 'And how much will *you*, Miles, have to tell him? There are things he'll ask you!'

He turned it over. 'Very likely. But what things?'

'The things you've never told me. To make up his mind what to do with you. He can't send you back—'

'I don't want to go back!' he broke in. 'I want a new field.'

He said it with admirable serenity, with positive unimpeachable gaiety; and doubtless it was that very note that most evoked for me the poignancy, the unnatural childish tragedy, of his probable reappearance at the end of three months with all this bravado and still more dishonour. It overwhelmed me now that I should never be able to bear that, and it made me let myself go. I threw myself upon him and in the tenderness of my pity I embraced him. 'Dear little Miles, dear little Miles—!'

My face was close to his, and he let me kiss him, simply taking it with indulgent good humour. 'Well, old lady?'

'Is there nothing—nothing at all that you want to tell me?'

He turned off a little, facing round toward the wall and holding up his hand to look at as one had seen sick children look. 'I've told you—I told you this morning.'

Oh I was sorry for him! 'That you just want me not to worry you?'

He looked round at me now as if in recognition of my understanding him; then ever so gently, 'To let me alone,' he replied.

There was even a strange little dignity in it, something that made me release him, yet, when I had slowly risen, linger beside him. God knows I never wished to harass him, but I felt that merely, at this, to turn my back on him was to abandon or, to put it more truly, lose him. 'I've just begun a letter to your uncle,' I said.

'Well then, finish it!'

I waited a minute. 'What happened before?'

He gazed up at me again. 'Before what?'

'Before you came back. And before you went away.'

For some time he was silent, but he continued to meet my eyes. 'What happened?'

It made me, the sound of the words, in which it seemed to

me I caught for the very first time a small faint quaver of consenting consciousness—it made me drop on my knees beside the bed and seize once more the chance of possessing him. 'Dear little Miles, dear little Miles, if you *knew* how I want to help you! It's only that, it's nothing but that, and I'd rather die than give you a pain or do you a wrong—I'd rather die than hurt a hair of you. Dear little Miles'—oh I brought it out now even if I *should* go too far—'I just want you to help me to save you!' But I knew in a moment after this that I had gone too far. The answer to my appeal was instantaneous, but it came in the form of an extraordinary blast and chill, a gust of frozen air and a shake of the room as great as if, in the wild wind, the casement had crashed in. The boy gave a loud high shriek which, lost in the rest of the shock of sound, might have seemed, indistinctly, though I was so close to him, a note either of jubilation or of terror. I jumped to my feet again and was conscious of darkness. So for a moment we remained, while I stared about me and saw the drawn curtains unstirred and the window still tight. 'Why the candle's out!' I then cried.

'It was I who blew it, dear!' said Miles.

XVIII

THE next day, after lessons, Mrs Grose found a moment to say to me quietly: 'Have you written, Miss?'

'Yes—I've written.' But I didn't add—for the hour—that my letter, sealed and directed, was still in my pocket. There would be time enough to send it before the messenger should go to the village. Meanwhile there had been on the part of my pupils no more brilliant, more exemplary morning. It was exactly as if they had both had at heart to gloss over any recent little friction. They performed the dizziest feats of arithmetic, soaring quite out of *my* feeble range, and perpetrated, in higher spirits than ever, geographical and historical jokes. It was conspicuous of course in Miles in particular that he appeared to wish to show how easily he could let me down. This child, to my memory, really lives in a setting of beauty and misery that no words can translate; there was a distinction all his own in every impulse he revealed; never was a small natural creature, to the uninformed eye all frankness and freedom, a more ingenious, a more extraordinary little gentleman. I had perpetually to guard against the wonder of contemplation into which my initiated view betrayed me; to check the irrelevant gaze and discouraged sigh in which I constantly both attacked and renounced the enigma of what such a little gentleman could have done that deserved a penalty. Say that, by the dark prodigy I knew, the imagination of all evil *had* been opened up to him: all the justice within me ached for the proof that it could ever have flowered into an act.

He had never at any rate been such a little gentleman as when, after our early dinner on this dreadful day, he came round to me and asked if I shouldn't like him for half an hour to play to me. David playing to Saul could never have shown a finer sense of the occasion. It was literally a charming exhibition of tact, of magnanimity, and quite tantamount to his saying outright: 'The true knights we love to read about never push an advantage too far. I know what you mean now: you mean that—to be let alone yourself and not followed up—you'll cease to worry and spy upon me, won't keep me so close to you, will let me go and come. Well, I "come", you see—but I don't go! There'll be plenty of time for that, I do really delight in your society and I only want to show you that I contended for a principle.' It may be imagined whether I resisted this appeal or failed to accompany him again, hand in hand, to the schoolroom. He sat down at the old piano and played as he had never played; and if there are those who think he had better have been kicking a football I can only say that I wholly agree with them. For at the end of a time that under his influence I had quite ceased to measure I started up with a strange sense of having literally slept at my post. It was after luncheon, and by the schoolroom fire, and yet I hadn't really in the least slept; I had only done something much worse—I had forgotten. Where all this time was Flora? When I put the question to Miles he played on a minute before answering, and then could only say: 'Why, my dear, how do *I* know?'—breaking moreover into a happy laugh which immediately after, as if it were a vocal accompaniment, he prolonged into incoherent extravagant song.

I went straight to my room, but his sister was not there; then, before going downstairs, I looked into several others. As she was nowhere about she would surely be with Mrs Grose, whom in the comfort of that theory I accordingly proceeded in quest of. I found her where I had found her the evening before, but she met my quick challenge with blank scared ignorance. She had only supposed that, after the repast, I had carried off both the children; as to which she was quite in her right, for it was the very first time I had allowed the little girl out of my sight without some special provision. Of course now indeed she might be with the maids, so that the immediate thing was to look for her without an air of alarm. This we promptly arranged between us; but when, ten minutes later and in pursuance of our arrangement, we met in the hall, it was only to report on either side that after guarded enquiries we had altogether failed to trace her. For a minute there, apart from observation, we exchanged mute alarms, and I could feel with what high interest my friend returned me all those I had from the first given her.

'She'll be above,' she presently said—'in one of the rooms you haven't searched.'

'No; she's at a distance.' I had made up my mind. 'She has gone out.'

Mrs Grose stared. 'Without a hat?'

I naturally also looked volumes. 'Isn't that woman always without one?'

'She's with *her*?'

'She's with *her!*' I declared. 'We must find them.'

My hand was on my friend's arm, but she failed for the moment, confronted with such an account of the matter, to respond to my pressure. She communed, on the contrary, where she stood, with her uneasiness. 'And where's Master Miles?'

'Oh *he*'s with Quint. They'll be in the schoolroom.'

'Lord, Miss!' My view, I was myself aware—and therefore I suppose my tone—had never yet reached so calm an assurance.

'The trick's played,' I went on; 'They've successfully worked their plan. He found the most divine little way to keep me quiet while she went off.'

' "Divine"?' Mrs Grose bewilderedly echoed.

'Infernal then!' I almost cheerfully rejoined. 'He has provided for himself as well. But come!'

She had helplessly gloomed at the upper regions. 'You leave him—?'

'So long with Quint? Yes—I don't mind that now.'

She always ended at these moments by getting possession of my hand, and in this manner she could at present still stay me. But after gasping an instant at my sudden resignation, 'Because of your letter?' she eagerly brought out.

I quickly, by way of answer, felt for my letter, drew it forth, held it up, and then, freeing myself, went and laid it on the great hall-table. 'Luke will take it,' I said as I came back. I reached the house-door and opened it; I was already on the steps.

My companion still demurred: the storm of the night and the early morning had dropped, but the afternoon was damp and grey. I came down to the drive while she stood in the doorway. 'You go with nothing on?'

'What do I care when the child has nothing? I can't wait to dress,' I cried, 'and if you must do so I leave you. Try meanwhile yourself upstairs.'

'With *them?*' Oh on this the poor woman promptly joined me!

XIX

WE went straight to the lake, as it was called at Bly, and I dare say rightly called, though it may have been a sheet of water less remarkable than my untravelled eyes supposed it. My aquaintance with sheets of water was small, and the pool of Bly, at all events on the few occasions of my consenting, under the protection of my pupils, to affront its surface in the old flat-bottomed boat moored there for our use, had impressed me both with its extent and its agitation. The usual place of embarkation was half a mile from the house, but I had an intimate conviction that, wherever Flora might be, she was not near home. She had not given me the slip for any small adventure, and, since the day of the very great one that I had shared with her by the pond, I had been aware, in our walks, of the quarter to which she most inclined. This was why I had now given to Mrs Grose's steps so marked a direction—a direction making her, when she perceived it, oppose a resistance that showed me she was freshly mystified. 'You're going to the water, Miss?—you think she's *in*—?'

'She may be, though the depth is, I believe, nowhere very great. But what I judge most likely is that she's on the spot from which, the other day, we saw together what I told you.'

'When she pretended not to see—?'

'With that astounding self-possession! I've always been sure she wanted to go back alone. And now her brother has managed it for her.'

Mrs Grose still stood where she had stopped. 'You suppose they really *talk* of them?'

I could meet this with an assurance! 'They say things that, if we heard them, would simply appal us.'

'And if she *is* there—?'

'Yes?'

'Then Miss Jessel is?'

'Beyond a doubt. You shall see.'

'Oh thank you!' my friend cried, planted so firm that, taking it in, I went straight on without her. By the time I reached the pool, however, she was close behind me, and I knew that, whatever, to her apprehension, might befall me, the exposure of sticking to me struck her as her least danger. She exhaled a moan of relief as we at last came in sight of the greater part of the water without a sight of the child. There was no trace of Flora on that nearer side of the bank where my observation of her had been most startling, and none on the opposite edge, where, save for a margin of some twenty yards, a thick copse came down to the pond. This expanse, oblong in shape, was so narrow compared to its length that, with its ends out of view, it might have been taken for a scant river. We looked at the empty stretch, and then I felt the suggestion in my friend's eyes. I knew what she meant and I replied with a negative headshake.

'No, no; wait! She has taken the boat.'

My companion stared at the vacant mooring-place and then again across the lake. 'Then where is it?'

'Our not seeing it is the strongest of proofs. She has used it to go over, and then has managed to hide it.'

'All alone—that child?'

'She's not alone, and at such times she's not a child: she's an old, old woman.' I scanned all the visible shore while Mrs Grose took again, into the queer element I offered her, one of her plunges of submission; then I pointed out that the boat might perfectly be in a small refuge formed by one of the recesses of the pool, an indentation masked, for the hither side, by a projection of the bank and by a clump of trees growing close to the water.

'But if the boat's there, where on earth's *she?*' my colleague anxiously asked.

'That's exactly what we must learn.' And I started to walk further.

'By going all the way round?'

'Certainly, far as it is. It will take us but ten minutes, yet it's far enough to have made the child prefer not to walk. She went straight over.'

'Laws!' cried my friend again: the chain of my logic was ever too strong for her. It dragged her at my heels even now, and when we had got halfway round—a devious tiresome process, on ground much broken and by a path choked with overgrowth—I paused to give her breath. I sustained her with a grateful arm, assuring her that she might hugely help me; and this started us afresh, so that in the course of but few minutes more we reached a point from which we found the boat to be where I had supposed it. It had been intentionally left as much as possible out of sight and was tied to one of the stakes of a fence that came, just there, down to the brink and that had been an assistance to disembarking. I recognised, as I looked at the pair of short thick oars, quite safely drawn up, the prodigious character of the feat for a little girl; but I had by this time lived too long among wonders and had panted to too many livelier measures. There was a gate in the fence, through which we passed, and that brought us after a trifling interval more into the open. Then 'There she is!' we both exclaimed at once.

Flora, a short way off, stood before us on the grass and smiled as if her performance had now become complete. The next thing she did, however, was to stoop straight down and pluck—quite as if it were all she was there for—a big ugly spray of withered fern. I at once felt sure she had just come out of the copse. She waited for us, not herself taking a step, and I was conscious of the rare solemnity with which we presently approached her. She smiled and smiled, and we met; but it was all done in a silence by this time flagrantly ominous. Mrs Grose was the first to break the spell: she threw herself on her knees and, drawing the child to her breast, clasped in a long embrace the little tender yielding body. While this dumb convulsion lasted I could only watch it—which I did the more intently when I saw Flora's face peep at me over our companion's shoulder. It was serious now—the flicker had left it; but it strengthened the pang with which I at that moment envied Mrs Grose the simplicity of *her* relation. Still, all this while, nothing more passed between us save that Flora had let her foolish fern again drop to the ground. What she and I had virtually said to each other was that pretexts were useless now. When Mrs Grose finally got up she kept the child's hand, so that the two were still before me; and the singular reticence of our communion was even more marked in the frank look she addressed me. 'I'll be hanged', it said, 'if *I'll* speak!'

It was Flora who, gazing all over me in candid wonder, was the first. She was struck with our bareheaded aspect. 'Why where are your things?'

'Where yours are, my dear!' I promptly returned.

She had already got back her gaiety and appeared to take this as an answer quite sufficient. 'And where's Miles?' she went on.

There was something in the small valour of it that quite finished me: these three words from her were in a flash like the glitter of a drawn blade the jostle of the cup that my hand for weeks and weeks had held high and full to the brim and that now, even before speaking, I felt overflow in a deluge. 'I'll tell you if you'll tell *me*—' I heard myself say, then heard the tremor in which it broke.

'Well, what?'

Mrs Grose's suspense blazed at me, but it was too late

now, and I brought the thing out handsomely. 'Where, my pet, is Miss Jessel?'

XX

JUST as in the churchyard with Miles, the whole thing was upon us. Much as I had made of the fact that this name had never once, between us, been sounded, the quick smitten glare with which the child's face now received it fairly likened my breach of the silence to the smash of a pane of glass. It added to the interposing cry, as if to stay the blow, that Mrs Grose at the same instant uttered over my violence—the shriek of a creature scared, or rather wounded, which, in turn, within a few seconds, was completed by a gasp of my own. I seized my colleague's arm. 'She's there, she's there!'

Miss Jessel stood before us on the opposite bank exactly as she had stood the other time, and I remember, strangely, as the first feeling now produced in me, my thrill of joy at having brought on a proof. She was there, so I was justified; she was there, so I was neither cruel nor mad. She was there for poor scared Mrs Grose, but she was there most for Flora; and no moment of my monstrous time was perhaps so extraordinary as that in which I consciously threw out to her—with the sense that, pale and ravenous demon as she was, she would catch and understand it—an inarticulate message of gratitude. She rose erect on the spot my friend and I had lately quitted, and there wasn't in all the long reach of her desire an inch of her evil that fell short. This first vividness of vision and emotion were things of a few seconds, during which Mrs Grose's dazed blink across to where I pointed struck me as showing that she too at last saw, just as it carried by own eyes precipitately to the child. The revelation then of the manner in which Flora was affected startled me in truth far more than it would have done to find her also merely agitated, for direct dismay was of course not what I had expected. Prepared and on her guard as our pursuit had actually made her, she would repress every betrayal; and I was therefore at once shaken by my first glimpse of the particular one for which I had not allowed. To see her, without a convulsion of her small pink face, not even feign to glance in the direction of the prodigy I announced, but only, instead of that, turn at *me* an expression of hard still gravity, an expression absolutely new and unprecedented and that appeared to read and accuse and judge me—this was a stroke that somehow converted the little girl herself into a figure portentous. I gaped at her coolness even though my certitude of her thoroughly seeing was never greater than at that instant, and then, in the immediate need to defend myself, I called her passionately to witness. 'She's there, you little unhappy thing—there, there, *there*, and you know it as well as you know me!' I had said shortly before to Mrs Grose that she was not at these times a child, but an old, old woman, and my description of her couldn't have been more strikingly confirmed than in the way in which, for all notice of this, she simply showed me, without an expressional concession or admission, a countenance of deeper and deeper, of indeed suddenly quite fixed reprobation. I was by this time—if I can put the whole thing at all together—more appalled at what I may properly call her manner than at anything else, though it was quite simultaneously that I became aware of having Mrs Grose also, and very formidably, to reckon with. My elder companion, the next moment, at any rate, blotted out everything but her own flushed face and her loud shocked protest, a burst of high disapproval. 'What a dreadful turn, to be sure, Miss! Where on earth do you see anything?'

I could only grasp her more quickly yet, for even while she spoke the hideous plain presence stood undimmed and undaunted. It had already lasted a minute, and it lasted while I continued, seizing my colleague, quite thrusting her at it and presenting her to it, to insist with my pointing hand. 'You don't see her exactly as *we* see?—you mean to say you don't now—*now*? She's as big as a blazing fire! Only look, dearest woman, *look*—!' She looked, just as I did, and gave me, with her deep groan of negation, repulsion, compassion—the mixture with her pity of her relief at her exemption—a sense, touching to me even then, that she would have backed me up if she had been able. I might well have needed that, for with this hard blow of the proof that her eyes were hopelessly sealed I felt my own situation horribly crumble, I felt—I *saw*—my livid predecessor press, from her position, on my defeat, and I took the measure, more than all, of what I should have from this instant to deal with in the astounding little attitude of Flora. Into this attitude Mrs Grose immediately and violently entered, breaking, even while there pierced through my sense of ruin a prodigious private triumph, into breathless reassurance.

'She isn't there, little lady, and nobody's there—and you never see nothing, my sweet! How can poor Miss Jessel—when poor Miss Jessel's dead and buried? *We* know, don't we, love?'—and she appealed, blundering in, to the child. 'It's all a mere mistake and a worry and a joke—and we'll go home as fast as we can!'

Our companion, on this, had responded with a strange quick primness of propriety, and they were again, with Mrs Grose on her feet, united, as it were, in shocked opposition to me. Flora continued to fix me with her small mask of disaffection, and even at that minute I prayed God to forgive me for seeming to see that, as she stood there holding tight to our friend's dress, her incomparable childish beauty had suddenly failed, had quite vanished. I've said it already—she was literally, she was hideously hard; she had turned common and almost ugly. 'I don't know what you mean. I see nobody. I see nothing. I never *have*. I think you're cruel. I don't like you!' Then, after this deliverance, which might have been that of a vulgarly pert little girl in the street, she hugged Mrs Grose more closely and buried in her skirts the dreadful little face. In this position she launched an almost furious wail. 'Take me away, take me away—oh take me away from *her!*'

'From *me?*' I panted.

'From you—from you!' she cried.

Even Mrs Grose looked across at me dismayed; while I had nothing to do but communicate again with the figure that, on the opposite bank, without a movement, as rigidly still as if catching, beyond the interval, our voices, was as vividly there for my disaster as it was not there for my service. The wretched child had spoken exactly as if she had got from some outside source each of her stabbing little words, and I could therefore, in the full despair of all I had to accept, but sadly shake my head at her. 'If I had ever doubted all my doubt would at present have gone. I've been living with the miserable truth, and now it has only too much closed round me. Of course I've lost you: I've interfered, and you've seen, under *her* dictation'—with which I faced, over the pool again, our infernal witness—'the easy and perfect way to meet it. I've done my best, but I've lost you. Goodbye.' For Mrs Grose I had an imperative, an almost frantic 'Go, go!' before which, in infinite distress, but mutely possessed of the little girl and clearly convinced, in spite of her blindness, that something awful had occurred and some collapse engulfed us, she retreated, by the way we had come, as fast as she could move.

Of what first happened when I was left alone I had no subsequent memory. I only knew that at the end of, I suppose, a quarter of an hour, an odorous dampness and roughness, chilling and piercing my trouble, had made me understand that I must have thrown myself, on my face, to the ground and given way to a wildness of grief. I must have lain there long and cried and wailed, for when I raised my head the day was almost done. I got up and looked a moment, through the twilight, at the grey pool and its blank haunted edge, and then I took, back to the house, my dreary and difficult course. When I reached the gate in the fence the boat, to my surprise, was gone, so that I had a fresh reflexion to make on Flora's extraordinary command of the situation. She passed that night, by the most tacit and, I should add, were not the word so grotesque a false note, the happiest of arrangements, with Mrs Grose. I saw neither of them on my return, but on the other hand I saw, as by an ambiguous compensation, a great deal of Miles. I saw—I can use no other phrase—so much of him that it fairly measured more than it had ever measured. No evening I had passed at Bly was to have had the portentous quality of this one; in spite of which—and in spite also of the deeper depths of consternation that had opened beneath my feet—there was literally, in the ebbing actual, an extraordinarily sweet sadness. On reaching the house I had never so much as looked for the boy; I had simply gone straight to my room to change what I was wearing and to take in, at a glance, much material testimony to Flora's rupture. Her little belongings had all been removed. When later, by the schoolroom fire, I was served with tea by the usual maid, I indulged, on the article of my other pupil, in no enquiry whatever. He had his freedom now—he might have it to the end! Well, he did have it; and it consisted—in part at least—of his coming in at about eight o'clock and sitting down with me in silence. On the removal of the tea-things I had blown out the candles and drawn my chair closer: I was conscious of a mortal coldness and felt as if I should never again be warm. So when he appeared I was sitting in the glow with my thoughts. He paused a moment by the door as if to look at me; then—as if to share them—came to the other side of the hearth and sank into a chair. We sat there in absolute stillness; yet he wanted, I felt, to be with me.

XXI

BEFORE a new day, in my room, had fully broken, my eyes opened to Mrs Grose, who had come to my bedside with worse news. Flora was so markedly feverish that an illness was perhaps at hand; she had passed a night of extreme unrest, a night agitated above all by fears that had for their subject not in the least her former but wholly her present governess. It was not against the possible re-entrance of Miss Jessel on the scene that she protested—it was conspicuously and passionately against mine. I was at once on my feet, and with an immense deal to ask; the more that my friend had discernibly now girded her loins to meet me afresh. This I felt as soon as I had put to her the question of her sense of the child's sincerity as against my own. 'She persists in denying to you that she saw, or has ever seen, anything?'

My visitor's trouble truly was great. 'Ah Miss, it isn't a matter on which I can push her! Yet it isn't either, I must say, as if I much needed to. It has made her, every inch of her, quite old.'

'Oh I see her perfectly from here. She resents, for all the world like some high little personage, the imputation on her truthfulness and, as it were, her respectability. "Miss Jessel indeed—*she!*" Ah she's "respectable", the chit! The impression she gave me there yesterday was, I assure you, the very strangest of all: it was quite beyond any of the others. I *did* put my foot in it! She'll never speak to me again.'

Hideous and obscure as it all was, it held Mrs Grose briefly silent; then she granted my point with a frankness which, I made sure, had more behind it. 'I think indeed, Miss, she never will. She do have a grand manner about it!'

'And that manner'—I summed it up—'is practically what's the matter with her now.'

Oh that manner, I could see in my visitor's face, and not a little else besides! 'She asks me every three minutes if I think you're coming in.'

'I see—I see.' I too, on my side, had so much more than worked it out. 'Has she said to you since yesterday—except to repudiate her familiarity with anything so dreadful—a single other word about Miss Jessel?'

'Not one, Miss. And of course, you know,' my friend added, 'I took it from her by the lake that just then and there at least there *was* nobody.'

'Rather! And naturally you take it from her still.'

'I don't contradict her. What else can I do?'

'Nothing in the world! You've the cleverest little person to deal with. They've made them—their two friends, I mean—still cleverer even than nature did; for it was wondrous material to play on! Flora has now her grievance, and she'll work it to the end.'

'Yes, Miss; but to *what* end?'

'Why that of dealing with me to her uncle. She'll make me out to him the lowest creature—!'

I winced at the fair show of the scene in Mrs Grose's face; she looked for a minute as if she sharply saw them together. 'And him who thinks so well of you!'

'He has an odd way—it comes over me now,' I laughed, '—of proving it! But that doesn't matter. What Flora wants of course is to get rid of me.'

My companion bravely concurred. 'Never again to so much as look at you.'

'So that what you've come to me now for', I asked, 'is to speed me on my way?' Before she had time to reply, however, I had her in check. 'I've a better idea—the result of my reflexions. My going *would* seem the right thing, and on Sunday I was terribly near it. Yet that won't do. It's *you* who must go. You must take Flora.'

My visitor, at this, did speculate. 'But where in the world—?'

'Away from here. Away from *them*. Away, even most of all, now, from me. Straight to her uncle.'

'Only to tell on you——?'

'No, not "only"! To leave me, in addition, with my remedy.'

She was still vague. 'And what *is* your remedy?'

'Your loyalty, to begin with. And then Miles's.'

She looked at me hard. 'Do you think he——?'

'Won't, if he has the chance, turn on me? Yes, I venture still to think it. At all events I want to try. Get off with his sister as soon as possible and leave me with him alone.' I was amazed, myself, at the spirit I had still in reserve, and therefore perhaps a trifle the more disconcerted at the way in which, in spite of this fine example of it, she hesitated. 'There's one thing, of course,' I went on: 'they mustn't, before she goes, see each other for three seconds.' Then it came over me that, in spite of Flora's presumable sequestration from the instant of her return from the pool, it might already be too late. 'Do you mean', I anxiously asked, 'that they *have* met?'

At this she quite flushed. 'Ah, Miss, I'm not such a fool as that! If I've been obliged to leave her three or four times, it has been each time with one of the maids, and at present, though she's alone, she's locked in safe. And yet—and yet!' There were too many things.

'And yet what?'

'Well, are you so sure of the litte gentleman?'

'I'm not sure of anything but *you*. But I have, since last evening, a new hope. I think he wants to give me an opening. I do believe that—poor little exquisite wretch!— he wants to speak. Last evening, in the firelight and the silence, he sat with me for two hours as if it were just coming.'

Mrs Grose looked hard through the window at the grey gathering day. 'And did it come?'

'No, though I waited and waited I confess it didn't, and it

was without a breach of the silence, or so much as a faint allusion to his sister's condition and absence, that we at last kissed for goodnight. All the same,' I continued, 'I can't, if her uncle sees her, consent to his seeing her brother without my having given the boy—and most of all because things have got so bad—a little more time.'

My friend appeared on this ground more reluctant than I could quite understand. 'What do you mean by more time?'

'Well, a day or two—really to bring it out. He'll then be on *my* side—of which you see the importance. If nothing comes I shall only fail, and you at the worst have helped me by doing on your arrival in town whatever you may have found possible.' So I put it before her, but she continued for a little so lost in other reasons that I came again to her aid. 'Unless indeed', I wound up, 'you really want *not* to go.'

I could see it, in her face, at last clear itself: she put out her hand to me as a pledge. 'I'll go—I'll go. I'll go this morning.'

I wanted to be very just. 'If you *should* wish still to wait I'd engage she shouldn't see me.'

'No, no: it's the place itself. She must leave it.' She held me a moment with heavy eyes, then brought out the rest. 'Your idea's the right one. I myself, Miss—'

'Well?'

'I can't stay.'

The look she gave me with it made me jump at possibilities. 'You mean that, since yesterday, you *have* seen—?'

She shook her head with dignity. 'I've *heard*—!'

'Heard?'

'From that child—horrors! There!' she sighed with tragic relief. 'On my honour, Miss, she says things—!' But at this evocation she broke down; she dropped with a sudden cry upon my sofa and, as I had seen her do before, gave way to all the anguish of it.

It was quite in another manner that I for my part let myself go. 'Oh thank God!'

She sprang up again at this, drying her eyes with a groan. ' "Thank God"?'

'It so justifies me!'

'It does that, Miss!'

I couldn't have desired more emphasis, but I just waited. 'She's so horrible?'

I saw my colleague scarce knew how to put it. 'Really shocking.'

'And about me?'

'About you, Miss—since you must have it. It's beyond everything, for a young lady; and I can't think wherever she must have picked up—'

'The appalling language she applies to me? I can then!' I broke in with a laugh that was doubtless significant enough.

It only in truth left my friend still more grave. 'Well, perhaps I ought to also—since I've heard some of it before! Yet I can't bear it,' the poor woman went on while with the same movement she glanced, on my dressing-table, at the face of my watch. 'But I must go back.'

I kept her, however. 'Ah if you can't bear it—!'

'How can I stop with her, you mean? Why just *for* that: to get her away. Far from this,' she pursued, 'far from *them*—'

'She may be different? she may be free?' I seized her almost with joy. 'Then in spite of yesterday you *believe*—'

'In such doings?' Her simple description of them required, in the light of her expression, to be carried no further, and she gave me the whole thing as she had never done. 'I believe.'

Yes, it was a joy, and we were still shoulder to shoulder: if I might continue sure of that I should care but little what else happened. My support in the presence of disaster would be the same as it had been in my early need of confidence, and if my friend would answer for my honesty I would answer for all the rest. On the point of taking leave of her, none the less, I was to some extent embarrassed. 'There's one thing of course—it occurs to me—to remember. My letter giving the alarm will have reached town before you.'

I now felt still more how she had been beating about the bush and how weary at last it had made her. 'Your letter won't have got there. Your letter never went.'

'What then became of it?'

'Goodness knows! Master Miles—'

'Do you mean *he* took it?' I gasped.

She hung fire, but she overcame her reluctance. 'I mean that I saw yesterday, when I came back with Miss Flora, that it wasn't where you had put it. Later in the evening I had the chance to question Luke, and he declared that he had neither noticed nor touched it.' We could only exchange, on this, one of our deeper mutual soundings, and it was Mrs Grose who first brought up the plumb with an almost elate 'You see!'

'Yes, I see that if Miles took it instead he probably will have read it and destroyed it.'

'And don't you see anything else?'

I faced her a moment with a sad smile. 'It strikes me that by this time your eyes are open even wider than mine.'

They proved to be so indeed, but she could still almost blush to show it. 'I make out now what he must have done at school.' And she gave, in her simple sharpness, an almost droll disillusioned nod. 'He stole!'

I turned it over—I tried to be more judicial. 'Well—perhaps.'

She looked as if she found me unexpectedly calm. 'He stole *letters!*'

She couldn't know my reasons for a calmness after all pretty shallow; so I showed them off as I might. 'I hope then it was to more purpose than in this case! The note, at all events, that I put on the table yesterday', I pursued, 'will have given him so scant an advantage—for it contained only the bare demand for an interview—that he's already much ashamed of having gone so far for so little, and that what he had on his mind last evening was precisely the need of confession.' I seemed to myself for the instant to have mastered it, to see it all. 'Leave us, leave us'— I was already, at the door, hurrying her off. 'I'll get it out of him. He'll meet me. He'll confess. If he confesses he's saved. And if he's saved—'

'Then *you* are?' The dear woman kissed me on this, and I took her farewell. 'I'll save you without him!' she cried as she went.

XXII

YET it was when she had got off—and I missed her on the spot—that the great pinch really came. If I had counted on what it would give me to find myself alone with Miles I quickly recognised that it would give me at least a measure. No hour of my stay in fact was so assailed with apprehensions as that of my coming down to learn that the carriage containing Mrs Grose and my younger pupil had already rolled out of the gates. Now I *was*, I said to myself, face to face with the elements, and for much of the rest of the day, while I fought my weakness, I could consider that I had been supremely rash. It was a tighter place still than I had yet turned round in; all the more that for the first time, I could see in the aspect of others a confused reflexion of the crisis. What had happened naturally caused them all to stare; there was too little of the explained, throw out whatever we might, in the suddenness of my colleague's act. The maids and the men looked blank; the effect of which on my nerves was an aggravation until I saw the necessity of making it a positive aid. It was in short by just clutching the helm that I avoided total wreck; and I dare say that, to bear up at all, I became that morning very grand and very dry. I welcomed the consciousness that I was charged with much to do, and I caused it to be known as well that, left thus to myself, I was quite remarkably firm. I wandered with that manner, for the next hour or two, all over the place and looked, I have no doubt, as if I were ready for any onset. So, for the benefit of whom it might concern, I paraded with a sick heart.

The person it appeared to concern proved to be, till dinner, little Miles himself. My perambulations had given me meanwhile no glimpse of him, but they had tended to make more public the change taking place in our relation as a consequence of his having at the piano, the day before, kept me, in Flora's interest, so beguiled and befooled. The stamp of publicity had of course been fully given by her confinement and departure, and the change itself was now ushered in by our non-observance of the regular custom of the schoolroom. He had already disappeared when, on my way down, I pushed open his door, and I learned below that he had breakfasted—in the presence of a couple of the maids—with Mrs Grose and his sister. He had then gone out, as he said, for a stroll; than which nothing, I reflected, could better have expressed his frank view of the abrupt transformation of my office. What he would now permit this office to consist of was yet to be settled: there was at the least a queer relief—I mean for myself in especial—in the renouncement of one pretension. If so much had sprung to the surface I scarce put it too strongly in saying that what had perhaps sprung highest was the absurdity of our prolonging the fiction that I had anything more to teach him. It sufficiently stuck out that, by tacit little tricks in which even more than myself he carried out the care for my dignity, I had had to appeal to him to let me off straining to meet him on the ground of his true capacity. He had at any rate his freedom now; I was never to touch it again: as I had amply shown, moreover, when, on his joining me in the schoolroom the previous night, I uttered, in reference to the interval just concluded, neither challenge nor hint. I had too much, from this moment, my other ideas. Yet when he at last arrived the difficulty of applying them, the accumulations of my problem, were brought straight home to me by the beautiful little presence on which what had occurred had as yet, for the eye, dropped neither stain nor shadow.

To mark, for the house, the high state I cultivated I decreed that my meals with the boy should be served, as we called it, downstairs; so that I had been awaiting him in the ponderous pomp of the room outside the window of which I had had from Mrs Grose, that first scared Sunday, my flash of something it would scarce have done to call light. Here at present I felt afresh—for I had felt it again and again—how my equilibrium depended on the success of my rigid will, the will to shut my eyes as tight as possible to the truth that what I had to deal with was, revoltingly, against nature. I could only get on at all by taking 'nature' into my confidence and my account, by treating my monstrous ordeal as a push in a direction unusual, of course, and unpleasant, but demanding after all, for a fair front, only another turn of the screw of ordinary human virtue. No attempt, none the less, could well require more tact than just this attempt to supply, one's self, *all* the nature. How could I put even a little of that article into a suppression of reference to what had occurred? How on the other hand could I make a reference without a new plunge into the hideous obscure? Well, a sort of answer, after a time, had come to me, and it was so far confirmed as that I was met, incontestably, by the quickened vision of what was rare in my little companion. It was indeed as if he had found even now—as he had so often found at lessons—still some other delicate way to ease me off. Wasn't there light in the fact which, as we shared our solitude, broke out with a specious glitter it had never yet quite worn?—the fact that (opportunity aiding, precious opportunity which had now come) it would be preposterous, with a child so endowed, to forego the help one might wrest from absolute intelligence? What had his intelligence been given him for but to save him? Mightn't one, to reach his mind, risk the stretch of a stiff arm across his character? It was as if, when we were face to face in the dining-room, he had literally shown me the way. The roast mutton was on the table and I had dispensed with attendance. Miles, before he sat down, stood a moment with his hands in his pockets and looked at the joint, on which he seemed on the point of passing some humorous judgement. But what he presently produced was: 'I say, my dear, is she really very awfully ill?'

'Little Flora? Not so bad but that she'll presently be better. London will set her up. Bly had ceased to agree with her. Come here and take your mutton.'

He alertly obeyed me, carried the plate carefully to his seat and, when he was established, went on. 'Did Bly disagree with her so terribly all at once?'

'Not so suddenly as you might think. One had seen it coming on.'

'Then why didn't you get her off before?'

'Before what?'

'Before she became too ill to travel.'

I found myself prompt. 'She's *not* too ill to travel; she only might have become so if she had stayed. This was just the moment to seize. The journey will dissipate the influence'—oh I was grand!—'and carry it off.'

'I see, I see'—Miles, for that matter, was grand too. He settled to his repast with the charming little 'table manner' that, from the day of his arrival, had relieved me of all grossness of admonition. Whatever he had been expelled from school for, it wasn't for ugly feeding. He was irreproachable, as always, today; but was unmistakeably more conscious. He was discernibly trying to take for granted more things than he found, without assistance, quite easy; and he dropped into peaceful silence while he felt his situation. Our meal was of the briefest—mine a vain pretence, and I had the things immediately removed. While this was done Miles stood again with his hands in his little pockets and his back to me—stood and looked out of the wide window through which, that other day, I had seen what pulled me up. We continued silent while the maid was with us—as silent, it whimsically occurred to me, as some young couple who, on their wedding-journey, at the inn, feel shy in the presence of the waiter. He turned round only when the waiter had left us. 'Well—so we're alone!'

XXIII

'Oh more or less.' I imagine my smile was pale. 'Not absolutely. We shouldn't like that!' I went on.

'No—I suppose we shouldn't. Of course we've the others.'

'We've the others—we've indeed the others,' I concurred.

'Yet even though we have them,' he returned, still with his hands in his pockets and planted there in front of me, 'they don't much count, do they?'

I made the best of it, but I felt wan. 'It depends on what you call "much"!'

'Yes'—with all accommodation—'everything depends!' On this, however, he faced to the window again and presently reached it with his vague restless cogitating step. He remained there a while with his forehead against the glass, in contemplation of the stupid shrubs I knew and the dull things of November. I had always my hypocrisy of 'work', behind which I now gained the sofa. Steadying myself with it there as I had repeatedly done at those moments of torment that I have described as the moments of my knowing the children to be given to something from which I was barred, I sufficiently obeyed my habit of being prepared for the worst. But an extraordinary impression dropped on me as I extracted a meaning from the boy's embarrassed back—none other than the impression that I was not barred now. The inference grew in a few minutes to sharp intensity and seemed bound up with the direct perception that it was positively *he* who was. The frames and squares of the great window were a kind of image, for him, of a kind of failure. I felt that I saw him, in any case, shut in or shut out. He was admirable but not comfortable: I took it in with a throb of hope. Wasn't he looking through the haunted pane for something he couldn't see?—and wasn't it the first time in the whole business that he had known such a lapse? The first, the very first: I found it a splendid portent. It made him anxious, though he watched himself; he had been anxious all day and, even while in his usual sweet little manner he sat at table, had needed all his small strange genius to give it a gloss. When he at last turned round to meet me it was almost as if this genius had succumbed. 'Well, I think I'm glad Bly agrees with *me!*'

'You'd certainly seem to have seen, these twenty-four hours, a good deal more of it than for some time before. I hope', I went on bravely, 'that you've been enjoying yourself.'

'Oh yes, I've been ever so far; all round about—miles and miles away. I've never been so free.'

He had really a manner of his own, and I could only try to keep up with him. 'Well, do you like it?'

He stood there smiling; then at last he put into two words—'Do *you?*'—more discrimination than I had ever heard two words contain. Before I had time to deal with that, however, he continued as if with the sense that this was an impertinence to be softened. 'Nothing could be more charming than the way you take it, for of course if we're alone together now it's you that are alone most. But I hope', he threw in, 'you don't particularly mind!'

'Having to do with you?' I asked. 'My dear child, how can I help minding? Though I've renounced all claim to your company—you're so beyond me—I at least greatly enjoy it. What else should I stay on for?'

He looked at me more directly, and the expression of his face, graver now, struck me as the most beautiful I had ever found in it. 'You stay on just for *that*?'

'Certainly. I stay on as your friend and from the tremendous interest I take in you till something can be done for you that may be more worth your while. That needn't surprise you.' My voice trembled so that I felt it impossible to suppress the shake. 'Don't you remember how I told you, when I came and sat on your bed the night of the storm, that there was nothing in the world I wouldn't do for you?'

'Yes, yes!' He, on his side, more and more visibly nervous, had a tone to master; but he was so much more successful than I that, laughing out through his gravity, he could pretend we were pleasantly jesting. 'Only that, I think, was to get me to do something for *you!*'

'It was partly to get you to do something,' I conceded. 'But, you know, you didn't do it.'

'Oh yes,' he said with the brightest superficial eagerness, 'you wanted me to tell you something.'

'That's it. Out, straight out. What you have on your mind, you know.'

'Ah then is *that* what you've stayed over for?'

He spoke with a gaiety through which I could still catch the finest little quiver of resentful passion; but I can't begin to express the effect upon me of an implication of surrender even so faint. It was as if what I had yearned for had come at last only to astonish me. 'Well, yes—I may as well make a clean breast of it. It was precisely for that.'

He waited so long that I supposed it for the purpose of repudiating the assumption on which my action had been founded; but what he finally said was: 'Do you mean now—here?'

'There couldn't be a better place or time.' He looked

round him uneasily, and I had the rare—oh the queer!—
impression of the very first symptom I had seen in him of
the approach of immediate fear. It was as if he were
suddenly afraid of me—which struck me indeed as perhaps
the best thing to make him. Yet in the very pang of the
effort I felt it vain to try sternness, and I heard myself the
next instant so gentle as to be almost grotesque. 'You want
so to go out again?'

'Awfully!' He smiled at me heroically, and the touching
little bravery of it was enhanced by his actually flushing
with pain. He had picked up his hat, which he had brought
in, and stood twirling it in a way that gave me, even as I was
just nearly reaching port, a perverse horror of what I was
doing. To do it in *any* way was an act of violence, for what
did it consist of but the obtrusion of the idea of grossness
and guilt on a small helpless creature who had been for me a
revelation of the possibilities of beautiful intercourse?
Wasn't it base to create for a being so exquisite a mere alien
awkwardness? I suppose I now read into our situation a
clearness it couldn't have had at the time, for I seem to see
our poor eyes already lighted with some spark of a prevision
of the anguish that was to come. So we circled about with
terrors and scruples, fighters not daring to close. But it was
for each other we feared! That kept us a little longer
suspended and unbruised. 'I'll tell you everything,' Miles
said—'I mean I'll tell you anything you like. You'll stay on
with me, and we shall both be all right, and I *will* tell you—
I *will*. But not now.'

'Why not now?'

My insistence turned him from me and kept him once
more at his window in a silence during which, between us,
you might have heard a pin drop. Then he was before me
again with the air of a person for whom, outside, someone
who had frankly to be reckoned with was waiting. 'I have to
see Luke.'

I had not yet reduced him to quite so vulgar a lie, and I

felt proportionately ashamed. But, horrible as it was, his lies made up my truth. I achieved thoughtfully a few loops of my knitting. 'Well then go to Luke, and I'll wait for what you promise. Only in return for that satisfy, before you leave me, one very much smaller request.'

He looked as if he felt he had succeeded enough to be able still a little to bargain. 'Very much smaller—?'

'Yes, a mere fraction of the whole. Tell me'—oh my work preoccupied me, and I was off-hand!—'If, yesterday afternoon, from the table in the hall, you took, you know, my letter.'

XXIV

MY grasp of how he received this suffered for a minute from something that I can describe only as a fierce split of my attention—a stroke that at first, as I sprang staight up, reduced me to the mere blind movement of getting hold of him, drawing him close and, while I just fell for support against the nearest piece of furniture, instinctively keeping him with his back to the window. The appearance was full upon us that I had already had to deal with here: Peter Quint had come into view like a sentinel before a prison. The next thing I saw was that, from outside, he had reached the window, and then I knew that, close to the glass and glaring in through it, he offered once more to the room his white face of damnation. It represents but grossly what took place within me at the sight to say that on the second my decision was made; yet I believe that no woman so overwhelmed ever in so short a time recovered her command of the *act*. It came to me in the very horror of the immediate presence that the act would be, seeing and facing what I saw and faced, to keep the boy himself unaware. The inspiration—I can call it by no other name—was that I felt how voluntarily, how transcendently, I *might*. It was like fighting with a demon for a human soul, and when I had fairly so appraised it I saw how the human soul—held out, in the tremor of my hands, at arms' length—had a perfect dew of sweat on a lovely childish forehead. The face that was close to mine was as white as the face against the glass, and out of it presently came a sound, not low nor weak, but as if from much further away, that I drank like a waft of fragrance.

'Yes—I took it.'

At this, with a moan of joy, I enfolded, I drew him close; and while I held him to my breast, where I could feel in the sudden fever of his little body the tremendous pulse of his little heart, I kept my eyes on the thing at the window and saw it move and shift its posture. I have likened it to a sentinel, but its slow wheel, for a moment, was rather the prowl of a baffled beast. My present quickened courage, however, was such that, not too much to let it through, I had to shade, as it were, my flame. Meanwhile the glare of the face was again at the window, the scoundrel fixed as if to watch and wait. It was the very confidence that I might now defy him, as well as the positive certitude, by this time, of the child's unconsciousness, that made me go on. 'What did you take it for?'

'To see what you said about me.'

'You opened the letter?'

'I opened it.'

My eyes were now, as I held him off a little again, on Miles's own face, in which the collapse of mockery showed me how complete was the ravage of uneasiness. What was prodigious was that at last, by my success, his sense was sealed and his communication stopped: he knew that he was in presence, but knew not of what, and knew still less that I also was and that I did know. And what did this strain of trouble matter when my eyes went back to the window only to see that the air was clear again and—by my personal triumph—the influence quenched? There was nothing there. I felt that the cause was mine and that I should surely get *all*. 'And you found nothing!'—I let my elation out.

He gave the most mournful, thoughtful little headshake. 'Nothing.'

'Nothing, nothing!' I almost shouted in my joy.

'Nothing, nothing,' he sadly repeated.

I kissed his forehead; it was drenched. 'So what have you done with it?'

'I've burnt it.'

'Burnt it?' It was now or never. 'Is that what you did at school?'

Oh what this brought up! 'At school?'

'Did you take letters?—or other things?'

'Other things?' He appeared now to be thinking of something far off and that reached him only through the pressure of his anxiety. Yet it did reach him. 'Did I *steal*?'

I felt myself redden to the roots of my hair as well as wonder if it were more strange to put to a gentleman such a question or to see him take it with allowances that gave the very distance of his fall in the world. 'Was it for that you mightn't go back?'

The only thing he felt was rather a dreary little surprise. 'Did you know I mightn't go back?'

'I know everything.'

He gave me at this the longest and strangest look. 'Everything?'

'Everything. Therefore *did* you—?' But I couldn't say it again.

Miles could, very simply. 'No, I didn't steal.'

My face must have shown him I believed him utterly; yet my hands—but it was for pure tenderness—shook him as if to ask him why, if it was all for nothing, he had condemned me to months of torment. 'What then did you do?'

He looked in vague pain all round the top of the room and drew his breath, two or three times over, as if with difficulty. He might have been standing at the bottom of the

sea and raising his eyes to some faint green twilight. 'Well—
I said things.'

'Only that?'

'They thought it was enough!'

'To turn you out for?'

Never, truly, had a person 'turned out' shown so little to
explain it as this little person! He appeared to weigh my
question, but in a manner quite detached and almost
helpless. 'Well, I suppose I oughtn't.'

'But to whom did you say them?'

He evidently tried to remember, but it dropped—he had
lost it. 'I don't know!'

He almost smiled at me in the desolation of his surrender,
which was indeed practically, by this time, so complete that
I ought to have left it there. But I was infatuated—I was
blind with victory, though even then the very effect that was
to have brought him so much nearer was already that of
added separation. 'Was it to everyone?' I asked.

'No; it was only to—' But he gave a sick little headshake.
'I don't remember their names.'

'Were they then so many?'

'No—only a few. Those I liked.'

Those he liked? I seemed to float not into clearness, but
into a darker obscure, and within a minute there had come
to me out of my very pity the appalling alarm of his being
perhaps innocent. It was for the instant confounding and
bottomless, for if he *were* innocent what then on earth was
I? Paralysed, while it lasted, by the mere brush of the
question, I let him go a little, so that, with a deep-drawn
sigh, he turned away from me again; which, as he faced
toward the clear window, I suffered, feeling that I had
nothing now there to keep him from. 'And did they repeat
what you said?' I went on after a moment.

He was soon at some distance from me, still breathing
hard and again with the air, though now without anger for
it, of being confined against his will. Once more, as he had

done before, he looked up at the dim day as if, of what had hitherto sustained him, nothing was left but an unspeakable anxiety. 'Oh yes,' he nevertheless replied—'they must have repeated them. To those *they* liked,' he added.

There was somehow less of it than I had expected; but I turned it over. 'And these things came round—?'

'To the masters? Oh yes!' he answered very simply. 'But I didn't know they'd tell.'

'The masters? They didn't—they've never told. That's why I ask you.'

He turned to me again his little beautiful fevered face. 'Yes, it was too bad.'

'Too bad?'

'What I suppose I sometimes said. To write home.'

I can't name the exquisite pathos of the contradiction given to such a speech by such a speaker; I only know that the next instant I heard myself throw off with homely force: 'Stuff and nonsense!' But the next after that I must have sounded stern enough. 'What *were* these things?'

My sternness was all for his judge, his executioner; yet it made him avert himself again, and that movement made *me*, with a single bound and an irrepressible cry, spring straight upon him. For there again, against the glass, as if to blight his confession and stay his answer, was the hideous author of our woe—the white face of damnation. I felt a sick swim at the drop of my victory and all the return of my battle, so that the wildness of my veritable leap only served as a great betrayal. I saw him, from the midst of my act, meet it with a divination, and on the perception that even now he only guessed, and that the window was still to his own eyes free, I let the impulse flame up to convert the climax of his dismay into the very proof of his liberation. 'No more, no more, no more!' I shrieked to my visitant as I tried to press him against me.

'Is she *here*?' Miles panted as he caught with his sealed eyes the direction of my words. Then as his strange 'she' staggered me and, with a gasp, I echoed it, 'Miss Jessel, Miss Jessel!' he with sudden fury gave me back.

I seized, stupefied, his supposition—some sequel to what we had done to Flora, but this made me only want to show him that it was better still than that. 'It's not Miss Jessel! But it's at the window—straight before us. It's *there*—the coward horror, there for the last time!'

At this, after a second in which his head made the movement of a baffled dog's on a scent and then gave a frantic little shake for air and light, he was at me in a white rage, bewildered, glaring vainly over the place and missing wholly, though it now, to my sense, filled the room like the taste of poison, the wide overwhelming presence. 'It's *he*?'

I was so determined to have all my proof that I flashed into ice to challenge him. 'Whom do you mean by "he"?'

'Peter Quint—you devil!' His face gave again, round the room, its convulsed supplication. *'Where?'*

They are in my ears still, his supreme surrender of the name and his tribute to my devotion. 'What does he matter now, my own?—what will he *ever* matter? *I* have you,' I launched at the beast, 'but he has lost you for ever!' Then for the demonstration of my work, 'There, *there!*' I said to Miles.

But he had already jerked straight round, stared, glared again, and seen but the quiet day. With the stroke of the loss I was so proud of he uttered the cry of a creature hurled over an abyss, and the grasp with which I recovered him might have been that of catching him in his fall. I caught him, yes, I held him—it may be imagined with what a passion; but at the end of a minute I began to feel what it truly was that I held. We were alone with the quiet day, and his little heart, dispossessed, had stopped.

APPENDIX

From James's Notebooks[1]

I. 'SIR EDMUND ORME' (22 Jan. 1879)

Subject for a ghost-story. [. . .]

A young girl, unknown to herself, is followed, constantly, by a figure which other persons see. She is perfectly unconscious of it—but there is a dread that she may cease to be so. The figure is that of a young man—and there is a theory that the day that she falls in love, she may suddenly perceive it. Her mother dies, and the narrator of the story then discovers, by finding an old miniature among her letters and papers, that the figure is that of a young man whom she has jilted in her youth, and who therefore committed suicide. The girl *does* fall in love, and sees the figure. She accepts her lover, and never sees it again!

II. 'OWEN WINGRAVE' (26 Mar. 1892 and 8 May 1892)

The idea of the *soldier*—produced a little by the fascinated perusal of Marbot's magnificent memoirs. The image, the type, the vision, the character, as a transmitted, hereditary, mystical, almost supernatural force, challenge, incentive, almost haunting, apparitional presence, in the life and consciousness of a descendant—a descendant of totally different temperament and range of qualities, yet subjected to a superstitious awe in relation to carrying out the tradition of absolutely *military* valour—personal bravery and honour. Sense of the difficulty—the impossibility, etc.; sense of the ugliness, the blood, the carnage, the suffering. Get *something* it is enjoined upon him to do—etc. I can't complete this indication now; but I will take it up again, as I see in it the glimmer of an idea for a small subject, though only dimly and confusedly—the subject, or rather the idea, of a brave soldierly act—an act of heroism—done in the very effort to evade all the ugly and brutal part of the religion, the sacrifice, and winning (in a tragic death?)

[1] The following extracts are the relevant passages from *The Complete Notebooks of Henry James*, ed. Leon Edel and Lyall H. Powers (New York, 1987), pp. 10, 66–8, 112, 144, 151–4, 109. Reprinted with permission.

the reward of gallantry—winning it from the apparitional ancestor. This is very crude and rough, but there is probably something in it which I shall extract.

Can't I hammer out a little the idea—for a short tale—of the young soldier?—the young fellow who, though predestined, by every tradition of his race, to the profession of arms, has an insurmountable hatred of it—of the *bloody* side of it, the suffering, the ugliness, the cruelty; so that he determines to reject it for himself—to break with it and cast it off, and this in the face of every sort of coercion of opinion (on the part of others), of such pressure not to let the family honour, etc. (always gloriously connected with the army), break down, that there is a kind of degradation, an exposure to ridicule, and ignominy in his apostasy. The idea should be that he fights, after all, exposes himself to possibilities of danger and death for his own view—acts the soldier, *is* the soldier, and of indefeasible soldierly race—proves to have been so—even in this very effort of abjuration. The thing is to invent the particular heroic situation in which he may have found himself—show just *how* he has been a hero even while throwing away his arms. It is a question of a little subject for the *Graphic*—so I mustn't make it 'psychological'—they understand that no more than a donkey understands a violin. The particular form of opposition, of coercion, that he has to face, and the way his 'heroism' is *constatée*. It must, for prettiness's sake, be *constatée* in the eyes of some woman, some girl, whom he loves but who has taken the line of despising him for his renunciation—some *fille de soldat*, who is very *montée* about the whole thing, very hard on him, etc. But what the subject wants is to be distanced, relegated into some picturesque little past when the army occupied more place in life—poetized by some slightly romantic setting. Even if one could introduce a supernatural element in it—make it, I mean, a little ghost-story; place it, the scene, in some old country-house, in England at the beginning of the present century—the time of the Napoleonic wars.—It seems to me one might make some *haunting* business that would give it a colour without being ridiculous, and get in that way the sort of pressure to which the young man is subjected. I see it—it comes to me a little. He must die, of course, be slain, as it were on his own battle-field, the night spent in the haunted room in which the ghost of some grim grandfather—some bloody warrior of the race—or some father slain in the Peninsular or at Waterloo—is supposed to make himself visible.

III. 'THE FRIENDS OF THE FRIENDS'
(5 Feb. 1895, 21 Dec. 1895, 10 and 11 Jan. 1896)

What is there in the idea of *Too late*—of some friendship or passion or bond—some affection long desired and waited for, that is formed too late?—I mean too late in life altogether. Isn't there something in the idea that 2 persons may meet (as if they had looked for each other for years) only in time to feel how much it might have meant for them if they had only met earlier? This is vague, nebulous—the mere hint of a hint. They but meet to part or to suffer—they meet when one is dying—'or something of that sort.' They may have been dimly conscious, in the past, of the possibility between them—been groping for each other in the darkness. It's love, it's friendship, it's mutual comprehension—it's whatever one will. They've heard of each other, perhaps—felt each other, been conscious, each, of some tug at the cord—some vibration of the other's heartstrings. It's a passion that *might* have been. I seem to be coinciding simply with the idea of the married person encountering the *real* mate, etc.; but that is not what I mean. Married or not—the marriage is a detail. Or rather, I fancy, there would have been no marriage conceivable for either. Haven't they waited—waited too long—till something else has happened? The only *other* 'something else' than marriage must have been, doubtless, the wasting of life. And the wasting of life is the implication of death. There may be the germ of a situation in this; but it obviously requires digging out. X X X X X

The idea, for a scrap of a tale, on a scrap of a fantasy, of 2 persons who have constantly heard of each other, constantly been near each other, constantly *missed* each other. They have never met—though repeatedly told that they ought to know each other, etc.: the sort of thing that so often happens. They must be, I suppose, a man and a woman. At last it has been arranged—they really *are* to meet: arranged by some 3d person, the friend of each, who takes an interest in their meeting—sympathetically—officiously, blunderingly, whatever it may be: as also so often happens. But before the event one of them dies—the thing has become impossible forever. The other then comes, after death, to the survivor—so that they do meet, in spite of fate—they meet, and if necessary, they love.—They see, they know, all that would have been possible if they *had* met. It's a rather thin little fantasy—but there is something in it perhaps, for 5000 or 6000 words. There would be various ways of doing it, and it comes to me that the thing might be related by the

3d person, according to my wont when I want something—as I always do want it—intensely objective. It's the woman who's the ghost—it's the woman who comes to the man. I've spoken to them of each other—it's through me, mainly, that they know of each other. I mustn't be too much of an *entremetteur* or an *entremetteuse*: I may even have been a little reluctant or suspicious, a little jealous, even, if the mediator is a woman. If a woman tells the story she may have this jealousy of her dead friend after the latter's death. She suspects, she divines, she feels that the man, with whom she is herself more or less in love, *continues* to see the dead woman. She has thought, she has believed, he cares for *her*; but now he is sensibly detached. Or if I don't have the '3d person' narrator, what effect would one get from the impersonal form—what peculiar and characteristic, what compensating, effect *might* one get from it? I should have in this case—shouldn't I?—to represent the *post-mortem* interview? Yes—but not necessarily. I might 'impersonally' include the 3d person and his (or her) feelings—tell the thing even so from his, or her, point of view. Probably it would have to be longer so—and really 5000 words is all it deserves.

I am doing for Oswald Crawford—in 7000 words—the little subject of the 2 people who never met in life. I see it in 5 little chapters, all very, very tiny and intensely brief—with every word and every touch telling. I have only put pen to paper; but before I go further I must be crystal-clear. *Voyons un peu* what must be immitigably brought out. The salient thing, up to the death of the woman, must be the condition, the state of things, or relation between the pair, brought about by its being—there being—so often a question, a lively question of their meeting, and nothing ever coming of it. They perpetually *miss* each other—they are the buckets in the well. There seems a fate in it. It becomes, *de part et d'autre*, a joke (of each party) with the persons who wish to bring them together: that is (in the small space) with *me*, mainly—the interested narrator. They say, each, the same things, do the same things, feel the same things. It's a JOKE—it *becomes* one—*de part et d'autre*. They each end by declaring that it makes them too nervous, *à la fin*—and that really it won't *do*, for either, at last, to see the other: so possible a disappointment, an anticlimax, may ensue. Each knows that the other knows—each knows just how the other is affected: a certain self-consciousness and awkwardness, a certain preoccupied shyness has sprung up. So it goes. This colours the whole situation so that, necessarily (as it happens), the thing is left very much to accident. It is the *idea* that it shall be so left. It's too *serious* to arrange it in any other way. *Chance* must bring the meeting about. So it's by way of being left to chance. It's a joke, above all for *me*:—that is, it's an element of the little action to perceive in the joke a little serious side that makes me say 'Tiens!' Ah, divine principle of the 'scenario!'—it seems to make that wretched little past of patience and gain glow with the meaning I've waited for! I seem to catch hold of the tail of the very central notion of my little '*cochonnerie*,' as Jusserand used to say. The LAST *empêchement* to the little meeting, the supreme one, the one that caps the climax and makes the thing 'past a joke,' '*trop fort*,' and all the rest of it, is the result of *my own act*. I prevent it, because I become conscious of a dawning jealousy. I become conscious of a dawning jealousy because something has taken place between the young man (the man of my story; perhaps he's not in his 1st youth) and myself. I was on the point of writing just above that 'something takes place just before the last failure of the 2 parties to meet—something that has a bearing on this failure.' Well, what takes place is *tout simplement* THAT: I mean that he and the narrator become 'engaged'. It's *on* her engagement that her friend, her woman-friend, wants, more than ever, to see the man who has now become the fiancé. It is this (comparative eagerness) and a vague apprehension that determines her jealousy. It makes her *prevent* the meeting when it really might have (this time) occurred. The other failures have been by accident: this one, which might have come off (the narrator sees that there would have been no accident), has failed from active interference. What do I do? I write to my fiancé not to come—that *she* can't. (She mustn't live in London—but [say] at Richmond.) So he doesn't come. *She* does—and she sits with me, vainly waiting for him. I don't tell *her* what I have done; but, that evening, I tell *him*. I'm ashamed of it—I'm ashamed, and I make that reparation. She, in the afternoon, has gone away in good faith, but almost painfully, quite visibly disappointed. She is not well—she is 'odd', etc. I am struck with it. The form my reparation takes is to take him the next day straight out to see her. Is she then, as we find, dead—or only very ill—i.e., dying? The extreme brevity of my poor little form doubtless makes it indispensable that she shall be already dead. I can't devote space to what passes while she is dying, while her illness goes on. I must jump that—I must arrive (with all the little *merveilleux* of the story still to come) at what happens *after* this event.—Or rather, on second thoughts, have I got this—this last bit—all wrong? Don't I, *mustn't* I, see it, on reflection, in another way? *Voyons, voyons.* Say the narrator with her impulse of reparation (having TOLD her fiancé)—*confessed* to him—in the p.m., as I stated it just now: say she goes ALONE out to Richmond. She does this in the a.m. of the next day. She finds her friend has died that night. She goes home, with the wonder of it; and there befalls the still greater wonder of her interview with him in the afternoon. He tells her his marvellous experience of that evening— how, on going home, he has found her there. BUT that only comes out—is shaken out—in the *secousse*—of *my* announcement that she's dead—that she died at 10 o'clock that evening. Ten o'clk.—the stupefaction, the dismay, the question of the *hour*, etc. I see this—I see this: I needn't detail it here. I see what has (to his sense) happened—how she hasn't spoken, etc.—has visibly only come to see him, to let him see her: as if to say, '*Shouldn't* we, now, have liked each other?' He puts it that way to the narrator. The narrator says, utterly wonderstruck: 'Why, she was dead *then*—she was dead already.' The marvel of this, the comparison of notes. The possible doubt and question of whether it was after or before death. The ambiguity—the possibility. The view we take—the view *I* take. The effect of this view upon *me*. From here to the end, the attitude, on the subject, is mine: the return of my jealousy, the imputation of the difference that seeing her has made in *him*; the final rupture that comes entirely from ME and from my imputations and suspicions. I am jealous of the dead; I feel, or imagine I feel, his detachment, his alienation, his coldness—and the last words of my statement are: 'He sees her—he sees her: I know he sees her!' X X X X X

The ground on which the idea is originally started and the claim made that they shall know each other is that of this extraordinary peculiarity that each have had in their pretended (*constatée*), recognized, etc., experience of having had, each of them, the premonition, on the announcement of the death of a parent—he of his mother, she of her father after death—had it at a distance, at the moment, or just before, or just after. This known, recognized, etc.—whether generally, publicly or not; at any rate by the narrator. I've had it from each—I've repeated it to each. Others—yes—have done the same. Yes, there must be—have been—as much publicity as that: to make the needed consensus—the thing that follows them up and amuses and haunts them—the 'point' of the 1st ½ of the *morceau*. If instead of beginning the thing as I began it yesterday I give my first 10 (CLOSE ten) pages to a summary statement of this just-mentioned hearsay-business between them, and how it went on for long, each knowing and knowing the other knows, etc.— then I have my *last* 10 (all of premised closeness) for the state of mind, the imputations, suspicions, interpretations, etc., of the narrator—as a climax. That leaves me thirty for the rest: say, roughly 10 of these for the engagement and what surrounds it relative to *her*. But I've only to reflect to see that under this latter head must come in—then and there—the question of the last occasion for meeting. Perhaps I must make *10* little chapters. Try it so: each of 25 close pages. Let us see what this gives. But isn't, on the other hand, the best way to do so to see first what *five* give? FIRST. The statement of the peculiarity of the pair, and the way in which, for 3 or 4 years, it was followed by their dodging, missing, failing. SECOND. The narrator's engagement. Her jealousy. The day the 2d woman comes, when she (the narrator) has put off the man. THIRD. Her compunction, her confession to the man. Her going to Richmond. Her return with the news—with a certain relief. Her seeing her fiancé. FOURTH. His story to her. The recrudescence of her jealousy. FIFTH. Their going on with their engagement—her wonder and *malaise* about him. Then its coming over her—the *explanation's* coming over her (of what she sees). Her imputation. The rupture. Now let me try the little subdivisions into smaller fractions—a series of tenths.

1–10. 1st. The 2 persons and their story.

10–16. 2d. The long, odd frustration of their encounter.

16–20. 3d. The engagement. The others to meet because of it. The nearing of the day—my jealousy. I'm engaged—if now at the last moment something should intervene! I will—putting him off.

20–25. 4th. Her visit—her waiting—my dissimulation—her departure.

25–30. 5th. My compunction, my confession—scene with him—pendant to preceding.

30–35. 6th. My going to Richmond. What I learn there; and my return with the news—with a certain relief.

35–40. 7th. My scene with him—his revelation. My stupefaction.

8th. The ambiguity—the inquiry (mine). The return of my jealousy.

9th. Our approaching marriage—my theory—my suspicions—my imputations.

10th. The rupture. He goes on, unmarried, for years. Then I make up to him (?)—seek a reconciliation. *Il s'y soustrait par la mort* (?).

IV. 'THE TURN OF THE SCREW' (12 Jan. 1895)

Note here the ghost-story told me at Addington (evening of Thursday 10th), by the Archbishop of Canterbury: the mere vague, undetailed, faint sketch of it—being all he had been told (very badly and imperfectly), by a lady who had no art of relation, and no clearness: the story of the young children (indefinite number and age) left to the care of servants in an old country-house, through the death, presumably, of parents. The servants, wicked and depraved, corrupt and deprave the children; the children are bad, full of evil, to a sinister degree. The servants *die* (the story vague about the way of it) and their apparitions, figures, return to haunt the house *and* children, to whom they seem to beckon, whom they invite and solicit, from across dangerous places, the deep ditch of a sunk fence, etc.—so that the children may destroy themselves, lose themselves by responding, by getting into their power. So long as the children are kept from them, they are not lost: but they try and try and try, these evil presences, to get hold of them. It is a question of the children 'coming over to where they are'. It is all obscure and imperfect, the picture, the story, but there is a suggestion of strangely gruesome effect in it. The story to be told—tolerably obviously—by an outside spectator, observer.

NOTES

(The references are to page and line numbers)

PREFACES

xxxvii.1. *I fear I can defend such doings*: James has just been discussing the ingenuity of his 'small game' in 'The Private Life'.

xxxvii.8. *printed elsewhere only as I write*: in Ford Madox Hueffer's recently founded *English Review*, Dec. 1908.

xxxix.9. *bêtises*: 'stupidities', 'follies'.

xl.32. *moving accidents*: Othello speaks of 'moving accidents by flood and field' (I. iii. 134–5).

xli.21. *'Arthur Gordon Pym'*: James may have had reservations about the literary form of Edgar Allan Poe's *The Narrative of Arthur Gordon Pym of Nantucket* (1838), but Prince Amerigo in *The Golden Bowl* (1904) sees the tale as an example of 'what imagination Americans *could* have' and finds the climactic scene, in which Pym's boat drifts southward beyond a curtain of whiteness, an appropriate metaphor for his own predicament (ch. 1).

xliii.33. *the celebrated Topsy*: when asked who made her, Topsy in Harriet Beecher Stowe's *Uncle Tom's Cabin* (1852), replies that 'I 'spect I grow'd' (ch. 16).

xliv.9. *Kensington Gardens*: these lay just across the road from James's flat in De Vere Gardens. The 'summer afternoon' (xliv.8) is not mentioned in the Notebook entries on the tale, made during the spring of 1892. Possibly the figure of the young man combined with the Marbot germ later in the same year. The reference to the 'London hum' (xliv.15) recalls Matthew Arnold on 'the girdling city's hum' in 'Lines Written in Kensington Gardens', and 'Owen Wingrave' might be taken as an illustration of the poem's observation that 'peace has left the upper world, / And now keeps only in the grave'. Owen himself reads Goethe instead of Arnold (going back to the fount of earnest romanticism) although James had discussed Goethe's influence on Arnold in an 1865 review of *Essays in Criticism* and was to link them again in his 1884 essay on Arnold.

xlvi.19. *the Thackerayan Brighton*: parts of *Vanity Fair* (1847) are set in Brighton.

xlvii.4. *that particular challenge*: that it pretends to a ' "link" with reality' which it is unable to demonstrate: a criticism apparently made of 'The Aspern Papers', the tale which James has just been discussing.

xlvii.18. *a grave old country-house*: Addington. See the Notebook entry on 'The Turn of the Screw' and the note to p. 244 below.

xlvii.27. *the mere modern 'psychical' case*: Reed argues that James's dissatisfaction with the undramatic ghosts recorded in the *Proceedings* of the Society for Psychical Research provides evidence against the hallucination theory. This is not entirely true. Although the S. P. R. generally explained apparitions as hallucinations produced by thought transference, F. W. H. Myers was by the late 1880s seeking to demonstrate some form of post-mortem agency. The dispute between Myers and Frank Podmore was thus somewhat analogous to that between Heilman and Wilson, and James would seem to be distancing himself both from hallucinations and from scientifically sanctioned apparitions. James had more than a layman's knowledge of psychical research: he knew Myers, Edmund Gurney and Henry Sidgwick (all founder members of the Society) and his brother William was the President of the Society's American branch from 1894 to 1896. He also had personal familiarity with the 'learned meetings' alluded to in 'The Friends of the Friends' (p. 106), having delivered William's paper on the medium Mrs Piper to a meeting of the S. P. R. on 31 Oct. 1890. Despite James's prefatory disavowal of any attempt to keep his ghosts 'on terms with the today so copious psychical record of cases of apparitions' (p. lii), both Roellinger and Sheppard have shown that there are numerous parallels between the accounts published in the *Proceedings* of the S. P. R. and James's ghost stories, particularly 'The Turn of the Screw'.

xlviii.9. *certain 'bad' servants . . . were believed to have appeared*: in the Notebook entry of 1895 James had unambiguously stated that the 'apparitions . . . return to haunt the house'. In a Notebook entry of 16 March 1892, James recorded an idea for a tale about a servant who is thought to do 'base' things ('reading of letters, diaries, peeping, spying, etc.'). Interestingly, the tale involved the servant 'turning out utterly innocent'. Elements of this germ, which James never turned into a story, seem to have influenced 'The Turn of the Screw'. Mrs Grose asks whether Quint 'only peeps' (p. 146), and Miles steals the governess's letter.

xlviii.15. *my own appreciation . . . thinness*: in the Preface to *The Spoils of Poynton* James argued that the merest 'virus of suggestion' was more fertilizing and more convertible than the 'disjoined and lacerated lump of life'.

1.31. *an amusette*: 'a toy', 'an amusing trifle'. James habitually speaks of his ghost stories in this tone. On 9 Dec. 1898 he told H. G. Wells that 'The Turn of the Screw' was 'essentially a pot-boiler and a *jeu d'esprit*'. Ten days later he wrote to Myers that the tale was 'a very mechanical matter . . . an inferior, a merely *pictorial*, subject and rather a shameless pot-boiler'.

li.12. *a reader capable . . . of some attention*: probably Wells, to whom James wrote on 9 Dec. 1898 that he had had 'to rule out subjective complications' on the part of the governess 'and keep her impersonal save for the most obvious and indispensable little note of neatness, firmness and courage'.

li.31. *déjà très-joli*: 'already a pretty enough task'.

li.35. *her explanation of them, a different matter*: Wilson argues that this comment is inexplicable unless the ghosts are hallucinations but Heilman counters that James is merely referring to his decision not to exhibit the governess's 'relation to her own nature' (p. lii).

liii.16. *demons as loosely constructed as those of the old trials for witchcraft*: another notoriously ambiguous crux. Is James claiming the imaginative latitude of a romancer in describing the supernatural or is he implying that the governess improvises the demons and is motivated by a zeal similar to that of the Salem witch-hunters? Lydenberg is one of a number of critics to have described the governess as a Puritan. O'Gorman has also written interestingly in this connection.

lv.9. *the charge of all indecently expatiating*: the charge was most forcefully made in the *Independent* (5 Jan. 1899). The reviewer felt that the children's souls had been defiled 'in a way . . . by no means darkly and subtly hinted', saw the tale as a study of 'infernal human debauchery' and concluded that 'human imagination can go no further into infamy' (Kimbrough, p. 175).

SIR EDMUND ORME

3.1. *The statement . . . I've altered nothing but the names*: this 'frame' for the main narrative is a technique which James had first used in 'A Landscape Painter' (1866). The device is particularly associated with his ghostly tales (it had also been used in supernatural stories by Hawthorne, Mérimée, Maupassant, and Vernon Lee), and reappears in 'The Friends of the Friends', 'The Turn of the Screw', and 'Maud-Evelyn'. The mediation of the frame made it possible for James to represent directly a ghostly encounter and yet to keep the tale within 'the field of second exhibition' (see James's Preface, p. xl). The frame also tends to ambiguate the main narrative: the executor figure testifies to the narrator's 'general veracity' but inevitably raises the possibility of a particular mendacity.

3.6. *these pages, in a locked drawer*: as in 'The Friends of the Friends' and 'The Turn of the Screw', the frame to 'Sir Edmund Orme' involves the additional device of the discovered manuscript. 'Sir Dominick Ferrand' also gives the retrieval of old letters an uncanny turn. The theme of posthumous publication is investigated at length in 'The Aspern Papers' (1888) and later in 'John Delavoy' (1898), 'The Real Right Thing' (1899), and 'The Abasement of the Northmores' (1900).

28.1. *régimes*: regimens, fitness programmes.

30.6. *the visiting on the children of the sins of the mothers*: a play on Exodus 20: 5. This passage, not present in the 1891 version, is a good example of James's increasing use of the vocabulary of the sacred in his later works.

31.28. *Saint Martin's summer of the soul*: St Martin's Day is 11 Nov. James promised himself 'a rich and long St Martin's Summer' in a Notebook entry of 13 July 1891.

OWEN WINGRAVE

39.5. *Owen Wingrave*: Leon Edel, who discusses James's ambivalent attitude to war (*Life*, ii. 171–3), points out that the 'Scottish' (actually, Welsh) name 'Owen' means 'young soldier', and accordingly translates the title as 'The Young Soldier Wins His Grave'. When James revised 'The Romance of Certain Old Clothes' (another tale of ghosts and family violence) for *Stories Revived* (1885) he converted Perdita and Viola Willoughby into Perdita and Rosalind Wingrave. The name Owen Wingrave also recalls Owen Warland in Hawthorne's 'The Artist of the Beautiful' (1844), and Holgrave in *The House of the Seven Gables* (1851), a novel whose presence is felt at several points in James's tale.

41.35. *Kensington Gardens*: see n. to xliv.9.

42.10. *now that the cord had snapped*: unusually in James this scene temporarily abandons Coyle's point of view and provides a clear autobiographical link to the origin of the story as recounted in the Prefaces (p. xliv). The image of the snapped cord is a curious one since James had quoted with approval Taine's remark that 'Turgenieff so perfectly cut the umbilical cord that bound the story to himself' (Notebooks, 19 May 1889). In some sense James is one of the 'watchers' mentioned a few lines later, just as he was later to become, according to Leon Edel, one of the 'ghosts at the windows' in *The Ambassadors* (Book Fifth, ch. 1; *Life*, I. 455–6 and II. 60, 414–15).

44.5. *corrupting the youth of Athens*: according to Plato, the deposition against Socrates accused him of 'corrupting the minds of the young, and of believing in deities of his own invention instead of the gods recognized by the State' (*Apology*, 24 B).

45.29. *Poor Philip Wingrave*: in *The Princess Casamassima* Hyacinth is told that the haunted chamber at Medley contains 'a horrible figure . . . a dwarfish ghost with an enormous head, a dispossessed eldest brother of long ago who had passed for an idiot' (ch. 22). James often dispossesses elder brothers in his fiction and was himself a second son. See Edel on the sibling rivalry in the James family (*Life*, I. 51–7, 207–8, 584–6).

47.17. *the Indian Mutiny*: the 1857 revolt in central and northern India against British colonial rule.

52.33. *Hannibal and Julius Caesar, Marlborough and Frederick and Bonaparte*: James is perhaps subtly contrasting Owen's victory in defeat with the careers of these men, who are as notable for their falls as for their triumphs. Hannibal was defeated by Scipio at the Battle of Zama and later poisoned, Marlborough was dismissed, and the fates of Caesar and Napolean are well known. The only exception is Frederick the Great, King of Prussia from 1740 until his death in 1786, who, by well-timed peace treaties in the early 1860s, retained his territorial gains in Silesia (1740) and Bohemia (1744) in spite of military defeats in the late 1750s.

66.20. *visibly marked for sacrifice*: one of a number of references to martyrdom in this tale. Soldiers also become sacrificial victims in 'The Story of a Year' (1865) and 'A Most Extraordinary Case' (1868). Boys die in 'My Friend Bingham' (1867), 'The Author of "Beltraffio" ' (1884), 'The Pupil' (1891), and of course 'The Turn of the Screw'. *The Other House* (1896) is unusual in that the victim is a girl.

67.26. *Paul and Virginia*: Bernardin de Saint-Pierre's sentimental novel *Paul et Virginie* (1788) told of young love on a tropical island.

THE FRIENDS OF THE FRIENDS

84.7. *the 'Long'*: the long (summer) vacation.
89.17. *an entêtement*: 'an obstinacy'.

94.17. *She looked at your photograph*: the narrator is incorrect, since her friend looked at the photograph during the visit which occurred immediately after the engagement (p. 89) and not during the final visit (pp. 92–93). It is possible that James has simply confused the two occasions and is not hinting at the narrator's unreliability. But he rarely made such errors and two further oversights by the narrator (see notes to 98.4 and 99.29 below) provoke the suspicion that she is being economical with the truth.

98.4. *as I had then said to myself*: it is in fact the narrator's friend who first mentions the 'relation' (p. 93); when the narrator agrees she is not speaking to herself.

99.29. *an affection of the heart which . . . . her physician knew her to have*: in fact the doctor becomes satisfied of 'a long-latent weakness of the heart' only 'after the fact' (p. 96).

101.29. *soit*: 'so be it'.

107.9. *Medusa-mask*: the narrator's jealousy becomes an appalling, almost externalized presence like that of the mythical Gorgon, Medusa, whose face turned onlookers to stone.

107.30. *she's dead for me. But she's not dead for you*: this formulation of the situation in the final scene prefigures the last chapters of *The Wings of the Dove* (1902), in which the haunted Merton Densher falls in love with the memory of Milly Theale. The original Notebook entry on this novel (3 Nov. 1894) is the first statement of the 'too late' theme (see n. to p. 239.1).

110.18. *a rare extension of being*: in 'Is There a Life After Death?' James wrote that immortality could only be conceived of as a 'great extension' for consciousness. Nevertheless he reluctantly accepted science's denial of an afterlife. In the end art was the great extension for James: it was the writer who carried 'the field of consciousness further and further, making it lose itself in the ineffable'.

THE TURN OF THE SCREW

115.23. *Griffin's ghost, or whatever it was*: Douglas seems to stop well short of full credulity. Surprisingly this is the only use of the word 'ghost' in the novel.

115.27. *turn of the screw*: Douglas's use of this phrase relates to literary intensity; the governess's 'turn of the screw of ordinary human virtue' (p. 225), on the other hand, connotes moral and potentially physical violence. These divergent senses determine James's use of the phrase elsewhere. When George Flack gives 'a turn to one of his screws' in *The Reverberator* (ch. 2) or, in one of

James's 'American Letters' of 1898, Theodore Roosevelt is said to be jingoistically attempting to 'tighten the screws of the national consciousness' (*Literary Criticism*, I. 663), the turning of the screw is narrow and exploitative. But in his Notebook entry on 'The "K. B." Case' James is happy to subject his ideas to 'the pressure and the screw' and the Preface to Volume XVI of the New York Edition rather proudly admits that 'The Tree of Knowledge' (1900) required an even greater number of 'full revolutions of the merciless screw' than 'The Middle Years' (1893). The difference between the positive and negative senses seems to depend on whether the screw is used on living material.

117.13. *Trinity*: E. W. Benson (see n. to p. 244) was an undergraduate at Trinity College, Cambridge, as were Sidgwick, Myers, and Gurney (see n. to xlvii.27).

118.22. *Raison de plus*: 'All the more reason'.

119.14. *on the night of the fourth*: this conflicts with the earlier assertion that Douglas's reading commenced 'two nights' after the first evening and with the later statement that the reading begins on 'the next night' after the second evening (pp. 115, 122). If this is an error it is an unusual one in James. It certainly adds to the uncertainties of the tale and anticipates the gap in the governess's time-scheme (see n. to p. 169.1).

119.31. *a house in Harley Street*: Cargill (who believes that 'The Turn of the Screw' was directly influenced by the Case of Miss Lucy R. in Breuer and Freud's *Studies on Hysteria*) contends that this reference already suggests a clinical interpretation of the governess. There are a number of resemblances between the Case of Lucy R. and 'The Turn of the Screw' (as there are between the former text and *Jane Eyre*) but the idea that it is a source seems unlikely and unnecessary. Sheppard has argued that at the period when the tale is set Harley Street was still entirely residential. It may also be significant that, from 1848 onwards, governesses were able to obtain diplomas from Queen's College in Harley Street.

120.29. *Bly*: like 'Paramore' in 'Owen Wingrave', 'Bly' is a doubly directed word and suggests both 'blithe' and 'blight'. The name may well have been initially suggested by the following sequence of names in James's Notebooks for 1892: 'Gaye (name of house)—Taunt—Tant (Miss Tant, name of governess)'. James spent Aug. and Sept. 1897 at Dunwich in Suffolk, 4 miles from Blythburgh and 6 from Blyford. Edel (*Life*, II. 242) thinks that the geography of Lamb House in Rye may also have influenced that of Bly. Other possible elements in James's imaginative crucible include Haddon Hall (see n. to p. 134) and a chateau with a tower, a valet and a young orphan boy at Amilly-Loiret in France where James stayed in Aug. 1876 (see Edel, *Life*, I. 481–3). Shortly after the visit to Amilly-Loiret James briefly encountered a 'depressed English governess' in Bayonne (Edel, *Life*, I. 483).

121.12. *Miles: miles*, the Latin for 'soldier', links Miles to Owen Wingrave and other sacrificial victims in James (see notes to p. 39 and 66). In *The Awkward Age* (1898–9) Vanderbank's dead brother is also called Miles.

121.13. *Flora*: one of a number of floral names in James. Both Daisy Miller and Pansy Osmond inhabit oppressive social or familial environments. In *The American* Claire de Cintré tells her niece the tale of Florabella, who 'suffered terribly' but eventually married a young prince and was 'carried . . . off to live with him in the land of the Pink Sky' (ch. 12). Fairy-tale endings fail almost as badly in *The American* as in 'The Turn of the Screw'.

124.11. *long glasses . . . head to foot*: Bluebeard's castle contains looking-glasses 'in which you might see yourself from head to foot' and Cinderella's sisters have looking-glasses in which 'they might see themselves . . . from head to foot' (*The Classic Fairy Tales*, ed. Iona and Peter Opie (London, 1974), 107, 123).

125.19. *one of Raphael's holy infants*: the Italian artist Raphael (1483–1520) produced many works on the Madonna and Child theme, including the Madonna of the Chair and the Madonna of the Goldfinch. Curiously and perhaps coincidentally he was orphaned at the age of 11 and made a ward of his uncle. James may also be playing on the contrast between the purity of Raphael's art and his scandalous private life.

134.27. *a small interval alone*: the passage that follows recalls James's description of Haddon Hall, Derbyshire, in his 1872 article 'Lichfield and Warwick', later published in *Transatlantic Sketches* (1875) and revised for *English Hours* (1905, repr. Oxford, 1981). Feeling like 'a successful adventurer' James approached the house along the bank of the Wye: 'the twilight deepened, the ragged battlements and the low, broad oriels glanced duskily from the foliage, the rooks wheeled and clamoured in the glowing sky; and if there had been a ghost on the premises I certainly ought to have seen it. In fact I did see it, as we see ghosts nowadays. I felt the incommunicable spirit of the scene with the last, the right intensity. The old life, the old manners, the old figures seemed present again' (p. 48). In 'The Turn of the Screw' James's detached enjoyment gives way to the governess's horrified bewilderment.

138.34. *went as soon as possible to my room*: this passage, and the

encounter with Quint which precedes it, travesties the betrothal
scene in ch. 23 of *Jane Eyre*. When Rochester and Jane return to
the house the housekeeper Mrs Fairfax observes them embracing
in the hall. Jane then runs up to her room. Charlotte Brontë's
novel is part of James's general imaginative inheritance but he
would have been reminded of it early in 1897, when he discussed
Clement Shorter's *Charlotte Brontë and her Circle* (1896) in one of
his 'London Notes' for *Harper's Weekly* (*Literary Criticism*, I.
1391–2).

140.27. *cherubs of the anecdote . . . nothing to whack*: the
anecdote may well derive from a pun on Exodus 25: 18–20. In his
Journal (16 July 1843), Emerson wrote that 'Montaigne has the *de
quoi* which the French cherubs had not, when the courteous
Archbishop implored them to sit down'. The governess is soon to
see the children's lack of punishable bottoms as a moral
bottomlessness.

147.18. *She faltered but a second*: Mrs Grose's recognition of
Quint from the governess's description is, as Waldock has shown,
the most serious objection to the hallucination theory. Goddard,
whose approach anticipates Wilson's, argues that the governess
browbeats and virtually hypnotizes the housekeeper into making
the identification; his comments are suggestive but ultimately
unconvincing. In the 1948 edition of *The Triple Thinkers* Wilson
conceded that he had 'forced a point' in arguing that the ghosts
were intended to be hallucinations. Cargill later suggested that the
governess finds out about Quint from Flora, who exhibits Bly
'secret by secret' and seems disposed to tell the governess 'many
more things than she asked' (p. 127). Silver points out that the
governess's curiosity is aroused by what seems to be an inadvertent
disclosure by Mrs Grose that there is or has been another male at
Bly who liked young and pretty women (see p. 130) and argues
that her suspicions may have taken shape during her investigations
among the servants (see p. 139). The governess later tells Mrs
Grose that she has 'made sure' that Quint is not from Bly or the
village (p. 145). In his 1959 postscript to 'The Ambiguity of Henry
James' Wilson drew on these arguments to return to his original
thesis.

147.20. *Peter Quint*: the name has an extraordinary connotative
range. Sidney Lind points out that '*quinte*' and '*quinteux*' are
French for 'vagary', 'crotchet', 'whimsical' and 'fantastic'. Middle
English 'queynte' means 'strange', 'curious', 'artful', 'sly' and also
refers to the female genitals—a combination which would have
appealed to Freud, who examined a similar etymological play in

his 1919 essay 'The "Uncanny" '. The rotary motifs in the tale indicate a possible reference to 'quintain': a dummy figure or target used in medieval tournaments which, when hit incorrectly, revolved to strike the tilting knight. O'Gorman ingeniously reads 'Peter Quint' as a coded biblical reference: 'Be sober, be vigilant; because your adversary the devil, as a roaring lion, walketh about, seeking whom he may devour' (I Peter 5: 8). Sheppard is particularly good on the literary allusions in the name, which range from Peer Gynt to Quinion in *David Copperfield* (combined with elements of Steerforth, his valet Littimer, and the serpentine Uriah Heep) and Quilp in *The Old Curiosity Shop*. Roellinger notes that one of the S. P. R. 's correspondents was named Wilson Quint.

154.7. *Sea of Azof*: a shallow gulf of the Black Sea whose currents, according to the *Encyclopaedia Brittanica* (15th edn.), 'flow in a counterclockwise direction, but . . . may reverse'. The surrounding territories have been the subject of disputes since the 11th century.

157.3. *Miss Jessel*: the name lacks the connotative breadth of 'Quint', although O'Gorman sees an allusion to the biblical Jezebel (see I Kgs 16: 31 – II Kgs 9: 37). According to *Brewer's Dictionary of Phrase and Fable* (8th edn.), a 'painted Jezebel' is 'a flaunting woman of bold spirit but loose morals'.

169.1. *after a lull*: astonishingly, this lull appears to occupy a period of some 7 weeks in the narrative, which spans the period from June (p. 123) to Nov. (p. 227). All the scenes up to and including the governess's two conversations with Mrs Grose after Quint's second appearance take place in June. There follows a period of 'rigid control' which probably lasts for 'a week' (p. 151) and precedes Miss Jessel's first appearance. The governess then refers to the lapse of 'a very few' days (p. 166). The 'lull' is followed by Quint's third appearance, which takes place approximately 7 weeks before the final scene. Novels cannot be expected to account for the passage of every day, but it is unlikely that James has merely disregarded the time-scheme. The temporal uncertainty in the frame chapter (see n. to 119.14) acts as an anticipatory synecdoche for this more extensive and disturbing blank.

169.23. *Fielding's 'Amelia'*: perhaps the governess is identifying with the sexually beset but virtuous heroine in Henry Fielding's novel (1751), but she is no more successful in controlling the implications of this text than she is with *Udolpho* or *Jane Eyre*. The governess is 'the youngest of several daughters of a poor country parson' from Hampshire (p. 119) and moves to Bly, in Essex, at the age of 20. This links her not to Amelia but to the fallen Mrs Bennet, 'the younger of two daughters of a clergyman in Essex' who moves to Hampshire when she is 19 (Book VII, ch. 2). Fielding emphasizes that Mrs Bennet is 'desirous of inculcating a good opinion of herself, from recounting those transactions where her conduct was unexceptionable, before she came to the more dangerous and suspicious part of her character' (Book VII, ch. 1).

171.5. *some criminal*: this scene seems to be recalled in *The Golden Bowl*. After Maggie Verver's discovery of the relation between Amerigo and Charlotte a 'crisis' hovers in the corridors of Fawns 'after the fashion of the established ghost' (ch. 35), and Maggie's horror is compared to a meeting with 'some bad-faced stranger surprised in . . . a house of quiet on a Sunday afternoon' (ch. 36).

173.18. *Mrs Marcet*: Jane Marcet (1769–1858) wrote scientific textbooks for children. Her *Conversations on Chemistry* (1806) and *Conversations on Political Economy* (1816) went through numerous editions.

173.19. *nine-times-nine*: in *Macbeth*, the First Witch condemns a mariner to 'dwindle, peak and pine' for 'weary se'nnights nine times nine' (I. iii. 22–3). This faint but distinct allusion undercuts and qualifies the rational schoolroom tone of the allusion to Mrs Marcet (see n. above).

178.30. *the old tradition of the criminality of those caretakers of the young who minister to superstitions and fears*: the tradition goes back at least to the Enlightenment. Locke objected to the 'foolish maid' who inculcated '*ideas* of goblins and *sprites*' on the mind of a child (*An Essay Concerning Human Understanding* (1690), II. xxxiii. 10). In *The Children* (1897) Alice Meynell wrote that 'it is generally understood in the family that the nurse who menaces a child with the supernatural . . . goes' (quoted in Lind, p. 293). James mentioned this book and described its author as 'an observer of singular acuteness' shortly before discussing Shorter's book on Charlotte Brontë (see n. to p. 138).

183.28. *both him and you.*': in the periodical version of the novel James prolonged the exchange between the governess and Mrs Grose. This provided a smoother transition to the next chapter but was probably cut in the text of *The Two Magics* because it prematurely revealed the governess's intentions. The periodical text continues as follows:

'Then what's your remedy?' she asked as I watched the children.

I continued, without answering, to watch them. 'I would leave *them*,' and went on.

'But what *is* your remedy?' she persisted.

It seemed, after all, to have come to me then and there. 'To speak to them.' And I joined them.

197.3. *all swept and garnished*: in Matthew 12: 43–4 Jesus describes how the 'unclean spirit' tries to return to the body from which it has been cast out but finds the soul, like a house, 'empty, swept, and garnished'. The governess's allusion seems inappropriate because according to her interpretation Bly is anything but purged. See next note.

205.21. *David playing to Saul*: a more distinct biblical reference to demonic possession, and one which turns on the governess still more sharply: 'when the *evil* spirit from God was upon Saul . . . David took an harp, and played with his hand: so Saul was refreshed, and was well, and the evil spirit departed from him' (I Sam.: 16: 23). Rochester tells Jane Eyre that 'if Saul could have had you for his David, the evil spirit would have been exorcised without the aid of the harp' (*Jane Eyre*, ch. 37). In 'The Turn of the Screw', however, Miles is David whilst the governess puts herself in the place of the possessed Saul.

231.13. *a fierce split of my attention*: the idea that the consciousness became split in hysteria was fundamental to pre-Freudian psychology (see William James, *The Principles of Psychology* (1890), chs. 8–9; Josef Breuer, *Studies on Hysteria* (1895), Sections I and III).

231.20. *a sentinel before a prison*: if Quint is the sentinel, is the governess a gaoler (see p. 189) or a criminal (see p. 178)?

233.9. *I've burnt it*: documents are also burned in 'Guest's Confession' (1872), *The American*, 'The Aspern Papers', 'Sir Dominick Ferrand', and 'The Wings of the Dove' (1902). Incineration is usually accompanied by renunciation in James.

APPENDIX: NOTEBOOKS

237.1. *Subject for a ghost-story. [. . .]*: the passage here omitted records an idea for a tale about ghostly knocking behind a walled-up door. Although James claimed in his Preface to remember 'absolutely nothing' of the origin of 'Sir Edmund Orme' (p. xlv), Sidney Lind has shown in 'The Supernatural Tales of Henry James' (pp. 114–16) that both Notebook entries were inspired by James's research for *Hawthorne* (1879). In *The American Notebooks* (7 Sept. 1835), Hawthorne sketched an idea for a tale about 'a mysterious knocking' on the wall of an old house and for a story in which a heartless young man wins the love of a girl only to find that he has 'conjured up a spirit of mischief'. In 'Sir Edmund Orme' it is Mrs Marden who conjures up the persecuting spirit.

237.13. *Marbot's magnificent memoirs*: Marcelin Marbot (1782–1854) accompanied Napoleon on campaigns in Spain, Portugal, and Russia, and was made a general shortly before Waterloo. His memoirs were published in 1891.

238.24. *constatée*: 'established'.

238.27. *montée*: 'worked up'.

238.33. *the time of the Napoleonic wars*: in the event James decided against a historical setting and used Coyle's point of view to create the required distance.

238.40. *the Peninsular*: the Peninsular War, Wellington's 1808–14 campaign to eject the French from Spain and Portugal.

239.1. *the idea of Too late*: an idea which haunts a number of James's later works, in particular *The Ambassadors* (1903) and 'The Beast in the Jungle' (1903).

239.38. *5000 or 6000 words*: the tale grew to '7000 words' in the next Notebook entry (p. 240) and eventually ran to some 12,000 words—a triumph of economy for James, who confessed to W. D. Howells in a letter of 11 Dec. 1902 that 'The Turn of the Screw' (50,000 words) had originally been planned, like *The Spoils of Poynton*, *What Maisie Knew*, and *The Sacred Fount*, 'as a story of the "8 to 10 thousand words" '.

240.5. *an entremetteur*: 'a go-between', 'a matchmaker'.

240.20. *Oswald Crawford*: editor of *Chapman's Magazine of Fiction*.

240.24. *Voyons un peu*: 'let's just see.'

240.30. *de part et d'autre*: 'on both sides'.

241.5. *'Tiens!'*: 'Hold on!'

241.5. *divine principle of the 'scenario!'*: the principle was first used by James during the 'wretched little past' of his theatrical venture (1890–5). In a Notebook entry of 14 Feb. 1895 he wrote that it provided a key that fitted 'the complicated chambers of *both* the dramatic and the narrative lock'.

241.8. *my little 'cochonnerie'*: 'my little mess', 'my little trick'.

241.8. *Jusserand*: Jean Adrien Antoine Jules Jusserand (1855–1932), French diplomat and author of *The English Novel* (1886).

241.9. *empêchement*: 'hindrance'.

241.10. *'trop fort'*: 'too much'.

241.28. *[say]*: James's brackets.

241.39. *all the little merveilleux*: 'all the little gems', 'all the little marvels'.

242.8. *secousse*: 'shock'.

243.6. *10 little chapters*: James eventually used seven, also adding the introductory frame (which is not mentioned in these Notebook entries).

243.40. *Il s'y soustrait par la mort*: 'he gets out of it by dying'.

244.1. *Addington . . . Archbishop of Canterbury*: the Archbishop was Edward White Benson (1829–96) and Addington Park, near Croydon, was an official residence. The visit occurred 5 days after the disastrous opening night of *Guy Domville* and James's note was made upon his return to London. In a letter of 11 Mar. 1898 to A. C. Benson James recalled the visit, during which his correspondent's father had given him 'the few meagre elements of a small and gruesome spectral story' about 'some dead servants and some children'. James's 'unbridled imagination' had caused him 'to see the inevitable development of the subject'. In *Memories and Friends* (1924) A. C. Benson noted that his father had taken 'a certain interest in psychical matters' but was unable to shed further light on the anecdote.

VARIANT READINGS

IN THE preparation of the New York Edition James spent the best part of four years haunting his own work, breathing upon 'the dead reasons of things' and nowhere scrupling 'to rewrite a sentence or a passage on judging it susceptible of a better turn' (Preface to *Roderick Hudson*). Different readers will have their own opinion about the value of this exercise. Less affected by revision than an earlier work like *The American*, the tales in this volume nevertheless received subtle adjustment. Some of the more significant changes are discussed or listed in the following pages.

I. SIR EDMUND ORME

In revising this tale for the New York Edition James made approximately 350 separate changes of wording to the 1892 text. The James of 1909 is less interested in defining his ghosts in philosophical or theological language and his narrator disclaims knowledge not to Orme's 'transcendent' but of his 'odd' essence (29.17). The later James deploys a more generalized vocabulary of the sacred: Orme is not simply 'dressed' but 'arrayed and anointed' (29.29). In 1909 social relations are more informal: 'Mrs Marden' twice becomes 'my friend' (20.19, 28.12) and 'Miss Marden' becomes 'Charlotte' on three occasions (21.6, 24.22, and 32.29). But 'the girl' also becomes 'the charming creature' (17.5) and 'the creature I loved' (35.1), both of which seem more predatory. In the 1892 version Charlotte 'hesitated a moment'; in 1909, more desperately beset, she is said to 'cast about' (22.36). In 1909 Mrs Marden defends the memory of her husband not against 'mysterious imputations', which are rather grand, but against 'vague innuendo' (5.17), which is significantly shabbier. The following list is a selection of the most significant revisions.

Page	New York Edition (1909)	First edition (1892)
8.28	both my frail vessel and its fine recipient	the cup and saucer
10.31	she almost interfered with the slaughter of ground game.	she really interfered with the slaughter of ground game.

Page	New York Edition (1909)	First edition (1892)
16.33	I overdid my gallantry.	I said, fancifully, to Charlotte:
17.7	looking at me as if she scarce liked me at all.	looking at me as if she didn't like me.
19.23	as if it stood for all I had ever dreamt of.	as if it represented the fulfilment of my dearest dream.
21.10	out of which came an air of a keenness I had never breathed and of a taste stronger than wine.	out of which unspeakable vibrations played up through me like a fountain.
21.19	I was much uplifted.	I was extremely nervous.
29.33	the beauty of an old story, of love and pain and death.	the beauty of an old story of love and pain.
30.6	It was a case of retributive justice, of the visiting on the children of the sins of the mothers, since not of the fathers.	It was a case of retributive justice.
30.9	the disposition to trifle with an honest man's just expectations	the disposition to jilt a lover
30.18	her eyes would on the spot, by an insidious logic, be opened	her eyes would be opened
30.26	She couldn't take back what she had given before she had given rather more.	She couldn't throw me over before she had made a little more of me.
30.36	she did strike me as capable of missing my homage even though she might be indifferent to my happiness.	she struck me as capable of playing with a man.
33.5	an adorable girl menaced and terrified.	a frightened girl whom I loved.
34.35	another sound, the wail of one of the lost,	another sound, like a wail of one of the lost,

II. OWEN WINGRAVE

When he returned to 'Owen Wingrave', James made about 100 separate changes of wording to the 1893 text. Although apparently satisfied with the general rhythm of the tale he nevertheless made a number of small but telling refinements to his characterizations. In 1893 Coyle was 'versatile'; in 1909 he is 'brooding' (57.26). 'Miss Wingrave' emerges as 'the strenuous lady' (50.36) and the 'charming depths' of Kate Julian's eyes become 'ambiguous depths' (70.1). Owen's 'monomania' is changed into a more altruistic 'stiff obsession' (60.4) and he is said to reject not 'military glory' but 'just soldiering, don't you know?' (44.3). His smiling defiance no longer has the faint insincerity of 'exaggerated glory' but instead seems to the disapproving Coyle a 'perverse high spirit in a wrong cause' (51.33). In 1893 Sir Philip is 'a merciless old warrior' but in 1909, expertly enriching the paradoxical relationship between kinship and violence, James calls him 'a merciless old man of blood' (46.36). The later James is usually but not always more polysyllabic; he tends to the intangible but his imagery is sometimes more startling in its concrete clarity. Some of these extended figures are shown amongst a selection of the more significant changes below. Particularly noteworthy is James's sharpening of the irony in the final line of the tale.

Page	New York Edition (1909)	First edition (1893)
40.7	aspirants	young men
42.34	a face from which you could no more guess whether he had caught an idea than you could judge of your dinner by looking at a dish-cover.	a face from which you could never guess whether he had caught an idea.
47.2	episodes in which his scrupulous forms would only have made him more terrible. He had his legend—and oh there were stories about him!	episodes in which his scrupulous forms would only have made him more terrible.
50.22	He didn't know in the least what this engine might be, but he begged her to drag it without delay into the field.	He didn't know in the least what it was, but he begged her to put it forward without delay.

Page	New York Edition (1909)	First edition (1893)
56.34	the sinister gloom diffused through the place.	the sinister gloom that was stamped on the place.
57.6	named to her in advance some of the appearances she was to expect,	mentioned to her in advance certain facts,
57.31	the young fanatic's	the dear boy's
59.36	they'll be hanged—and also drawn and quartered—	they'll be hung
70.1	'What then would you have said without that tie?'	'Do you want then so much to send him off to be killed?'
76.21	renewed nervous derision.	another laugh.
77.16	a pale acceptance	a tremulous acquiescence
78.13	He was all the young soldier on the gained field.	He looked like a young soldier on a battle-field.

III. THE FRIENDS OF THE FRIENDS

Some 80 separate verbal alterations accompanied this tale's graduation to the New York Edition, perhaps the most significant of which was the changed title. 'The Way It Came' vaguely suggests the 'strange law' mentioned in the tale but 'The Friends of the Friends' more pointedly emphasizes the story's repetitive and reflective patterns. Most of the other changes involved minor adjustments of rhythm. James did, however, suggest more strongly the narrator's tendency to convert supposition into fact. A 'presentiment' becomes a more definite 'sharp foreboding' (91.16). The neutral 'I perceived' becomes the more assertive 'it was plain' (98.2) whilst a merely formal 'I assured him' becomes the more defensive 'I maintained' (100.35). The suggestion of 'a kind of soft stubbornness' becomes the stated 'a soft stubbornness' (103.6).

Page	New York Edition (1909)	First edition (1896)
91.26	they were approaching, converging. They were like the seekers for the hidden object in the game of blindfold; they	they were approaching, converging. We had talked

Page	New York Edition (1909)	First edition (1896)
	had one and the other begun to 'burn'. We had talked	
93.25	I remember the high quaver and the little break of her laugh.	she declared with a laugh.
94.13	'Did she say of me'—and I remember the just perceptible catch of breath in his pause—'what she had a right to say?'	'Did she say of me— what she had a right to say?'
99.5	'She evidently "pleased" you!'	'She evidently pleased you!'
106.7	so distinguished and so selected.	so distinguished.

IV. THE TURN OF THE SCREW

The revision of this tale involved some 200 separate changes of wording to the text of *The Two Magics* (1898). The effect of these has been the subject of considerable debate: Edel argues that the revisions support the hallucination theory because 'the nature of the governess's testimony is altered from a report of things observed to that of things experienced' (Introduction to 'The Turn of the Screw', in *Henry James: Stories of the Supernatural* (London, 1971), p. 430); Lind agrees that the New York version imparts 'greater subjectivity' (p. 307) to the narrative, but contends that its ambiguity is maintained, whilst Sheppard argues that the revisions were 'stylistic, and merely stylistic' (p. 253). In a letter to his agent J. B. Pinker on 11 Sept. 1914 James himself seemed concerned above all that Secker adhered to the 'authentic punctuation' of the New York text in their edition of the tale. In the New York Edition he had made approximately 500 changes of punctuation, almost all of them involving the removal of superfluous commas. The New York text does, as Edel claims, alter the perceptual to the conceptual (see 124.19, 170.16, 174.12, and 222.5 below) but it does not change the balance in favour of the hallucination theory: only the second of these examples relates to a ghostly appearance. The shift from seeing to knowing is part of a general tendency in later James to deal with centres of consciousness rather than points of view. Moreover the governess is perfectly prepared to accuse

Flora not of seeing but of knowing the spectres (see 213.17 below) without concluding that they are hallucinations, although admittedly this might be read as an indication of her indifference to the border between the subjective and the objective or even, more simply, as a recognition of the fact that Flora is not at this point looking across the lake towards Miss Jessel. It is, however, more subtly significant that the governess speaks of *noticing* and *recognizing* rather than *perceiving* (see 171.36, 193.1, and 223.14 below), engaging in active and even anticipatory perceptual construction rather than receiving visual information passively. It seems that the drift of the revisions is not to support one particular interpretation but to guard against easily founded suspicions of the governess's behaviour (see especially 153.11, 155.15, and 174.6 below). The second of these alterations is particularly important as it prevents an open conflict between the governess's subsequent statement that Flora had said 'not a word' (p. 156) and her assertion that Flora indulged in 'the gabbling of nonsense' in order to 'divert my attention' (p. 162). This process of preventing the reader locating clear evidence against the governess was already evident in James's revision of the periodical text of the tale for publication in *The Two Magics*. In the final scene he cut two of the governess's three somewhat grotesque references to her 'triumph' (at 232.30, 232.35, and 236.22 in the present text). He also changed the overtly violent 'rude long arm' of the periodical version (which in *The Two Magics* was still a somewhat puritanical 'angular arm') into a merely disciplinarian 'stiff arm' (226.3). The 'whimsical bent' of the New York governess's father (184.36) is merely odd, but his 'eccentric nature' in *The Two Magics*, and still more his 'eccentric habits' in the periodical version, might have suggested the possibility of hereditary insanity. The New York Edition does, however, raise new and more delicately attenuated doubts about the governess (see particularly 134.16, 140.8, and 178.12 below). James emphasizes her tendency to move from speculation to assertion (see 163.15, 188.12, and especially 212.17 below). In the periodical text the governess daydreams about being on a wedding journey with Miles and feeling shy, at an inn, before the waiter. But she quickly returns to reality when she notes that 'the maid had left us.' In contrast both her successors seem to continue fantasy into life when they observe that 'the waiter had left us' (227.9). On two occasions, however, (160.28 and perhaps also 162.4) the New York governess is more restrained in her inductions. Some of the more significant changes between the text of *The Two Magics* and that of the New York Edition are shown

below. See also the note to p. 183 for the original ending to
Chapter XII.

Page	New York Edition (1908)	First edition (1898)
120.13	the death of his parents	the death of their parents
124.19	I felt	I perceived
126.34	suffered some wrong	suffered some delay
134.16	would have to be fenced about and ordered and arranged,	would have to be enclosed and protected
140.8	instead of growing deadly used to them	instead of growing used to them
141.2	I should have found the trace, should have felt the wound and the dishonour.	I should have found the trace.
153.11	a disguised tension,	a disguised excitement
155.15	all spontaneous sounds from her had dropped	all sounds from her had previously dropped
160.28	seemed least to be questioned.	was least to be questioned.
162.4	must have been for both parties a matter of habit.	was a matter, for either party, of habit.
163.15	the particular fact	the circumstance
170.16	I knew that there was a figure	I saw that there was someone
171.36	I noticed	I perceived
174.6	plenty of call for nerve.	plenty of chance for nerve.
174.12	I had conceived	I had felt that
178.12	his dreadful little mind	his little mind
183.2	a person enjoying his confidence and whose prime undertaking	a governess whose prime undertaking
187.12	I drew my actual conclusions.	I made my actual inductions.
188.12	a wild irrelevance	a kind of wild irrelevance
193.1	I recognised	I perceived
195.23	in my turmoil	in my bewilderment
196.29	my desertion.	my absence.
212.17	She was there, so I was justified; she was there,	She was there, and I was justified; she was there,

Page	New York Edition (1908)	First edition (1898)
	so I was neither cruel nor mad.	and I was neither cruel nor mad.
213.12	a figure portentous.	the very presence that could make me quail.
213.17	you know it as well as you know me!'	you see her as well as you see me!'
222.5	I now felt	I now perceived
223.14	I quickly recognised	I speedily perceived.

THE WORLD'S CLASSICS

A Select List

HANS ANDERSEN: Fairy Tales
Translated by L. W. Kingsland
Introduction by Naomi Lewis
Illustrated by Vilhelm Pedersen and Lorenz Frølich

ARTHUR J. ARBERRY (Transl.): The Koran

LUDOVICO ARIOSTO: Orlando Furioso
Translated by Guido Waldman

ARISTOTLE: The Nicomachean Ethics
Translated by David Ross

JANE AUSTEN: Emma
Edited by James Kinsley and David Lodge

Northanger Abbey, Lady Susan, The Watsons,
and Sanditon
Edited by John Davie

Persuasion
Edited by John Davie

WILLIAM BECKFORD: Vathek
Edited by Roger Lonsdale

KEITH BOSLEY (Transl.): The Kalevala

CHARLOTTE BRONTË: Jane Eyre
Edited by Margaret Smith

JOHN BUNYAN: The Pilgrim's Progress
Edited by N. H. Keeble

FRANCES HODGSON BURNETT: The Secret Garden
Edited by Dennis Butts

FANNY BURNEY: Cecilia
or Memoirs of an Heiress
Edited by Peter Sabor and Margaret Anne Doody

THOMAS CARLYLE: The French Revolution
Edited by K. J. Fielding and David Sorensen

TOBIAS SMOLLETT: The Expedition of Humphry Clinker
Edited by Lewis M. Knapp
Revised by Paul-Gabriel Boucé

ROBERT LOUIS STEVENSON:
Treasure Island
Edited by Emma Letley

ANTHONY TROLLOPE: The American Senator
Edited by John Halperin

GIORGIO VASARI: The Lives of the Artists
Translated and Edited by Julia Conaway Bondanella and Peter Bondanella

VIRGINIA WOOLF: Orlando
Edited by Rachel Bowlby

ÉMILE ZOLA: Nana
Translated and Edited by Douglas Parmée

A complete list of Oxford Paperbacks, including The World's Classics, OPUS, Past Masters, Oxford Authors, Oxford Shakespeare, and Oxford Paperback Reference, is available in the UK from the Arts and Reference Publicity Department (BH), Oxford University Press, Walton Street, Oxford OX2 6DP.

In the USA, complete lists are available from the Paperbacks Marketing Manager, Oxford University Press, 200 Madison Avenue, New York, NY 10016.

Oxford Paperbacks are available from all good bookshops. In case of difficulty, customers in the UK can order direct from Oxford University Press Bookshop, Freepost, 116 High Street, Oxford, OX1 4BR, enclosing full payment. Please add 10 per cent of published price for postage and packing.